ISBN-13 978-1-939820-82-2
Printed in U.S.A.

Cover Design and Interior © format by

PENETRATE

THE PORTALS OF TIME

JACKIE IVIE

To my dear writer friend and owner of equestrian stables,
Sandy Shacklett.
Your expertise, experience, and willingness to share
both were absolutely invaluable to me.

Thank you!

CHAPTER ONE

EVERYTHING WAS READY. ENGINES ON. Runway cleared. Dawn just breaking. The perfect time for a flight.

Neal barely listened as Eric went over the last of the checklist. As if it mattered. As if anything mattered except getting back to Miami. Reaching his office. And drafting yet another break-up letter with another girlfriend. Then again, he hadn't dated Lindsey for a year yet. Maybe he could send a text this time.

Women.

Under the beauty, and around the personality, they all seemed to have the same traits. They were conniving. Manipulative. It must be encoded into their DNA. No matter what you gave them, or the attention you showered on them, they wanted more.

They wanted a little gold ring.

With a really large diamond.

As if that would solve all the world's problems. Well. Not in his world. Neal had a lot of companies in his portfolio. Most of them energy-conserving, or energy generating. Right now, he was working with a developer on a concept for solar-powered flight. Because the future needed it.

It sure didn't need another Straithmore.

That's why he'd taken care of accidental reproduction. Permanently. In his early thirties. Aside from the fact that right now he was in his late forties and that was no age to be starting a family, it wasn't medically possible. Lindsey should have done her homework just a little better before she tried the pregnancy ploy.

Anger flashed through him. Along with it came a tingling sensation up his left arm. He already had a myriad of dots floating before his vision. Large and small, and making blurry spots he had to concentrate around. All signs he'd had before. And didn't need again. He needed to remain calm here. Unemotional. Despite the thought, Neal subconsciously reacted. He pushed the throttle. The plane jumped forward.

Eric stopped his recitation of the pre-flight checklist. Neal really liked Eric. The kid was his protégée. Hand-picked three years ago from a sea of applicants. Because Neal had suffered a transient ischemic attack very few people knew about. Classified as a minor stroke, that episode had forced Neal to face reality. And mortality. And if he wanted to continue his empire building, he needed to hire an assistant. He'd required someone bright. Efficient. Loyal. Energetic. Open-minded. And closed-mouth. Eric had proven to possess all of those qualities and more. Perhaps Neal should do what the Romans did millennia ago. They'd found the best candidate for their progeny and adopted him.

He felt, rather than saw, Eric turn his head toward him. Neal ignored him, pushed farther on the throttle, and taxied onto the runway.

"Just keep it under mach one, okay, boss?"

"This engine won't do mach one, Eric."

"So far," the kid answered.

Neal's lip lifted on one side. The one Eric couldn't see. That was the only response he gave. They were piloting his newest acquisition, a Cessna Citation X, rated at 617 mph. Mach 0.935. It carried a spiral motif on the tail, as did all his acquisitions. That spiral was embossed into the leather seats. He'd had it tattooed onto his left shoulder. Eric had recently gotten one in exactly the same place. It was designed after the signet ring Neal always wore.

This particular Cessna was the fastest private jet he could purchase. Neal had never opened it up all the way. Today might be the day. Because time was wasting. Time was always wasting.

Time was his number one priority.

Always.

Too bad Lindsey hadn't figured that out.

He'd called an impromptu board meeting for ten o'clock. The flight from Aruba to Miami-Dade should take just over two hours. He calculated another fifteen minutes for any in-flight issues. He mentally added to the time budget. He'd need an hour to reach his condo, ninety minutes under a worst case scenario. Should take thirty minutes to shed the linen pants and intensely-colored tropical shirt that marked what was supposed to have been a fourteen day vacation. And it would still be happening if Lindsey hadn't tried the tears and blackmail program on him last night...

Focus, Neal.

The thirty minutes included time to shower. Shave. Dress in a three-piece suit that had become his trademark attire. He assumed Eric would do similar preparations. They would then need a short helicopter trip – maybe twenty minutes – to reach his company headquarters...

They were cutting this close.

The jet lifted from the ground with an adrenaline-kicking rush that sent all kinds of pleasure rocketing through him. The same thing happened no matter how many times he flew, or what jet. Commercial planes wouldn't ascend as quickly as a private plane. But the Cessna was in a league of its own. Moments after lift-off, they were at cruising altitude. If he cared, he could look back and watch the island of Aruba disappear into an expanse of turquoise-colored water. A glance down showed all kinds of sparkles as dawn light touched the wave-topped surface of the Caribbean Ocean. Neal moved his gaze to the limitless vista of sky. They had some high cirrus clouds this morning, their composition of ice crystals making them resemble strands of filament. As if a master artist had just applied brush-strokes of white amidst a field of barely-there blue.

It was probably awe-inspiring. Maybe he should take a moment and just enjoy. Neal took a deep breath.

"Bad night?" Eric asked.

"Not open to discussion," he answered.

"Fair enough."

Neal forced his attention back to the span of electronic monitors and controls that comprised the cockpit. Everything was working properly. Displays were clear. He gave a sidelong glance to his personal assistant. Eric appeared to be concentrating on the view. It wasn't faked. The kid really wasn't interested in what happened with his boss. That was another reason Neal liked him. That, and his devil-may-care attitude. The kid had a crop of sandy-colored hair that needed a serious combing this morning. That was Neal's fault. He hadn't given the kid more than fifteen minutes warning that they were flying out. Eric had been expecting at least another week in paradise. Complete with hot and cold running ladies. And lots of booze. He looked like he'd slept in the clothes he was wearing, too. And yet, managed to look alert, awake, and entirely capable.

Neal looked back out the window. Shook his head. To be in his twenties again. Able to recuperate so quickly. Effortlessly...

But wait.

The dots were clearing.

His vision might get ultra-sharp now. As if everything was being viewed through enhanced-vision goggles. If that happened, he needed to down a clot-blocker tablet, turn the flight over to his co-pilot, don an eye mask and earplugs, in an attempt to envision serenity. Calmness. A sense of oneness with the universe. Something called *fudoshin,* according to his personal physician, Doctor...what was his name?

Chen?

Quong?

Uh oh.

He couldn't bring the man's name to mind? Looked like he was heading toward another stroke episode. He reached into his chest pocket and pulled out a clot-busting tablet. Pushed it through the foil backing with his thumb. Surreptitiously stuck it in his mouth. Grabbed his water bottle from the pocket on the left edge of his chair. Flipped the top open.

"We got a weird cloud, boss. Or...something."

"Where?"

The word was slurred. Neal hoped that was due to the pill's presence beneath his tongue. And that Eric wouldn't notice. He chugged a couple of swallows.

"Two o'clock. Closing fast."

"What?"

Neal leaned forward. Scanned the area beyond Eric. The kid was right. There was a definite dark mass on that side. It was moving closer as well as getting larger. And darker. A flash went through the cabin. Every monitor flat-lined. And then a riot of sensors started going off. Simultaneously. Red light infused the cabin with a dull glow.

"What the hell? The instruments are all going crazy!"

He didn't need Eric to inform him of it. A glance had already shown even their archaic altimeter was spinning. As was the compass. And fuel gauge.

Neal flicked the radio switch on his headset.

"Mayday! Mayday! This is NC4082. Aruba to Miami."

"This is Luis Munoz Marin International. Go ahead."

What the hell?

They'd reached San Juan, Puerto Rico air controllers? That wasn't possible. They hadn't been flying but a few minutes. They couldn't possibly be this far off course, nor could they have flown in an easterly direction. They'd have been flying into sunlight. And he knew that hadn't happened.

"Mayday! We've got system malfunction! Zero visibility!"

"Come again, NC4082?"

"Mayday! Electronics are dead. Massive cloud cover! Zero visibility!"

"There's not a cloud in the sky. Over."

Neal pushed for speed. The fuselage shuddered and complied.

550 mph.

600.

610.

They weren't escaping it. If anything, the mass was closer. Bigger. And darker. And then it started swirling. The plane started shifting with it. Going from side-to-side with large sweeping motions. If either man were the seasick type, that would be a foregone conclusion.

Eric caught his glance. The kid was straining to hold the plane level. And then the left engine stalled.

"Oh. Shit." Eric muttered.

Neal began reciting. "Luis Munoz Marin International! This is NC4082. Aruba to Miami. Mayday! We are in a dark cloud. Electronics malfunctioning. Engines malfunctioning. The cloud is spinning now!"

"NC4082? Come again? NC...? Come...?"

The air traffic controller's voice faded in and out, the words interspersed with static sounds. And then the plane started rolling. Neal caught a breath. Watched as lights began erupting, either in his brain or in the mass surrounding them. He couldn't tell. This could be another TIA. Or the big one. He should have taken this flight alone. Not dragged Eric into infamy with him. He should have adopted the kid, too, although it wouldn't have mattered. He'd given him control of everything in his will.

If the kid survived this.

Eric Donegal was a good man. Young. Strong. Capable. And still working the wheel against an unknown force of unbelievable magnitude.

Blackness started encasing them, going from a swirl of shadow along the edges of everything, and narrowing with each revolution of the plane. It was a strange blackness, interspersed with a series of near-blinding explosions, accompanied by intense heat. As if they'd somehow flown right into a Fourth of July fireworks exhibition.

"We're being swallowed by a UFO!"

Eric yelled it.

Neal couldn't respond.

He was losing consciousness, and actually welcomed it. And just before he blacked out, it occurred to him. He and Eric were about to become a Bermuda Triangle statistic.

Of all the fates he'd projected for himself, this exceeded them all.

CHAPTER TWO

1803

WELL, NOBODY COULD SAY SHE didn't truly love her sister,
Lileth.

Ainslee tensed slightly at the sound of horse hooves, alerting her to the
duke's approach. *Thank all the saints!* He hadn't changed too much. He
might have spent a good portion of time at sea in the ongoing war with
Napoleon. Since the truce, the duke might have been down south in London-town, known as a den of iniquity. He might have altered to the point
he no longer wore Highland dress, preferring the stovepipe trousers, tight
jackets, and cravats of the English peerage.

Didn't much matter.

Niall Straith was still out and riding in the pre-dawn mist, exactly as he'd
done when she'd last seen him. Back then he'd been a gangly youth, astride
a huge stallion, his hair a dark reddish shade worn long and straight, whip-
ping about behind him, while his *feile-brecan* had done little to disguise a
lean muscled frame. He'd had wide shoulders, a hint of shadowy whisker
on his chin and upper lip, an angry expression.

He'd ridden by her then. He hadn't appeared to see her. But that was
normal in her life. And necessary.

Ainslee slid her palms along her woolen skirts. The duke was probably
astride his latest acquisition, the big gray stallion just arrived from some
foreign breeder. The Arabian stud everyone in his stables spoke of, using
awe-imbued tones.

Ainslee pushed closer to the stone slab that shielded her. Imagined the ground trembling as he neared. She crouched lower as he passed by her hiding spot...and then she jumped out.

The horse reacted poorly, rearing onto his hind legs. Ainslee dodged and ducked wicked-looking hooves, while Straith fell ignominiously right off the back of his steed. And worse. His foot was caught in a stirrup. His horse proved to be skittish and uncontrollable, and entirely dangerous. Before she could even react and grab the reins, the stupid thing took off, dragging the duke with him. They topped a slight dale, disappeared from view, and when the horse reappeared on the other side, it wasn't dragging anything.

Oh no!

This was not what she'd planned.

Not at all.

A groom rounded the hill on his own horse, saw her, and stopped. He waved.

"Catch the horse!"

Ainslee yelled and pointed to where the new equine acquisition was almost out of sight. Then she grabbed her skirts up, and started running toward where the duke had disappeared. This was bad. She hoped he wasn't injured! And she doubly hoped he wouldn't know this was her fault.

If Straith was hurt...

It didn't bear thinking of. She didn't have much time as it was. He had to listen to her. He couldn't be injured. Or unconscious. Or anything other than awake and alert and able to understand. Anything else was dire.

Ainslee didn't check to see if the groom obeyed her. She didn't even consider the fact that he might not. But he'd already raced past, easily outdistancing her. She caught a glimpse of his horse's rear as they cleared the far side of the vale intent on catching the Arabian horse. And then she saw the duke.

Her eyes went wide. Her heart stopped. Her breath caught. Ainslee smacked a hand to her mouth to prevent any sound from escaping. The duke was in a heap of body and clothing, and his head was planted beneath him.

Backward.

"Oh, dearest God! I've killed him!"

Tears stung her eyes as she whipped around. She slapped her other hand atop the first to hold back a shocked scream. Her knees trembled and then dropped her. Thistle-covered grass enwrapped her. Painfully sharp. Dew-kissed. Moist. Fragrant. Her belly roiled sickeningly. She swallowed continuously against any illness, and blinked rapidly until her vision cleared.

Her situation had just changed from ominous to absolute disaster. She had to think! Escape. She could manage it. She had time. She could run for home. Pretend this hadn't happened. Maybe she'd be lucky...

No.

It wouldn't work. She was never lucky. Her shoulders sagged. Besides, she'd been spotted. It wasn't a far stretch to piece together what had happened. The groom would return to Straith Castle. Gather clan to retrieve the duke's body. Then they'd come for her. And even if they did believe her explanation, she wouldn't survive the beating Father was certain to give. A tear dropped before she could stanch it. She whisked it away with a shaky hand, tightened her jaw, and forced any further ones away. She was grimacing as the meadow came back into focus.

As usual, there wasn't any way to change her fate.

She might as well just face it.

Ainslee took a deep breath, straightened her shoulders, and stood up. It wasn't easy. Her legs shook, as did her arms when she clasped them about her. She was cold. And wet. Her skirts were stuck to her with the amount of moisture she'd soaked up. She was an abject failure. She ought to be used to it.

Ainslee was just pulling a hank of sodden material from her lower legs when the sky blazed into life about her. A massive shockwave penetrated the air, sending a blinding arc of multi-hued light with it. A boom of what had to be thunder happened. The force slammed her onto her back and then it locked her there.

Ainslee was stunned. Shocked. Absolutely and completely terrified.

She didn't move for a very long time. The thunderous noise faded away. A gust of wind reached her, rustling meadow grass and thistle stalks. Another gust followed. Several more moments passed. Her heart slowed to normal. Her quaking calmed. She'd experienced lightning strikes, but never that closely. Strands of her hair were actually lifted from her head. She brushed them down with hands that shook.

And then, she heard a groan.

Ainslee sat, swiveled, and watched the duke roll over awkwardly. Onto his back. And then he lifted a leg, bending it.

Oh heavens!

Ainslee was on her feet and racing toward him a second later, tripping in her rush. She slid down the last bit of slope, landing in a mess of saturated skirts and petticoats directly beside Straith. Sod had been disrupted in the ground all about him, adding muck to her appearance. She didn't care. It was a small thing next to the fact he wasn't dead. He was *breathing*. He didn't even look that injured.

Except for a nasty cut at his hairline.

Ainslee pulled a handkerchief from a pocket and pressed the fabric to his wound. He grunted and swatted at her hand, and when he missed, he just let his arm fall limply back at his side.

Well.

That answered some things. Gossip was that he'd gone soft. Effeminate. She hadn't believed it, but the tales appeared to have some substance. His hands didn't look like they did much work, if any. Then again, she'd been told his hands didn't do more than lift a lady's fingertips to his lips.

To kiss them.

"Your grace! Straith? Can you hear me?"

She left off ministering to the cut. It didn't look fatal and she mustn't forget the reason for her appearance this morning. Her reaction to him didn't matter. Nor did his appearance. Conduct. Or anything other than her mission. She hadn't had much time to start with. Now, she had less.

If Father knew where she was. And what she was doing. And who she spoke with...!

Ainslee trembled. She couldn't continue the thought. She didn't dare. She shook the duke before she lost her nerve completely. "Your grace! Wake up! Please? You must wake up! Come along, your grace. Please?"

He definitely did more than kiss a lady's hand. She didn't imagine the strength that seized her wrist and yanked her almost atop him. The only thing preventing it was her other arm as it stopped the fall. Her hand hit the ground on his far side, propping her up. He wasn't touching anything except her wrist, but near-contact sent heat through her. It penetrated the wet skirts. Warming. Steadying. Bolstering.

"We've little time. You hear?"

Her lips were near his ear, framed by strands of hair that had escaped a queue. And that meant he hadn't cut his hair. He'd tied it back and tucked the length beneath his collar. Ainslee tried to discount it. She pursed her lips. Cleared her throat. Moved her eyes. She'd believed the rumor that he'd dispensed with his hair. She'd listened and secretly mourned it. Straith lairds claimed the most glorious, thick hair. The new duke was no exception. It had been striking when he was young. It was said to be even more so now that it had darkened to the color of roasted chestnuts. He was also said to possess such handsomeness he set all the lasses in his vicinity to sighing. Ainslee looked him over. The last hadn't been a lie. Ainslee's heart stuttered. She almost sighed before catching it.

"What? The hell?"

Oh. My.

She hadn't known his voice had changed. Not this much. He had a strange accent, but he'd been away, visiting foreign ports. And in London-town. That might explain it. But nothing explained the depth of it. Nor her reaction. Bass tones rumbled through the air, lifting shivers along her skin. They affected her words as she stumbled through them.

"Ain...slee! You have to...uh. No! You *must* ask for Ainslee today! You just have to!"

"I need. A drink," he replied.

"Aren't you listening?"

He groaned again.

"Today! When you visit MacAffrey, you have to ask for Ainslee! You ken?"

"Ken?" he asked.

She pushed up, gained her knees beside him, and pulled at her captured hand. He released it.

"You've an appointment with the MacAffrey laird this afternoon! You're asking for his daughter's hand! Make certain to ask for Ainslee!"

"All right. That's it. Where's Eric?"

He opened his eyes and settled his penetrating gaze on her. Ainslee's heart stopped and then the darn thing felt like it swelled. Each beat almost pained. She'd forgotten he had stunning eyes. Gray-toned. Mercurial. It was akin to looking at hammered silver. This time when she swallowed, it was more of a gulp.

"Well?" he asked.

"I do na' ken...anyone of that name."

He frowned, put a hand to his wound, lifted her linen and then stared at it uncomprehendingly. His nose pinched up, as if in distaste. Ainslee looked from the cloth to him. Back at her cloth. It was a scrap of old linen, frayed at the edges. Despite continual washing and letting it bleach dry in bright sunlight, it had been stained before she'd used it on him. Now it was streaked with blood from his wound. But if she'd known she'd be proffering her handkerchief to him, she'd have brought one of Lileth's lace-bedecked ones.

"What? Is this?"

He had a strange way of breaking sentences, pausing distinctly between the words. It was already difficult to keep his gaze. With his voice and the way he spoke, it was even more so.

"My...handkerchief?" she offered.

He moved the cloth toward her, holding it with his forefinger and thumb as if that was too much contact. She took it, and despite her best effort, her hand visibly trembled as she tucked it back into her pocket. This was not going well. He wasn't listening. Or he didn't understand. And it had taken every bit of bravery she possessed to accost him this morn. She glanced toward him. Looked away. Struggled against the instant sting of tears again.

This was truly odd. Completely unlike her. She was known for stoicism. She rarely cried. The punishment was too severe.

"Okay. Level with me. I crashed-landed. Right?"

Ainslee watched the view blur into a wash of thistle amid heather, the color a mass of purple, green, and the dark brown of peat. She blinked rapidly and somehow conquered the urge to sob.

"Speak up, girl."

"I do na' ken your meaning," she whispered.

"Oh! For the love of—! Look. The one thing I detest is wasting time."

"Exactly! And that's why you have to—!"

"Don't start the 'ask for Ainslee' spiel again. Just. Don't. Oh! My head."

He'd tried to lift his head. Dropped it back to the sod. She watched him put a hand to his forehead and use a gingerly-looking motion to tap on his wound. He lifted his fingers away. Stared at them for a moment. Looked over at her.

"What. The hell. Happened to me?"

"You fell off your horse."

"Impossible."

"He reared. You fell. Your groom has gone to fetch him. I canna' stay! But first say you'll ask for Ainslee when you visit the MacAffrey laird. You must!"

"Young woman. Please. Make some sense."

"You've an appointment today! 'Tis part of the Straith will! You have no choice! You have to ask for the hand of a MacAffrey lass. Everyone expects you to ask for Lileth. But you can na'! You just can na'!"

"I have to do what?"

"You can na' ask for Lileth. Please? I'm begging you!"

She'd never been this emotional. Ever. Ainslee's eyes filled with stupid tears again. It was stupid. Irrational. She blinked and struggled, and was rewarded finally as his image cleared.

"She'll kill herself. She's vowed it."

He lifted an eyebrow. The move highlighted and defined and put dawn glow on how many shades of gray his eyes contained. The cut at his forehead seeped again. He didn't act like he felt it.

"You're making this up."

Ainslee shook her head.

"You truly expect me to believe that a woman? This...Lileth? She'd kill herself? Rather than wed with me?"

Ainslee nodded.

"You can't be serious."

Ainslee nodded again.

"Bullshit."

Ainslee's eyes went wide at his crudity. "But, it's true!"

"Women hound me for a ring, young woman. You wouldn't believe the plots they hatch. I've even had one post video online to force my hand."

"Vid...eo?" She stumbled over the unfamiliar word.

"This is a set-up, isn't it?" he interrupted. "Any moment now, news crews will be buzzing about, filming this. Am I right?"

Ainslee frowned. He must have taken a terrible blow to his head. He was speaking gibberish. And she was out of time. The sun was burning away the concealment of mist with every passing second. She craned her neck and looked, not in the direction the groom should be appearing. She scanned the path she needed to take. She was going to be late. She'd have to run every step. She looked back at the duke. Sighed in resignation. "I... have to go."

"Just when we were having so much fun?"

"Will you ask for Ainslee today?"

He didn't act like he heard her plea. He tried to sit. Crumpled back to the turf again with a groan.

"Oh. Hell. My head."

"You mustn't move. Your groom will be here soon with your horse."

"I don't have a horse."

"But, you do. You own scores of them! Each more impressive than the next. Your stables are immense!"

"No. I own bikes. Large ones. Powerful. Garages full."

"But...your grace!"

"Can we dispense with the 'your grace' nonsense? It makes my head hurt worse."

"Forgive me, your grace."

"That's it. Enough. Please. Cease calling me that. My name is Neal. Use it."

Ainslee couldn't believe it. Her mouth dropped open. Her eyes had to be reflecting the shock. He said his name in an odd fashion, but he'd still said it. She'd heard him. She was having trouble with comprehension. It wasn't possible. She was being allowed to address the Duke of Straithcairn by his given name?

Her?

Was this morning truly happening?

His eyes narrowed as he watched her. They looked less like hammered silver and a lot more like lead. That was a disquieting thought.

"This is some...uncharted island. Right?"

"Island?"

"It's not Bermuda. Even I can tell that. But we have to be somewhere in the Atlantic. Someplace off the beaten path. Someplace...fairly uncivilized. Yes?"

Uncivilized? Ainslee stiffened. Had he really just used that word and tone to describe his homeland? As if he was a Sassenach and not pure Highlander? And worse. Perhaps, he was including everything in it with his opinion.

Like her.

"Hail there!"

They both turned at the voice, coming over the slight hill.

"Oh, dear! 'Tis your groom! I must go."

Ainslee was on her feet. He forestalled her by grabbing her hand. And then he pulled, hunching her forward. She probably looked as awkward as she felt.

"Your grace! Please?"

"Neal."

"I canna' be seen here with you! Na' alone! You do na' ken!"

Of all the horrid consequences of this morning, what happened right now had to be the worst. She may have forestalled tears, but she hadn't alleviated anything. Shortly, she'd be sobbing outright. The humiliation was beyond imagining. Ainslee swiped at her cheeks with her free hand. Sniffed loudly. And then – thankfully – he released her.

"All right. You win! I'll figure this out myself. Run along, little girl. Run. Far! And fast!"

His taunt followed her, wafting on the wind with the volume of it. Tears blinded her flight through the swift scramble up the hill. A glance backward showed the groom just topping the next dale, riding his steed while leading the duke's horse. He lifted his hand toward her. She ignored it and started running, unseeing of her every footstep. She had to get home. Hide. Somehow conceal the perfidy of this morning. It was inconceivable how massively she'd failed. She hadn't received his promise. She hadn't managed to get him to understand! She hadn't even managed stealth.

And she couldn't seem to stop weeping.

CHAPTER THREE

NEAL WATCHED THE WAIF SCRAMBLE away from him, intent on escape. He couldn't blame her. If his head didn't feel like it was about to split, he might have been a little less insulting. And a lot more charming. He owned and operated various companies throughout the world, marketing Straith energy-conserving products in every country he could get a business licensed and operating. You didn't get listed as one of the top five-hundred wealthiest men on the planet if you didn't have global influence.

That meant the last thing you did was go about insulting clients on their own turf.

And then he placed her accent.

She'd been speaking with a Scottish brogue. Thicker than the ones he'd dealt with before, but still. He'd swear the little urchin was Scottish. Which meant he'd somehow landed in Scotland.

That was all well and good, and gave him a baseline for this experience. But little more.

The how of his arrival escaped him. The why portion was an unfathomable realm. Figuring out what had happened was beyond imagination. But the where was clear. Real. And inescapable. He was in Scotland. Extremely rural Scotland, but nobody could call it uncivilized. And he'd just done so. To a native Scotswoman.

Great.

He'd been around all kinds of customs, endured every manner of hardship, learned and then achieved success at protocols regardless of their strangeness, without even raising one of his eyebrows. Neal Straithmore hadn't achieved business success without possessing and using an ability to think quickly, keep up with internal and external events, accommodate as required. Fill in gaps if needed. Deal with unforeseen issues. Use his money and influence to advantage. Gain leverage. And then use it.

But most of all, he knew to keep his counsel.

Regardless of how confusing things appeared on the outset, he wasn't a novice at much anymore. He was adept at handling crisis, soothing ruffled feelings, alleviating tension. He just needed to gather facts.

If he could figure them out.

It was still sharp in his mind. He'd been overly annoyed at Lindsey's ploy to get him to the altar last night at his beachside bungalow. He'd reacted with his usual avoidance technique. He'd had a few stiff drinks in the interim, but hadn't said a word to her after her little announcement, that had been given to him with all kinds of ultimatums and dramatics. After which, she'd let him be. Maybe she thought she'd delivered a *coups-de-grace*. He'd sat in his chair all night, brooding into his brandy snifter. She'd been sleeping with the slightest smile on her face when he left. He hadn't packed a bag. Left a note. Alerted her to anything. He'd called for a meeting with his board while on the way to the airfield. Phoned Eric to join him. Minutes later, they'd left Aruba in his Cessna Citation X.

And then things had taken a distinct turn downward.

He'd been in the midst of a mini-stroke episode, or perhaps it had been the real thing. He'd taken one of his prescription pills. He'd never had a bad drug reaction, but there was always a first time. That could explain the weird spinning cloud that had appeared and sucked them into it, somewhere in the Bermuda Triangle area. He hadn't died. He couldn't have. He sure didn't feel dead right now. And he wasn't on an alien planet with large-eyed humanoid creatures he couldn't communicate with. He wasn't even in a strange place if he considered it. He'd somehow been regurgitated into the wilds of Scotland.

There were worse circumstances.

And much worse locales.

He needed to consider another option, however. He could be unconscious. This could be a drug-induced delusion. Even now, he could be on an operating table, pumped full of morphine, while medical personnel worked at saving his life.

But just then Eric came into view.

The relief at seeing his protégé was palpable. Weakening. His voice even came out an octave higher than his normal range. "Eric! Oh! Thank God."

The fellow jumped from his horse and knelt at Neal's side. The plaid kilt he wore spread onto the ground between them. An instant inspection revealed Neal's mistake here. Where Eric's hair had been slept-in and could have used a combing, this fellow's head-full was long, shaggy, and needed a good barbering. But the two men could be twins. Except this lad was a good deal younger than his doppelganger.

Speaking of which...

Neal lifted his hand again, the one with fingers still smeared with blood from his wound. He'd noted an oddity the first time he'd looked at it, but he hadn't assigned reason. Now he did. The hand was familiar, but looked like it had when he'd been younger. Before age spots appeared, his veins thickened, and the skin thinned. He was also missing the spiral signet ring from his little finger, too.

Without one sign of a tan mark where it had been.

It occurred to him that there was another option. Despite the implausibility of it. He needed to consider Quantum Physics. It was improbable, but potentially possible. He might actually have experienced Einstein's theory of relativity first-hand. And, if he really stretched his imagination, he could add in an Einstein/Rosen bridge portion. That vortex he and Eric had flown into could have been a wormhole.

Neal Alexander Straithmore might not just be on a different island entirely, he could be in a totally different time period, as well. He might even inhabit a different body.

Oh, no. No. No way in hell.

He needed to consider things. Draw it up and look it over. Visuals always helped. Hopefully he'd have some time before fate stuck him into another wedding noose situation. That was ironic. What were the odds he'd get sent back in time and have to avoid yet another woman wanting a ring?

Neal frowned.

"Be you all right, your grace?"

Neal thinned his lips and looked away before he answered. The who portion of his new reality was rapidly starting to annoy. It could easily frustrate. He hadn't liked being called 'Mister' even when it was correct protocol to do so. Assigning titles added an invisible layer of stratification in any situation. That usually went hand-in-hand with subordinate positioning. And that tended to stifle creativity.

Since he dealt with innovative solutions to the planet's diverse issues, he required creativity. His human resources departments actively sought out and hired people who spoke their minds, regardless of salary or position. His companies wanted the best. And they paid for it. Most of his employees were satisfied with the arrangement. Unless they decided they wanted to strike out on their own. Become a competitor. He had an entire legal firm to prevent that from happening. That's why his employment contract read like it did. He had a lock on intellectual productivity, as well as future ideas that might be generated from working for him...or even construed as such.

And that was just about everything.

He was known as an employment shark in most business circles. Neal didn't care what monikers got assigned to him. Some of his company's most productive and lucrative ideas had come from an idea spouted out at a meeting, or in the elevator, or out in the parking lot...even the café. That's how you grabbed at genius. You drew it up. Added and enhanced. Trademarked and patented.

And Straithmore Enterprises owned a lot of trademarks and patents.

This could be the opportunity he'd been searching for! He needed to check the lay of the land. Scope out the financial landscape. Depending on the timeframe he'd landed in here, he could potentially get an energy-saving concept into the core of industry *before* it even became an environmental issue.

Save the planet.

Gain a legacy.

Add to his bank account.

The possibilities were mind-blowing. Sounded like he had an edge already with his social position. That was almost embarrassing. He'd heard that people who'd been regressed had never been menservants or laborers or slaves in their past lives. Oh, no. They'd always been an Egyptian pharaoh. Alexander the Great. A Roman conqueror. A king. Chieftain.

Or even a Scottish duke...

"Your grace?"

He turned back to Eric's lookalike. "What's your name?" he asked.

"Rory, your grace. I work in your stables."

"Rory. Of course. Forgive me."

"Nothing to forgive, your grace. There are a lot of stable hands. It is na' an easy thing to keep us straight. And you've but recent arrived."

Neal pondered that for a moment. His lips twitched, but he somehow kept the amusement from showing. "I have?"

"From down London-town way. I've na' been there me-self. I hear 'tis a verra...uh. Exciting place."

"How...fortuitous for me."

Holy shit!

The duke was new to the title? And new to the area? And had a name so close to his that he'd actually answer?

Neal couldn't have set this up better.

"Your grace?"

Neal lifted his head tentatively. Nothing felt like it had before – as if a sledge hammer smashed into his skull with the motion. He sat next, using just as much caution. His head didn't react to that, either. He hadn't been mistaken about his physical age and condition. He had his sleeves rolled up. His forearms were bare. They looked a lot more muscled and firm than they had last night.

"What...day is it, Rory?"

"'Tis a Monday."

Neal started. "Really?"

"Aye."

"And the month?"

"June."

The fellow's confusion was obvious. Neal's heart ticked up a notch. It was incredible. Impossible. And yet...

He'd left Aruba on a Thursday. In October. Because Lindsey had requested a vacation to escape the chill of fall. She hadn't given a hint about the engagement ring she really wanted. Neal subconsciously tensed at the thought before he let it go. Lindsey was a blip in his past. Actually... she might not even be that.

"Year?" he pressed the groom.

"Year, your grace?"

"I have...suffered a head injury, Rory."

"Aye. You took quite a spill. I told you Thundercloud was a mite spirited this morn."

"You appear to have been correct. And I am still a bit nonplussed by my concussion."

"Your grace?"

Crap. The kid didn't know what that meant? Was the word concussion even in use? "I'm uncertain of...things. Like the year. Nudge my recollection. Remind me."

"'Tis the year eighteen hundred and three, your grace."

"1803? Holy hell. I'm at the very birth of the stock market!"

"Your grace?"

"Oh. Uh. Yeah. Never mind me, lad. It's the...head injury talking." Neal needed to get someplace and figure out logistics. Strategies. Decide what commodities to begin his investment portfolio with. Steel! That would be the first thing. No. Wait! It would be iron. Steel wasn't available yet. He looked back at Rory. "We...need to get back to...um. Where do we live?"

"Castle Straith."

"We live in a castle?"

"'Tis the Straith Clan ancestral home."

Neal cleared his throat. "Well. Of course it is." *And probably archaic as all get-out.* "Well, Rory. Is there a conveyance about for my use?"

"I've brought your horse."

"The one that threw me?"

"He's properly mollified, your grace."

Neal cast a glance upward. The horse was an immense animal from this angle, young. Muscled. It wasn't gelded, either. It was pulling against the rein Rory held, more than once showing the whites of his eyes. Neal didn't know much about horses —buying stock in living things was a waste of money unless it was edible — but that horse didn't look remotely mollified. Or calm. Or anything other than ready to bolt. Neal made a face. He liked his horsepower condensed into the cc kind. Apparently riding a motorcycle just became a nice memory. Motorized craft weren't due for some decades yet.

Unless he started the industry.

Hmm. That was a thought with a lot of potential.

"Will you be needin' an assist, your grace?"

"You could say that," Neal replied.

"Do you need an assist, your grace?"

"What? Why did you re-ask that?"

"Because you said I could."

Neal gave a heavy sigh. Being a duke in the early nineteenth century might be a bit taxing. He'd have to keep his own counsel about everything. He waved off Rory's hand and stood, noting instantly that he wore trousers. They were fashioned strangely, with a bit more room in the seat than he liked, and a lot less negotiating room everywhere else, but familiar-feeling. He had a cloth cinched about his throat to the choking level. The jacket didn't have much breathing room to it, either. He might as well have a girdle about his waist. Neal pulled at his throat covering until it gapped open and then started unfastening jacket buttons, starting at the bottom of the garment.

Well.

Appeared as if finding a decent tailor was going to be a prime objective in his new life. He decided to make a mental listing of what he needed to do. Draw it up on a chart later. He could jumpstart modern menswear, too.

That was before he discovered that the boots were even worse.

Some idiot had crafted them both identically, as if the left and right foot were alike. A shoemaker was going high on his list of requirements, too. He wore socks that were obviously woolen. He could feel the familiar itch of that fiber, but they were the only cushioning he could feel. There wasn't any insole support. The boots were outsized to top it off, and they slanted downward due to the heels. He might as well be standing on slick boards atop a ski slope. His toes slid forward as he stood there, regarding his mount with the same expression of distaste the horse appeared to exhibit.

"What is my horse's name, again?" he asked.

"Thundercloud."

"Well. That's apt."

The horse's head was level with Neal. Thundercloud didn't look quite as intimidating from this angle, but he was still an animal that outweighed Neal by hundreds of pounds, possessed an agenda that differed from that of his owner, and he had the ability to put it into play. But things could be worse.

Neal could be wearing a kilt.

The groom sprang onto his own mount without much hint of effort, showing a lot of leg as his attire flapped about him. He settled into a section of leather that barely resembled a saddle, simultaneously shoving his boots into the stirrups. The kid hadn't even used one. Neal considered his groom's leg for a moment. It hadn't looked hard, but he wasn't trying it that way. He wasn't entirely naïve of this. He'd seen this done more than once. Usually on film. By accomplished riders.

"You want the reins, your grace?"

"Uh. No. You better keep them. For now."

"You certain-sure?"

"Oh. Yes."

He'd seen horses mounted. He'd never tried it. Horses were mounted from the left. Neal moved a few paces to his right and faced the animal's side. He put his left hand on the front part of his saddle. It had a raised area that lifted a lot higher than Rory's saddle. That leather bit had a name, too…if he could just think…

Oh. Yes. It was a pommel.

His right hand gripped to the hunk of leather at the back of his saddle. Neal lifted his left foot toward the stirrup, but then had to use his left hand in order to wedge his boot into the damn thing. It was a tight fit. Completely unequal battle. Shoe leather against iron. The sides of his boot compacted slightly before he had his foot in, and then hopped about trying to grab the pommel again. Shoemaker moved above tailor in his mental list of requirements, while Rory sounded like he was trying not to laugh.

Finally!

Neal latched onto both ends of the saddle, heaved himself up. Lifted his right hand to toss his leg over the animal's back, stretching out across the animal's back, and that's when the horse bucked. Neal promptly went flying off the far side of the animal, landing ignominiously on his butt as his foot slipped out of the boot.

The landing took his breath. Sent his vision swirling. A lot of horse was jumping around him, hooves flashing. He was rather grateful for Rory's expertise as he brought Thundercloud back under control.

And that's when he got angry.

CHAPTER FOUR

"DID HE AGREE?"

Ainslee put a finger to her lips as Lileth's maid, Elvie, finished shutting the door. Trust her sister not to know the slightest thing about subterfuge and secrecy. And it was her future at stake! Ainslee waited another moment before coming fully out from behind the tapestry, crossing to the chamber door, and then lowering the bolt, barring it.

"Well?"

She crossed quickly to the bed, opened her shawl, and dumped all sorts of breakfast goodies onto the coverlet beside Lileth. She'd brought crisped bacon strips, lightly browned scones with butter dripping from them, and even a portion of salmon – fresh-caught that morn, before being filleted, breaded, and then grilled to mouth-watering perfection. Although the feast had been crushed in her shawl, it looked immeasurably more appetizing than the crusts of bread and tureen of water Elvie had just delivered.

Lileth gasped. "How did you steal so much?"

"Nobody notices anything I do. You ken as much. And they already claim I eat like a horse, so who's to note?"

"With na' an ounce of extra to show for it. Still."

Ainslee grinned, bounced onto the bed, and then sobered as her sister's eyes filled with tears.

"So, tell me! Please? I've been awake all morn, fretting. I won't be able to eat a bite."

"I told you to rest. Worry will na' help. Here. I even put honey on your scones." Not very much, though. Her shawl was already sticky. She'd have to dip it in the loch at the first opportunity.

Her sister took a dainty bite, looking lovely and feminine and exactly what the Duke of Straithcairn should receive in a wife. Lileth was a full-blooded Scot, a product of the Sinclair and MacAffrey clans. She claimed vivid green eyes, red-gold hair that rippled to her waist, and womanly curves that promised healthy bairns.

Ainslee had suspected Father let her sister's majority pass without accepting any of the offers he received because he was holding out for a prize catch, but even she couldn't have guessed he'd set his sights on the Duke of Straithcairn! Their antecedents went back the Robert the Bruce! Why... the Laird of MacAffrey wouldn't even have been allowed to sit at the same table with the Straithcairn laird in the past. And yet Father had managed to arrange a union between the two clans. It was still unbelievable, akin to attaining the moon. She eyed her sister worriedly.

"Are you certain...you do na' wish to wed with him? I mean...truly certain?"

Lileth dropped the scone, her eyes immediately welled with tears that only made her more beautiful, and then she covered her face with her hands. That got followed by her wailing again, exactly as she'd already done for two days since this had started.

"Why are you crying now?"

Ainslee reached for the handkerchief in her pocket, pulled it out and then shoved it back before Lileth noted it. She'd forgotten. It was worse stained than before. And crusty with the duke's dried blood now. She lifted a napkin instead. "Stop, Lileth. Please? You ken it breaks my heart."

"But...you failed!"

"I did na' say that."

Her sister looked up, her lashes spiked together with moisture. When Ainslee cried, she looked like a bedraggled street urchin, not someone that should be immortalized in a painting. She sighed and looked away, toward the headboard, not really seeing the MacAffrey clan emblem that had been painstakingly carved into it.

Lileth was the beauty of the family. It seemed unnecessary that she also possessed a large dowry, settled upon her second birthday with the death of her mother. The MacAffrey laird had been inconsolable, everyone said. Until his trip abroad. When he'd returned with an Irishwoman for his second wife, it had surprised everyone. They'd called it a love match. That didn't seem possible. She didn't think Father knew the meaning of the word. Regardless, the Laird of MacAffrey welcomed a second daughter within a year of his return, but one who didn't look remotely Scottish. Ainslee had hair as dark as the night and deep, sapphire blue eyes. She'd also inherited black, lush lashes, giving her a look some called 'eyes put in by the devil's smudged fingers'.

The combination of pink and white porcelain fine skin, dark hair, and black, thick lashes, should have rendered her with the moniker of pretty. And it might have, if she wore something besides her older sister's cast-offs, ever gained enough weight to fill any of the clothing out, and stopped fidgeting long enough for anyone to notice.

Ainslee wasn't even a year old when the laird's second wife passed away, a still-birthed daughter with her. The laird hadn't mourned her demise for any length of time or with any dignity. The gossips made certain Ainslee heard the story of how he'd up and wed the youngest daughter of the MacHugh clan within two weeks of the tragic deaths.

Two, short weeks!

But who could blame him? The Laird of MacAffrey wanted sons. That's all anyone seemed to care about. And nobody found fault with that.

His third choice of wife was a woman of lusty size and a boisterous nature. She'd given the laird not one son, but five of them, and another due this fall; all of them red-cheeked and red-haired, raw-boned, and supremely healthy. But not one of them possessed much handsomeness. Even with red-rimmed eyes and tear-streaked cheeks, the oldest daughter, Lileth, was the beauty in the family. She reigned supreme in that regard.

Always had.

Always would.

"Then, you succeeded?"

"I...did na' say that, either."

Lileth's eyes filled with tears again. Ainslee almost swore aloud.

"If I can na' be with Robert...I'll die!"

"I just need to make certain you are certain. I mean, Robert has little to recommend him, and—"

"I don't care!"

Lileth glared at her. The expression was better than tears. Ainslee regarded her for a moment.

"I just want you to be sure. Straith is a duke! He is rich. He's got a fine castle and a matchless stable. You should've seen the horse he rode today! Thundercloud is his name and—"

"I don't care about horses, Ainslee. I'm not like you."

Lileth was right there. For sisters, they were as different as night to day. Lileth didn't spend a moment of thought on horses, while they were Ains-lee's life. That was one thing that reassured her over this plot. Although, secretly. The duke's stable was part of the compensation package for taking Lileth's place. She was giving up any chance for love in exchange for access to his horses.

And an escape from here.

Such thoughts were grim and did nothing. Ainslee stood. Looked down at her sister. Tried to smile reassuringly. "Stay in your rooms today. Use any excuse."

"Why?"

"What man would ask for me if he sees you first? Unless, of course, you're determined to ruin your looks by more sobbing."

The flattery worked. Lileth straightened and immediately started dabbing at her tear-soaked cheeks. "But...I'm under orders from Father."

"Be ill. Have a feminine complaint. Do whatever you have to! But don't be seen."

"What if...Straith asks for me?"

"Then we'll know I failed, and you'll have to elope. Father will be verra angry. You might be disowned. But that could happen anyway. You ken as much."

"Robert says he doesn't care! Besides, I have *my* dowry. Father can't take that from me. No one can!"

That was true. Lileth had a large dowry from her mother. She was a beauty. Her father was a laird. The Duke of Straithcairn was a stellar match. But her heart had been taken by a music tutor who was a second son of a second son of some obscure baronetcy in Cornwall somewhere. If Ainslee hadn't seen them together, she'd have assumed the worst. But she knew the truth. When Robert was with Lileth, it seemed like a light enveloped them. Nobody else got to enjoin it. Both of them radiated such happiness, it was a crime to separate them.

Ainslee had never known love, but it looked like a truly wondrous event. Magical. Amazing. It should be in everyone's future. But for her? If the duke did as she'd begged?

That would be never.

She cleared her throat. "You see? You have nothing to cry over and everything to look forward to. So, finish your breakfast and do na' leave any crumbs! You ken how Elvie is. She'll tell."

"Ainslee!"

Her father's booming voice penetrated the halls. It throbbed through the chamber door, rattling the bolt. It matched his size, and his emotions. He was a large man with an even larger temper. Ainslee was at the tapestry that hid the secret opening before the sound finished vibrating through the room.

"I must go."

"What have you done now?" Lileth asked.

Ainslee waved a hand in response and disappeared into the black void that was the crawlspace. It didn't take much to set her father's ire against her. It was better to stay out of sight. Ainslee didn't waste any time. She knew the hidden passages that honeycombed the castle almost as well as she knew the stables. If this were a normal day, she'd be running the narrow flight of steps to her tower room. That wasn't feasible now. Father had probably already sent someone to check for her there. They might even be there waiting. She headed instead to the passage that connected to the second floor rooms, and the library. If she wasn't in the stables, she was in the library. And there were lots of alcoves and niches to hide within. She could pretend she hadn't heard Father calling.

Hadn't heard him? His voice was loud enough to shake the rafters of the chieftain room.

"Ains! Lee!"

His voice broke her name in two sections when she heard it next, and that through a panel she passed. The passage she turned down wasn't often used. It was dusty and contained more than a few cobwebs, but eventually she slid out from behind a bookshelf, shook her hair, and then her skirts, and hoped she looked like she'd been thoroughly engrossed in a book.

She'd just started down a ladder when she was spotted.

"I've found her, Father!"

It was her second-born, half-brother, William. He was fourteen and already developing brutish tendencies. She had to attend to just about every horse after he'd ridden it. The spot between Ainslee's shoulders tensed. William wasn't trust-worthy. But she was in luck. Their next younger brother, Ronald, was at his heels. Even at just ten years of age, Ronald was like an angel. Everyone adored him.

"There you are, you lazy wench!"

Father's hand encircled her upper arm and yanked her from the steps. He slammed her to her feet and let go before she had her balance, sending her crashing back into the ladder. That hurt. Actually, everything to do with Father hurt.

"Where have you been?"

Ainslee's heart hammered. Her throat closed off. Her mouth went dry. She'd have moved her hands to her breast to help with the thudding of her heart, but her father detested fear. Demonstrating it only got her more of his attention.

"Well?"

His voice was thunderous and loud. Due to the height of the library ceiling, it echoed. Ainslee lifted her shoulders slightly. Defensively.

"Answer me!"

"I…was reading, Father."

"Are my bookshelves of such dust, you appear to have been swimming in it?"

Ainslee darted her eyes to his before looking down at herself. She could usually gauge his anger with one glance. Today was no exception. He was in a rage. It was going to be bad. The time he'd spent searching for her had only swelled it. She watched his fingers tighten on the riding crop in his hand.

"I…was looking…near the back," she explained.

"For what in particular?"

"A book on…science." Her voice dropped.

"Are you na' under orders to stay from books and reading? And did na' I just give this punishment but three day ago?"

Ainslee's entire body went cold as he started slapping the riding crop against his thigh. *Oh, dearest God!* She'd forgotten. In her rush to protect Lileth, she'd failed to recall that he'd forbidden her the library.

"Well?"

"I…forgot." The last word was whispered. There wasn't enough moisture in her throat to say more.

"Ronald? Go to your room," Father commanded.

"Now?"

"Must I suffer disobedience throughout my home? Aye! Now! Return to your rooms this moment, or I'll attend to you next."

Laird MacAffrey slapped a bookshelf with his riding crop, causing several volumes to jump. Ainslee followed suit. Her heart had turned into a wild caged thing. She didn't care who noticed as she clenched her hands tightly together at her bosom. Ronald took off at a run. The door slammed behind him. That left William as a witness. It wasn't helpful. She already knew he liked to watch.

Ainslee shut her eyes, sent a quick silent prayer, and the very next moment got rescued.

"Father. Please. I'm already late for my ride. I need Ainslee at the stable. My horse, Eros, will na' accept a bridle for some reason. Can you na' punish her later?"

The MacAffrey laird's pride and joy, Ainslee's eldest half-brother, stood at the door, lazily saying the words that saved her. Mitchell MacAffrey was three years her junior, but towered over just about everyone. Already six feet tall, he was strong, thick-boned, spoiled, self-centered, and extremely selfish. He was everything that made her father proud. And all of that was perfect for saving her right now.

He was standing just inside the portal, slapping his own riding crop against his thigh while he waited; the epitome of a MacAffrey clan heir being put-out at having to wait for something. Father sighed heavily.

"Go then, lass. But do na' think this will na' be taken up with you later."

Ainslee raced around her father and then skirted William, grateful for strength and agility as her legs didn't even betray how they quaked. Mitchell gave her a grudging nod, and motioned for her to follow him. He needn't have bothered with that directive. She was so close to his heels, she was in danger of tripping.

CHAPTER FIVE

THE FIRST HINT THAT THEY neared Straith Castle came a good span of time later. Neal didn't have any way of checking time. That was ridiculous. It was 1803. It wasn't the dark ages. Even Scot dukes should possess and carry a timepiece. Maybe not a wrist watch, but he should have a pocket watch, at least. He patted the open sides of his jacket for anything solid. Metallic. Checked his trouser pockets next. Got nothing but material.

He'd have to go by instinct. Experience. It felt like an hour had passed. Could have been more. Or less.

The castle grounds were an incalculable amount on acreage. There wasn't any warning that he'd reached them, either. He'd been following a track that ran through a field of ripening grains when a chunk of dark stone appeared at his left, just off the beaten surface. It was followed by more rocks. The stones were impacted into the ground. Worn smooth with erosion and age. Large. More than a man could lift, and that hypothesis was only based on the surface area. There could be much more boulder beneath the sod for all Neal knew. Perhaps that explained why these people had just left them haphazardly looming from the ground, creating a tripping hazard for any unsuspecting traveler.

Or his horse.

Neal steered his mount to the right. The animal instantly obeyed. Thundercloud didn't exhibit any fight. That was exhilarating; exactly as it had been the first time it had happened. *Good thing.* The rage that had colored his vision a reddish tone, gotten him atop this beast and clamped in place, and then pulled the reins from Rory, had long since vanished. Neal didn't know the procedure for staying atop this beast if it acted up and decided to buck him off again, although clamping his thighs about its girth and grabbing a fistful of mane had already proven to work. He couldn't remember the last time he'd been that mad, or the reason for it. He never lost his temper anymore. He rarely even raised his voice. Anger was an emotion, and he couldn't afford those. Exhibiting emotion in any transaction was a surefire way to lose the objective.

Every negotiator knew what to project when they first approached a bargaining table. No emotion. Little expression. Zero sense of approachability. Neal hadn't been labeled as a heartless man for no reason.

The stones got more numerous as he continued. Rory was somewhere behind him. Neal didn't look to verify it. He heard him occasionally. The kid had a slight cough, and his horse a strange wheeze. Either could prove troublesome. Or, both. Neal wasn't a chemist, but he knew the rudimentary power of bacteria. And penicillin didn't exist. He supposed he could figure out something with molding bread, but he really didn't want to worry over it.

He had a market takeover to plan.

Everything else was a waste of mental and physical energy.

The rocks became more numerous, jumbling together as they rose to stirrup level. Neal continued on. The conglomeration of stone grew thicker as well as higher. It had reached the height of his saddle when Neal deduced the purpose for it. It was a wall. Stoutly made. The stones were now shaped and fitted together, easily eight or nine feet in width. He moved his gaze above it and got the instant reason for such a wall. Beyond it was nothing but sky and water. And a large spit of land that jutted out into the span, getting splashed with white-crested waves.

It was an awe-inspiring view. Worthy of note. And extremely ill-advised.

Neal had visited several castles, spent an entire summer on the enterprise. He'd received quite the education in castle building. There'd been a reason. He'd contemplated buying one, and wasn't spending resources on a piece of history if he didn't know what it entailed. He'd decided in favor of acquiring and then restoring a ruin located somewhere in the interior of the continent. And why? Because castles were already drafty affairs. Interior climate control was impossible to maintain. Any castle built on a seacoast, especially at this altitude, would be open to the elements. He hoped it wasn't built on a cliff. He'd have to deal with erosion, too.

It was obvious the original builders had chosen the location for the view. They hadn't given one thought to the consequences. Owning this bit of real estate meant a constant battle with nature just to keep any struc-

ture intact, let alone habitable. Perhaps there was another location on his
property better suited for building. He could always relocate. Use modern
techniques. Confound the hell out of any historian centuries from now.
Neal snickered, made a mental note to put it on the list for consideration,
and looked back up the path.

The wall at his left was now being paralleled by one that had been mean-
dering along the hill below them on the right. The view beyond it was
of more water, making an inlet with a high cliff of more dark rock on
the opposite side. The scene was beyond impressive. It was breathtaking.
Absolutely majestic.

Someone had an exact idea of the impression they'd wanted to make
when they'd chosen this location. Neal was experiencing it. Perhaps he
needed to rethink the relocation plan. Heating and venting options could
always be installed. Foundations could be shored up. He'd have to check
into construction techniques. He wasn't even sure if the Roman Empire's
use of concrete had been rediscovered yet. If not, he'd figure it out. He
could use steel-reinforced cement on his castle. He knew for certain he
was on the cusp of the industrial revolution. That's why iron and then steel
were at the top of his investment list.

Neal pulled on the reins. Thundercloud stopped. Rory joined him within
moments.

"Your grace?"

"Who owns that land? Right...there?" He pointed toward the headland
across the bay and swept his arm outward to encompass all of it.

"I believe...'tis Straith land."

"I own it?"

"Now that, I...can na' exactly say."

"Why not?"

"I'm na' entirely certain...I should speak."

Neal considered the lad for a moment longer before speaking. "Rory. I
had a bad spill. I can't think clearly. I don't remember...much. Can't you
just tell me?"

"'Tis na' wise to speak ill of the dead, your grace."

"Who died?"

"Your uncle, may God rest his soul."

"The late duke?"

"Aye."

"Recently?"

"Eight months past. Almost nine."

"Nine months! And I just managed to get here?"

"Aye. Two days past."

"Hmm. Sounds like I need to invest in transportation. Stat."

"Your grace?"

"Oh. Um. Never mind me, Rory. I've...suffered a head injury." He put his hand to his temple and tenderly dabbed at the spot. "But, tell me. Why did it take me so long to claim my inheritance? Surely travel doesn't take that long."

"They say you were...powerfully hard to persuade."

"Really? Why is that?"

The lad flushed. "Well, the gossips say—uh."

The kid's voice stopped. Neal lifted his brows. "Yes?"

"I...should na' have said anything."

"How about I fill in blanks? You just nod."

"I do na' ken—"

"I was found in London? Isn't that what you said?"

The lad nodded. His skin reddened even more. Neal barely caught the chuckle.

"Well. London must have quite a lot of enticements for a young man on the prowl. I must have been having a very good time. Is that what you're trying to tell me?"

Rory nodded again. Thundercloud shifted beneath Neal. He clamped his thighs on the horse's sides. Thundercloud stopped fidgeting. Neal managed to stifle displaying the rush of pleasure at the horse's obedience, as well as the amusement at Rory's discomfiture.

"Did my uncle own that land?"

Rory nodded.

"Isn't it part of the inheritance?"

The lad nodded. And the shook his head.

"All right. Forget nodding. Just explain."

"'Tis na' my place, your grace."

"Then, whose is it?"

"Uh."

"If you can't answer my questions, who am I supposed to ask?"

"You have a steward."

"I do?"

Rory nodded.

"Well. He's not here with us now, is he?"

The lad shook his head. Neal sighed heavily. Thundercloud shifted again. Neal tightened his legs. The horse stopped moving.

"Can't you just tell me? I won't say anything about where I got my information. You have my word."

"Well...rumor is your uncle was na' right in the head. He lingered on a long time after his attack. Visited with all manner of solicitor fellows and lawyers, and the like."

"And that means...?"

"I am na' privy to the...contents of the will, your grace. Truly. All I have is rumor."

Uh oh.

This could involve the little sprite who'd accosted him. She'd told Neal he had an appointment this afternoon with some laird, but the name escaped him. *Ah!* He should have a better recollection of events. He'd always had perfect recall before. She'd mentioned a name that began with an 'A'. She'd pleaded with him to use that name today. Not the other one. He needed to use the 'A' name when he visited. It was required. She'd said it involved something in the Straithcairn will...

The spot between Neal's shoulders clenched up. There'd been a lot of plots hatched to try and get a marriage noose about his neck. He wasn't a good candidate for a husband. He liked his freedom too much. But to escape this one, he was going to need all his wits about him, and a lot more information. He looked up toward the sun. Afternoon was rapidly approaching.

Damn. Apparently, time was still his top priority. "You said I have a steward?"

He surprised Rory with the question and way he asked it. The kid jerked. He didn't have any trouble with his horse, however.

"Aye."

"Does he have a name?"

"Aye. Garrick Straith."

"Ah. He's a relative of mine?"

The kid met his gaze, but wouldn't hold it. He looked away rapidly. Toward the path they should be moving along.

"We should get going," Rory told him.

"Rory."

The kid sighed. "Aye?"

"Is this Garrick a relative of mine or not?" Neal waited. Rory's mount pranced for a bit. Quieted. The kid finally nodded.

"Close relation?"

"Uh. Aye."

"There's something you are not telling me, isn't there?"

The kid's skin went rosy-shaded again. "'Tis na' my place—"

"Damn it! Just give me the answer. Or I'll ask the next person I meet."

"You do na' want to do that."

"Why not?"

The kid sighed heavily. "You may na' wish to put much trust in Garrick."

"My own steward? Why not?"

"Gossip has it he will inherit the dukedom...should you fail."

"Fail? At what? I haven't even started anything yet."

"I do na' ken the particulars. Na' exactly." The kid colored again. The difference between Rory and Neal's twenty-first century assistant was clear. Eric was a lot more confident. He'd never blushed this often. Or this noticeably.

"But you know something," Neal pressed.

Rory nodded.

"Well. Spit it out. It can't be that bad."

"'Tis rumored you are required to wed with the MacAffrey lass."

Oh. Crap.

That was a distinct wrinkle. This marriage noose sounded tough to wriggle out of, if not impossible.

Then again...nothing said that Neal Straithmore needed to be a Scottish duke in order to take over the stock market. Being a member of the peerage might actually be a deficit. Being located in the wilds of Scotland could be exponentially worse. Messages would take forever. Financial transactions might be impossible to oversee. He actually needed to be in New York. Wall Street.

It was 1803!

In June!

Shivers ran along his skin at the realization hit him. Somehow, he'd passed through a time portal. While that was mind-blowing, the possibilities before him were even more so. He was on the verge of history! Young. Fit. And he'd retained his financial savvy! The potential for fortune-making was astronomical.

The view faded into insignificance as Neal looked inward. He didn't need this castle. Or a dukedom. He didn't need anyone. All he needed were his wits...and maybe a small stake. Pennies. He wasn't a history buff. He knew the financial markets, resource and asset management, strategies for renewable energy. He should still be able to figure out what stock to buy, how long to hold it, if and when to sell. He could easily be one of the wealthiest, most influential men on the planet before the decade was out, as well as fix the pollution issues of the twenty-first century.

"We need to get moving, your grace."

Rory's voice brought Neal back to the present with a jolt. He shook his head. Blinked. Focused. Scanned the incredible vista before him again. And then he experienced a sudden flash of something emotional through his chest. It held a hint of sadness. Even to him.

That was odd.

"Oh. Yes. Of course."

He turned Thundercloud's head forward, nudged the horse with his knees, and was rewarded with the horse's immediate movement. He'd been apprehensive without reason. Riding a horse wasn't all that difficult. Just took a little practice.

Like riding a bike.

Yeah. Right, Neal.

His lips twisted at his foolishness. This didn't remotely resemble being atop any of his bikes. There could be several reasons why he wasn't having trouble with Thundercloud at the moment, none of them based on Neal's proficiency. The horse was probably tired. Hungry. Or he could just be biding time...waiting for the opportune moment to unseat Neal again.

The wall on the left rose higher as they progressed. The right side matched it, lifting upward to twenty feet. Twenty-five. Thirty. Thirty-five. Neal was approximating, but he didn't think he was far off. It looked close to the size of a four story structure. If the sun was at its apex, the area was probably fully illuminated. Right now, the base of the passageway was beset with a lengthy shadow that swallowed them up. He was surrounded on both sides by what would be solid black rock, except for darker slits in the stone every twelve feet or so. They were at varying levels through the wall. Neal didn't have to ask the purpose of this construction. It had been part of his summer of castle education. The slits were for archers. If he looked higher up, he'd probably spot openings called murder holes, used for raining boiling liquids down on intruders. Castles were defensive structures, and this passageway was one hell of an obstacle for an attacker.

It was a massive display of power.

Might.

Authority.

Despite everything, goosebumps lifted on his skin. He wasn't claustrophobic, but this approach made his heart pound quicker. He might as well be entering the maw of a large black tunnel. Each breath came with a heavy sensation. The only thing that muted the effect was the width of the space. He'd gauge it at twenty feet wide, never narrower. The ground changed to what looked like cobblestone. Sounded like it, too, if the impression of hammers hitting on rock as shod horse hooves traversed it was an indicator. Neal couldn't see much at the moment, either. There was a distinct curve coming up, leading to the left.

The walls finally met high above his head, the mass of black stonework rising to form a Romanesque arch. This one had a woven-leather and iron-studded gate hanging down from it. *Wow.* He was looking over a port-cullis. He'd seen ancient ones, while touring castles. Never like this. They hadn't looked this nasty. The spikes were lifted just high enough a rider atop a horse could get beneath it. Neal ducked his head even though he had several inches leeway.

And if he wasn't already slack-jawed, that would have happened as the castle came into sight.

CHAPTER SIX

COFFEE.

That item went to the top of Neal's mental list of investments. Steel, transportation, and men's fashion took a backseat to coffee beans. Someone needed to make sure coffee beans were picked at the peak of ripeness. Slow-roasted. Ground evenly. Settled in a filtered well, so steamed water could be passed through them. None of which had been done to his pot of coffee before it got delivered. He was investing in a coffee plantation somewhere in South America and giving the instructions at his first opportunity. The world needed a decent cup of java, ASAP.

That took care of his first fortune.

Neal took one taste of the liquid in his cup and nearly spit it back out. It was a chore to swallow. For the first time in his life, he added sugar and copious amounts of cream. He made a face as he doctored the brew, but the one he made after downing the mixture was worse. He had a mirror that confirmed it.

His reflection proved several things, actually. It was a long cheval-style affair, set on dowels so it could pivot up and down. It had been in the room between this one and the suite belonging to his duchess. He'd hauled it in here himself after three menservants had delivered three pails of heated water to this chamber. He'd wanted one for soaping, one for rinsing, and the third one just because he was annoyed.

He hadn't been when the groomsman, Rory, had deserted him at the front door. Or, rather, the lad had taken the mounts away after Neal dismounted and left him to face an array of uneven stone steps that led to the front door. At the second floor. Apparently, Straith Castle had been started as a tower house prior to being added and enhanced.

Neal had recalled that lesson as he'd considered the mass of dark stone.

There were reasons why living areas began with the second floor. The first floor was dark and cool, both necessities for food storage. There was a problem with pests, rats in particular. They also liked cool, dark places. There was always a risk of drunken clansmen riding into the place while still on horseback – a feat more than one nobleman had attempted in the past. This design was also a defense mechanism against a horde of invaders, assuming they survived a pelting of arrows and boiling oil during their approach. Having to mount a massive set of steps to accomplish a takeover would be an additional hurdle.

All of which went through Neal's head before he'd shrugged it off. What did it matter how the castle had been constructed? By whom? And when? He needed to start discounting things. Financial world domination was the objective. Everything else was ancillary.

Everything.

Neal had started up the steps at a jog, taking them two-at-a-time, barely winded as he reached the top. The extra room in his trouser seats for such an exercise was a decided plus point. Perhaps he'd best rethink altering menswear too much. His new body was another bonus to his new reality, too. He was the same height – six feet, four inches – but he was several pounds heavier. The additional weight wasn't flab. Neal had been in great shape in his thirties, but he didn't recall possessing this much muscle. Strength. Or energy.

He reached the stoop. The castle had a large, iron-studded, wooden door. It was propped open, held that way with an iron statue in the shape of a reclining dog. Neal bounded onto a raised entrance stone. Dropped down onto a wooden floor with a thud that echoed. And then he'd entered a span of room large enough to hold a stockholder meeting. With all of his companies. At once.

And then he'd just stood there, absorbing the space, while working to keep his jaw from dropping.

The room was dim and carried a distinct chill, even for a sunny morning in June. Nobody was about. An arrangement of long, heavy-looking, wooden picnic tables and benches graced one side of the room. Hotel-sized rugs were scattered about the floor, looking like pools of color amidst all the dark wood. They each held a smattering of furniture. Couches. Chairs. Tables. Lamps. The amount of space was mind-numbing. He couldn't imagine what energy it must take to keep this area at a comfortable temperature, or if that was even possible.

The ceiling was a good span above him. He couldn't tell the construction material, but the support beams spanning the width were wood. Each one looked like it had been hewn from a single immense tree. There were windows in the highest level, sending sunlight down in multi-hued spears of illumination. The light touched on what they had displayed up there. Neal had lost the battle against his jaw. It had dropped. He'd spent years amassing a weapons collection. It was rarely seen outside of his vault. But he'd never seen the amount of weaponry he was looking at now.

The entire back wall held spiral displays created from taking hundreds of swords, placing their tips together, and fanning them outward, using the hilts as the circle's circumference. Large spiral displays were at both ends of the wall, interspersed with smaller ones, presumably fashioned from a like amount of daggers. He couldn't tell in the lighting and from this distance, but that's exactly what it looked like.

Eight.

Nine.

No.

They had *thirteen* of the displays up there.

Someone had taken flintlock rifles and done the same thing along the walls on both sides of the room, alternating them with smaller spirals made from smaller weapons – he'd guess pistols. A glance over his shoulder showed that the wall behind him was almost entirely taken up with a collection of shields. All kinds of shapes. Several different materials. This was unbelievable. Stunning.

Neal was looking at an array of armament that would shame the acquisitions department of any institution he could name. There was an incalculable amount of wealth and power on the walls about him. The impression was of dominance. Command. Supremacy. It left the viewer with an uneasy feeling. As if they'd lost significance.

He felt it.

He knew it was intentional.

And he owned all of this?

No. Wait.

It didn't matter who was the Duke of Straith-whatever. Who owned the castle. How they acquired it. Neal didn't care about people. Their machinations. Petty problems. Human failings. He needed to remember his goals.

Market takeover.

Save the planet.

Period.

He lowered his head. There were four massive stone fireplaces along

each wall. Eight in all. That was probably an attempt to warm the place, as
well as provide light. He wondered if they burned wood. And from where
would they get it? The waste was incalculable. It was beyond wasteful.
Those fireplaces probably didn't even work well. Neal couldn't imagine
how dark and cold this place was at night. He could guess.

But...wait. Wasn't Benjamin Franklin around doing the kite and key
and lightning experiment about now? *Hmm.* Electricity was a viable stock
option. If Neal lived long enough to see it offered. Or maybe he could
manage to jumpstart that industry, too. He had another item for his portfolio.

He really needed to get this written down!

Neal moved his attention to the staircase gracing the back wall. It had
been constructed using more of the dark stones. There were two lengths
of steps rising in tandem along the side walls. They curved inward, and
met at a large landing that looked capable of holding members of an entire
board of any of his companies. It was well above the floor. Ten feet or so
beneath the lowest display of swords.

Those must be a pain in the ass to dust.

He'd smiled at the instant thought. Then realized, the estate must have
an army of employees. He wondered what that must cost. In 1803 terms.

And then he ignored it.

Who cared?

He had larger plans.

There was a shadowy space beneath the landing. Neal could just make
out a set of doors. Massive, carved wooden affairs, containing long handles
fashioned of antlers. The entire room was medieval. Masculine-themed.
The ladies of the house must not have exercised much influence. But, that
might have been normal for the area and time period. What did he know?

One door opened.

And Garrick Straith walked into the room.

Neal didn't need to ask the fellow's identity. He just knew. His steward had dark hair. It was pulled back into a pony-tail, exactly like the one
Neal sported. Garrick was fit. Not unattractive. Save for the dark beard
he wore, Garrick was close to Neal in size and appearance. He rapidly
closed the distance between them, his strides making a thumping sound
that turned into a mass of noise resembling a band of drummers without
much rhythm. Garrick had been pretty damned impressive as he'd neared,
his kilt flapping along his thighs. Neal got a sensation of something malev-
olent. That was highly unlikely. He didn't believe in emotions. That didn't
stop the goose bumps from lifting along his skin. Even if he hadn't been

warned by Rory, he'd have still known not to trust the man. Neal was instantly on edge. And extremely wary.

"So! You've finally returned, have ye?"

The steward hailed him loudly, using a Scottish brogue Neal didn't think he'd ever achieve, even if he wanted to.

"Good morning, Garrick," Neal had answered.

Garrick had frowned. "Yer voice has changed."

"Really?"

"Aye."

"That's...odd."

They'd looked each other over. His steward hadn't said anything for several seconds. If Neal had a timepiece he'd have heard it ticking away as the time passed. He'd tensed without conscious volition.

"The clan's gathered. Prepared. Ye've na' got much time."

"Before what?"

"Did ye forget yer meetin' today? With the MacAffrey laird?"

"Oh. That."

Neal's voice had lowered on the last word, clearly demonstrating his distaste. It had been at the periphery of his thought process to simply forego the coming event. Run away. Snatch a berth on the nearest ship going west. Disappear. Just let things happen here in the wilds of Scotland as they might. It was at that moment, standing beside Garrick, that Neal decided otherwise.

"Aye. That. Ye've got two hours. Mayhap less."

"What's the plan?"

"There's some-what powerful strange aboot you, mon. Be ye serious?"

Neal had lifted an eyebrow. The man's speech was thick enough to render it a foreign tongue. "I took a spill from my horse. Hit my head." He lifted a lock of hair from his forehead to display it. Winced as his fingers touched the spot.

"I warned ye that horse was too much fer ye."

"Yes. Well. Apparently, you weren't the lone one with that advice. Is that the way to my chamber?"

Neal pointed to the portal Garrick had come through and started walking that direction. His steward fell into step with him.

"Of course na'."

"I took a nasty spill, Garrick. Didn't you hear? I seem to have lost a good bit of memory because of it. Most of it...of recent origin."

"Truly?"

The hope in the man's voice was grating.

"It comes and goes. So. If that isn't the direction to my room, what is?"

The man pointed up to the landing. "Chieftain's rooms are oop there. Where they've always been."

Well, of course the duke would have the most regal path to his chamber. Neal should have figured that out. He selected the staircase on the right, jogged to it, and was halfway up when he noticed Garrick was directly behind him. Neal had stopped. Turned around. Regarded his steward for long moments. He was one step above the man. He could tell the additional height bothered Garrick. That was pleasurable. Neal had been hard-pressed not to show it.

"Why are you following me?"

"I am yer steward, Niall. Ye've been away most of yer life. Yer not familiar with our coostoms...so ye said. You'll be a-needin' my advice."

"Oh. Not anymore."

"What?"

The fellow was taken aback. His head went back along with his shoulders. Neal decided that reaction was even more pleasurable to observe. It took an act of will to hide that emotion, too.

"Tell you what? Why don't you leave me alone to shower and shave? Change my attire. Grab a bite to eat. And then...we can meet back here in...? How about an hour and a half? How does that sound?"

"Shower?"

Crap. They didn't have showers, either? Neal was extremely grateful for his position above Garrick. It was easier to look and act condescending.

"Just see that three large buckets of warmed water are delivered to my chamber. Oh! I'd also like breakfast. With coffee. Lots and lots of coffee."

"Ye want yer breakfast delivered? To yer rooms?"

"Yes. I do."

"But—"

"You seem to possess excellent hearing, Garrick. Comprehension is another matter entirely. Sounds like it will take a bit of work, but we all have to start somewhere. Don't we?"

Garrick had narrowed his eyes and tightened something in his jaw, if the nerve twitching at one side was an indicator. Neal had waited. And then the man had spun around, gone back down the stairs, and his step when he reached the ground floor wasn't near as jaunty as it had been.

CHAPTER SEVEN

NEAL GRIMACED AGAIN AT THE bitter taste from the coffee he'd just swigged. Put the cup back onto its saucer. He rarely stopped at one cup. He did now. For self-preservation. He regarded the rest of his breakfast selection with an even more jaundiced eye. Most of it looked inedible. Maybe it was due to the distance from the kitchen. He couldn't tell. But the meats were greasy and cold, the yolks of two fried eggs broken and congealed. There was a bowl of baked beans. Chunks of something black and sour-smelling. Thank goodness someone had included a small pot of oatmeal! And scones. Those were familiar. Hearty. Delicious. He wrapped a sausage link within a pancake that tasted of oats and potatoes and chomped on it as he considered the wicked-looking bruise at his temple in the mirror. Nasty-looking thing.

And he was running out of time.

Even when given an entire new adulthood to work with, time was still a priority.

He had about twenty minutes left, give-or-take. He needed to prepare and he didn't have much help. The menservants hadn't been any, but he hadn't asked, either. None of them would meet his glance. Neal guessed it had something to do with the breakfast, and his requirement of it in his room, but he didn't have anyone to verify it. Unless he considered the gent who'd arrived on the heels of his breakfast, and who hovered even now, beside the bed. Silently watching. Neal caught the fellow's gaze in the mirror before the man also looked away from him.

The man had given his identity. He was the laird's valet.

Another blasted Scotsman.

Neal wondered over trustworthiness, although he hadn't sensed anything like the emotion he'd felt when in Garrick's presence. Neal turned about. Approached the bed. He wore a floor-length robe, fashioned of some soft fiber he couldn't identify at the moment. It was lined with satin and finished with a silver embroidered crest at his left chest area, directly above his heart. The emblem was so heavy with thread it weighed down the material.

His valet stood patiently, hovering beside a selection of Highland attire. There was a white linen shirt. A ruffled bit of material hung from the neck. It had buttonholes. He guessed it was a facsimile of a tie. Or...what had they called neckwear back then? Cravats. *Yeah*. That was it. Two circles of white linen fabric were resting above the shirt. They were mystifying. A short black jacket with embroidered epaulets came next. Looked like it had been fashioned from velvet. A length of red, white, and black plaid was spread out across the coverlet beside the jacket. Neal guessed it would become a kilt of some kind. A round purse-thing rested beside the plaid, made from some animal's pelt. It was heavily embossed with silver. Tasseled plaid socks in the same color scheme of red, white, and black were beside it, followed by four silver-handled daggers. Two smaller knives came next. A large, jeweled and gilt-trimmed scabbard rested toward the foot of the bed, ready to hold the sword that lay beside it. That wicked-looking weapon graced the footboard, glinting with the amount of polishing it had been given. The last item looked like a bonnet for his head.

There wasn't anything resembling underwear.

Anywhere.

Neal continued his inspection, moving his glance across from the sword. On the other side of the bed, the valet had set out a completely different set of clothing. Knee-high boots rested on the coverlet, so clean and shiny, they nearly matched the sheen coming from the sword. Little round straps came next. They probably held up the socks beside them. A dark blue coat was next. A pair of long trousers of a tan shade. Didn't look like they had as much excess room in the seat as those he'd worn earlier. *Excellent*. Beside the pants was a length of starched white linen that would be wrapped about the throat in another choke-collar. *Ah*. That was a real cravat. Next to that was a white button-down shirt, and at the area just below his pillows were items even he recognized: knee-length, off-white drawers that buttoned to a like-material sleeveless shirt. Apparently, if he dressed in the attire of an English gentlemen, at least he'd have underwear.

This was getting complicated.

Neal looked at his valet, back down to the bed. He didn't have to ask which outfit the valet favored. The man's demeanor spoke for him. He supposed as chieftain of the Straith Clan, there was only one option.

Neal sighed heavily. "Your name's Millbourne? Isn't that what you said?"

"Your grace?"

"What can you tell me of Miss...uh. Is it...MacAffrey?"

"Lileth?"

Oh good. Neal smiled to himself as the fellow filled in one blank. The woman everyone expected him to ask for was named Lileth. "No. The other one. The one that begins with an 'A'."

The man jerked slightly, then frowned. "Ainslee...MacAffrey, your grace?"

"Yes. That's it. Ainslee. You know anything of her?"

The man cleared his throat and then put a finger beneath his collar. Neal regarded him silently.

"I'm uncertain how to proceed with the answer, your grace."

Neal leaned against the dresser behind him. It scudded along the stone floor before he realized his mistake. He was larger and heavier. The furniture wasn't secured to the floor. He stood back up before something drastic happened, like the thing fell.

"Is there some secret I'm not privy to? Come on, my good fellow. Speak up."

"I'm wondering...what your grace has heard."

"Call me Neal, all right? I'm a bit...out-of-sorts here. I've but recently arrived. I just suffered some sort of head injury...that um...scrambled my brains a bit. I need help. Information. And I am not asking my steward for it. So. Are you going to assist me or not?"

The man lifted his head and met Neal's gaze. Neal got an instant sensation of warmth. A sense of benevolence. The exact opposite of what he'd felt with Garrick. He instantly felt at-ease. As if he was around Eric again. That was curious.

"We'd have never allowed the lass the run of the estate if you'd been here."

Neal's eyebrows rose. "The run of the estate?" he echoed. "She lives here?"

"Oh. No. Nothing like that. But she visits. Oft. Mostly the stables."

"The stables? A girl?"

"The lass has the touch of the fey to her fingers. All note it."

"Fey?" The word was harshly spoken. Neal couldn't help it. He was not accepting fairy nonsense. *No way.* Not without a fight, anyway. He refused.

"I've been a witness to it, your grace. Near all she touches heals. She's a wonder with horses. She's the reason your stable is as healthy as it is when hoof-rot decimated most others. There's nae horse born she canna' calm."

"Oh. *That* kind of fey."

"Check with MacCreary, our head groomsman. Actually, you could check with all the stable hands. You'll hear the same. But, afore you do, your grace, I wish to take full responsibility."

"For what? And really. You can call me Neal."

"I allowed her to visit the estate while the auld laird, your uncle, was ill. But I also allowed it to continue afore your arrival. I'll see it stopped immediately-like."

"Oh, I don't know, Millbourne. No harm, no foul. Right?"

"Your grace?"

Neal unfastened his robe tie. "It's Neal. And I'm going to need your help with this, as well."

"With what?"

"My...uh. Attire. I wouldn't wish to reflect poorly on the Straith Clan, and I'm a mite...uncertain as to the wearing of...um. This." Neal motioned to the length of plaid.

"You'll wear the *feile-breacan* today?"

"Uh. Yeah. If that's what it's called."

"Oh, your grace! Aye! It will be an honor to assist you."

"What would it take to get you to call me Neal?"

"'Twould be a mistake, your grace."

Neal sighed again. "Why?"

"It is na' my place. Your cousin looks for any reason to negate yer claim. Ye mustn't give him one."

"Garrick?"

"Aye."

"He's my cousin? Buggers."

"His mother is the late duke's younger sister. As well as your father's, I should add."

"I take it she's still alive?"

"She resides in the east wing along with your other cousin."

Other cousin? Crap. There was another one like Garrick? That was an unpleasant turn of events. "Why is he a Straith, then? Isn't his mother wed?"

"Of course! She's been widowed. Garrick's father was a Blair. But, since the duke's left no son, the duchy of Straithcairn could easily have gone to your cousin. I believe that...to be the prime reason he assumed the Straith surname."

"And that took place recently, I take it?"

"Upon your uncle's death."

"I see. So. I was difficult to locate, harder to persuade, and Garrick was thinking he had a lock on the duchy until I showed up. Is that my situation?"

"None said you were difficult to locate, your grace."

"Really? I must have been having a *very* good time in London."

"So I have been told."

"But...my uncle stuck a fly in the ointment, didn't he? In order to assume the inheritance, I've got to wed a MacAffrey lass. Sight unseen. How am I doing? Is that my situation? In a nutshell?"

"Nutshell?"

"You know...take the major facts of an issue. Condense them. Quick and dirty. Wrap them up. Tie them in ribbons. I'm speaking metaphorically, of course. Nothing concrete. Oh! That reminds me. I'm going to need paper. My list is getting larger by the moment. I need paper to get this down. Lots of it. Rolls, if we have it. Is that possible?"

"Rolls of paper?"

"Well, yeah. Newspapers have them. We should be able to get them. And pens! No! Markers. Big ones. In every color. I work better when I have lots of space to make visuals."

"Markers, your grace?"

The man's eyebrows were lifted. *Damn it.* Neal had been on a roll. Thinking aloud. He'd have to keep a better watch on his tongue.

"How about we discuss it later? After my meeting? And, come on Millbourne. Isn't there any way I can get you to call me Neal? When we're alone? And nobody is around to hear?"

The valet considered him for a long moment. And then the man smiled. "And you must call me Mason, your gra—I mean, Neal."

"Mason. Got it. So. You ready for our next hurdle?"

"Your *feile-brecan?*"

"That, and the will. Sounds as if you've got real knowledge of it. Am I right?"

"I was one of the witnesses to the signing. I actually have a copy."

"A copy?"

"Signed by all involved."

"Excellent!"

Neal shrugged out of his robe, was startled again at the view of unblemished skin where he'd sported a spiral tattoo, then turned to eye the attire on the bed. The valet lifted the shirt and assisted him into it. Neal started buttoning. A lot of pearl buttons had been stitched onto the fabric, in series of two. They were going to be hidden by the ruffles. What a waste. Sewing machines hadn't been invented yet. Some poor woman had put every one of these pearls in place. Or, maybe it had been a child. For all he knew, child labor laws hadn't been enacted yet, either. It was 1803. A lot of work needed to be done on the social level still...

What the hell?

This thought process was perplexing, as well as disconcerting. What was it to him who sewed his clothing? And under what circumstances? Neal had seen all kinds of human conditions in his travels. Viewed economic situations that shouldn't support a dog. After a span, he'd learned to ignore them. He rarely even noticed. Such travails were part of life. He didn't allow it to become his issue.

Not then.

And he wasn't about to start now.

He finished the buttons. Started attaching the ruffled front piece. "I need to know about the will, Mason. Refresh my memory."

"What do you recollect?"

"Parts. But I'm a bit...uh...vague on the betrothal stuff. Give me the exact wording, and—now, wait...just a minute here."

The shirt was finished. He'd watched Mason wrap the coils of linen at Neal's wrists and slide little chains through them, making a cuff and link affair, securing the sleeves in place. Menswear really needed to get updated. And then the valet had approached and tossed a hank of the plaid over his Neal's shoulder.

"You need to hold still, your—I mean, Neal."

The man circled behind him, came back around to the front, wrapping material as he moved.

"Come on. You're not joking? This is it? I don't get anything else? No underwear? Nothing? Doesn't the wool...um. You know? Itch?"

"Well. That's one of the uses of the sporran, Neal."

Mason Millbourne pointed to the purse-thing. He was chuckling. And it wasn't all that funny.

CHAPTER EIGHT

FOR ONCE, AINSLEE DID AS she'd been ordered. She stayed in her tower room.

It wasn't an onerous chore, in the worst of times. She loved every inch of the old stone edifice, even if it was freezing cold in the winter and unbearably stuffy some nights in the summer. On those nights, she could always climb the ladder and sleep atop the highest part of the castle, watching the stars, secure atop the wooden latticework tower ceiling that an ancestor of hers had seen constructed.

She also loved the tower because it was an access point to the secret passages. She'd found it by trial and error one particularly severe winter when she couldn't keep the fire going. One section of her room was so much colder than anywhere else, while it seemed to have a continual breeze. By standing on a chair and hanging on one heavy shield, she'd twisted the thing a half turn, and it had come away from the wall, opening right out like a door! That shield hid a crawlspace just large enough for her, and beyond that, all sorts of halls and steps that linked her to the entire castle.

That passageway meant freedom.

And nobody else knew about it.

This evening, however, she was obeying because she had preparations to attend to, and not because any chance encounter with Father might remind him of her promised punishment. It seemed ridiculous to think the Laird of MacAffrey might still be planning and devising a beating for his younger daughter. He sounded like he was in great spirits. His laughter rang out more than once since the Straith laird had arrived.

Ainslee hadn't been able to see the official arrival, since her tower was on the opposite side of the entrance gate, but the walls weren't high enough to completely obscure the Straith retinue as they'd approached on the road. The day had altered since this morn – a normal event – and the skies were now gray-cast, with low-hanging clouds that promised rain. She'd still been able to make out the duke, easily seen since he was the only mounted man. He'd been surrounded by a double row of clansmen that denoted his Honor Guard. Directly behind them would be the bard, an elder clansman who kept the oral history of clan. He was followed by pipers, blaring out the clan marching tune. Although she couldn't see it, behind the pipers should be the clan spokesman known as a *bladier*. After him came an uncountable number of clansmen, all wearing the red, white, and black plaid denoting the Straith Clan. It looked extremely impressive. She almost gave into her curiosity and snuck down the passageway so she could watch their greeting. The only thing that stopped her was she didn't wish to upset her appearance.

It had come at too great a price in time and effort already.

She'd drawn cans of peat-colored water from the pump and lugged them all the way to her room. Fourteen in all. Then, she'd dragged one of the small wash tubs up the steps, stopping to catch her breath more than once. It took most of the afternoon and was laborious, but she didn't wish help, or notice, and she especially wished to avoid any curiosity. There hadn't been enough water for a full bath, but it worked for washing her hair, and then the rest of her. She'd even purloined sweet-smelling soap bits from her stepmother's closet to use.

The laird's younger daughter had been sent to her room with an early sup. She was under orders to stay put throughout the Straith's visit, no matter how long it should last. The new duke wasn't to see her. He wasn't to meet her. He wasn't to know of her existence.

It was going to cause a small riot if he really did ask for her hand, rather than Lileth's.

Ainslee spent a massive amount of time washing and rinsing her hair before she had it combed and pulled back to dry. That was just one punishment for being a lady. She'd much rather take a swim in the loch, but with all the clan gathering in the meadows, it was too risky. So, she'd bathed up here and didn't even complain while toting the used water, can-by-can, to the window, climbing up into the alcove, and tossing it out.

Her tower was in the oldest section of the castle, the walls over ten feet thick even at this height. They were so wide she could sleep in the window's well if she wanted. It was still a far cry from the wall thickness at castle's base, however. Measurements down there stood at thirty-three feet.

Bathing and clean-up weren't what took the longest, though. She'd spent hours twining her hair into long ropes of braids, winding and pinning them atop her head in all sorts of arrangements, trying for height and dignity.

And failing.

Nothing looked right. The mass of hair was too much.

She'd finally settled with wrapping two small braids at her temples, winding them about the crown of her head, pinning them together at the back, and then letting the rest fall free. Few knew her hair reached her knees, being even longer than Lileth's. That was fine with her. But Ainslee was cheating. Lileth's hair had a natural wave that thickened and shortened it, and Lileth stood a half-head taller than Ainslee.

At last, her *coiffure* was finished, and then she had a real issue: proper attire.

What should one wear when meeting a betrothed, supposedly for the first time? And why would she think she had an option? Everything she owned was thread-bare, or torn, or stained, or in need of altering. And they were all in pastel colors that brought out Lileth's beauty. Hideous shades on her. They made Ainslee look washed-out and ill. It couldn't be helped, however. They were all she had.

And then she remembered. She did own a yellow dress, with little gathers at the bodice to create an illusion of fullness for the twelve-year-old girl it had been designed for. Lileth had hated it on sight and banished it to Ainslee's wardrobe closet, where it had had been hanging amidst wildflower sachets for years, forgotten.

Ainslee rushed to her wardrobe. Tossed open the door. The dress was just as she remembered, dusty, but new-looking. The color was vivid. The fit was acceptable, too, although she looked like a child. That was hardly her fault. She didn't have another option. She never did. She didn't care, either. Ainslee had long ago decided she hated everything about being female. Her gender was a handicap. A bore. A burden. A decided curse. She'd have given anything to be down in the great hall right now, at the chieftain table, discussing terms...knowing what was happening, rather than banished to her tower, and left guessing.

But, if she had been born a boy, she'd be the MacAffrey Clan heir. Life would be so much different!

She wouldn't think about it. She'd spent enough time hating her gender. There was nothing left to do now except wait. Pray. And hope.

CHAPTER NINE

WELL.

This was borderline educational, but that was about it.

Neal stopped trying to move the conversation into his reason for being there after the fifth attempt, this time by the presentation of huge platters containing meats. He hadn't planned on staying past sundown, but the decision was taken from him by the length of the proceedings.

He'd been met at the gate and escorted inside, noted that the room wasn't nearly as large or impressive as the one at Castle Straith, and then they'd moved on. He'd been led to an alcove area, something they called a chieftain room. Garrick had followed at Neal's heels. Behind him were the clansmen denoting his Honor Guard.

Neal hadn't known what an Honor Guard was, or that he had one. The thought still gave him a rush of pleasure. They were a commanding sight. Imposing. They were all massive men, as tall, or taller, than either him or Garrick. They were physically fit. Identically arrayed in Straith colors. They were also all sporting full beards.

As if it was part of the attire.

Neal glanced about and got that answered. Aside from him, every man in the assemblage – with the exception of MacAffrey's heir, who was too young yet – had facial hair. Perhaps Neal shouldn't have shaved earlier. Even five o'clock shadow would have sufficed.

Discard it, Neal.

Not your issue.

He was here for one reason. Circumvent Garrick's claim. Get the betrothal portion of the will handled. Nothing in the will said he had to wed with anyone. All he had to do was get the engagement portion taken care of. After that, he could do as he liked. Wed if – and when – he so wished. Or not at all. He'd still be Duke of Straithcairn.

For life.

Mason had even winked at him while speaking of it.

So. Neal had one mission tonight, arrange an engagement. It couldn't be hard. He'd been running from one for years. And, as soon as this was accomplished, he could move onto what really mattered. All he had to do was get through what amounted to an oddball bit of protocol.

Easy.

He just needed to use patience. Bring out his negotiating skills. Neal snuck a hand beneath his sporran and scratched surreptitiously at his groin. He also needed to ignore the continual scrape of a woolen garment against bare skin, as well as the sensation of air. The day had turned into a storm-filled one, with a lot of accompanying wind gusts. He hadn't even noted them until dismounting the horse. Garrick, and everyone in his Honor Guard got an eyeful then, which wasn't all that embarrassing. Neal wasn't a small man. But nobody else seemed to have this trouble. Then again, he *had* just returned from London. He wasn't used to wearing what amounted to a knee-length skirt with attached, one-shoulder shawl. Why, he was so accustomed to wearing trousers his own valet had set them out today.

Twice since then, Neal had smacked a hand to the back of his left thigh, certain his ass was on display. He didn't have that problem on his right side. The claymore in its scabbard hung from the belt at his waist. That kept the plaid secured on that side. It felt like the material was continually slipping though, despite the four daggers stabbed through it from behind his belt. The two smaller knives were labeled as *skean-dhu*. Mason had tucked them into Neal's socks, one per foot, where they rubbed occasionally against his ankles in case he needed a reminder of their presence. It was a lot of weaponry. The men about him looked similarly armed. Neal wondered if this was how one dressed for a ceremony at the neighbor's, what must they take into battle?

It was a farce. He felt like a complete fraud. This attire was more difficult to wear than any English gent's could possibly be. But it would all be over soon. He could change back into clothing he recognized, even if it was poorly fitted. He just needed to get through the next hour or so.

The official introductions had turned into a long, incredibly drawn-out affair. Whiskey was brought out. A dram poured out and swigged by just about everyone. One thing was immediately clear. The Scots really did make great whiskey, and apparently, they always had.

From the chieftain room, the Laird of MacAffrey had moved the assemblage back into the great hall. Neal had been escorted to a dais, climbed onto it, and shuffled into position before one of two throne-like chairs at the center of the raised platform. He'd been accompanied by Garrick and the Honor Guard. Garrick was at Neal's immediate left. Five men were on his left. They were the ones who'd be seated. Seven more clansmen stood behind.

Good thing everyone knew their place. Neal was clueless.

MacAffrey's entourage had done pretty much the same maneuvering, except his heir sat at his far side, followed by an Honor Guard. The MacAffrey laird had said some more words of welcome, and they'd sat. Drunk more whiskey. Made more toasts. Someone in Neal's camp had signaled the Straith *bladier* to present himself and bring up the reason for their meeting. The man had done his duty, assumed the orator spot before the dais and announced that the Duke of Straithcairn had come to speak about a matter of legal proceedings.

Their host – who requested to be called Dughall – had stalled the proceedings, by loudly thanking the man for the announcement. Dughall had then waved his arm, and called loudly for refreshments. Neal had lifted his brows and watched the table spread with platters of all kinds of unidentifiable things that turned out to be stuffed sheep tongue, blood puddings, haggis, flat oatcakes called bannock, and cold smoked salmon. All of it was accompanied with large tureens containing ale, while they continued to pour out raw whiskey.

Before partaking of anything on the platters, Niall had thanked the man for his generous repast and finished by remarking he'd come not on a neighborly visit, but to conduct business. That announcement didn't get him any action. It merely got him toasted again. Nothing was said about a betrothal. Nothing about the purpose of his visit.

Nothing but stalling.

Neal wasn't eating much. He nibbled and tasted, trying not to show that he had no idea what he was eating, or if it was even edible in its current state. Nothing had been refrigerated. Everything seemed to come with a lot of sauce around it. He was probably flirting with food poisoning. Or any number of digestive ailments.

And time kept passing.

They brought out torches. Stuck them in high holders that looked like lamp posts. Lit them. That added a lot of smoke to the gathering, but little light. Neal's nose itched enough he had to dab at it occasionally using the cloth Mason had tucked into the sporran. Neal's eyes stung. His belly roiled on him more than once. He was borderline inebriated. And they were no nearer his objective than when he'd first arrived.

This was truly great whiskey, though. He obviously needed to look into acquiring stock in it. *No.* Not just acquiring stock. He might as well own and operate a distillery. He'd need legal advice on how to trademark the operation here in the UK, but somebody needed to get this whiskey out to the rest of the world. Neal added it to his mental list. Right beneath coffee.

Wait a minute, Neal.

This was stupid. The amount of alcohol he'd consumed was fogging his thinking. There were too many variables when investing in grain-based products. It wouldn't be a good idea until the government came up with crop insurance programs. Even then, it wouldn't be a massive money-making machine like steel. He wished he'd been a little more interested in history. He'd know for certain what to invest in, and when.

Too bad it wasn't closer to the twentieth century. He'd be first in line to purchase Bell Telephone stock. *No!* He needed to invest in Ford Motor Company. And make certain to back anything Nikolai Tesla was inventing. Neal was in a truly unique position. He actually had the ability to see that electricity was the energy source of an engine, and not fossil fuel! That hadn't even occurred to him until right now.

Perhaps that was the rationale behind his teleportation to this exact year. Into this place. With his memory intact. There might be a higher power at work. It was possible...but he wouldn't really know unless he succeeded. And then, it would be his future self that saw it.

Wait a minute.

Would he actually be re-born in the latter part of the twentieth century again? If so, would he be Neal Straithmore, CEO of Straithmore Enterprises? And, if that happened, what kind of stock would that Neal have in his portfolio? If energy conservation and environmental issues weren't money-generating enterprises...just what would be?

The din ebbed and rose about him. Neal wasn't paying much attention. Funds needed to be sent for his first acquisition. It wasn't going to be coffee. Or whiskey. Or menswear. He'd been right the first time. He needed to corner the market in iron and then steel. That way, he'd have some sort of control when the automobile industry started.

He really needed to get this idea on paper, so even if he wasn't around, a future Straith could see it to fruition.

Future Straith?

Neal jerked involuntarily. The move straightened his back. Bumped his shoulders against the back of the chair. Where in the hell had that thought come from? He'd never wanted kids. For a reason. As far as he could tell raising children was a complete crapshoot. You could have the same set of parents. Same parenting involved. Same schooling, education opportunities, financial resources. Get completely different outcomes. Children were a financial, emotional, and mental drain. And worse of all, was the time depletion involved.

But...if he didn't have any...would that mean Garrick's progeny would eventually inherit?

What a horrid thought.

Neal snuck a glance to his left. It was a chore to sit beside Garrick. Neal hadn't been mistaken earlier when they'd first met. An unpleasant vibe really did emanate from the man. What if the man's children took after their sire? Did Neal really want them having this information? The ability to corner the stock market? Gain unimaginable wealth? And with it, unmitigated dominance? And why did that thought make every muscle in his body tense up?

Damn everything.

It was his destiny to control the stock market, and in so doing, save the environment. The absolute last thing he wanted was this much knowledge and power in the hands of an evil son-of-a-bitch. This was getting more and more problematic by the moment. He needed to get it written down. Look it over. Connect the dots. Evaluate things.

And if they ever manage to finalize this betrothal nonsense, he would.

Another round of whiskey was poured. More toasts given. More stalling occurred. Neal accepted a drop or two more in his tankard. He'd given up trying to keep up with his host's drinking, resorting to taking a slight sip for every toast. He'd never been a drinker, not even in his early twenties in college. He knew enough not to go head-to-head with a man who was.

All of which was getting him absolutely nowhere.

Neal dabbed at his nose, before turning to his right, and addressing his host. "MacAffrey! My good man! You do know that I am here on business? Yes?"

He spoke loudly enough the man had to have heard. But MacAffrey ignored him, speared another joint of roast mutton onto the platter before him, split open a roll next, shoved a huge pat of butter within it, smashed it shut, and then, *finally*, the man answered.

"Aye. That I do."

"Do you have a chamber for our use?"

"What the devil for?"

"It's a private matter!"

"What you have to say can be heard by all."

Neal raised his brows. "Very well. I'll begin."

"Grant! Start up a pipe!"

Strains of pipe music started infiltrating the scene, adding unnecessarily to the cacophony. Neal had to yell his next words.

"I've come to solidify a union with our clans!"

The man replied with his own yell. "Thought as much, your grace. So, we did."

The lone piper had been joined by more of them, adding more sound to the din. Neal's head started pounding. He put a hand to his forehead, only to connect with his wound. That smarted. He winced. This was ridiculous.

"I'm seeking a betrothal with your daughter!"

"Lileth, is prepared to receive you, too…just as soon as——. As soon as—— well." The man hiccoughed. "We need more to eat! And more whiskey, MacGruder! Bring out another keg! All around!"

Another keg? And more stalling?

"I am here about the betrothal, Dughall!" He had to speak over the din. He didn't have much choice.

"And a fine duchess Lileth will make."

"Lileth? Who said anything about Lileth? I've come to ask for your daughter, Ainslee!"

Neal shouted it. His host looked stunned. Everything else seemed to stop. Movement. Sound. Everyone stopped talking. The pipers ceased playing, although wails of sound leaked out of their pipes as air got expelled. The Laird of MacAffrey's mouth kept opening and closing, looking like a fish out of water. A big, loud, drunken, red-bearded fish.

"*Ainslee?* Did you say——? I thought I heard——? Surely, your grace is mistaken. Or…I heard you wrong?"

The man was sputtering. That might have been amusing in another time or setting. Neal should probably be grateful Dughall's voice had lost quite a few decibels. He wasn't. He was annoyed. His head was throbbing. And his belly wasn't thrilled with him, either.

"You do have a daughter named Ainslee? Yes?"

"Aye. That, I do. But…*Ainslee?*"

The man's voice reflected shock or something close.

"I'm here to betroth your daughter. I've asked for the hand of Ainslee. We can set a date for the wedding at a later meeting."

"You can na' be serious! She——! She——! Why, I do na' believe she's even left the schoolroom."

"Is she of marriageable age?"

"'Tis most unexpected. I mean, surely you jest. *Ainslee?*"

Neal gritted his teeth at the man's obstinacy. He could really use an acet-aminophen. But they hadn't been invented. *Hell.* Aspirin hadn't even been invented yet, that he knew of. The smoke wafting about wasn't helping. He narrowed his eyes. "I asked if Ainslee is of marriageable age."

"She is," the man admitted, albeit in a grudging manner.

"I fail to see the trouble then. Let us settle. Allow me to meet with her."

The man's eyes looked like they might pop out. When he answered, he was stammering. "M-m-meet with her? To-to-tonight?"

"Well. Yes. Perhaps you'll grant us a bit of privacy, too? Just long enough to give her the Straith betrothal ring. If need be, I'll accept a chaperone."

"You are toying with me, your grace. And it is na' pleasant, let me assure you. Surely you mean Lileth."

"My offer is for Ainslee. Unless, she's affianced elsewhere?"

"But—. But—. Wait! You may wish to reconsider. Lileth has a large dowry. The woman comes with two thousand pounds! Two thousand, man! Sterling! 'Twas settled upon her by her mother, who was a member of the Sinclair Clan!"

"We've already wasted time, Dughall. Now, we are wasting words. I came here to betroth your daughter. Nothing in the documents state *which* daughter; just as nothing specifies my name as the reigning duke. Now, I ask again, and this is the final time, for the hand of your daughter, Ainslee. Is your answer yes. Or no?"

MacAffrey's face turned a mottled shade of red before he answered, amidst more stammering and sputtering. "But...your grace! We all assumed...! We thought—! Lileth is first-born. 'Tis right and proper that she be wed first."

Neal waited several long moments as he contemplated their host. The standing members of his Honor Guard stepped forward. Those who'd been sitting shoved their chairs back and also stood. Nobody had a sword drawn, but the menace being displayed was obvious. It simply remained unspoken. Something of the tension taking place on the dais must have filtered through the crowd about them. He could hear the shuffling of feet. Whispers. Groans.

"Does this mean you're...turning down my offer?"

Neal asked it with a loud enough voice nobody in the vicinity could fail to hear it correctly. And then he waited. The Laird of MacAffrey was frowning. They both knew if the offer was declined, the agreement would be nullified. MacAffrey would lose the Duke of Straithcairn as a son-in-law, and Neal would be free. He watched the man's comprehension of it, and knew exactly when it happened. The fellow's shoulders sagged visibly. And he sighed.

"I will have Ainslee shown to the library. My man, MacGruder, will show you the way. *Ainslee?* By God in heaven, I can na' believe it."

The man stood on unsteady legs and shoved at his son until the lad also stood. Neal followed suit, and then had to wait before Garrick finally rose, as well.

"Get a move on, Mitchell! You heard the man. Ainslee! Send a message to your mother! Send another to Ainslee! And somebody get me another whiskey! I am going to need it."

The man looked older of a sudden. Feeble. He was still shaking his head as he left the platform.

CHAPTER TEN

SHE'D GIVEN UP HOPE AND was well into plans for Lileth's
elopement with her Robert, when a heavy knock came. Ainslee stopped
pacing, swiveled from the far wall, sent a silent prayer of thanks heavenward, and crossed straight to her door. She should've asked who knocked
first. It was her second half-brother, William, standing in the gloom of her
hall. He looked pleased. That didn't bode well.

"William."

It wasn't a greeting. It was a statement of unpleasant fact. Her voice
reflected it. She would have shut the door on him, but couldn't have succeeded. He was a product of a MacHugh and MacAffrey union, and, as
such, he towered over her and outweighed her by at least two stone.

He sneered. She smelled whiskey on him.

"My. My. Aren't ye fancied-oop this eve? Almost like you were expectin'
someone."

"What do you want?"

"Father sent me to fetch you."

Her heart dropped with a sickening motion. A chill ran through her. She
knew the color drained from her face. She felt it. The combination was
debilitating. She barely kept it from sounding in her voice.

"Father?"

"Aye. He is requiring yer presence. In the library. Right now."

"The...library?"

Her voice warbled slightly, but he heard it, and was thoroughly entertained by it, if his grin meant anything. The younger MacAffrey lads were
all tucked in for the night and Lileth had managed to portray an illness

so severe the Lady of MacAffrey was in attendance at her stepdaughter's bedside. That meant there wasn't anyone Ainslee could call on to get out of her predicament.

All of which ran through her mind while William watched.

She didn't need to ask what had transpired. It was obvious. The all-mighty Duke of Straithcairn hadn't done as she'd begged this morn. The bastard had asked for Lileth. The men had then spent a large amount of time celebrating, allowing even the younger MacAffrey males to tipple a dram or so. Then someone had triggered Father's memory about Ainslee's transgression and the punishment he'd promised. It had probably been William.

Punishment was always meted out in the library.

There wasn't any other reason for a summons that sent her there.

Why, oh why, hadn't she considered this possibility? And why hadn't she asked who was on the other side of the door before unbarring it? And why did Straith have to be an unprincipled cad, with little care for other's troubles? Ainslee lifted her skirts with a hand that trembled, worked at conquering it, and then moved past William into the hall.

"Why didn't he send a servant? Or, have you taken to delivering messages now?"

"Oh. I offered," William replied.

Ainslee started walking, ignoring him as much as possible. Her free hand skimmed along the banister as she descended the spiral stone steps. The satin slippers didn't make much sound. She didn't hear William, either. Actually, she couldn't hear much over the sound of her own heartbeat as it grew louder and faster with each step. She didn't have to hear William to place him, however. She knew he'd be right behind her. He wouldn't miss this.

She wouldn't demur. She wouldn't cower. She wouldn't sob. Or beg. And she definitely wouldn't cry out. No matter how many times Father hit her. Or how hard. She wouldn't make a sound. She daren't. It might be heard. She hadn't seen the Duke of Straithcairn or any of his retinue leave yet. For all Ainslee knew, they were still in the great hall, toasting the betrothal of Lileth, while they waited for their host to return from the library.

She'd failed.

For some strange reason, that fact was a harder thing to deal with than her fear. She didn't want to look too closely into why, so she didn't. She simply put one foot before the other. They reached the third floor landing. Ainslee walked from the spiral steps into the hall, her steps barely making sound on the span of wood covered with the long woven rugs, either. This hall led to the salons, the ladies solar, the study…and finally—

…the library.

She stopped at the large double doors, her nose nearly touching. They'd fashioned these doors so tall that torchlight didn't penetrate the gloom near the top of the doorframe. Ainslee pulled in a shuddered breath, straightened her shoulders, blinked rapidly at the moisture atop her eyes, and then reached for the handle. It was solid iron. Heavy. Well-used. Cold to the touch. It turned down without a hint of delay or effort when it normally required a wrenching.

The door opened inward into a room lit by a huge chandelier, since it was too hot for a fire. The library was a two-story room, built in an octagonal shape. Book-filled shelves lined every available wall, interspersed with two long windows that looked out at the MacAffrey loch. The room also contained free-standing shelving units. They were arranged, radiating outward from the center area, like spokes in a wheel. There were lots of shadowy recesses. Ainslee moved through them without a sound. Somewhere she heard the hint of a clock ticking away at time. It actually carried over the sound of her pulse.

She was heading toward the center of the room. Father always stood there, beside a massive desk all the MacAffrey lairds must have used. But he wasn't there. Ainslee sent a quick glance about the spot, and then back the way she'd come. The door had been pulled shut behind her. William hadn't even followed her in.

Ainslee forced herself to scan the area again. It looked deserted. There was only that large desk, a table, two sofas, assorted chairs. And then she saw a man silhouetted against one of the long windows.

He moved.

Ainslee dropped her eyes and stood rooted in place, trembling visibly. Why, oh why, was it so hard to be brave tonight?

Why?

"Well. Well. What have we here? It was *you* this morn. I should have guessed."

Ainslee's head snapped up. She stared across the lit area, and then up. He'd stepped fully into the light. Flickers from the candlelit chandelier danced through the area, highlighting every bit of Straithcairn brawn.

Oh! Thank the saints! It was the duke!

Relief whooshed through her with a rush, resembling a burn running with a torrent of water. She felt light-headed. Woozy. Faint. Ainslee reached out and grabbed onto the nearest object. It became the back of a sofa, the wood hard and solid in her hand. She clamped tighter to it as little dots danced about her vision, making the duke's image warp and then clear.

Warp.

Clear.

"Y-y-your...grace." The words trembled.

"Miss Ainslee MacAffrey."

The library acoustics gave a resonating timbre to his voice as he said her name. His voice was warm. Deep. Musical-sounding.

"Your...grace." This time, she cleared her throat first.

"You should probably call me Neal."

"Your grace."

Her voice was stronger. Her legs felt the same. Ainslee sketched a deep curtsey before standing back up. She didn't release the sofa.

"We need to move past the greeting portion of this, Ainslee. We're being timed. I've probably got but a minute left. You must reside in the Hebrides, as long as it took to fetch you."

"You...asked for me?"

"Of course. Wasn't that the plan?"

"Yes...but—?"

"But, what? Never mind. Whatever it is, we'll discuss it later. We don't have much time. I need to give you the Straith emerald engagement ring, and if you weren't so damned young, I might...steal a kiss."

She gasped. He regarded her for a bit and then snickered.

"Very well. We'll forego any kissing."

He stepped toward her, gaining illumination along his straight nose, full lips, strong chin... Her heart gave a start at his nearness. Ainslee's eyes widened as she felt it. She'd known he was handsome, but it hadn't meant much until right then.

"You truly...asked for me?"

He sighed heavily. "Give me your hand. Or...? You don't want a bended-knee proposal, do you?"

"What? Why?"

"Why would you want a man on his knees? Or why am I here asking for you? Because, if you're questioning the latter, quite frankly, *I'm* not even sure. I believe it has something to do with lesser evils. Add in a large, unbelievable dose of quantum physics, along with a heretofore undiscovered altruistic nature I apparently possessed, but have kept hidden, even from myself. All possibilities. There could even be something in the whiskey I wasn't informed about. Your call."

He'd walked around the desk while he'd spoken and stood before her, looking down. She didn't know how to answer. His words were strange.

Bewildering. And being this close to him had an odd effect on her throat. As if a knot had lodged there. She hadn't known he was this large. He hadn't looked it when lying on the ground this morn. The man was enormous. Ainslee was dwarfed. Even if she'd worn her riding boots with heels, regardless of how out of place they'd look, it wouldn't have helped. She glanced up at him, and then back to the ruffles at his shirt front at her eye level.

"Your hand, my dear?"

He put his out, palm upward. Ainslee regarded it for a moment before craning her neck to look back up at him.

"Look. I don't bite. All right? Not recently, anyway."

"Bite?"

"I'm joking. Trying to alleviate your fears."

"I'm...na' frightened."

"Left hand please? You looked ready to keel over when you first saw me. Don't bother denying it. I didn't just parachute in here, you know. Oh. Wait. Maybe I did."

He stopped and chuckled. "Sorry. Private joke. I need your hand, dear. For the ring. I mean, you are accepting me, aren't you?"

Ainslee nodded and placed her hand in his, and experienced a jolt of something completely unrelated to fear. She'd have jerked her hand back if he hadn't already held it. She watched him slide the ring on first her ring finger, then her index finger, and then her middle finger where it dangled. It was useless. Her fingers were too small. He settled with crooking her fingers into a fist to hold the ring in place.

"There. Should work for the time being. As long as you don't go around hitting anyone. Pulling weeds. Doing dishes. You know. Stuff like that."

"Your grace?"

She glanced up. He was smiling. Her heart stuttered. She moved her gaze to his mouth and chin before anything else happened.

"You really need to call me Neal. All right? We are affianced, after all. I'm pretty sure you can stop the 'your grace' stuff, especially when we're alone."

The breath she eased out trembled. She hoped he didn't notice. His voice was unsettling. His touch even more so. Her entire body felt tingly all over, aware and alert, as if she'd just risen from the waves of the loch after a clandestine swim. Before the sun rose and the mists cleared. On the coldest of morns. Except this sensation didn't make her feel remotely cold. Anywhere.

"Hmm. If I'd known the color of your eyes, I'd have been tempted to ignore the custom, and bring a sapphire ring. I'd have made certain it was smaller, too," he remarked. "By the way, we need to set a wedding date. You can figure that out, can't you?"

"I can be ready tomorrow."

He grinned at her. He had a beautiful smile. Very white teeth. Perfectly straight. Her heart stuttered again. Ainslee's eyes widened. She swiftly moved her gaze back to the ruffles at his shirt front. Pulled on her hand. He released it.

"Oh. I think you'll need at least a week. Maybe two. If this dress is an example of your wardrobe, I'm in severe danger of being accused of cradle-robbing. I was told you were somewhere in the age range of nineteen. But, you look about twelve in this get-up. You're going to need some new clothing. Something age-appropriate. Tell your sire to send me the bill. And there isn't a woman I know of that would turn that offer down."

Her heart gave another stumble. That was beyond worrisome. She wasn't supposed to react to the duke. Or any man. And she didn't dare feel anything! She set about squashing the reactions. Now. Right now.

"Verra well, your grace. Two weeks."

She took a step back to make it easier. Glanced back up. Couldn't move her gaze.

Again.

"Oh. No rush. I was just making conversation. Tell you what? Why don't we meet up in two weeks...to discuss possible dates? And please. It's Neal."

He folded his arms, and tilted his head to one side, giving the impression of looking her over as he might a horse or similar acquisition. Ainslee couldn't shake the sensation. Her back straightened, and that just put every bit of her breasts against the tight bodice of the gown, defining portions of her anatomy no one ever saw. She watched him glance there and then he looked at something over her head. She watched a nerve twitch in his jaw. For the longest moment, neither of them moved. Nobody even breathed.

"Ainslee?"

Her eldest half-brother stuck his head in, his voice accompanying the door opening. Ainslee immediately stepped toward the duke. The move was instantaneous and instinctive. Self-preserving. And completely foreign.

It also blocked her from view.

"Oh...g-good eve, uh...your...grace. Have you seen my...uh...my sister, Ainslee, by chance?"

Mitchell's words were slurred and nearly unintelligible. He stumbled into the door. It slammed into the wall. Smacked back against his shoulder, making him stagger backwards before catching it.

"As a matter of fact..." The duke began drawing out the words, but Mitchell interrupted him.

"The laird's been yellin' for her."

"Tell him there's no need. We've about finished."

"I doona' believe I can save her a beatin' this...go-round. She's so stup't. She kens better than to set him against her when he's in his cups."

"Set him against her?" The duke repeated, without one inflection to his voice.

"You hush your tongue, Mitchell MacAffrey!"

Ainslee moved out from behind the duke before her brother said anything more. His face lightened and he smiled drunkenly at her.

"Oh. Hello, Ains...lee. Come along. Father's yellin' for you."

Mitchell gestured for her. Ainslee moved another step away from the duke. She didn't look up. She couldn't. She could barely move without somewhere showing signs of abject shame. Embarrassment. If only a hole would open in the floor before her! She'd have dropped into it with alacrity. She dropped a curtsey in his direction. She didn't have enough moisture in her mouth to speak, so she whispered.

"I must go."

"Oh. I don't think so," he answered.

The duke snatched up her hand and used it to pull her against him. Ainslee gave a soft gasp as he gripped her to his left side. He glanced down, his expression harsh, and nothing like the one he'd given her earlier. And then he looked across the library at her brother.

CHAPTER ELEVEN

NEAL.
  Neal.
What are you doing, buddy?

Neal castigated himself silently, while Ainslee trembled at his side. Just like that, he'd gone off the script. Without any warning. This was the opposite of his objective. He was here to dot some 'I's, cross some 'T's. Get the hell out of Dodge. If the little waif lived in an abusive environment, what the hell did it matter to him? She wouldn't be the first woman. Besides, she didn't have any obvious bruising. No signs of trauma. She was obviously used to it. This wasn't his concern.

He almost groaned.

There wasn't one inkling to why he was doing this. Something weird was happening here. He didn't recognize it and he damned sure didn't like not knowing what it was.

So what if Ainslee was small? So excruciating young? What did it matter that she was – *face it, Neal* – the waif was mercilessly attractive. *So what?* Neal had been around stunning women his entire adult life although Ainslee MacAffrey might overshadow them all. Even dressed in a poorly fashioned dress, in an excruciatingly bad color choice, she had a beauty that transcended normality. It was almost ethereal.

He'd recognized it instantly. He'd nearly whistled when she'd first approached. She had a waterfall of midnight-colored hair falling across her shoulders and down her back, incredibly vivid sapphire hued eyes set amidst black lashes that wouldn't need mascara even if it was available at this point in time, and pristine skin that a cosmetic counter couldn't possibly enhance.

So what, Neal?

Argh.

He had to factor in her first reaction to him. Perhaps that was why he was standing here now, preparing to go head-to-head with her abuser. Ainslee's face had lit up when she'd recognized him. He guessed the reason for it now. He didn't think he was far off. She'd been expecting another man entirely. And that made her bravery as she'd approached him even more remarkable.

Neal stiffened as he regarded the MacAffrey heir. The move tightened his arm and lifted Ainslee from the floor, plastering her to his left leg. The closeness of her, as she melted into his protective arm caused an unfamiliar surge of electricity to course through his body.

He rocked back slightly with the force of it before returning upright. But, all of that had to have been in his mind. Ainslee hadn't moved, and her brother didn't appear to have noted anything.

What in the hell?

Mitchell grinned drunkenly across at them. Wove in place. And then he wagged a finger in their direction.

"Ye need to release..me, uh. Me. Me..." The lad stopped. Licked his lips. Hiccoughed. "Her. Ains...lee. Me sister."

Neal cleared his throat. Glanced down at Ainslee. "I don't believe we've finalized our plans. Have we, darling?"

He attempted a smile. Another jolt went through his belly and lower limbs. It messed with his intent. His eyes widened, any attempt at a smile died, and he shifted his gaze before anything more alien happened. The area where her brother stood was a viable option. And he knew he could deal with Mitchell, at least.

"Be off, lad. Find your father. Tell him to attend me here. Right now. And while you're at it, request my Honor Guard."

"But—."

"I said to be off. *Now.*"

Neal used his most authoritarian voice, the one described in one magazine article about him as being *predatory.* Bestial. Almost feral. Neal hadn't minded the description. It was an imaginative use of words by a journalist to sell papers. Hadn't meant it was real. But he did possess something that got masses to listen. It wasn't a rise in volume. It was more how he lowered his tone and projected it outward. He'd always possessed this ability. That was one reason he'd managed his first takeover. While his quarry had waited for a mic and sound system, Neal had been addressing the crowd. Swaying them with words every stockholder wanted to hear. Positive return. Zero risk. Profit. Profit.

Profit.

...*always profit.*

His voice throbbed through the library now, sending bass tones filled with command that expected obedience. The MacAffrey heir stood straighter, and then he did an off-kilter bow before leaving. The door shut behind him with a bang.

"You...should put me down now," Ainslee whispered at his side.

"Oh. You believe so, do you?"

The words left this mouth, but he didn't move anything. His body was giving him trouble. That was as foreign as it was unbelievable. He might as well be on another planet. His strength was already an oddity. What was happening, even more so. It didn't take the slightest effort to continue holding her aloft with one arm. Exactly where she was, while nerve endings fired through him, sending messages filled with warmth.

No.

This was closer to scorching.

And then even worse things happened. The wool plaid of his kilt-thing, the velvet jacket, and the finely woven linen shirt that barely covered his ass and loins, weren't remotely sufficient to prevent what was happening. He held a softly curved, wickedly desirable, and fully mature female against him. His body immediately recognized it and went on the alert, despite his effort at stopping it. This was ridiculous. Impossible. Intensely personal. He wasn't bestial. Or feral. And he sure as hell wasn't craven. Controlling testosterone had never been a problem. That Neal could remember, anyway.

Well.

It was now.

Neal tightened every muscle he possessed, but it was useless. His dick was operating at another frequency. It lengthened. Hardened. And prepared. The scratch of wool didn't temper it. He couldn't even feel the fiber until his erection rammed into the obstruction of his sporran. Neal shoved down on the bag with his right hand, and continued the pressure, although he hoped it looked more like he was negligently resting a palm there. Mason hadn't mentioned this use for a sporran. That might be one of the reasons the valet had been so amused.

"My father...will be here any moment."

"I certainly. Hope. So." He broke the words into separate sentences, spoken from between gritted teeth. It was the best he could manage. He didn't look down toward her. He didn't dare.

"You must set...me down."

Her whisper didn't help things. It was akin to having a bellows working on an already massive fire. This was completely out of his realm of experience. Neal sucked in a breath. Held it. The move lifted her even closer. Neal shut his eyes. Little blasts resembling fireworks filled the space behind his eyelids.

Breathe, Neal.

Just.

Breathe.

Neal shoved air out. Sucked in another large breath. Held it. Shoved it back out. Repeated the process. The fireworks effect fizzled and started fading. "Really?" he finally managed to answer.

He felt her give a nod. Or give something that could be a nod.

"Maybe I don't. Want. To."

She gasped. "Your grace!"

"It's. Neal."

That came out harsher than he intended. He felt her trembling again. "Please?"

Oh, shit.

She had a hint of tears to her voice. Neal pulled in another heavy breath. Released it. Opened his eyes. Glanced down. *Yep.* She had a gloss atop her eyes. Now, they really resembled gemstones.

He looked away. Toward the door. It was opening and closing almost silently. His brain kicked into gear.

Finally.

A large fellow filed in. A similarly large fellow followed at his heels. The first had gone to the right upon his entrance. The second man went to the left. The next man went to the right again. The next one went left. Neal counted six of them. Seven. Eight. More. Man after man entered and silently wove their way through the bookshelves at the outer edges of the room. He recognized them. It was the members of his Honor Guard. Their presence sent impressions of cool through him, instantly calming a level of testosterone-fueled madness that had seemed insurmountable.

Pride filled him as they assembled in the space behind and to both sides of where he stood with Ainslee. It was an amazing feeling. Unless he counted Eric, Neal had never had anyone protecting his back. And now, he did. Just like that. Neal looked over his right shoulder and then his left. Nodded each time. And then he had to clear his throat against an onslaught of something that might be emotion.

"Ahem. Gentlemen."

One of them stepped forward to Neal's right side. He must be their leader. Not that Neal had any experience or information to go by, that the title felt right. The man bent his head in deference and then looked back at Neal. The fellow was a good two inches taller than Neal and looked a great deal heavier. He could easily be one of those fellows in competition at a Highland game somewhere, tossing a telephone-pole thing. The pole had a name. Neal couldn't recall it at the moment. He'd figure it out later.

"What's your name?" he enquired.

The fellow's eyebrows shot up, and his lips twisted. Otherwise, he didn't give much sign that Neal had probably just violated all kinds of protocol.

"You do na' recognize me, your grace?"

"I...had an accident this morn. Hit my head." Neal moved his right hand from the sporran to carefully lift the hair at his temple. The leader's eyebrows lifted and he whistled. Neal quickly replaced his hand atop the sporran before it had a chance to stick out farther.

"Your grace...be all right?"

"It's not as bad as it looks. I have some memory loss. Head pain. Comes and goes."

"Me name's Iain, your grace. Iain Staithmore."

Whoa! Neal started. He had a hard time stopping further reaction. He could be looking at his great-great-great-whatever grandfather. And that was a supremely pleasant thought. He grinned. Leaned a hair closer to the man. "Iain. Tell me. Where's my cousin, Garrick?"

"He's...na' a-boot at present. Word is he returned to the castle."

"Really?"

"Aye."

Neal's mind raced, filling in blanks. Perhaps everyone in Straith had gotten lucky and his cousin had returned to pack. Leave. Seek his fortune elsewhere. That was unlikely.

Next option was that Garrick had returned to lick his wounds. Develop a new strategy. That would merit consideration. And vigilance. It was the likely reason. And a bit worrisome. Neal made a mental note to put it on his charts. If Mason found the paper so Neal could start filling it.

There was another possible scenario. Garrick could have returned so he could play the part of town crier. Be the first with the story. The center of attention. Neal snickered.

"Well. I think he left a bit too soon. Know what I mean?"

"Your grace?"

"He's going to regret missing this."

The leader's lips moved into a shadow of a smile. Neal was hard-put not to chuckle. All of which helped considerably against the raging emotion he'd been struggling with. Something so like...

Just name it, Neal. Quit being such a coward.

He'd been dealing with lust.

Not just any lust, either. The desire had been on a massive scale. Unwarranted. Unprovoked. And fairly unbelievable. He still experienced it for the woman glued to his side. If anyone looked at how he pressed down on his sporran, they'd have probably guessed it, too. Neal made a face, pulled in another breath, and thanked his lucky stars for the arrival of his Honor Guard.

Their presence had sent what amounted to a spray of cool spray onto a bonfire. The mental exercise he'd just done over Garrick's absence had helped, too. Hopefully, it was enough. Feeling sufficiently fortified, Neal had one last hurdle to clear. He licked his lips and looked down at Ainslee.

And his heart flipped over.

Damn it.

The door smacked open with a bang. Neal jumped. Everyone turned that direction to watch the Laird of MacAffrey stomp toward them. He had a lot of men behind him. The room started filling with MacAffrey clan. A rough estimate put the amount of thirty. Neal could see more MacAffrey clansmen in the hall behind, unable to shove into the rapidly filling room.

The space between the bookshelves filled to a claustrophobic level. Neal scanned the ranks. Straith clan were outnumbered at least three-to-one here. There was another problem, as well. Nobody on MacAffrey's side appeared to be remotely sober.

"Well, your bloody grace Straithcairn! I am here! As you so ordered! You have the gall to have me fetched. Me! Ordered about? In my own home!"

Dughall's complexion matched his hair as he finished shouting. Ainslee had gone board stiff in Neal's arms. And she was trembling again. Neal waited for the sound of her father's voice to die.

"Greetings, Dughall," Neal finally answered.

"You've spoken with my daughter?"

"She wears the Straith emerald betrothal ring as we speak."

"I'll be thanking you to release her, then. Ainslee? Hie to your room!"

Ainslee would have moved, but Neal didn't allow it. He made certain of it by pulling her tighter with his arm. Her father's eyes bulged out, he took a step closer, grabbed a large breath, and used it to spew whiskey-tainted words their direction.

"You think to disobey me, lass? Now? Before all? It'll be the last—!"

Neal interrupted him. "Enough! Control yourself, Dughall. We've a lady in our presence."

"Ainslee's nae lady, Straithcairn! She's a lazy slut with naught for a recommend, and even less to redeem her!"

Ainslee gasped. Neal reeled backward a hairsbreadth. He wasn't the lone one. He sensed movement throughout the ranks of his Honor Guard about him. Shock ran his veins, sending an icy sensation. It annihilated any remainder of his lustful impulses as he realized the extent of abuse Ainslee had suffered. No wonder it hadn't left scars. Verbal abuse rarely did.

The man's clan didn't appear to have the same sentiment as their laird, however. Neal noticed they were starting to desert. Men were slipping from the room, and the hall looked less crowded. Neal narrowed his eyes, lowered his chin and then his voice, and when he spoke he made certain this announcement projected through the room, and out into the hall.

"As most of you know, I came here to arrange my future marriage with a daughter of the MacAffrey laird. I did this due to an agreement that binds my hands. We are all agreed on this? Can I get an 'aye'?"

There were some sounds of agreement, but her father shushed it with a wave of his arms.

"Aye! We are all agreed. Of course we are. But come, Straith. Reconsider. Look at who you've chosen. Ainslee is a…well. I have said all I will a-boot it. You should wed my Lileth. I am na' the lone one thinking you've lost your eyesight, as well as your sense. Most are in agreement with me. We've even drunk to it."

Nobody said anything for a bit. It was as if his words had to settle and get considered. Neal lowered Ainslee to her feet, but didn't release her. He swiveled her to face her father. The back of her braided crown reached his mid-chest. Then, he wrapped his other arm about her and pulled her to him. It was meant to look like an embrace. He knew he'd achieved it when the laird's face darkened to a dark red color again. And then Neal spoke, making certain nobody misunderstood.

"Well, Dughall. I do believe I've changed my mind."

CHAPTER TWELVE

O H, DEAREST GOD!

The duke's statement sent a shard of agonizing pain through her chest. For a fraction of time, Ainslee didn't think her heart could absorb it and continue beating. Nothing had ever hurt this badly.

Ever.

She dropped her gaze to the floor beneath her, and fought waves of misery that brought overwhelming sobs with them. She shook visibly. She hated that. The duke's arms flexed about her. She would have flung them off if she had any chance of success. The way he'd enwrapped her made everything so much worse. His arms were looped just beneath her breasts, holding her so closely he probably experienced every thump of her heart against his forearms. Each one carried anguish. She couldn't escape any of this, and it just kept getting worse. She started crying. Absolutely nothing halted it. The floor beneath her blurred. A tear slipped down her cheek. Another. They started dripping off her cheeks, and each one felt like it scalded.

"Well. It's a-boot time! I'll have Lileth fetched."

Her father's voice had changed markedly, as if a magician had waved a wand, altering the laird's mood into one of satisfaction and joviality. He almost smacked his lips. Ainslee's shoulders sagged. Not a whole lot, but enough the man holding her must have felt it, for his hold tightened even more. She pulled in and held breaths that shuddered.

Why did she have to lose control now?

And why in front of everyone?

And why, oh why, hadn't she just let Lileth deal with her own future?

"You misunderstand me, Dughall. I have not changed my preference of bride. I chose your daughter, Ainslee. I'm well satisfied. I merely wish to... shorten the length of our engagement. Considerably."

"What?!"

Her father's voice carried the same sense of stupefaction that hit her, as well as everyone else in the room.

"You heard me. I came today to betroth a bride. Very well, I've done so. Now, I find myself, for lack of better word, longing for more. And I want it sooner."

"S-s-sooner?"

Her father stuttered. She'd never heard such a thing. Ainslee sniffed. The duke's arms tensed about her again.

"Very well, Dughall. I'll be blunt. I want to marry your daughter. And I don't want to wait. Right now. Tonight."

"Tonight?"

"Well...I wouldn't wish you to think my request is due to any worry over Ainslee's health or safety, should I leave her in your care for a fortnight. I'm simply...well...I'll just state it. I'm a bit eager for a consummation."

"Your grace!"

"Straithcairn!"

Several exclamations rang out through the room. They swallowed Ainslee's gasp. The duke had shocked just about everyone. She blinked, sending another tear down the trail on one cheek, and then watched it drop onto the velvet of his jacket sleeve. She narrowed her eyes on the spot as it got absorbed, and then she stopped any others from joining it. She couldn't believe it. The Duke of Straithcairn was saving her. Saying words of nonsense, but the result would be the same. She needn't stay a moment longer beneath this roof. He was a very good actor, too. He was fooling everyone. His words continued to amaze and astound. Even she found him believable.

"So. What say you? Does Clan MacAffrey have anyone here with the authority to preside over a wedding ceremony?"

"Surely, you are na' serious?"

Her father expostulated. His voice sounded unsure. The duke chuckled.

"Really? Don't I sound serious?"

"Come, your grace. 'Tis a fine jest, but I'm a fair bit stewed at present. As are we all. We'd best repair to the chieftain room and further discussion."

Her father was wrong. They weren't all stewed. The duke's reply didn't sound the least bit drunk. He sounded irritated. Provoked. Angered. Ainslee watched where his arms were linked about her, and trembled at a menace she could feel.

"I tire of repeating myself. You find an official right now or – Iain?"

The duke swiveled slightly to his right.

"Your grace?" The man beside him answered.

"There's a law in this country, isn't there? Something about declaration being as good as the event. It's still on the books. Legal. Binding. Yes?"

"Aye. That, there is."

"Good." The duke moved, turning back to face her father. "Well, Dughall. Your choice. Which is it to be?"

"Now, listen here, Niall Straith—"

The duke interrupted her father. "I am not used to being thwarted, MacAffrey. Or delayed. Or ignored. And I've *never* had my vision and mental capabilities questioned. I'm not allowing it to continue. I'd rather wed your daughter with an actual ceremony, but I've exhausted my repertoire of niceties. I'm finished with speeches and toasts, and delays. Therefore, I'm invoking the Law of Marriage by Declaration, or whatever it's called. I. Neal–ahem. *Niall* Alexander Straith, being of sound mind and body, do hereby declare myself wedded to Ainslee MacAffrey, second daughter of Laird Dughall MacAffrey, and she is wedded to me. Does that work, Iain Straithmore?"

"Aye, your grace."

"Good. Your turn, sweet."

Sweet.

He'd just called her sweet.

For a moment, that's all she registered. He lifted her and at the same time bent to touch his lips to her ear, causing an instant blizzard of shiver, and an ocean swell of heat.

"For pity's sake, lass – speak up!"

Ainslee lifted her head and cleared her throat. "Oh! I...also declare myself wed. To...uh...his grace. The Duke of Straithcairn."

"Neal Alexander Straith." He listed the name for her.

"Aye. Him. Straith."

There was a bit of chuckling at her statement. It matched the bubbles frothing within her, making her feel buoyant and light, and giddy. The duke answered. He also sounded amused.

"That's close enough. You all heard us?"

There was a chorus of 'ayes', and some loud yelling that could mean anything, and then the duke swung her fully into his arms, cradling her right against his chest. Ainslee shut her eyes and put her nose against his neck, just above his collar. The area vibrated with his next words, this time spoken so loudly, they were heard above everything else.

"There! 'Tis done. We're wed. And what has been proclaimed let no man put asunder, and all that jazz! Now, we're leaving! Laird MacAffrey? My thanks for your hospitality. My wife thanks you, as well. Iain!"

"Your grace?"

"Make a path for us. Alert any clansmen still capable of walking. Find the bard, the *bladier* fellow, and the pipers. Oh! And fetch a plaid for her grace. 'Tis a powerful cold ride, and I'm beyond waiting for feminine frippery."

"Frippery?"

She spoke around an odd sensation no one had warned her of. Everything on her was singing. Rejoicing. Laughing. She was afraid to voice anything, in case the combination of blissfulness erupted.

"You're leaving with me now, Ainslee. Right now. You're not fetching a shawl. You're not packing. You're not leaving my sight. Got it?"

She nodded, the motion rubbing her cheek against his collar.

"You can ride, can't you?"

She pulled her head back, opened her eyes, and glared up at him. He winked.

"Oh. Hi there. Glad to see you're not fully cowed. I was worried for a bit there."

If he mentioned he knew she'd been crying, she might never speak to him again. He didn't. He walked between bookcases to the library door, marched down the hall, and jogged down the wide staircase leading to the great hall, an Honor Guardsman at each side the entire way. Masses of Straith clansmen poured from everywhere to surround them. The duke was tall. She knew that. She just hadn't realized the extent of it. He stood above most of his clan.

"Thank God! Here comes a man with a bit of plaid. I may have to set you down, wife. You ready?"

Wife. He called her wife. *Oh, my*.

"Well?"

"Why would na' I be?" Ainslee asked.

"Feminine nature. Womanly weakness."

"I would have you know I have never been weak, your grace. Ever."

"You may wish to portray it. And, please. It's Neal. Gentlemen! Find other chores than hanging about me. See to preparing my horse. And you!" He used the arm at her back to point at someone. "You look fit. Sober-ish. Can you get to Straith Castle? See to...whatever needs to be seen to?"

He waited a few moments and then bent his head close to hers. Ainslee could sense movement about her, but she didn't truly see it. Her vision was entirely filled with him.

"Now that we've a bit of privacy, we can speak. Make it quick-like. My Honor Guard are not slackers. We've a few moments before they'll return. At best."

"I'm na' weak, and I'm na' prone to feminine faints. Or whatever you are suggesting," she told him.

"Ainslee. You just took part in a wedding that will gain no small measure of notoriety. Such a thing could be enough to cause female vapors."

"I *am* a Highlander," she informed him.

He looked away from her, out the open door, still holding her well above the floor. Ainslee heard and smelled moisture. A downpour.

"It's raining," he informed her.

"I'm na' afraid of rain."

"Only an idiot travels on a night like this. Astride one horse. And with a woman in his arms."

"But, you're no idiot. And I'm full waterproof. Wait. Did you just say… one horse?"

He glanced down at her and winced, before looking out again. "Aye. That's all I brought. His name is Dragon-something-or-other."

"Dragonheart?"

He shook his head. "No. That doesn't sound right."

"Dragonbreath?"

"That's it."

"Good choice. He's well-trained. Large at the withers. Strong. Stands almost eighteen hands. Na' the slightest bit skittish, either. Even to a thunderstorm."

He smiled slightly, but kept looking out into the elements. "Can you control him?"

"Easily."

"Good."

"Good?"

"We are about to make a grand exit. I'd hate to ruin it by falling off the horse. Think of the embarrassment."

"But, you are a fine rider. The best! Everyone kens that."

"Really? Consider this a forewarning, my dear. I took a blow to the head. It…changed me. Whatever you might have known…is probably altered."

"But I hadn't seen you for years! Afore this morn, I mean. I recognized you, though. Na' that I was visiting with you afore you left, though. You were near grown, and—well. Um. I mean—"

His lips twitched but he didn't smile. Ainslee was blushing, but she blazed through the rest of it, anyway.

"I was verra young...when you left."

"I'll bet."

"Your grace? I...need to be thanking you."

"For what? And please. It's Neal."

"I ken what you just did. I only wish I knew proper words of gratitude to use."

"No words necessary. It was the plan, remember?"

"Aye. But not this. And...you should set me down now. I do na' believe any would note it."

"Oh, yeah? Well...maybe I like holding you."

She lifted one eyebrow and regarded him. He was looking at something over her shoulder and wouldn't meet her gaze.

"I'm na' dense, your grace, albeit that is my father's opinion. I know you said all that to save me. It was brilliant. I think it fooled everyone."

"It's Neal. And I've got news for you, Missus Straith. I am not that good of an actor."

"But I still thank you. Most sincerely."

"I don't want your gratitude! Damn everything! How long does it take to prepare one horse?"

He shifted her and yelled the last words out into the elements.

"I can walk," she offered.

"Ainslee. Please. I'm in the middle of a grand exit, trying to portray an impatient bridegroom here. The least you can do is play along."

"What would you wish me to do?"

Her lips were pursed throughout the question, and she watched him touch a glance to them and then away. The bottom of his face went a mottled pink shade. He didn't have a beard that might have hidden it. Ainslee watched it happen.

And wondered.

CHAPTER THIRTEEN

DRAGONBREATH WAS AN IMPRESSIVE HORSE. He'd been decked out with a tasseled blanket beneath a leather-tooled saddle with silver smelted to the edges. His entire equipage was trimmed with silver. Such accoutrements made him a fit mount for the Duke of Straithcairn. The horse was a Clydesdale and one of the largest in the Straithcairn stable. But he was also the most docile. He'd been groomed to perfection. Dressed for show. He was definitely muscled and wide at the withers. Near eighteen hands in height so they'd told Neal, which was supposedly an immense size.

Oh, yeah?

Well, right now, Dragonbreath wasn't large enough.

The stallion was certainly docile, however. He'd stood patiently while Neal handed Ainslee to Iain's care, shoved a boot into a stirrup and mounted, shimmied about, tucking loose ends of material beneath his thighs and butt. The horse hadn't even shifted when Ainslee had been handed up to Neal. Good thing. She wasn't in a position to control a wild horse. She was bundled up in two lengths of Straith clan plaid. She was so small, she didn't even make a large, unwieldy bundle.

It wasn't just sprinkling, either. The sky was pouring rain on them, stealing breath and saturating wool to the point of heft and weightiness. Water ran in rivulets off every surface, including each bit of Neal's attire, the blankets atop Ainslee, and the one beneath the saddle. Neal's hands and legs were wet and cold. His feet were resting in the equivalent of small ponds within his boots. The deluge turned the road into a muck-filled trail that sucked at Dragonbreath's hooves. It obscured the path and blurred the elements. This sort of rainfall should be enough to keep a man's attention fully on the journey he was undertaking, and off the woman in his arms.

It wasn't.

Ainslee should be soaked as well. She had to be. Her wrapping was so dark and wet at the moment, the pattern and color couldn't be deciphered. Neal had earlier tried to keep some of the water off her by lifting the hank of plaid that had previously covered his shoulder up over his head and beyond his forehead. It made an overhang of sorts. That chivalrous offering got him hunched forward with his arms fully about her, in order to provide even more shelter. That sort of position should have been uncomfortable and awkward.

It was neither.

It sent primal commands he had to thwart, basic needs and hungers he couldn't seem to stop, and a deep-rooted sensation he didn't dare pursue. Nothing he tried seemed to work against them. The reactions firing through his loins were bothersome. Completely unacceptable. Irritating. And thoroughly exasperating. He acted like an unfledged youth facing his first woman.

Mason had informed him of his age. Niall was twenty-six. That was young for accomplishing a distinguished career in His Majesty's Navy. He'd earned his first medal at twenty-one, and the second just before being forced to give up his commission with this inheritance. Twenty-six was young. It was especially youthful to be carrying the title and responsibility of a dukedom.

Then again, in almost two hundred years from now, Neal had already parlayed his inheritance into a small fortune and assumed control of his first company at twenty-six. By thirty, he'd made his first million. Didn't change the perspective here, however. Twenty-six was still young. *But, damn everything!* His body might be that age, but his mind sure as hell wasn't. He'd been approaching the half-century mark. He was old enough to be Ainslee's father. That fact should be enough to keep his mind strictly where he wanted it.

It should, but it didn't.

Ainslee snuggled into his belly; her head at his shoulder, her nose directly atop his heart. Each breath she exhaled sent tingles through his chest. The experience sent waves of hormone-fueled reaction right against his efforts at containment. She had a lot in her arsenal. And he was a failure at defense.

Focus, Neal.

Market takeover and save the planet.

That had to be the reason he'd been zapped into this exact period in time. Thus far, he accomplished a little side-trip to stop an evil bastard from influencing things in a tiny corner of Scotland, and managed to gain a wife rather than a fiancée. Fair enough. What had happened was actually providential. The steward couldn't possibly inherit now. Not for some time anyway. The estate had a duke, and now it had a duchess. She was young. Healthy. In possession of her mental faculties. Garrick was a fly in the ointment, but there was probably a procedure for firing the man. Neal wondered what it was. If gut instinct was any indicator, Mason Millbourne would make a great steward. Ainslee would have an advisor she could trust, Iain Straithmore and the rest of the Honor Guard to protect her back, and full authority to manage things.

Situation handled.

All Neal needed to do was get her ensconced at Straith Castle and he'd be on his way to New York. And destiny.

Too bad his body wasn't in agreement.

His dick continually jumped into alertness, thickening and straining with an amazing degree of consistency against first the linen of his shirt, then the woolen kilt, and when it reached the pommel of the saddle, his member smashed the sporran upward, into the bundle he held in his arm. He only hoped she wouldn't know what it meant as it happened yet again.

Damn it.

Mind over matter, buddy.

Market takeover...

Neal subconsciously thrust toward Ainslee, before yanking his ass backward with a motion that was fairly obscene. And undeniable. He didn't have any control over this? *What the hell?* He was acting like a stud in mating season. It couldn't just be the gift he'd received of a young man's body. Neal had been this exact age once. It hadn't been that long ago. He'd been physically fit. Maintained a full social calendar. Dated women who'd reacted favorably to his company. He'd had sexual urges. He'd acted on them if necessary. He remembered most of the encounters.

Okay.

Maybe he only remembered *some* of them.

But he'd swear he'd never dealt with this level of testosterone-fueled desire. It was unfathomable. Rain fell as if heaven had turned showerheads on to full blasting level. It was dark. He was out in the open. Had all kinds of company around him. He was wet. Shiver-inducing cold.

Well...parts of him were.

And there went another twinge from his dick.

The horse did an extra large sway to one side, as if in accompaniment. Neal instinctively tightened his legs about the horse, grabbed Ainslee tighter to him with one arm, and held onto the reins. The horse caught the stumble with some shuffled steps. The world gradually re-righted. Neal let out a trembled breath he hadn't known he'd held.

That had been close.

Good thing the horse knew what to do. Ainslee could hardly control Dragonbreath in her current position. She'd have to be astride it. Her legs spread over a lot of horse. Right in front of him...

Argh!

That had been really stupid. He hadn't needed that bit of imagery. Longing already hammered at him. Yearning thumped through him with every heartbeat. Craving filled every breath. This ride was filled with the lowest, basest sensations, in a combination that was difficult to stifle, and he had to envision Ainslee in that position?

Neal stifled a groan, lifted his head, and scanned the darkness beyond Dragonbreath's head. There wasn't much to see. It was probably past midnight. Rainfall obliterated the path, and obscured everything except the closest of his Honor Guard. No one had noticed his horse's near-disaster, or maybe, they'd assumed he'd just handle it.

Neal relaxed his thighs gradually and settled back down into the saddle. He didn't loosen his grip on Ainslee. This hold kept her above his groin. He needed a bit of space, and distance, and gap between them. His arm started burning. He had to loosen the muscles. Ainslee's bulk settled right back into his lap. And then she wriggled.

This time the groan was audible. And loud. Ainslee parted the plaid about her, stuck her face out, and spoke.

"'Tis faster if you go through Huntsman's Dale."

"Right. Whatever that is."

His voice sounded like a rock shale slide tumbling down a hillside. She seemed to consider it for several moments. He didn't dare glance down to see what expression she might have on her face. Or even if he'd be able to see it in the gloom. Wouldn't have mattered. He already saw her in his mind.

"It's the valley that connects your property with the MacAffrey land. 'Twas where you rode this morn. And where...we met."

He grunted.

"You were riding Thundercloud. He...wasn't harmed?"

"The horse?"

"He's your newest stud. Arabian. I'd never seen him afore. He's quite impressive."

He made a noncommittal grunting noise. If he put any sound to it, it might come out as a whine. Or – heaven forbid – a plea. It was better to act dense. Or tired. That was a thought. He could try portraying abject exhaustion.

Neal eased his shoulders back, tipped his head, and forced a yawn, making a great show of it.

"Oh. It is late. And you've been injured. We've some time yet, but you could sleep. You did well bringing Dragonbreath. He's an impressive stallion. Perfectly proportioned. His gait, even and settled. 'Tis akin to being rocked to sleep. That wouldn't be possible if he had to pick his way through Huntsman's Dale and the pass. Is that why you took the road?"

"No."

The word came from between his set teeth. She must've inferred something, though, because she scooted a bit, mashing parts of her right against him. Feminine parts. Soft. Delicately-rounded parts. He could swear he felt exactly that, and everything about his nether region made certain he was aware of it. Primed for it. Readied. Eager. Even with all that material about her.

Neal looked out at the rain-filled night, and started putting little breaths into the air. He was panting. *Good Lord*. And she just kept speaking, sounding blissfully unaware of what she was doing to him.

"This road adds miles to the journey. You ken it follows the boundary wall? I've often wondered if it was built by a past duke to designate his property, or if it was here long afore then, and the boundary was just set there. It's a grand structure, that wall. I've walked it on occasion. Every section. Some of them are wide. And some are really thin. I've fallen from it more than once."

And then she giggled.

Neal's entire frame reacted, his arms gripping her to him as every muscle moved in tandem, lifting them both up from the saddle. He had to consciously force his body back down. And then he sat there, holding her up against his belly, vibrating to a curse of sensation only his new wife seemed to wield. One more feminine affectation like that giggle, and he was going to have to get drastic.

Falling off the horse even sounded like a viable option.

He was eyeing the slime of the roadbed when a man loomed out into the road.

CHAPTER FOURTEEN

NEAL STARTED SLIGHTLY. DRAGONBREATH DIDN'T react. The horse lumbered several more steps before Neal remembered to pull up on the reins. And it was foolish. He'd known about this. They'd obviously reached the meadow where the entourage had left the horses. That was the reason they'd taken the road. If Neal had possessed wits that worked he'd have told her. Ainslee twisted, using him as a propping post in order to look about.

"Oh. Of course. We took the road because you left the bulk of horses at the standing stones. I should've guessed. Look. They've even built a shelter. Oh, Hello, Sam. Henry. And look. Even Will is here."

She was right. Light was denting the elements, coming in spurts from a fire built between two of the megalithic stones. It was being kept alive by a length of heavy plaid spread across the area. There was just enough shelter for three clansmen, all looking miserably sodden, and thoroughly confused.

One of them stepped out at her greeting and doffed his tam. He approached the side of Dragonbreath. The fire lit one side of his face. He had a puzzled expression on it.

"Uh…Miss Ainslee? Be that…you?"

"The lady you address is now Her Grace, the Duchess of Straithcairn! She was lawfully wedded to His Grace, the Fifth Duke of Straithcairn, Niall Alexander Straith –by proclamation afore witnesses. Let it be known throughout the Highlands! That this union took place on this day! The thirteenth of June! In the year of our Lord, 1803!"

The clan bard may be advanced in years, but the man possessed a grand voice. He knew how to use it, even after a rain-soaking and a hike of over three miles. He only stopped twice for breath. The man's intonation was proof of why he held the position. It was also proof that Neal had been right earlier. Their wedding was notorious enough to be orated.

"The...*Duchess*? Holy Je—! I mean—uh. Your grace!"

The man sputtered and then he went down onto his knee. Right into the muck beside them. Neal took the lead, and answered, using his own orator voice.

"Rise, man! We're rain-soaked and tired...with a fair bit of ride ahead of us still. And mount up – all of you! Oh! And someone fetch a horse for my wife!"

"Niall?"

Oh hell.

She'd said his name.

The whiff of sound she made was barely audible, but viciously effective. Neal's heart constricted, missing a beat. He waited another moment and then tipped his head down. He'd been wrong about the amount of light cast by their bonfire. It was shedding way too much of it at the moment. Everything about his new wife's almost unearthly beauty was highlighted and caressed by fire-glow. The raindrops just made her glisten.

"Are there...enough horses?" she asked.

"Some...can ride double."

Oh, good. His voice worked. His reply was gruff, but audible.

"Um. I...am na' dressed for it."

His eyebrows rose. "None can tell what you wear."

She looked down for a moment and then back at him. There was a glimmer of moisture atop her eyes, now. He didn't guess at the stutter his heart gave him this time. It was massive and had a catch to it that was near pain. He was still examining the affliction when she spoke again, in a whisper that was barely audible.

"It's different now. Somehow. A-a-after that announcement. Did na' you hear? I'm a *duchess*."

Neal's lips twitched at how awed she sounded. He held the amusement back with an act of will. That was odd. He didn't think he had any will-power left. "True," he finally replied.

"Do na' you see?"

She moved her glance to somewhere between Dragonbreath's ears. There wasn't much to see there. He knew. He had the spot about memorized.

"Not really. But...I did suffer a head injury?" He posed it as a question, in the event it helped.

"The wedding that happened...just makes it all *worse*."

"Worse?"

That was a bombshell. His voice reflected it. Marriage to him - when she'd practically orchestrated it - was worse?

Than what?

Wasn't this what she wanted? Hadn't she begged him? What had he done to make it so horrid? He'd been a perfect gentleman.

Neal quickly amended that.

He'd *tried* to be a perfect gentleman. He thought he'd hidden the lust. He must have failed. Why else would she slur a union with him? It was a conundrum. If his mind was the prime portion of his anatomy in control at the moment, he might be able to figure it out.

No. Wait.

He was trying to alter thousands of years of gender relationships. He was a male. Woman might as well be another frickin' species. No male had ever figured them out. It was a useless endeavor.

"I mean...I ken why you wed me. It's our...secret. It's just—"

She sucked in on her bottom lip, and since they hadn't tamped the bonfire yet, the light was assisting in showing the blossom of a blush at her cheeks. All of it combined to not just make her ethereal-looking, but massively so.

"What?"

"Forgive...me. I'll ride my own mount."

She looked small, and young, and unsure, and incapable of sitting atop a horse, let alone controlling one. Neal put a finger beneath her chin and lifted it so she had to face him. He had to ignore a roar of sound that went through his ears with every pulse beat and then he had to concentrate in order to hear around it. His own voice sounded strange.

"Ainslee. I'm...at odds here. I don't know how women think. Can't you just tell me?"

His gaze was hooked. Deep sapphire-colored eyes locked with his.

Shit.

Times two, Neal.

He shouldn't have touched her. He shouldn't be gazing into her eyes. He should have had the sense to dismount. Move. Say he needed to take a leak or something. He should be doing a thousand different things.

"These men. Some were in the library. They...*heard*."

The last word was spoken so softly, he had to guess at it.

"So?" he asked. Or thought he asked. Now, he couldn't even hear himself over the pulse in his ear.

"Could you just—? I mean, I ken it would be hard…but, please? Could you pretend…a little longer? Please?"

"Pretend?"

She had tears skimming her eyes. That made deep pools of mystery out of the blue. Someone did something with the blanket atop the shelter, sluicing the water onto the fire. Their actions sent sizzling sounds and smoke smell into the air. It also dimmed the light.

"That you…want me?"

She had her eyes squeezed shut, as if afraid of what might be on his face. She wasn't the lone one. He was afraid of what expression he wore.

"You are…so young," he replied.

"Full grown."

"That what you call it?" Neal bent his head and whispered the words against her nose.

"I'm…nineteen."

"Barely hatched."

His words hovered atop her lips. His breath mingled with hers. Each moment sent a charge with it. Neal groaned, closed his eyes, and pressed his lips to hers.

Neal had experienced near-death in his lifetime. Car wrecks. A skiing accident. An explosion of a plant he'd been touring. With resultant fire. And hearing loss. And then, there had been the Bermuda Triangle incident this morning. That had been the epitome of mind-blowing experiences.

And yet, what happened the instant he kissed Ainslee annihilated even that.

Brightness flooded his vision, granting him flight. Sweetness plowed his veins, gifting him with a sense of wonder. Excitement grabbed his heart, sending awareness with each beat. Thrill after thrill coursed his veins. He vibrated with a sensation of immeasurable bliss. Delight. Pleasure.

He didn't know how long the kiss lasted. He'd been in another realm. There was just this one glorious span of time, this woman, and an incredible sense of wonder. And then someone cleared their throat.

"Uh. Y-yes? What…is it?"

The duke lifted his head and turned to ask it. His voice warbled momentarily. Ainslee gasped and hid her face in the space below his chin. Shivers alternated with blushes, and those succumbed to such an ecstatic sensation, it took long moments before she again felt the velvet of his jacket that she'd gripped in each hand, the feeling of muscled thighs she sat atop, the moistness in the air, and the chill of a rain-filled night.

The duke had kissed her!

She hadn't just accepted it, either. She'd kissed him back! It wasn't possible to face anyone at the moment. Especially him. So, Ainslee held onto him and vibrated with waves of reaction she didn't know how to control. She'd call it shock, but it couldn't be. What had happened had been too beautiful. Too amazing. Too unbelievable.

She'd received her first kiss!

Sweet heaven!

And it was everything Lileth had eulogized about to her little sister, using awestruck tones. A kiss was all of that.

And more.

Ainslee still quivered with how much more the kiss had contained. The tremors subsided slowly, pushed aside by what had to be embarrassment. The duke must think her unbelievably brazen! Desperate.

She was fully capable of riding her own horse. She just wanted to stay right where she was, held within his embrace as though she was treasured. Wanted. Safe. It was a bubble of fantasy, but she hadn't wanted it burst. Not yet. Time enough for everyone to know the marriage was a sham. That he'd wed her because she'd begged him to. And that he'd done it by proclamation this eve - without one hint of warning – because he pitied her.

What she'd done was unbelievably forward. And ungrateful. She'd been asking for the moon, when he'd already delivered the stars. But, in his arms, for the first time she could recall, she'd felt protected, secure...and something more. She'd been cocooned in a hum of something exciting.

She trembled anew at the recollection. One of his arms tightened about her.

This was terrible.

Wonderfully, magnificently terrible.

She'd also asked for some sign from him so the note of respect that had been in Sam's voice wouldn't disappear, turning him back into a stable-hand who treated her like one of them. But she hadn't asked for a kiss! She'd never meant for the duke to do something so drastic.

Oh...dear.

It really had been terrible. And wonderful. And it was especially terrible because it had been so wonderful.

"Begging your pardon, but we've brought a mount for Ainslee—uh. I mean, her grace."

"Oh. Very good. Ainslee?"

Her nose tingled with the vibration of sound as the duke said it. She shook her head. He inhaled deeply, moving her with it, and then blew a sigh out over her head.

"The duchess has changed her mind. She'll continue the journey with me."

Ainslee gasped again. The duke cleared his throat. And when he spoke he was using the amazingly deep, broad voice he'd used before. In the library. When he'd pronounced them wed.

Ainslee trembled at the memory. Sighed softly.

"So? What are we standing about for? Mount up! Cease wasting time! I mean. Gents. Come on. I am a newlywed! I would truly like to reach my castle sometime tonight!"

There were answers given, amidst a lot of laughter. Ainslee didn't pay attention. She was too aware of what it felt like to have her heart sing. Her entire body tingled. The sensation reached every bit of her. The tips of her fingers. Edges of her toes. She'd thought him a wonderful sight when she'd first seen him - over a decade ago, riding hard through the grass. Now, she knew he was truly wonderful.

Even if it was a sham to be wed to him, she was thrilled by it.

"Ainslee."

He turned and lowered his head in order to speak just to her, his chest rising, while the move dislodged her. She shook her head again. She couldn't answer. She couldn't look at him. Even if it was raining and dark. It was still too soon.

"You need to release me a bit, love."

Love?

Oh, my stars. He'd just called her love.

Her ears heard it, but it took a moment for the rest of her to grasp it. Surprise lifted her head and she peered at him. It wasn't raining as hard, or they hadn't extinguished the fire enough. He was easy to see. He was looking at her with a stern expression on his face, almost a frown.

"I cannot continue to ride this way."

"What...way?"

"With you...uh. Clinging to me. We truly might fall from the horse. They'll think—. Well. I won't even go into what everyone might think. I daren't."

Ainslee moved her gaze to his ruffled shirtfront.

Oh, dear.

She'd been embracing him. Before an audience. Her entire face was hot with the reaction.

She consciously loosened her fingers, releasing his jacket from where she'd gripped it. She moved her hands back beneath the double layer of plaid covering her, laced her fingers together, and placed them against her legs, near her knees. It only took a few seconds, but it felt too long.

"Not like that. Face sideways again. Lean back. There. This might work. If I'm lucky."

She must have moved too slowly, because he gripped one arm about and pulled her against him, before nudging Dragonbreath forward. She'd been right. Dragonbreath was a wise choice. The horse had a great stride. Seemingly tireless. Strong. His canter resembled a rocker chair. It would be easy to sleep atop him.

And especially easy to pretend to it.

CHAPTER FIFTEEN

THE DUCHESS'S SUITE AT CASTLE Straith was a spectacular set of rooms. Ainslee had been awestruck when she'd first seen
them. Everything was designed in an ivory tone with golden accents. The
walls were wainscot, light oak on the bottom, while the tops were papered
with ivory silk, overlaid with golden filigree. They soared to a height close
to two-stories. The ceiling was plastered with three flower-themed circles,
each holding a chandelier. Little ropes led across the ceiling and down the
walls and were secured in loops around ornate holders to allow the lighting
or extinguishing of the tapers.

The chandeliers were dark at the moment, although crystals glinted occasionally from the mass of shadow as candlelight reached them.

The bed frame, armoires, wardrobes, and bureaus had been designed
with the same light oak wood, and were decorated with more filigree. Set-
tees graced the walls, while a chaise lounge rested just past the footboard.
The furniture pieces were upholstered in ivory and gold silk damask that
had streaks of red woven through it. They matched the bedding, except for
the coverlet. That item was crafted of scarlet-shaded material, and heavily
embroidered with gold threads.

There were three doors in the bedroom. One led directly to the hall
outside, and from there to the massive staircase leading to the great hall.
One door led to a dressing area. The other opened into a salon, with
more carved wooden furniture, although it was of a darker hue and much
heavier. That room had a door at the end of it that led directly to the chieftain's bedchamber. She knew because she'd once peeked.

The duchess suite in Castle Straith was spacious, beautiful, awe-inspiring.

Majestic.

Ainslee had snuck about this room once. She hadn't touched anything. She was afraid to. Even now, ensconced in the bed, high on its own pedestal, clad in a nightgown borrowed from the housekeeper's niece, she was almost afraid to move.

A linen sheet, so finely woven it was slick-feeling, covered the mattress beneath her, while another one, edged in lace, tucked her in. Woolen blankets in the Straith colors added weight and warmth. Four enormous pillows, each of a size she could sleep atop, were along the headboard, two directly behind her, propping her up. The scarlet coverlet had been folded down and moved to a stand. A candelabra with two lit candles flickered from her night stand, giving glimpses of the treasures accumulated in the room. It was after two in the morning, but she couldn't sleep. She should be exhausted. It had been an incredibly long day full of all sorts of emotions and tribulations, not the least of which was her presence right here.

She was in the duchess suite at Straithcairn Castle!

In the actual bed!

Sitting atop the bed as if she belonged there!

It felt like any moment the door would open and she'd be denounced as a fraud and chastised for taking liberties. A door did open - the one leading to the salon. Ainslee's eyes widened as the duke walked in, turning to face the door as he closed it behind him. The latch clicked in the stillness.

Ainslee's hands went to the area just above her breasts, touching on a lace-edged neckline so new it scratched, and a little row of buttons that were all fully fastened. It didn't help. She still wore a nightgown. She was *en-dishabille*.

With a man.

The duke took a breath that lifted his shoulders, turned around, and walked toward her. Her jaw dropped. She'd been impressed by how he looked this morn in Sassenach clothing. She'd been awed by his appearance in Highland attire, especially the Straithcairn *feile-brecan*. There wasn't a description for what she felt when seeing him in this.

He wore a floor-length robe, fashioned of material in the Straithcairn plaid. His belt and lapels looked to be red velvet. He had his hair tied back and a bit of bare chest on display at the junction of his robe. Everything about his attire was masculine. Virile.

Vaguely threatening.

"What…are you doing here?" she asked, with a voice that trembled.

"Not what you think. Trust me."

"But—"

"I have little choice in the matter. Mason is in there." He pointed back toward the door he'd used.

"Ma...son?"

"My valet. Surely you recall the man. He knows enough of you."

"Oh. Mason Millbourne. Aye. I ken him."

"He had a fellow named Barnes assisting him. I didn't know there was such a thing as an under-valet. Bother it."

"Oh. That's Thomas Barnes. He was elevated from footman upon your arrival. He's verra full of himself over it. Verra proud."

"Trust you to know."

"Is that...bad?"

"Hardly. But that's not the point. I have two personal servants. And while that's odd, it gets worse. Both men are fonts of propriety and correct behavior. That Mason is the worst. By far."

"Propriety?"

"The man's a stickler about it. Everything needs to be right and proper and in its place. He actually stayed up this late to make certain I was properly seen to. And that everything's as it should be. He's not the lone one, either. The entire castle is filled with them. Hovering about. Seeing to every whim. They're everywhere."

"What are you talking of?"

"Servants. Roaming about the place. As if it isn't the middle of the night and everyone should be abed. This is ridiculous. I could employ every type of servant I wished, but there's a huge loss of privacy involved. Servants mean you have to deal with a lot of eyes and ears about. And all of them are taking note."

"The estate could hardly run without them."

"You're not listening, Ainslee. Or I should be a bit more direct. Mason is in my chamber. Right now. He's even whistling as he putters around. Whistling. Some damnable tune that is now stuck in my head. In an off-key. At this time of night. And that means I had to come in here, for...uh...a bit."

"You did?"

He smiled slightly. "Remind me not to send a messenger ahead of my arrival again. Especially one capable of raising the dead. What? You think they had the entire front of the castle lit up, and everyone at full attention, for just anyone's arrival? In the midst of a monsoon? In the dead of night?"

"You're the duke. They were waiting your return."

He moved closer and stood looking down at her, elevating the temperature and making her heart thud so heavily it was probably noticeable. She still had her hands in place atop her chest, however. He wouldn't know.

"Mason is very pleased with events. He also told me he is not overly surprised. Just pleased. As is everyone else in the castle. Or so he assures me."

"With what?"

"My selection of duchess, of course."

"Me?"

He sat on the edge of the bed, making it shimmy with the move. Ainslee did her best to pretend not to notice.

He's sitting on the bed!

"Who else have I been speaking of? Of course, you. They're supremely pleased with my choice of wife and thoroughly impressed with the method I employed to gain one. According to Mason, I may hearken back to one of my ancestors. The second duke. Rakish fellow, he was. Mason is full of tales of valor and…well, romance. I'm telling you, I had to vacate my chamber. The man's gone soft, regaling me about the romance of it all. They're all quite pleased to have you as their new duchess. I suppose I should be grateful. That's one less worry."

"What…are you worrying over?"

"Leaving."

She started. He saw it.

"We had to discuss it at some point. I can't stay. It's almost a crime. And my intentions are—not of a higher nature, trust me. You don't understand. Things…are not as they appear."

"They're na'?"

He looked at her for a long moment, stilling everything, even time. Ainslee didn't even miss it. He moved his gaze away. And somewhere clocks started ticking seconds off again.

"You've got Mason. Barnes. The Honor Guard, led by Iain Straithmore. The comptroller, MacGruder, and his wife. The head housekeeper, a Missus Paige. The head groom, MacCreary…countless groomsmen, maids, a lot of stable hands that you probably already know. They're all ready to assist you."

"With…what?"

Her voice caught. She couldn't help it. She already felt like a charlatan. It was deflating to realize how much she must appear it, as well.

"Running the estate. Watching over things. Taking care of the Straith legacy. Subverting Garrick and his ilk. Oh. You'll need access to funds. I'll put that on the list for tomorrow. I'll find where the accounts are and make certain you have access."

"You'll set up accounts? For me?"

"I don't know the extent of the finances, but it won't be long before you'll have enough for anything you want. I'll have to wire it from—oh. Crap. There's no such thing yet. Damn it! This just keeps adding up."

"What does?"

"All the things I have to do, so you'll have what you need."

"Where…will you be?"

He tilted his head and looked back at her, seizing her eyes with the expression in his. The lighting gave his eyes a silver hue, almost like polished mirrors. A flash of something went through her ribcage, startling and yet thrilling. It elevated her pulse rate. Her breathing. She couldn't move. Not even to blink.

"Anywhere…but here."

Ainslee gasped. She didn't dare speak. She was afraid of what might come out if she opened her mouth.

"You don't understand. And I can't explain." He stopped, and everything about him went strangely quiet, tense. "Please don't look at me like that. Please? This is already…" He stopped again. It sounded like he gulped. "Well. It's late. I've got a trip to plan. And you're the Duchess of Straithcairn now. I understand there's a lot of responsibility facing you. Think you can handle it?"

She nodded again. Swallowed. Blinked. Swore she wouldn't say anything to make him regret picking her. He moved his gaze to the fists he'd made of his hands. He didn't seem to move for the longest time. He just sat there, statue-still. He might even be holding his breath.

"You ever read about New York. In the…United States of America?"

"New York?" She didn't have to feign the confusion.

"Mason tells me you read prodigiously. You claim to have read most of the books in your family library and even started on those here. Surely you've read something about New York. If not, find some and purchase them."

"I've…read about it."

"I believe I'll take a trip that way. I'll try and send you a missive or two. Move over."

He shoved the blankets toward her, and leaned forward to grab one of her pillows. Then he stopped and looked right at her, close enough to touch, far enough apart she didn't dare. The way he'd positioned himself put a light crease in his forehead. The candlelight was being fickle, too. It put most of his face in shadow. Except the tip of his nose, slight cleft of his chin. He was incredibly handsome. This view was going to be imprinted on her memory whether she wished it or not. Ainslee swallowed.

"Are you going to help me or not?"

Her eyes went wide. "Uh…"

"Come on, Ainslee. It's our wedding night. I already proclaimed to all and sundry how impatient and eager I am. You've been about the stables. You know what happens between a stallion and mare."

"But—"

Her voice stopped. It matched her heart.

"You got me into this. Now, you're just going to have to help me finish it."

He grabbed two pillows and tossed them onto the floor. And then he dropped onto them, disappearing from her view except for his head.

"What are you doing?" she asked.

He was back to his feet before launching onto the bed, making it rock with his entrance. Then he was on hands and knees, and giving her an expression that looked like a snarl. And then he started pushing himself up and landing hard over and over all about the center of the mattress, dislodging her and the other pillows with each bounce.

"What does it look like I'm doing?"

"You're jumping on the duchess's bed!"

She was shocked. Horrified. It sounded not just in her voice, but was demonstrated as she slid out from beneath the covers to stand at the other side, staring at him, wide-eyed. Her words stopped him in mid-bounce. He landed, arms and legs splayed awkwardly, and just stayed there, his bare feet creasing one end of the duchess's ivory-shaded sheets, while his hands crunched sections of plaid fabric into balls.

"No. I'm jumping on *your* bed, Ainslee."

He went to his knees, swinging one of the pillows at her as he did so. Those pillows were large. They were over-stuffed, and he was accurate. Ainslee slammed onto her buttocks, and that hurt.

She was on her feet a moment later and now she was angry. "Why don't you just go jump on yours?" she demanded.

"Because Mason's in there! I already…told you!"

He sent the other pillow at her. It wasn't coming as quick or hard. She caught it although it knocked her backward a step.

"You're crazed," she told him.

He regarded her with a look that sent shivers down her spine. And then he reached down, grabbed a blanket, and pulled it up toward his chest, twisting it into balls of fabric within his hands. And if he didn't stop, he was going to tear it.

"I'm trying to look and sound like I'm making wild passionate love to you, Ainslee Straith. The least you can do is figure that out!"

You mean...you don't want to?

She almost asked it aloud. Some sort of self-protective instinct rose up and stopped her right in time. She lowered her chin to the pillow she held, and suffered wave after wave of shivers. She'd known he'd been acting... but did that include the kiss he given her while atop Dragonbreath?

She didn't know why she questioned it. The proof was right in front of her.

She'd been wrong. This was what real pain felt like. She'd rather take one of her father's beatings.

The expression on her face must have translated to something she didn't want it to because he put his head down and started emanating the deepest throbbing cry into the room. He sounded enraged. Antagonized. Angered. Frustrated. His yell went on and on, moving him with it, his back arching to send the sound. His eyes were crunched shut. He was turning red. Still he yelled. Thick cords grew visible from beneath the skin in his neck. He was shaking, too, making the mattress move with it. Everything about him looked taut and angered. Bestial.

Ainslee stared without meaning to, while her skin rippled over and over with something that had her completely spellbound. Mesmerized. Shocked. And yet, enthralled.

His cry ended. He released the blankets and launched up, spinning to land on his back atop the mattress. The bed frame gave a heavy thump, rocked, and then stilled. Ainslee couldn't move. It didn't feel like her limbs belonged to her anymore. She watched as he just lay there, glaring at the unlit chandeliers in the ceiling, his chest rising and falling with exertion. And then he started laughing, as if it was amusing.

Ainslee jumped slightly, and hugged tighter to the pillow. She was still doing so as he sobered, turned his head, and with one look rooted her to the floor.

"This is insane," he told her.

She didn't answer. She didn't even nod.

"You look like an imp. A really small one."

She straightened her shoulders, and that raised her head.

"Trying to protect yourself from a big bad wolf. With just a pillow. You do not have to, love. I'm no wolf."

"I never said you were," she replied.

"True."

He turned on his side to face her, crooking his arm to support his head. His robe had come unfastened a bit, giving her a large view of his chest, while one knee and thigh peeked through the bottom opening. He was massive. Muscled. Impressive. Her nipples actually seemed to tighten and itch against the muslin nightgown in response. Her grip on the pillow tightened.

"Your hair is very long. I've never seen anything like it. The length. Or the shade. It resembles twilight. Nah. A shadow. Oh, brother. Listen to me. Mason's romantic rambling must have rubbed off. Have you never cut it?"

Ainslee didn't answer.

"How do you deal with all of it?"

"I…manage."

"It has to be an issue when riding. A horse would find it very distracting, especially if it wasn't broken completely. I was told you like riding the wilder ones. You like the excitement. Or maybe it's the feel of a massive stallion between your legs that needs taming. Good God. I'm pathetic. Forget I just said that."

His voice had deepened for some reason. He reached out his free hand toward her. "Hand me the pillow."

She hugged it closer. He grinned.

"Very well. Hand me a different one."

"Why?"

"So I can use it to rest my head on, of course. That's what they're for."

"U-u-use it?"

"Must you act so naïve? Now?"

Oh no! She was going to cry.

Not again.

It was going to be really horrid this time. It was very late. She'd been up almost a full day and night. There were conflicting emotions running through her. She was in a strange place. He was practically a stranger. All of that, combined with his tone, was a difficult combination to fight. She blinked rapidly against the blur and heard him sigh.

"I keep forgetting how young you are. And innocent. You asked of the pillow?"

Ainslee didn't answer. She sniffed. Blinked some more. Sniffed again. The tears slowly abated, as did the urge to cry them. His image grew clear again, too. It looked like he'd waited for her. And he was smiling.

"I'm going to put my head on a pillow and lie here a bit so it will look like I slept here. In this truly mussed bed. With you. That way, no one will think I just consummated our union and then left you to sleep alone. The pillow?"

He gestured with his fingers.

"You're na' sleeping here?"

"Do you want me to?" he asked.

Ainslee's eyes went huge and her heart gave a vicious thump. She stumbled back a step on legs that didn't seem to support her. She had the pillow clutched so tight, feathers drifted out.

"And that is exactly what I thought you'd answer. I guess sleeping on your chaise is out, too. Just as well."

His voice was gruff. She watched him roll off the far side of the bed and toss a pillow up from the floor, then another. He stacked them in a haphazard pile and then punched a dent into them with a fist. He straightened, pulled his robe together, re-tied his velvet belt, and then he walked over to his connecting door. All without looking once at her. He opened the door.

"Good night, Ainslee. Sleep well."

He said it softly from over his shoulder. And then he walked out.

CHAPTER SIXTEEN

TINKLING CHIMES SET IN MOTION by a slight breeze awoke Neal. Rustling sounds accompanied it. He cracked an eye open on unfamiliar surroundings, groaned, and flopped over.

"Ah! Good day, Neal. I see you've awakened."

Neal lifted his head. Stared at the valet. Dropped his head again.

I'm still here.

Unbelievable.

"I take it you'll awaken now?" the man continued. It took a second for his name to register.

"Mason."

"At your service...and I've brought a bit of repast. Something the duchess sent up. Just let me get the drape pulled for you."

"No! Wait!"

The man either pretended not to hear, or was ignoring Neal, because his footsteps crossed the chamber toward a wall full of windows. The man added insult to injury by whistling the same damned Highland tune from last night as he moved. In the same off-key notes. By the sound of it, he'd reached the floor-to-ceiling window and shoved one side of the drapery open. Neal waited with narrowed eyes for the assault of daylight as the man moved to the other side of the window casement, making certain the entire twelve foot span of glazed glass was free of covering.

No sunlight lit up the room. Neal turned his head that direction. Looked out. The reason was obvious. The sun was a no-show. The view was a span of gray-shaded opacity. Moisture ran down the outside of the glass. Apparently, the rain hadn't let up. The amount they were receiving looked considerable. He'd always heard that of Scotland. This was the first time the numbers for their average rainfall registered.

The roads would be a quagmire.

If they were even passable.

"Looks like a vicious day for travel," he remarked, pushing himself up and shoving hair behind his ears. Neal never wore it this long. Not since college, anyway.

"That it is. For certain. Coffee?"

"Ugh. Is it the same brew as yesterday?"

"Of course. It's a special order. Comes in every month at the port. 'Twas the late duke's favorite brand."

"How's the tea, then?"

"You'd rather drink tea?"

"You're right. Forget it. Water will work. I'm famished, all of a sudden. What have you brought?"

Neal rubbed his jaw. He could use a shave. Or...perhaps he should start a beard. He'd have a nice scruff in a couple of days. Might make him look as rakish as his ancestor. He wondered if his wife might care. If she had a preference...or if she even cared. Neal frowned. Ainslee probably didn't remember what he looked like.

And after his performance in her room, she might be actively trying not to.

He watched Mason fuss with some silver topped dishes over at a table, recognizing the tinkling sound that had awakened him.

"I did na' bring more than a bit of smoked kipper, some bannock, and a poached egg, your grace."

"*A* poached egg."

"Aye."

"Just one? What the hell? Go back to the kitchens. Get more. Tell them I require ham. Bacon. A half-dozen eggs at the least, oh! And scones! With butter."

"That...could be unwise, Neal."

Neal rolled to the side of his bed and sat up. He'd stumbled in here sometime before dawn, exhausted, pissed-off, and sporting the hard-on that had jerked him awake and caused his fall from a too-short, and overly hard sofa in the room that separated this chamber from Ainslee. He couldn't remember the last time he'd had an erotic dream that vivid. Nor, how it had ended. If he was in his forty-nine year old body, he'd be feeling all kinds of aches. Neal stood up and stretched, and then looked across to where Mason stood, holding a silver coffeepot that emitted steam in one hand, while the other held a pad to support it and block the heat. There was a large silver platter atop the table beside him. It held Neal's meal. The meager repast looked even smaller in the midst of all the silver.

Well.

He might as well knock back some coffee. If he swigged it, he might be able to get past the taste. Neal regarded Mason silently. He dwarfed the man. He hadn't realized the valet was so small. His influence certainly didn't match his size.

"All, right. I give. Why would it be unwise?" he asked.

"You'll spoil her grace's tea."

"Her what?"

"Her grace has invited some of the castle residents to tea today."

"Who?"

"She's invited the bard, the vicar, the comptroller, and the castle librarian. I believe your cousins, Garrick and his brother Lachlan are on the guest list...along with their mother, your aunt Margaret. The kitchen has been working non-stop to make sure of the menu."

"What the hell time is it?"

"Three-forty."

"Three-forty! In the afternoon?"

"Exactly. And her grace was getting a mite concerned. That's why she sent me up here. With your repast. You drink your coffee black, still? No cream? Sugar?"

"I instructed you to call me at first light! Damn it! I had plans."

He advanced on the man, who responded by putting the coffee pot down to pull out one of the high-backed chairs. And then Mason just stood there, waiting. Patiently. With the strangest smile on his face.

"Well? What have you to say for yourself? And I warn you, Mason. I am *not* used to having instructions ignored. Nor will I tolerate it."

"We did call for you, Neal. Promptly at first light. You were verra unhappy with us. Verra. You ordered us to stay the hell out of sight. You tossed a boot at Barnes, with perfect accuracy, I might add. I do na' think he actually believes you'd toss us out on our ears, but he's new to the position. He'll learn."

Neal groaned again and turned instead to walk over to the window. He couldn't see through the cloud mass. This was unacceptable. He didn't want children. Still. It wasn't just selfishness. Over-population of the planet was a real issue two hundred years from now. So. He needed to leave. Put his plan into play. Somehow ignore the fact he was in a young man's body, complete with a lot of needs. And that he was wed to the instigator of them. She was such an amazing woman. One, with all kinds of power.

She didn't realize the ones she wielded. And the extent of them.

Argh.

What sleep he'd gained had been filled with images of Ainslee and this one-sided desire for her. Nothing on him felt rested. And now, he was unable to escape? Or even think about leaving? He looked out at a view of ocean, blurred with the slide of rainwater on the glass.

He might as well swallow the bitter pill of defeat being shoved down his throat and move on. He'd work on a defensive strategy. But for that, he needed to find out which side Mason was on.

Neal sighed heavily, fogging the glass, and then turned around. His hands went to his hips and met the velvet of his belt. He looked down. He still wore the robe from last night.

"All right Mason, tell me. If I ordered you to stay out of sight, why are you here now?"

"I'm made of sterner stuff. I tended to the last chieftain and all manner of gentlemen afore him. It will take more than a boot to my head to deter me. Aside from which, her grace asked me to. Would you like to try cream?"

"And a lot of sugar."

The valet looked surprised. Neal approached. "And I should dress. What time is this tea, anyway?"

"Four o'clock."

Neal blinked several times in rapid succession with surprise. "I have twenty minutes?"

"Fifteen now. That's why her grace sent me. She was getting worried. I've set out your attire already. It's just a matter of putting your clothing on. And you can be a mite late. Nae man is perfect."

"That is a kilt, Mason."

"True. As well as the accoutrements required to be worn along with it."

"Dirks? Knives in my socks? A claymore *and* a smaller sword? What is it with this country? I'm going to a tea, not a declaration of war."

"Straithcairn chieftains need look the part. It will be expected of you."

"Well, maybe I don't want to wear that. Maybe I want to wear trousers today."

"I do na' think that would be wise, Neal."

"Again with the wise stuff? Why not, this time?"

"This is the first tea your new wife is overseeing. Your first appearance as a wedded couple. You are the Duke of Straithcairn. Chieftain of an honorable and proud clan. To appear in anything less than Straithcairn plaid in your own home would create a bit of gossip. And there are those who live for that sort of...ill will."

His attire would create gossip?

Neal considered Mason for longer than he should. He knew Ainslee didn't possess anything except what she'd arrived in. Her attire was bound to create gossip. Unless she'd found some material and a seamstress and been especially busy. And he doubted it.

"Well, Mason. Maybe I don't want to get up and dressed and attend a little tea party. Maybe I want to just order a bottle of Scot whiskey and get roaring drunk. And let the gossips be damned."

"I would normally allow you to do all of that, Neal...except for her."

"Her? Oh. Let me guess – my wife."

"The gossip will reflect on her as well. I would na' wish a whisper of ill will to reach her."

Well. That gave Neal his answer. Mason was definitely in Ainslee's camp. Neal sighed again, this time in resignation. "Fine. Give me the coffee. I won't even have time to shave."

"'Tis of nae account. You should grow a proper beard anyway. Cream?"

Neal nodded, waited for the cup, and then tossed it back. It was still a chore to swallow. This wasn't coffee. It was syrupy tan liquid. He just wanted to get the hell out of here. Get to New York. Start trading on the market floor.

No.

That wasn't true.

What he really wanted, he knew he couldn't have.

CHAPTER SEVENTEEN

PRECISELY TWENTY-FIVE MINUTES LATER, NEAL jogged the wide set of stone steps from the chieftain's chambers to the great hall, a kilt swishing against his thighs, knives throughout his belt and socks, a sporran at his groin, his small sword and claymore bouncing. The sensation of air down below was still weird. At least Mason had let him out of the chamber without a tam. He wore his head uncovered. His hair back in a tail. None of that was his reason for lateness. It was because he'd refused to attend without shaving first.

And that was that.

The great hall had a couple of servants in it. Dusting. Humming. Both women looked up as he stepped from the stairs and approached the door beneath them. His steps echoed. The attire rattled. Neal actually heard a very feminine sigh from one of the maids. That was flattering.

Neal found himself in a foyer area with three halls leading from it. Mason was a font of information once Neal had acquiesced. *Good thing.* The castle was a maze of interconnected halls lined with tapestries with an occasional window on one side, and a lot of stonework on the other. Mason had informed him to go right a fair distance until he reached a short set of steps. At the top, the passage would branch off yet again. He needed to take the hall on his right again. In the event he was worried, there would be a tapestry portraying the castle, rendered in dark blue on the wall of the correct passage. He needed to walk another fair piece. Reach another set of descending set of steps. The blue salon was at the base of them.

Blue salon.

Neal peeked into rooms as he passed. More than one of them had a blue color scheme. Mason told him he'd reach the correct one if the walls were a light blue shade, with a gallery worth of large paintings adorning them. The room didn't have any windows. For a reason. It had been a lady's solar back in medieval times, its fireplace backing to one in the Great Hall.

Neal didn't get lost. He could tell which room before he got there from the laughter. The intermittent buzz of conversation. Someone spoke, louder than the others. Neal immediately recognized Garrick, and whatever he said brought on another bout of laughter.

That was disconcerting.

Garrick wasn't that amusing.

A man stood to one side of the door. Neal recognized him instantly. It was the stable hand, Rory. Eric's doppelganger looked a lot more like Eric with his hair pulled back and secured. Rory straightened at Neal's approach, and took a step toward the door in order to push it open for him. Neal stopped him with a finger to his lips.

"Good day...um, Rory, isn't it?"

The kid grinned. "You recognize me?"

"Sure. But...aren't you a stable hand?"

"The steward had me promoted."

"Garrick?"

"Aye."

Neal grunted. "When did this happen?"

"This morn."

"Well. That's an...interesting development."

"'Tis a big step up. Every mon in the stable was shocked when they heard."

"Really?"

"Aye."

"Well. My cousin obviously recognizes a good man when he sees him."

Neal smiled. The kid's grin widened and then moved his head toward Neal. The next words were barely above a whisper.

"Na' to worry, your grace. I did na' tell him a word a-boot yester-morn."

"Yester-morn?"

"He is verra interested in the accident. But I would never betray you. Or Ains—I mean, her grace."

Well. Well. Well.

The plot thickens.

This answered the question behind Garrick's untimely departure from the fest last night. The fellow had obviously worked on his next bit of strategy. Neal had known Garrick was trouble. He hadn't realized the extent of it, nor did he know how many were involved. Perhaps that was the reason for Neal's continued presence here at Straith Castle. He couldn't leave. Not yet, anyway. Ainslee needed a champion to secure her position first.

Well.

Her husband certainly looked the part.

Even Neal had to admit, when faced with his reflection in the chamber mirror, that he might feel archaic. But he looked pretty damned regal in this get-up. There was something more, too.

He looked dangerous.

Perhaps that had been Mason's point.

Neal patted the hilt of the claymore at his hip. Mason had been pleased when the sword had been strapped into place. So was Neal. On the two previous dukes, this sword had scraped the floor if worn at the hip. Most Straithcairn dukes wore it strapped to their back. Neal's height made that a non-issue. He had a much shorter sword hanging from his left side, along with four silver-handled daggers sticking out of his belt.

He heard a bit of clattering within the blue salon that was probably crockery, and then his wife said something. Neal's heart jerked within his chest. He stood there beside Rory in semi-shock, his mind revolting against a tremor that scored his frame.

Shit.

He'd been borderline afraid of this. Being in her proximity. Listening to her. Looking at her. And it just didn't make sense. He'd just met her! She was a teenager. It wasn't possible to have feelings like this.

It just wasn't and he didn't.

And that was that.

Neal peeked into the room. Ainslee was perched atop a chair that appeared to be a bit higher than the others in attendance. Neal stooped down to check. Stood back up.

Yep.

It had been done on purpose. Her chair was set atop a block. Her feet weren't even touching the floor. The servants had probably had a hand in her positioning, although it didn't help much. She was still a tiny thing. Excruciatingly young.

And entirely perfect.

Neal's heart stuttered again. He sucked in a breath. Held it to a slow count of ten. Exhaled.

Damn it.

He'd checked the room for a reason. He needed the 'lay of the land'. Questions answered. Who sat where? What was the potential ranking?

Where did he need to direct his attention? Who should he speak with first? And with what volume and tone? That was of prime importance before girding any group of people – especially if they were hostile board members enraged at a possible takeover. Neal never approached without a strategy. He was an expert at setting things up. So, why – the moment he saw his wife – must he lose even that ability?

Despite everything, his gaze went to her.

And stayed there.

Ainslee sat at the back of the room. A fireplace framed her position. This particular fireplace appeared to be constructed from an assortment of light-gray-colored stones and topped with a thick-cut wooden mantle. It wasn't lit at the moment. The fire-screen held flowers. Bouquets of them. So many, he couldn't see the black void behind them.

Ainslee must have found her way into a wardrobe from somewhere. She wore a sea-green colored gown with a cinched-in waist and yards of fabric below that. Her skirt looked wide enough to parachute with. Neal had attended several masquerade charity balls with women who seemed to ceaselessly enjoy dressing as Marie Antoinette. He recognized Ainslee's fashion automatically. Her skirts had been crafted to wear the pontoon things beneath them. That dress was probably forty years out-of-date and absolutely stunning.

His new wife was a beauty. That dress didn't hide one bit of it.

It seemed to be fitted exactly to her, outlining a figure he'd already spent way too much thought on, mostly of an uncontrollable erotic nature. Her hair had been piled atop her head, although a long section slid over one shoulder, and snaked down the side of a breast before pooling in her lap. Neal had hoped his wife's unearthly beauty was a product of his imagination. A trick of the candle light. Now, he knew the truth.

She was so blasted beautiful, it should be illegal.

Damn.

No. Double damn.

Neal pulled his head back so the groan wouldn't announce him.

"'Tis na' that bad, your grace."

Rory whispered it at his side. Neal looked sideways and down at the man. Rory was wrong. This set-up wasn't just bad. It was horrid.

"I mean, she did na' request the pipers to attend."

Neal snorted, coughed with an attempt to stifle it, and that just got him announced. In the midst of a coughing fit. Without warning. And Rory proved to have a competent voice for it.

"His Grace, Laird Niall Alexander Straith, fifth Duke of Straithcairn!"

Neal smacked his chest and entered the room, and silently cursed how his heart stumbled. He knew the reason. His wife looked up, her lushly-lashed eyes widened slightly, and then a light blush shaded the tops of her cheeks. He'd never seen anything to compare her to. He didn't try. He didn't care who else was in the room. He didn't see them or note them. He thumped once more on his chest with a sideways fist and walked right up to Ainslee, looked into perfect sapphire-shaded eyes, held out his hand, and somehow managed to nod his head and speak.

"Forgive my tardiness, love."

She looked down quickly. Her lashes dusted her cheeks, while another blush stole across her skin. But he had what he wanted. She gave him her hand. Her fingers trembled slightly within his. An odd weakness hit him in the back of his knees. Neal lifted her fingers to his lips and touched a light kiss across her knuckles. She trembled again, his blasted heart stuttered again, and then somebody behind him had to go and move his attention.

"Greetings, your grace! Niall! You seem to be taking to the Scot life, just fine. Regardless of what Lachlan, here, has told us."

Niall turned sideways toward the speaker. It was the bard. He'd forgotten Ainslee had invited him. Just his luck. And then he asked himself, *why not?* If they had to provide grist for the rumor mill, might as well do it all the way. He'd already portrayed a man struck with love at first sight. Might as well act the part of smitten swain, after-the-fact, too. And if he had to do that, who better to witness it than the man with the largest voice in the clan?

"I merely said he wasn't long for the Scottish life. There are a lot of attractions in London-town. I'm sure he misses them."

The man who'd spoken was a younger version of Garrick, giving Neal an instant identity. An arrival of dislike was just as rapid. Lachlan was sitting in the chair at Ainslee's right. Neal motioned him to move and then glowered until Lachlan complied, shifting one seat over. Neal hooked one of the vacated chair's legs, scooted it close to Ainslee and her tea setting, and managed to sit gracefully amid a rustle of plaid and a clink of weaponry. He was proud of the fact he hadn't given up his hold on her fingers, either.

"Well, cousin?"

Neal turned to look at Lachlan. The fellow could have used a pedestal beneath his chair. He barely reached Neal's shoulder while sitting down. Lachlan looked like he hadn't inherited much of the Straith stature. He wasn't very happy with that fact. It was readily apparent in his sneer as he looked up at the top of Neal's head and then back down. Neal would have snickered except Ainslee's hand moved slightly within his. He squeezed her fingers, just enough to keep them captured. She returned the gesture, the movement so slight, he almost missed it. Neal's heart flipped again.

It was an energizing, enervating, exciting feeling. It was also wrong. On every level.

Neal. Neal. What are you doing, buddy?

He went over the litany of reasons why feeling anything for Ainslee was a bad idea. She deserved someone with a much different moral fiber than Neal Straithmore. She was so young. On the cusp of life. *Hell.* Neal was practically jaded. She exuded goodness. Light. Warmth. He was a heartless cold bastard. At least, that's what he'd been called more than once. He hadn't argued it. He hadn't given it a second thought.

"London is an extraordinary city," Neal finally answered. "If a man is unattached. You should try it, Lachlan, if you can spare the time."

"Time? 'Tis funds we lack, na' time. We've all the time in the world, do na' we, Garrick?"

"Ah. Greetings, Garrick. I missed seeing you. Sitting there." Neal looked across the space toward his like-sized steward. Gave the man a slight smile. Garrick returned it.

"You act as though we have access to Straithcairn wealth like you."

Lachlan complained from Neal's side. Neal turned back to him. "Correct me if I'm wrong, someone. But I didn't have access to much from Straith-cairn, either. Until recently. Seems I managed well enough."

"You were the heir. 'Tis different, I'm certain."

It was turning into a pity-fest. Neal wasn't interested in playing. He scanned the attendees. Frowned. "I don't see your mother here today. Is she well?"

It was a safe comment. Everyone except Ainslee was male.

"She...uh. Well. Aye. That's it. She is unwell. She'll join us for sup. I'm certain."

"Attractions, you say?"

The man who spoke had an appetite for food and spirits. His girth and ruddiness betrayed it. He was probably the vicar. He wore a lot of brown-shaded attire. And a large cross. It was a safe assumption.

"Why, naught down south can ever match the Highlands! The burns run deep with fish! There's a great deal of red deer the farmers need thinned down, and do na' forget — we've got the best grouse shooting anywhere. There's always the possibility of a jaunt to Inverness, too. They've got a new theatre sure to bring major actors, and even with the war re-starting, the shops are full. London might have its attractions, but nothing akin to ours. Admit it."

The man missed a major point with his listing. London didn't have Ains-lee. And she was magnetic. Despite the misgivings, Neal glanced toward her. He couldn't help it. Her fingers were quivering within his grasp. The allure was too great. She'd been awaiting his gaze, because she caught it easily, and then held it. He'd been slightly off on his earlier descriptions. She didn't have perfect sapphire colored eyes. She had eyes so striking they reached out and dragged him right into their depths.

"Still and all, 'twas nae certainty that ye'd be duke, was it, Niall? Uncle could have disregarded your claim...what with yer mum being Sassenach and all."

Garrick said it. Neal dragged his attention from Ainslee. He felt a rush of ire that probably showed, although he tried to hide the scowl.

"Must have been quite the surprise. Eh, your grace?" The vicar spoke up again.

"It was a surprise. Not unwelcome...although I would rather have my uncle still with us."

"Here. Here. God rest his soul," the Vicar replied, and lifted his teacup as if in a toast.

"I still say you'll head back. And when you do, might I hope you'll take me with you? I could be your assistant," Lachlan offered.

What a wretched idea. Neal regarded the littler man for a long time as several acerbic comments ran his mind, none of which he'd voice.

"I suppose I'll consider it, Lachlan...in good time. You say the fishing's good?" Neal turned his attention to the vicar. He spoke, but could be saying anything. His mind wasn't on the conversation. It wasn't due to Garrick, although Neal kept the man in his peripheral vision. It was because he still had Ainslee's fingers within his. He moved his thumb along the ridges of her knuckles, and back. She was so small. Petite. Her bones so fragile-feeling. Perfect.

Elegant.

"You thinking to take a pole and try your luck?"

"Perhaps. Once the rain lets up."

"I believe I shall accompany you," Garrick said. "We'll make a wager of it."

Neal gave his cousin his full attention. Added another slight smile. This time the fellow didn't return it. Neal lowered his chin. Almost snarled. And then he answered with a deep tone that projected as much menace as he dared exhibit before his wife.

"Oh, I don't know, Garrick. Perhaps we should go...grouse hunting instead."

"Your aim has improved, has it?"

"Oh, yes. In fact...I look forward to proving it."

"I say, might I have another spot of tea? And a couple of scones? And perhaps one of those iced cakes?"

The vicar was oblivious to the tension. Hopefully Ainslee was, too. Neal didn't move his gaze from Garrick. He didn't blink, either. He caught movement from the corner of his eye as the others glanced from him to Garrick and back. Neal watched his cousin swallow. The vicar stood and approached Ainslee. Neal released her hand so she could refill the man's cup, moving with an inherent grace and elegance. It wasn't the only thing she exhibited. The impression of innocence about her was almost visual.

And that made her the perfect prey.

CHAPTER EIGHTEEN

A INSLEE HADN'T KNOWN THE DUKE'S mother was English, although it didn't matter. She was half Irish. But it explained so many things! His nose, for instance. It was thinner, not near as prominent as his cousins. It didn't resemble any of the portraits gracing the walls, either. And then she needed to consider his piercing gray eyes. He was the lone Straith with those! Sometimes they resembled a storm-tossed sea. At others, they were more the shade of the clouds as they were today – rain-filled and dark. And sometimes, they looked like polished silver. Ainslee could gaze into them for hours, listening to her heart beat faster while each breath grew shallower.

His matriarchal lineage could even explain why he'd stayed in London-town for so long, seemingly ignoring his responsibilities. He might have been visiting family.

So.

The duke's father had chosen a Sassenach for a wife. He wasn't the only Straith to have done so. Niall's grand-father, the third Duke of Straith-cairn, had a younger sister named Iliff. Iliff had wed a man named Findley, a union that was still whispered about if Ainslee enquired. The marriage hadn't lasted. Iliff had been widowed shortly after the ceremony and had returned, childless, to her ancestral home.

Iliff Findley had been a seemingly-fragile, tiny woman of unique coloring – possessing dark red hair and white skin. There was a miniature in one of the salons, painted of her before she'd wed. She'd died soon after returning to Straith Castle, hopefully she'd been mourned, but then she'd been largely forgotten.

As had her wardrobe.

Iliff's husband must have possessed some measure of wealth if her clothing was a sampling. Everything had been fashioned in colors to complement her. She'd had them crafted from the deepest shades, the most brilliant hues, supremely vivid tones. Every outfit seemed to have accessories to match. From gloves to shawls, the thinnest of chemises to the thickest petticoats, every necessary item was included, and all crafted in myriad tones to match the dress. There were cloaks, reticules, stockings, garters, corsets…everything. The ensembles were old-fashioned, musty-smelling, and needed altering.

But to Ainslee, it was absolute treasure.

Even if the clothing was laughably ancient, it was a godsend, making her feel ladylike and elegant when she most needed it.

It had started this morn when a note was delivered from Niall's aunt, asking if Ainslee was going to oversee the running of the castle or if she needed training first. That had been followed by another message an hour later. That one Ainslee tore up and tossed in the waste-bin. She didn't need anyone telling her she wasn't a fit wife for a Duke of Straithcairn, and that he should have married Lileth. She already knew what everyone thought. The bottom of the note had degenerated into a scrawl of words, chastising Niall for keeping the dukedom, when he should have given the title to Garrick so he could wed the proper MacAffrey – the one with the dowry. There had been more. The note had been filled with so much vituperative language it burned Ainslee's eyes to read it.

So, she'd torn the missive into pieces and pulled the cord for help. And the housekeeper, Missus Paige, who Ainslee had known and loved for years, had sent her daughter, Mira, who was now a chamber maid. Mira had brought two other women, Beth and Doreen. Both women were trained as lady's maids. On their heels had come the castle seamstress, Mistress Aggie. Between them, they'd not only remembered Lady Iliff's wardrobe, but found which set of rooms in the cavernous fourth floor held it, and which keys worked on the locks.

All of which had combined to see Ainslee hosting her very first tea in that eye-catching green gown.

The fact that the duke had attended, dressed in a magnificence that stole her breath, was perfect! He'd treated her with exactly the right combinations of words and gestures, too. It had been an amazement she wouldn't have believed if she hadn't been there. Niall Straith was a consummate actor. He'd played the role of love-struck husband so well he could take the stage if he wanted.

He'd fooled everyone with his portrayal.

And now, he needed to do it again.

Tonight she was the hostess of a castle dinner worthy of the duchy of Straithcairn. This time, Ainslee wore a copper-hued evening gown that Mistress Aggie had worked on all day. The seamstress had removed the topaz-studded ribbons from the neckline in order to make it more fashionable, taken yards of material from the skirt to thin it, and worked an absolute miracle to get it ready for tonight. Ainslee was taking even more care with her appearance than before. Niall's aunt, Lady Margaret Blair, would be there. Lady Margaret was very aware of her social status. Ainslee had avoided the woman for years. The lives of the very high and mighty had never interested her.

Well...maybe their horses.

Ainslee watched her reflection as Mira and Beth worked with her hair, heating locks with an iron, and wrapping them about rods in order to get some curl and buoyancy, only to ultimately fail. They'd finally resorted to her usual style – braiding, only this time they'd plaited thin locks of hair, entwining the previously discarded topaz-studded ribbon through the tresses as they worked. The hair at the top had been pulled off her face and woven into something resembling a medieval cap, worked into a mass at the crown of her head and then it was left loose, making a waterfall of hair down her back.

They'd managed to get it above her knees, but it was still going to require some awareness to keep it under control. It was a unique style. Eye-catching. Almost outrageous. Then again, so was her dress, but she didn't have a choice. Mistress Aggie had been exact on her measurements, and there wasn't time to let anything out.

The copper satin was like a second skin, molding to her breasts, upper arms, waist and hips, while the neckline gave her more than a moment of concern, despite their assurances that the new fashions were so immodest, they were shocking! Women wore nothing beneath their light gauze gowns, and even wet them down in order to appear near-naked!

Well. If Niall was used to that, he probably wouldn't take a second glance at her.

What was she thinking?

He might not even notice. They both knew he'd chosen her because she'd begged him. He'd hastened the union due to pity. And he'd kissed her because she'd asked him to. Imagining anything else was sheer fancy. She didn't know for certain why he'd pretended to consummate their marriage last night, but she could guess. He might have been securing her position so he could leave because he knew Lady Margaret's nature and had heard her aspirations for her son. The reason could be baser, too. Perhaps he didn't wish any gossip of his manhood questioned. Ainslee knew how men spoke. She'd been in the stables and heard them. She'd blushed at what she'd heard. That could easily be the reason for the duke's appearance in her room last night. But what did she know?

The only one she could ask was the duke.

And that was impossible.

Ainslee watched her reflection as the women created a vision. She was so completely out of fashion in Lady Iliff's clothing that the only choice was to create an entirely new one. Unique. She hoped the duke would help. She desperately needed him to keep up his playacting a little longer, praying he'd continue acting the part of loving newlywed, for just one more evening. That's all she asked. All she needed.

Please God...

Ainslee might need some training on how to be a lady, and exactly how to stand and move and look like a duchess, but she'd never allow such a hate-filled woman as Lady Margaret to give it to her.

"Lordy, Miss Ainslee—I mean, your grace. You are...well. You will definitely set some jaws to wagging tonight," Mira said it as Ainslee turned this way and that at the mirror.

"She needs jewelry."

Doreen spoke from the door, where she'd been standing guard, while giving opinions throughout the dressing.

Mira stood suddenly, a broad smile on her face. "Of course! The Straithcairn collection includes a topaz necklace. I have seen it in one of the portraits when I've dusted them. I shall be right back! I'll just go and see about it."

Mira bobbed a curtsey and rushed from the room. Doreen opened the door for her, and then latched it shut again. Somewhere in the room behind Ainslee someone was fluffing out cloth. Or straightening one of the chairs. Or something that engendered a swishing sound. Ainslee didn't move her gaze to check. She was too fascinated with her image. The door leading to the duke's chamber opened, and the duke's voice preceded him as he just walked right in.

"Ainslee? Mason tells me it would make a grand display if we know what colors you are wearing tonight. That way, I can match my cuff studs and brooch to—"

Ainslee swiveled at the sound of his voice and watched him walk in, talking mainly to the floor, and then he looked up, and stopped dead. He had a strange look on his face. She'd call it shock, but she didn't know him well enough to peg it. His words ended with a garbled sound, his eyes widened, and his mouth dropped opened. And she wished he'd stayed silent, since the next burst of words were mostly expletives, peppered with negatives.

"Oh, my *God*! Damn it, Ainslee! Son-of-a-bitch! No. Hell no. And another no. *Ah*!"

The last word was a massive growl of sorts. It reverberated through the chamber, gaining more than one gasp. Ainslee immediately looked down. They'd spent hours creating this attire and it was all a waste. He wasn't pleased. That much was obvious. Nobody said anything. Nobody moved. Waves of goose bumps traipsed across her skin. She could feel them against the satin. It wasn't a nice sensation. Nothing about this was.

"Forgive me," she told the bit of floor beneath her slippers.

"For. What?" His answer was in two clipped words.

The spot beneath her slippers was swimming oddly. That was odd. She didn't feel any urge to cry, although she might expire of the embarrassment. This would have been so much easier if she didn't have her new maids watching and listening.

But it couldn't be helped.

And what one couldn't help, one had to endure.

Very well.

The duke could attend the sup by himself. She was going to request Beth to undo all the work on her hair, Doreen to assist with removing this dress that so upset him. Then she'd don her borrowed nightgown and dismiss everyone, so she could hide in her rooms. She didn't need anyone bringing up her shortcomings. Not even the duke, who didn't even know all of them.

"You are...na' pleased with my appearance." It was whispered, but she said it. And nothing betrayed any kind of emotion.

"What?"

The word was abrupt. Irritated. He was clearly angered. He used the deep loud voice he could wield so easily. This was so patently unfair. Must he go and make this even more difficult?

"This ensemble...is all I have."

He said something beneath his breath that sounded like another expletive. One, she'd never heard outside of the stable yard. She could hear him walking nearer, his steps sure and solid, and then he did something so amazing, her eyes widened. He went to a knee in front of her, reached for both of her hands, and brought them to his neck, just above his chest.

Then he held them there, her fingers touching the slight stubble beneath his chin. And he was visibly trembling.

Her heart went into palpitations.

"Ainslee. Kid. This is getting..." There was a distinct pause before he continued. "Beyond complicated. And I—well. Let's just say. I'm way out of my league here. And I know it. So. I'm going to try. And find. The right words to untangle this. But it's not going to be easy. Trust me."

He'd broken the words into distinct sentences, but he did that often. It seemed to give whatever he said an aura of importance. Once he'd finished, he pulled in such a huge breath, it enlarged his stature. But that was ridiculous. He was already massive. Immense. And kneeling at her feet. Which was absolutely unbelievable.

The duke is kneeling at my feet!

The wonder of it was as thrilling as the actual fact. He was attired in a Straithcairn kilt and shirt. He hadn't donned a jacket yet. His shirt was stretched at the seams with his physique and the position he'd assumed. That gave her a perfect look at how muscular and wide his shoulders were. It also gave her a view of how long and thick his hair was, since he hadn't tied it back yet. He wore a fringed sporran that draped from his bent knee, while the sword at his hip skimmed the floor right beside him.

The sight was beyond thrilling.

He blew the air out with a heavy sigh. His breath feathered across her lower arms, raising shivers.

"You are not remotely displeasing, Ainslee. To me. Or to anyone. You are the most beautiful woman I've ever seen. Ever. And...you don't know what I'm talking about right now, but I have to tell you – that's saying something." His frame trembled again.

Oh, my.

"I reacted as I did...because—well. Because—uh. Just spit it out, Neal. It ain't that hard, buddy."

The last words were barely audible. Totally mystifying. And something else. Ainslee fought a smile. She hadn't known the duke talked to himself. Or that he could sound so unsure. It was thoroughly endearing. His fingers tightened on hers. And then he took another deep breath.

"I'll just admit it. I'm a severe. Failure. At control."

He broke the words into separate sentences again.

"Control?"

Ainslee straightened a bit with the surprise. Her move pulled more of her bosom from the bodice of the gown. The duke moved his gaze to hers.

And the world shifted.

Words felt like they got hurled back and forth. Raw words. Filled with emotion. His chest rose and fell with increasing rapidity. His nostrils widened as he inhaled. Her nipples hardened into tight knots against the satin dress. Itching. Straining. She almost glanced down, but it wouldn't have mattered. The duke acted as if he knew!

His upper lip lifted into a snarl next. And his eyes narrowed. Ainslee's heart seized up, and then started beating in a frantic motion. She caught a flash from between his eyelashes, but his eyes didn't look remotely silver. Or gray. They were multi-hued glass shards refracting light. He looked wild. Untamed. Extremely dangerous. His unbound hair just added to the impression.

"Do you understand what I'm saying?" he finally asked.

She nodded. And then shook her head.

His response was a complete shock. He slammed his eyes shut and arched backward, and sent a howling sound into the chamber. He didn't stop until he ran out of breath. Waves of bass tones reverberated through her room. Ainslee's knees shook first. Her entire body followed. She held back any further reaction, but heard what sounded like gasps from her maids.

The duke finished his cry and looked back at her. He was frowning, and his eyes were the color of lead. Ainslee darted her glance toward the mirror. It was far safer. She watched his reflection release her hands. Gain its feet. Heard the clinking of weaponry as it settled back into place about him. He might be gazing at her in the mirror. He could be checking his own reflection. She didn't peek to check. She didn't dare.

"I'm going to leave now, Ainslee."

"L-l-leave?"

Her heart fell. Her stammer reflected it. He wouldn't leave her to face everyone by herself. Would he?

"For my own chamber."

Ainslee dared a glance upward. Got snagged and then held by his gaze. A roar of ocean crested through her ears. A thunder of horse-hooves accompanied it. The breath got sucked out of her, leaving her weak enough to fall.

And fall hard.

Someone knocked on the connecting door. One of her maids opened it. Some talking ensued. She barely heard it. It took a moment to note that Niall's valet, Mason was speaking.

"...nae need to shout, your grace. I've found the answer myself. I've got the topaz studs. MacGruder is on his way with the rest. He'll be here momentarily. You may na' ken the history behind this particular set. If

I recall correctly, it was the third duke who bought the stones, but your uncle who had them set. Or maybe it was his wife. She had a great eye for presentation. Your grace?"

The duke blinked and turned his head from her. Ainslee wavered in place. She felt as washed out and weak as she had one summer day, after she'd slipped and fallen into a burn, and been pulled under by the swift water. She'd fought her way to the shore, and had lain on the bank. Weak. Wrung-out. Shaky.

That's exactly how this felt.

The duke moved away. She heard him and his valet speaking. She sensed the maids moving about. Most of it failed to register. She reached out and grabbed onto one side of her cheval looking-glass, holding it like a lifeline as the duke and his valet moved toward his door.

That's when the duke's words filtered through. The door wasn't fully closed behind him. He must not realize he was ruining the act he'd just put on.

"You heard me, Mason. I need whiskey! Right now! Double-shot. Why? Because I've damn-well earned it, that's why!"

Beth hurriedly shut the door. Too late, though. Nobody said anything. They didn't have to.

CHAPTER NINETEEN

WHISKEY DIDN'T WORK.
But he'd already known that.

The liquor still had its uses. The shot he'd downed earlier cleared his head, braced him momentarily, but then it had dissipated, leaving him as shaky and frustrated as before. Neal could have tried stepping out onto the stone balcony again. The Chieftain's chamber had a large balcony on the seaward side. He'd looked over the edge. Considered things. If a man was desperate, he could conceivably drop onto the rock ledge beneath, work his way along the cliff, and with a great deal of luck, escape. Should any attackers actually make it that far into the structure.

The balcony was as sturdily built as the rest of Castle Straith. A balustrade ran the edge, waist-high at the center, but rising significantly on both sides. That had created two dark, three-sided enclosures. One contained a rain barrel for his use as it caught the stream of water sluicing from the roof. Neal shoved the rain barrel to one side and found that he had a unique, but credible shower.

A really cold one.

The effects of that had long worn off, too.

Neal gave a short sigh, glanced down at his problem – the woman holding onto his arm, and then he quickly darted his gaze back to the hall they traversed. Ainslee walked beside him, taking two quick steps to his one, which just made the amount of cleavage she'd put on display bounce. This was his fault. He didn't have to escort her the entire way. He could've met up with her at the landing above the great hall. Or used the foyer beneath the stairs. Heck, he could have even arranged to catch up with her outside the grand salon with adjacent dining room, with minimum contact.

But.

No.

Mason had arranged this, but Neal hadn't fought it, either. At a subconscious level, he must want this contact. Which made no sense. Zero. Zilch. Nada. He was already dealing with an incomprehensible level of testosterone-fueled need. He had to go and add to it?

He forced his mind to go over the reasons it was a bad idea to pursue any thoughts of bedding Ainslee. Again.

Mind over matter, buddy.

Focus.

This wasn't his life. It wasn't his body. Ainslee was *not* his wife. The only thing that Neal Straithmore could claim was his intellect. He hadn't been reborn here. He'd traveled backward through time and usurped another guy's body. There had to be a reason for it. He'd been dropped into the dawn of the nineteenth century. He didn't think it was so he could hijack somebody else's life.

And make wild, passionate love to—

A jolt of electricity shot down both legs as he yanked his mind from the instant vision. Neal stopped. Ainslee followed suit. A glance in her direction showed the shadow of her dark lashes on her cheeks. She didn't look up to see what the matter might be. That was no surprise. He'd been an absolute ass last night in her chamber, but at least they'd been alone. This time, when he'd acted like a rutting beast, he'd had witnesses.

Argh.

Mason hadn't acted like Neal's foray into the duchess's chamber was of much import. The valet had been whistling that same stinkin', off-key Highland tune as he assisted Neal with the topaz studs that secured his cuffs. And then Mason had brought up his belief again about the new duchess and her gift. The man truly believed Ainslee was fey. She could work magic with any creature. He was certain Neal had noted it by now. How could her own husband miss it?

Bullshit.

Neal kept his opinion unvoiced. The valet was free to think as he wanted, and use what information he had. But Mason was dealing with things from an early nineteenth-century perspective. With limited knowledge to draw from. Neal was a world-traveler who'd had every available benefit of education and technology from the twenty-first century. He'd heard it all; practically seen it as well. Almost everything had a root cause that had already been discovered. Catalogued. Discussed. Had documentaries filmed.

Magic had been disproven time and time again.

That wasn't proof that unexplained things didn't happen. *Hell.* Neal had experienced one. Didn't make it magical. The only thing his presence here right now proved was that forces existed in the physics arena that hadn't been scientifically explained.

Yet.

He'd heard of people like Ainslee, however. They used the title '*Whisperer*' for publicity purposes. Made money with it. Titled their reality shows the same way. It was inserted after the name of the animal they specialized in. Didn't make anything magical.

Or fairylike.

Or enchanted.

Despite the internal warnings rocketing through his skull, Neal tipped his head toward the mass of her braided hair situated at his shoulder level and inhaled. She smelled so sweet. Clean. Fresh. Like a wildflower, bravely struggling for life…blooming where nothing else could. Warm. Alive. Utterly female…

Desirable.

Damn it.

Neal stiffened. Blinked rapidly. Swallowed. And began walking again. Ainslee started up her double-step beside him. Mason was off a bit. Ainslee wasn't fey, but she was a magnet for all sorts of warm and loving emotions and sensations. With the exception of his cousins and their mother, the entire household seemed genuinely fond of the new duchess. Neal looked away from the shining crown of hair they'd created atop her head, and barely avoided hitting a suit of armor by the merest span of space.

And she giggled over it.

Neal's entire frame seized up. This was the problem cold showers didn't correct. Whiskey didn't even dent. He moved again before anything else happened. They passed a hall that branched off. Went straight. Started up a flight of steps. Turned to the left at the top. The castle was a maze. Ainslee had stopped him at his first almost-wrong turn. Gestured wordlessly to the correct hall. After that, she used slight turns of her body to direct him. Good thing. Neal was lost. And his mind wasn't assisting with much. The woman had too much allure, and it was displayed way too well. He hadn't thought she possessed much bosom, but what she had was shoved up so a massive topaz necklace could rest atop her cleavage. She probably owed her new curves to a corset. A black lace one. One of the really sexy ones… from the past.

Well. Of course she would, Neal. That was the only kind they made.

Neal tripped, and caught it with a couple of danced steps. Ainslee actually kept step beside him, although her hand tightened on his arm throughout the maneuver. He was in luck they weren't on a staircase. His clumsiness could have sent them both flying.

Great.

Just great.

Neal looked heavenward. Took a deep breath. Exhaled. This wasn't going well, and he had an entire room full of people awaiting them. He needed vigilance. Wariness. His observation skills at their most keen. Garrick would need watching. Lachlan, a bit of monitoring. Their mother was probably the spider in a proverbial parlor, awaiting a fly.

"Uh. Sorry about that," he finally said.

"The rugs should be weighted at the edges. Secured better."

"What?"

"Before someone takes a nasty spill. Forgive me. I'll speak...with the staff."

Neal smiled. If she hadn't trembled through most of that she would have sounded like a gracious hostess of advanced years. Helping him save face as she took the blame for his near-disaster. It was still a good try.

"You're really cute. You know that?"

He made the mistake not only of saying it, but of looking down at her while speaking. His ears stared buzzing. She had her brows drawn together, a puzzled look on her face.

"You call me bow-legged?"

"What? That's not what cute means. Um. Nowadays."

"What does it mean?"

"Well...uh. It means...something like...pretty. And darling. And endearing. A few more things like that. I think I'll just shut up now before my mouth gets me into even more trouble. All right with you?"

Well.

He'd cured her frown. Her eyes had gone wide, her mouth had the same affliction, and a blush colored her cheeks as she quickly looked down. She appeared to focus on the topaz stud Mason had pinned into Neal's lace jabot at the space right between his pecs. Or thereabouts.

"Oh."

Oh? That's all she had to say?

"Um. Niall?"

She said his name. Well. The other guy's name. It meant the same thing. Neal's heart caught at the fact she'd used it, and the hesitant way she'd done it. He almost thumped his free fist against his chest until his heart restarted on its own.

"Yes?"

"I...need to be thanking you."

"For what? Not falling? And dragging you with me?"

She snorted. And then she looked up at him and stole his next breath. His heartbeat again. She damn near took every wit he possessed, too.

"For...not deserting me."

"What?"

"I ken...you wished to...leave."

"When?"

"Today."

"It's raining cats and dogs outside."

"It is?"

Neal almost rolled his eyes. "It's an expression, Ainslee. It doesn't mean real cats and dogs—forget it. I couldn't go. The roads are a mess. A carriage would be stuck within a half mile."

"You could have taken Huntsmen's Dale."

"That would require riding a horse. And that's not likely to happen, babe."

"Babe?"

"Uh. That's another...bit of slang. Means the same as cute. Sort of."

"Well...I still wish to thank you. Especially since...you do na' wish to be anywhere near...me."

"Where did you get that idea?"

"From you. Last night. In my room."

Her voice had lowered to the slightest whisper. He had to bend to hear it.

"Oh. That. Well, darling. That may have been what I said. But it is light-years away from what I meant. Trust me."

Her eyelashes fluttered as she looked away. And the fingers atop his arm tightened.

"What is it now?" he asked.

"You just...called me darling."

Neal straightened. He called himself every kind of fool. Her reaction was the same she'd given him last night when he'd offered to stay in her bed chamber with her. She was exhibiting something close to panic. Or fright. Or...what did he know? Could easily be dislike. He looked over her head at the wall. Tried ignoring the solid knot of ache overtaking his chest. There was a large rendition of a seascape opposite where they stood. With a lot of stitches to it. Somebody had taken a lot of time putting a lot of thread into it. It went out of focus as he stared. Neal blinked his eyes rapidly to clear them.

"And I—well...I just want to thank you," she continued.

Neal cleared his throat. Tried for a non-committal tone. Completely unemotional. He should have waited. It sounded like he was chewing on gravel. "No need."

"But...the Lady Margaret. She'll....attend?"

"My aunt?"

She nodded.

"Well...the woman can't feign illness forever."

Ainslee was quick. She had a conspiratorial smile on her face as she looked up at him. And damn him for seeing that much! Her glance darted away again.

"She is na' verra fond of me."

"I don't think I'm in her good graces, either," he replied. "You ready to proceed, then?"

She nodded. He moved automatically. One foot before the next. Whatever he was feeling for Ainslee had to cease. And, if he couldn't stop it, he needed to at least put the emotions on a back burner. He had unknown people to face. Problematic social codes to follow – some he might not even be aware of. A lot of unspoken tensions to alleviate. Hidden agendas to discover and abort. Potential hostilities to decipher and nullify.

And a massive woman problem.

You can do this, Neal. This is your forte.

They reached the landing outside the grand salon without further mishap. Neal waited for a moment before approaching. He could hear sounds of a crowd through the opened doors. Sounded festive. Large. He sucked in a deep breath.

"We're about to gird the lions in their den, Ainslee. You ready for this?"

She gave him a quick grin and squeezed his arm. Nodded. They were spotted. And then announced.

"Their graces, the Duke and Duchess of Straithcairn!"

Applause erupted at the end of the announcement. Neal barely heard it. He walked into a room ablaze with candlelight and filled with people. He didn't hear or see much of it.

Because of the woman on his arm.

CHAPTER TWENTY

SHE KNEW NIALL WAS JUST pretending. But it was getting more and more difficult to resist. Every single time he acted in love with her, it sent a sharp, insistent, fire-like pain lancing through her breast. Ainslee didn't dare analyze it. She was leery of what it might be. She hadn't ever wanted to be female, and now she was fancying something worse? Something she was afraid of feeling, but might blurt out if she wasn't careful? She couldn't pretend the way he was able to, and if he didn't cease, she didn't know what might happen. She wasn't an actor like him. She didn't think any other man was.

And what a man...

Niall Straith was so manly. Well beyond her scope of experience and imagination, and she'd been around males most of her life. The duke was just so different. Every bit of him exhibited fully mature male. Massive. Heated. Solid. Virile...

It was at that exact moment, she realized she'd been wrong her entire life. She was grateful to be a woman.

She only wished she was *his* woman.

Ainslee trembled and her cheeks warmed. She was being absurd now. Over-reaching. He'd done everything she begged him to do. He'd made her his duchess! She hadn't thought through what she'd asked. She'd never dreamt of achieving such a grand status. Or what gaining such a husband might mean. All she'd focused on was saving her sister. Lileth should be here, standing beside the duke at this very moment, graciously acknowledging the guests. Not Ainslee.

Ainslee had toyed with the duke's future without one thought to what it meant. She needed to stop anything else from happening. It was bad enough she'd forced him, becoming a wife he didn't want. There was no excuse for adding unrequited love to this. None. Ainslee's feet stopped. The duke stopped. He looked down at her. She didn't check. She felt him waiting as she watched the parquet flooring waver with unblinking eyes.

Oh, dearest God!

She hadn't just admitted she was falling in love with him. Had she? Oh, no. No. It couldn't be. This was terrible. The consequences beyond imaging.

"Oh, my. How…ghastly."

Ainslee looked up as Lady Blair approached, skirts of some blue gauzy material fluttering about her. The material was made see-through by the firelight behind it. Ainslee could easily see lower limbs…and even garters atop plump knees that held the woman's stockings in place. Ainslee held her breath and blinked rapidly on the shock. The view didn't change. Good heavens! The woman looked almost naked.

Ainslee looked up higher. The bodice might have been double-layered with material, but it wasn't sufficient for coverage there, either. Lady Blair possessed an enormous bosom. Large, dark nipples.

Higher, Ainslee.

She forced her eyes to the woman's face. Niall's aunt colored her hair with a preparation that contained soot as its base. As it wore off, the gray hairs at the roots became more and more apparent, giving her the look of a skunk. She must have recently applied it, for no tell-tale white line was in evidence. The woman also covered her complexion with a liberal application of face powder atop a cream base that contained arsenic. Ainslee knew all that from listening to the servants over the years.

That gave Ainslee a start. Hadn't Niall said something about how the employment of servants equaled loss of privacy? She'd never had a high position in society, but at that moment realized how right he was. Ainslee already knew Niall Straith's assets were vast. They just kept increasing. He was beyond handsome. Fit. Manly. Charming. Educated. Intelligent. Now, she knew he had insight, as well.

And he was wed to her.

The thought brought such pleasure, her knees went weak. She swayed against him. The duke glanced down. She couldn't meet his eyes, but gave him what was probably a sickly-looking smile. He brought his free hand across his chest to place it atop where hers rested. And then he just held it there. Ainslee was cocooned in an instant sensation of warmth. Comfort. Solidness.

She looked quickly back to Lady Blair before any of that reflected anywhere on her features for anyone to see. Niall's aunt had the height of a Straith, placing her well above Ainslee. From that vantage, it was easy to see a distinct line between real skin color, which was mottled with light brown and pink spots, and where the powdered paint had been applied. The woman fancied herself a beauty, and she might have been. Some years past. But she wasn't admitting defeat. Gossip was the woman was desperate to hang onto her youth, and punished any lady's maid who failed to achieve it.

The effort was wasted, especially with her expression at the moment. She looked all the way down to Ainslee's hem and then back. She had her nose wrinkled as if smelling something vile. That expression put a lot of lines into prominence throughout her face. Ainslee subconsciously stiffened and stepped nearer to the duke. That was nonsensical. She had to face the woman sooner or later. She was just grateful Lady Blair's sons weren't accompanying their mother at the moment.

Something in the duke's forearm tightened beneath her fingers. When he spoke, he sounded as shocked as Ainslee felt. And twice as disgusted. He also separated the words, making them even more dramatic. She rather liked that affectation of his.

"Surely. This can't be. Aunt...Margaret?"

"Niall. My...dearest nephew."

"Well. Your presence must mean you've recovered your malady and can join us this eve. How...fortunate for all involved."

"Oh! You are such a flirt, Niall. Always were, though. Weren't you, lad?"

The woman laughed. Batted her eyelashes. She'd coated them with a mixture of soot and lamp-black. Little specks of black dusted the woman's cheeks. Ainslee had to look away before she did something disastrous. Like snort the giggle she held back. Niall answered with a slow drawl.

"Please don't say you mean that."

"What?"

"Surely I had better taste."

Lady Margaret pulled her head back. "I beg your pardon."

Ainslee snorted. Both Niall and his aunt looked to her. Niall moved her slightly forward. She had no choice but to take a step.

"Have you met my wife? Ainslee? My aunt, Lady Margaret Blair."

Ainslee watched the woman give her another once-over. The woman's expression markedly changed.

"We've met."

"I certainly hope you amend your opinion somewhat, Aunt Margaret, before I'm forced to take medieval measures over it."

Something about Niall had altered, getting larger and more menacing. It matched the steely note in his voice.

"How so?" Lady Margaret enquired, without the slightest difference to her tone or physical stance.

"I refer to my newly wedded state. Ghastly is *not* the description I would put to it."

"Oh. That. Of course na'. I was referring to…well. I was speaking of the temperature of this room. I had to request a servant to light the fire. This room is ever cold, even in high summer. Most of the rooms are, but especially this one."

"I hadn't noticed."

"Such a thing should have been checked."

"We've not had time to check temperatures outside our chambers, Aunt Margaret. We're but newly wedded. Last night, in point of fact. And I've made certain my wife isn't cold. Haven't I, sweet?"

The duke turned to her and bent his head. Ainslee's heart thudded sharply. There wasn't anything she could do to prevent it. She glanced up at him, but he was looking over her at something beyond.

"Well. It still should have been seen to afore requesting we assemble here."

"Good point. Be certain to make a note of that, my love."

Another endearment rolled off his tongue, stalling her breathing without any effort on his part. It didn't match his expression. He had his teeth tightly set, or something else that sent a nerve into prominence along one side.

"You are not listening to a word I say, Niall."

He faced his aunt again, hauling Ainslee closer to his side with the move. "Truly? How…odd. I do hope you'll excuse us. We have other guests."

"I am referring to proper etiquette. A real hostess always makes certain of her guest's comfort, afore the event…not during."

"Perhaps you should wear more."

"Perhaps you should have wed the correct bride," his aunt retorted.

There was a large gasping sound. Ainslee hoped it hadn't come from her. Everyone had gone completely silent with the same inhaled breath, while somewhere out in the halls something fell, sending an echo into the room. Niall was as still as a statue, but he appeared larger somehow. His answer was in his deeper tone. There was a threatening thread beneath the words.

"If I'm not mistaken, the estate probably has something called a Dower House. I'm sure it's musty. It may even require a bit of work, but I believe we can get it habitable within the week. I'd suggest you prepare yourself."

"The...Dower House?"

Lady Margaret's voice trembled.

"You heard me. It's meant for the widowed duchess when a new one takes her place. It's not usually given over to poor relations, but this isn't a usual event, is it? I'd suggest you pack. And I'd take thicker gowns. The one you're wearing would let any draft through."

Lady Blair could be immune to the duke's tone. She laughed, as if she wasn't facing banishment.

"Oh, Niall. You are such a tease. This is the latest fashion from London. Surely you recognize it. You were just there. My maids ordered me all the fashion journals. They assure me this is what all the highest ladies of society wear."

"*Haute Couture* requires the proper figure, dearest aunt. Perhaps your employees failed to mention that part," Niall replied.

"Well!"

Ainslee was in shock. Her legs were trembling. Her fingers clenched on the duke's arm to prevent her knees from giving out.

"But there won't be many to note your fashion chops, or lack thereof, in the Dower House. Now. We really do need to move on, Aunt. We've other guests."

Lady Blair stopped him with a quick move. Her body blocked their progress.

"Surely you are na' serious? You expect me to live in that monstrosity? The Dower House?"

"Actually, I believe I'm merely offering the Dower House, should you fail to alter your current opinion of my wedded state. 'Tis a fair alternative. Would you like me to elaborate?"

"What of Garrick?"

"What of him?"

"Have you forgotten? He's your heir. Are you sending him away, too?"

"Garrick's a grown man. He can live where-all he likes. And I think...isn't there something called a Grand Tour? Maybe I should send him on that. Although...wait. It's 1803, isn't it? That means Napoleon has restarted his war. That puts a damper on things in Europe. But there's always London."

"What of me?"

Lachlan joined them from the duke's other side, acting as if the drama of the moment wasn't happening. Maybe it wasn't. Perhaps only Ainslee felt as if she'd taken a blow to the belly.

"Ah. You, too? Why not? London doesn't have anything I want. Sounds like I'll be rather busy here. As your mother just pointed out, I've a lack of heirs. You and your brother have been laboring under the false aspiration of inheriting for long enough. I've a wife now. Following that event, there are usually babies. Lots and lots of them."

Ainslee had been wrong. It wasn't a blow to the belly. It was higher and grabbed her heart. And then squeezed it. Babies? He was talking about creating babies?

With her?

Oh, dear God. It was play-acting, but she felt faint. Her hand gripped to his arm like talons.

"Well, Aunt Margaret?" An upward glance showed Niall's attention still fully on his aunt.

"Well what?"

"You ready to proffer an apology?"

The woman pulled her face out of the scrunched look and attempted a smile in Ainslee's direction.

"I spoke hastily...your graces. You have my sincerest congratulations on your...union."

The words were false. Filled with an underlying acidic tone. Ainslee recognized it. She'd heard Lady Blair use it before.

"I believe it's proper to curtsey when speaking to a duchess, Aunt Margaret. Unless one's position in society is of a higher status...and that would only be a member of the royal family. Which you are not. Am I right?"

Oh no.

He wouldn't.

He didn't.

Lady Blair would never forgive such an insult.

Ainslee's mouth opened and then shut and then opened again. Nothing came out. The duke must've known what she was about, for he sent her a look that instantly quelled any utterance. Then he turned to watch Lady Blair lift her diaphanous skirts and sink into a curtsey. Ainslee's gaze kept darting from his aunt to Niall. The skin beneath her face paint was a purplish tone. Niall didn't have an expression that Ainslee could decipher. He looked hard. It matched the rest of him. There wasn't a gentle look to any portion of him.

"Well done, Aunt Margaret. Now. You truly must excuse us. We're neglecting our other guests. Come, darling."

He pulled Ainslee's with him. She managed a step. Another. She was having trouble walking?

"You're shaking," he said softly.

"I...know."

"Buck up, love. We girded the dragon in her lair. And just look. We're both still breathing. Nobody is bleeding. It wasn't that bad. Admit it."

CHAPTER TWENTY-ONE

L OVE.
   The word carried a hint of emotion when said with such a depth of voice! She'd been wrong. It wasn't her knees or her heart having an issue. Her throat closed off with the knot that formed in it.

"Would you like some champagne?"

She shook her head. It was the best she could manage.

"You really need to cease shaking. Someone is bound to notice. They might even think it's me causing it."

It is you!

"You're not holding it against me, are you?"

"Wh…at?" The word was split it two, coming through lips so cold, they probably looked blue.

He bent toward her, whispering to her earlobe. The spot sparked. Tingled. And absolutely terrified.

"Requiring my aunt to show proper respect and abeyance. I won't allow you to be treated as a pariah in your own home. Come along, Ainslee, it is not that frightening."

"I'm…na' frightened."

"You're shaking. Still."

"I'm sorry."

"In a moment, I'm going to haul you over my shoulder and return to our chambers with you. I may even jog."

She pulled back and stared up at him before realizing that mistake. She darted her glance away. Toward the wall. The window. The doorway. Anywhere else felt safer. She didn't dare lock gazes with him.

"You don't believe me? Oh, come on. They already think I'm lustful and uncivilized. Might as well convince them. Besides…it's a better alternative than allowing everyone to watch your reaction at the moment."

"My…reaction?"

That idea was too horrid to even consider. The way he affected her was obvious to everyone? She didn't know what to do. He'd championed her, called her all sorts of endearments, and added to it with that announcement of how he wanted to create babies with her. She was still reeling. Shocked. Awed. Stunned. Dazed. She was terrified of the giddy, effervescent feeling.

She didn't know how to hide any of it.

"Try not to show it. Can we agree on that much?"

She nodded.

"I'll attempt to stay away. Should be easier once they announce the sup. We're on opposite ends of the table. The room seats twenty. Per side. You're practically in the next village. You ready?"

"For what?"

His shoulders slumped slightly. And then went rigid again. "Helping me with this! For the love of—! You might at least look at me. Maybe give a lover-like expression with it?"

He didn't know what he asked!

"Come along, Ainslee, play fair. Attempt a smile or something. You're ruining a really great scene, and I'm trying to portray undying love here. The least you could do is act your part."

Ainslee looked up at him, and couldn't look away. The entire room about them blurred as it seemed to slowly rotate about them. Everyone disappeared into the kaleidoscope of form and color. There was just the duke and her, suspended somehow, his hand holding hers atop his arm, his hair pulled back, revealing his handsomeness. He had such intense gray eyes, sometimes as warm as a string of candlelit Scot gray pearls; at others, as cold and glossy as molten silver. They drew her, mesmerized. Made it impossible to hide what she felt for him. She might as well be floating.

She may not know much of love, but she knew she was in it. Deeply. Fully. Forever.

"Your graces? The dinner is ready."

The announcement intruded sharply, breaking the spell. Niall blinked and then shook his head slightly. He looked almost as surprised as she felt. And then he winked.

"Much better. I'm almost fooled. If you weren't still shaking, that is."

She was listening but didn't comprehend much. It had something to do with the feel of his hand still holding hers atop his arm. The closeness of his chest rising and falling with each breath right before her. The way a stray lock of hair slid down his forehead. The way he licked his lips...

"Perhaps now, no one will guess how much you abhor me."

"Abhor...you?"

"You have a better word for it? Come on. You're seated between the vicar and Lachlan. I don't envy your conversation." He steered her around the end of the table and down one side, and then waited while a footman pulled out her chair.

"Niall?"

He froze in place, whether at the use of his given name, or the frantic way she said it, his hand lifting hers from his sleeve.

"Yes?"

"I don't—"

Ainslee stopped with her mouth still open to refute it. To tell him the truth. She didn't abhor him at all. She loved him! Reality flared up from somewhere to save her from an embarrassment beyond comprehension. What was she thinking? Doing? She couldn't blurt out something so personal and private! Something he'd detest hearing.

She'd rather die.

The large form of the vicar settled his girth into the chair to her right, making the wood squeak. Lachlan had arrived as well, and stood behind the duke, waiting. Ainslee shut her lips, shook her head, and dropped into her chair with an inelegant plop.

He put a kiss atop her fingers before releasing her hand. She watched his kilt sway as he walked to his own seat, so far away she wouldn't hear anything he said. She could barely see the top of his head over the table centerpiece. This dinner was going to feel interminable.

But it was her doing.

She'd orchestrated it.

CHAPTER TWENTY-TWO

"WELL. YOU CERTAINLY SET THE servant's hall a-twitter this evening, Neal."

Neal looked down at Mason. The man was working at the fastenings of his ruffled jabot. They'd already removed his weapons, boots, socks, jacket, kilt, cuff studs and then the cuffs. The coiled bits of material sat atop a bureau at approximately Mason's eye level. Menswear needed an update, but this Highland wear was really over-the-top. He'd thought Scots just tossed on a kilt, grabbed a sword, maybe dabbled on some blue paint, and *voila!* They were ready for anything. Shirts were optional. So were socks and boots.

Shows what he'd known.

"Really?" he finally answered. "Why's that?"

The valet had finished with the jabot and probably would have started on Neal's buttons, if he hadn't gotten there first. Neal's fingers flew down the shirt-front opening without looking as the valet watched him.

"Why...the way you handled the situation."

"What situation are we referring to?"

"Lady Margaret will probably stay in her wing for a fortnight after the set-down you gave her."

"That old bag?"

The valet snorted, and then coughed. He was probably trying not to laugh.

"Please don't tell me I used to flirt with that woman. Just. Don't. Good God. I mean. Surely I didn't."

"Well...you have changed markedly since your accident, Neal. I am na' the lone one to have noted it."

"For the better, I hope."

"Perhaps."

"Oh, come on, Mason. As far as I'm concerned the old me was a complete moron."

"Moron?"

"You know. Dunce. Dork. Fool. Idiot. Twit."

"Oh. I wouldn't go that far, Neal. You had your moments."

"Like flirting with an old woman who should know better than to wear next to nothing when she possesses a stomach-churning figure? Come on, here. That takes balls. And with her attire, I could almost spot them."

Mason's coughing fit lasted longer this time. Neal shrugged the shirt off, hung it from a post on his shaving stand, and reached for another floor-length robe that rested atop his bed. These robes were all constructed of the same basic plaid color scheme, but this one had a black satin belt, and the same material for a lining. It slid onto his skin with a cool sensation that immediately started warming. It felt deliciously decadent.

"Lady Margaret has been the chatelaine of Castle Straith for many years. You've been here four days. I believe you flattered her as a method of keeping the peace."

"Oh. I see. I was doing the 'discretion is the better part of valor' thing."

"Oh. Neal. You know your Shakespeare."

"Doesn't everyone? So. I was keeping the peace, huh? I suppose I trusted Garrick for the same reason?"

"Now that, I can na' say."

"You know...now that I think on it, Garrick wasn't at the supper tonight. I wonder what that portends."

"Perhaps he's come down with the same ailment as his mum."

"Oh." Neal snickered. "We can but hope. Right. Well, then. I don't think you need to wait around tonight. You might as well seek your own bed."

"You are certain?"

Neal walked to the door leading to the salon that led to Ainslee's room. Rotated the handle. Pulled the door open. Turned back around to address his servant. Spoke.

"Well. Yeah. The duchess and I have other plans. We are newlyweds, you know."

Mason chuckled. "Verra good, Neal. I shall wait for your call in the morn."

"Good night, Mason."

Neal stood in the doorway and waited as the valet puttered around, retrieving the discarded clothing. And then he started whistling. Neal sighed. Walked into the connecting room. Pulled the door shut behind him. He eyed the hard sofa he'd fallen from last night. Looked across the room to Ainslee's door. And had an immediate reaction from his dick.

Great.

He shoved down on it as he walked past the hard sofa. Let up a little. That didn't work. His problem was pretty hard to miss. Neal pulled both sides of his robe closer. Re-tied his belt. Looked down. Frowned. He could really use a sporran about now. Ainslee might not welcome the sight of him in her bedchamber as it was, but the last thing he wanted was her to catch sight of him and do something maidenly.

Like scream.

Neal stopped. Tilted his head. He couldn't hear Mason, but he needed to wait at least a half hour. The man could still be about. And Neal wasn't about to be rumored as an eight-second guy. He looked over the hard sofa again. Set his shoulders next. Approached the door. And started a pep-talk. Because this couldn't continue. He might have to take things into his own hands.

Literally.

Neal. Buddy. It's a door. A bit of wood. Some varnish. A handle. Lock. Some studs. Brackets. Still and all…just a door. Plain and simple.

He'd reached it. And he was wrong. It wasn't just any door. Nor was anything about it plain and simple.

It was *her* door.

He almost backed away. He didn't have a Scot valet mutely nudging him tonight. There wasn't a consummation to play-act. There wasn't even a sign that Ainslee wanted him to visit, unless the thin line of light beneath the portal was a clue. She had her candles lit. But that could mean anything. He hadn't had a chance to speak with her during, or after, that lengthy sup. No. He'd been stuck at his end, ignoring his aunt while she gave him the same treatment, all the while trying to catch a glimpse of his wife. After that, they'd all had to listen to Lady Margaret's supposed skill at the pianoforte.

Neal didn't have much to work with here. Some brief glances his wife sent him from her end of the table.

And two words:

'I don't…'

He'd heard it clearly and perfectly. How could he do anything but, when she'd prefaced that little snippet with his name? He loved hearing his name coming from her lips! What was he thinking?

He already loved just about everything about Ainslee.

Holy shit.

Neal reeled as the truth hit.

He loved her?

That had to be what this unbelievable level of emotion signified. He was in love! The man called a cold heartless bastard had a heart, after all. And the little imp, Ainslee owned it.

'I don't...'

The words hammered through his skull again. She didn't what? He'd asked her not to show her abhorrence, and she'd replied with those two words.

She didn't.

She didn't...what?

What, Neal?

She didn't wish to discuss it? She didn't think now was the time and place. She didn't have an answer. Or maybe – just maybe – it was what he needed, wanted, and would give his entire fortune to have. Maybe she'd meant that she didn't abhor him.

Neal pulled in huge breath, then let it out with a force that ruffled the stray hairs at his forehead.

If only that's what she'd meant! If she didn't abhor him...then the trembling she'd suffered might mean something else, entirely. Something that sounded like absolute heaven.

He could sure use a big gulp of whiskey about now.

For the false courage.

Maybe he should have drunk something with dinner. He hadn't touched the champagne offered before and during supper, the different wines that accompanied every course. Nor had he taken more than a sip from his port after dinner. He'd had a goblet that held water. Because somebody had to make certain the supper wouldn't reflect badly on her.

He needn't have worried. Just as they'd altered her chair for the tea, the castle staff made certain of things. Everyone below-stairs seemed to be in on it. They wanted the duchess to be absolute perfection. And she was. Neal had no idea what he'd eaten, but it had been delicious. Each dish received applause. None of it had given him a stomach ailment. Or even the hint of one.

He'd ordered the removal of the floral centerpieces, however. He wanted to view his wife, even if she was yards away and deep in conversation with her dinner companions. He knew why now. He was in love with her. The staff appeared to share the sentiment. Neal didn't know the proper workings of a supper like this. But he was certain the old bag sitting on his right did. That made it extremely gratifying to watch a note slipped to Ainslee along with a little silver dinner bell. He'd watched her read it and then hand it back to the man. And smile at him.

That was one of the times he'd gotten her glance as she caught him watching.

Immediately following the dessert, she'd rung the little silver bell beside her plate, rose, and requested the ladies to follow her, leaving the gentlemen to drink port. Neal stood to watch them leave, while other gents made half-hearted efforts to stand with him. He didn't want more conversation with men. He didn't need liquor.

He knew exactly what he needed, wanted, and craved.

It was behind the door he faced right now.

Neal slid a hand over his face and jaw, checking for stubble. He placed the other hand in front of his groin and shoved down at his cock. He'd just have to keep her attention on his face. It shouldn't be that hard. He was not the novice here. He had enough experience to find out what she'd meant with her two words without giving anything away.

If not, he'd just have to wing it.

The handle turned easily in his hand. He pushed the door open and walked in, portraying a nonchalance he was far from feeling. He'd almost reached the center of the room before noticing the obvious. His preparations had been for naught. Her chamber was empty.

And Garrick hadn't attended supper.

Neal's entire body went cold. Instantly. And completely.

He raced back to his chamber, tossed off the robe, tore open drawers until he found a pair of trousers, shoved his legs into them. Donned socks. Grabbed a pair of boots. And took off for the great hall.

And it still took way too long.

CHAPTER TWENTY-THREE

THE STABLES OF STRAITH CASTLE had no equal…a least, not in Scotland. They were a behemoth of a building, exceeding the entire size of her childhood home, the MacAffrey stronghold. The original building had been constructed from the same stone as the castle and connected to a barbican wall. The third duke had doubled the space last century, adding a racing stable. He'd used the same rock, but since it was hewn later and from a different section of the Cairn quarry, the delineation between the two halves could be seen if the light was right. The previous duke had made improvements to the design, as well, adding stalls and a plastered ceiling to keep dust from the eyes of his horses. On the side given over to his racing thoroughbreds, the previous duke had even had the plaster fashioned into a design of Scot thistles, as if the horses cared.

All of that was on display, even this late at night. Ainslee didn't note any of the stable attributes as she approached what sounded like a heaving tornado at the back of the older building. It was still raining; not as hard, but enough to thoroughly saturate the crown of braids her maids had so laboriously worked onto her head. Water had then wet the large mass of hair she'd secured beneath her robe. It couldn't be helped. They had an emergency at the stables. She didn't have time to get dressed. She'd barely had time to grab a robe, shove her feet into boots, and toss on a cloak. Her hood had fallen during her rush, and belt on her robe wouldn't stay fastened. She yanked it again, before lifting the edge of her skirts above the stable muck.

"God's teeth, Will! What did you go and fetch the duchess for?"

"I did na' fetch her. I went for Rory. He went and woke the lass named

Mira. 'Twas her that fetched Ains—I mean the duchess!"

"Have ye all lost yer minds?"

Ainslee shook her head, sending droplets of water about her. "Oh, cease that, MacCreary. Please? Can't I go back to being Ainslee? Just for tonight? Wills tells me we've got colic from bad feed. Have you separated it out yet? How many horses ate it? Have we lost any yet? And did any of the thoroughbreds partake?"

"Only eleven, thank the Lord. Draft horses. But we've got it handled. You should na' be here, Miss Ainslee. I mean, yer grace. Oh, Will. The duke is gonna want yer arse. And I am na' gonna interfere!"

A crash interrupted him. It was followed by a cry from the back of the building. And then loud cursing.

"Oh, heavens. That's Nightfall. Wills told me he's taking it bad."

Ainslee lifted her skirts higher in order to jog. MacCreary, the head groom was at her side. Thank goodness he'd decided to cease arguing her presence. Nightfall was their pride. At almost nineteen hands in height and colored a dark charcoal shade, he was the largest, sturdiest, and most impressive Clydesdale the duchy of Straithcairn owned. He'd already sired more than ten progeny that appeared to match him. He was also an unruly and temperamental horse, difficult to control even without a colicky situation.

"He broke Henry's shoulder already, kicked Zeke so hard in the—uh. Well. He'll na' wish to eat anytime soon, and even with three men holding him we're losing the battle."

"He hasn't lain down, though? You ken if he rolls, he could twist his innards, and—"

"And we could lose him. I am the head groom, your grace. I'm na' fresh-birthed." MacCreary interrupted her, looking as offended as he sounded.

"Would you just call me Ainslee?"

"Na' likely. You're the duchess now. You should na' be here. Especially na' – forgive the words – in little more than your night-rail. I'll have Will reprimanded for fetching you."

"You'll do no such thing! You ken how important Nightfall is. I'm the lone one who can manage him. You there! Loose those ropes! Afore you choke him!"

Ainslee slid between two stall bars, dodging hooves as Nightfall reared. The horse's movements sent the three men holding him scudding along the straw-strewn floor. She could already see the line of chafing they'd raised on Nightfall's shoulders. It felt like everyone held their breath. And then she was at the stallion's neck, latching her arms about him and going aloft with his next attempt to rear, while speaking calmly and precisely into the closest ear.

"Hush, my *breagha* one. So verra handsome. And strong. There is nae horse your equal. And we'll need that *curinan* to fight this. But you must cease this, my *laidir gesur*. Calm. That's a good, strong boy."

The stallion stopped lunging the longer she spoke, repeating over and over again barely-intoned Celtic words for his handsomeness, his strength, his vitality. Soon, she was back on her feet and easing one of the ropes from his neck, then the next was removed, and finally, the last one was pulled off, gesturing for them to leave as she tossed each line to the man holding it.

"Has he been drenched yet?" she turned her head to ask. The stallion jerked slightly, but otherwise didn't react.

"He will na' let us near enough!" Someone shouted.

"How does she do that?"

One of the newer lads added that. MacCreary answered with a gruff order for silence. Their statements upset the stallion, and he tossed his head more than once, lifting her easily each time. Ainslee held tighter and started speaking again, in the same low, calm tone, for the horse's ear only.

"There, Nightfall. Good *gesur*. That's a love. My big handsome *gaol*."

The tone and cadence of her words worked more than the content. She could be speaking complete nonsense, and Nightfall would've had the same response. There wasn't a sound to be heard outside her whispering as he calmed again. Her feet reached the ground, and Nightfall just stood there trembling, impressive and immense, and in pain.

Ainslee turned her head slightly, matching her cheek to the stallions, and spoke toward the grooms, using only a slightly louder volume. "Mac-Creary? You there?"

"Aye."

She kept her voice calm. Her words modulated, as her hands slid along the stallion's neck, withers, and chest. "We have a water bag handy?"

"Right here."

"We'll need a fresh one."

"This one has herbs in it already."

"He does na' want that one. He needs fresh water. And newly picked herbs. Do na' you, *gesur*?"

The horse seemed to understand, for he nodded his head twice at her query. There was more than one gasping sound from behind her.

"You see? He does na' want the swill from the trough. Save that for the others. Nightfall is special. He needs a new bag, pulled from a rain barrel.

With fresh herbs."

Ainslee continued her soothing tone, speaking sometimes to the men behind her, but mostly to Nightfall, stroking where she could reach without moving her lips from his ear. That was the only way to keep him calm and still; trembling beneath her fingers, but otherwise giving no sign of his distress.

The animal beside her had enough power to toss her right through a plank of his stall if he wanted. Everything on him exhibited it. It was akin to touching a tightly coiled length of rope, only one with a lot of life to it. Nightfall exhibited barely-leashed strength, impossible size, and muscle. Ainslee moved toward his nose, crooning to him the entire time. That way, when she ducked beneath his head, it didn't startle him too much, although he pulled against his halter and his ears went up. Moments later, he was calm again to the point he nuzzled her shoulder. The grooms watching probably thought her crazed. MacCreary would know why she went for this position, though. She needed to be between the stallion and the wall. That way, he wouldn't try and lie down; or if he did, he wouldn't roll, because she'd be in the way.

She wondered if they could even see her. Her like-shaded head didn't even clear Nightfall's withers. And yet something indefinable kept him standing beside her, docile as a small foal. It was her gift. But any loud, abrupt, or sudden noise could alter everything.

"Well. Do na' just stand there gawking, men! You heard her grace. Fetch some clean water."

"Do everything softly, though," Ainslee told them from behind the horse. "Do na' do anything rapid near the stall. Or loud. There, *gesur*. Good lad."

The horse trembled, and calmed again. And then he started to lie down.

Ainslee was instantly in front of his chest, both hands at his halter, holding his head aloft, despite how much it weighed. Her arms strained. The horse whinnied. Stomped. Snorted.

"Nae, *gesur*. Na' yet! Na' yet. Oh, Nightfall, I ken. 'Tis painful. So painful. But 'twill pass. And I'm here. That's a love. Calm, my handsome one. Calm."

Her voice carried a hint of tears. The horse lowered his head and nuzzled her forehead, nearly knocking her over.

"Do we have the drench yet?" she asked quietly, as if for Nightfall's ears only.

"Na' yet. But anytime now," MacCreary answered.

"'Twill be a long night, *gesur*. But, do na' fret. I will be here for you." Ainslee turned her head toward the row of grooms watching from the other side of the stall.

"MacCreary?"

"Aye?"

"Ye'd best send someone with a message to my...husband."

Husband.

Oh, my. She said it. Her ears had heard it. Her heart was throbbing through her chest at actually voicing it.

"Ah, Jay-zus, Will! Ye did na' even leave a note tellin' him where she was?"

"I did na' go into the castle! I keep tellin' ye. I'm from the stables! Covered with manure. Wet through to my birthday suit. Ye think they're gonna let me just waltz into Straith Castle?"

"Hie yer arse back oop there and tell him, then!"

"Will?"

Ainslee still hadn't altered her voice. Everything she said was in the same soothing tone. As though she spoke to Nightfall still. She was inaudible unless a listener strained. The stable went silent every time she spoke.

"Aye?"

"Tell him I may na' be back tonight."

"What? Now that I will na' allow!"

MacCreary answered with a harsh tone that clearly upset the horse again. Nightfall tossed his head and then stomped. Time and time again. Ainslee hung onto his neck throughout. The horse finally settled back down. The sound of a unanimous sigh of relief was loud.

"Well. There you have it," she finally spoke.

"What do we have? A duchess in the stables. Lordy. The Lady Blair will enjoy this."

"She already thinks me a hoyden with little manners. Does na' she, Nightfall?"

Ainslee soothed a hand along his cheek. Rubbed his ear. Turned her head to address where MacCreary stood. The amount of groomsmen outside the stall appeared to have tripled. Everyone had the same slack-jawed expression. Ainslee looked away and endured a flush that sent heat through her entire body.

"What will one more incident matter? Besides, we do na' have much choice here."

"But, yer grace—"

"Do we have anyone else who can drench Nightfall?"

MacCreary was silent. Someone else answered.

"We do na' have anyone else that can get near him right now."

"Exactly. Well then. I shall do it."

"Ah! Thank the Lord! They're bringing the bag. Finally."

MacCreary's relief was obvious. The stall door opened. Nightfall's eyes widened, and his nostrils flared, but he didn't move beyond that. Ainslee continued stroking him as someone brought in a bladder full of the herb/ water mixture. It was attached to a long membranous hose. Their rush to leave the stall kicked up straw from the floor. Ainslee turned back to the horse.

"This will na' be pleasant, my *gesur*. But I'll be gentle. You ken?"

The horse whickered, and then nodded. There was another rumble of reaction from her audience as they watched what looked like a horse responding.

"Can I get some help holding the bag?" Ainslee asked.

"I need a volunteer. Where's that Will? He's responsible fer this."

"Ye sent him to the castle with a message. Remember?"

"Oh. Bugger. Oh, no. We're in deep now, gents. Yer grace."

MacCreary's voice changed. The stall opened. And then Niall walked toward her. Ainslee's eyes widened and she gasped. Nightfall had almost the same reaction, although he also started trembling again. The duke was in long trousers that clung to his legs, and shirtless above that. He was wet. Hanks of hair fell to his shoulders. He approached slowly. Picked up the bag with a move that sent all kinds of definition along his back and arms. Came closer.

Everyone held their breath.

And Nightfall allowed it.

Niall had reached the horse's flank. He walked slowly along Nightfall's side, keeping the hose above his shoulders, while pinching the open end. He reached the other side of the horse's head and looked at her with an unfathomable expression. Ainslee was trembling almost as much as the horse.

He held the hose toward her. She'd seen his eyes in all kinds of lighting and conditions. Right now, they looked like molten silver. And just as warm.

"Am I doing it wrong?" he asked in a low tone.

Nightfall's trembling slowed. It wasn't visible to the others, but Ainslee felt it. She shook her head.

"Then...what?"

"Nightfall allowed you in here."

He glanced to the horse. Back to her. "Oh. I think he's just tolerating me. He doesn't like it at all."

"How...can you tell?"

He whispered the answer.

"He knows you're here to help. I don't know how. This is way out of my line of expertise. But I think he's only accepting me...because he's in pain. Every creature eventually reaches a point where they just want the pain gone. No matter what they need to go through. And don't ask me how I know that. Because I'm winging it here. I actually have no idea."

"Niall?"

"Do your thing, sweetheart. We'll discuss it later. We'll discuss a lot of things later. When big boy here is better. Okay?"

"O...kay?"

"It's a term for asking if you are in agreement. It's from...another place. And time."

"Oh."

"Don't worry. It will be part of what we'll discuss. You ready, then?"

She nodded, and took the hose from him.

CHAPTER TWENTY-FOUR

D AWN WAS PEEKING THROUGH CLOUDS still swollen
and dark, but doing little more than spitting raindrops, before things
at the stable changed. Throughout the night Ainslee had worked the hose
into, and then out of, the stallion's mouth. Neal held the bag above the
horse's head and squeezed. Toward morn, he applied a lot less pressure
than the first few times, when he'd sprayed the horse, Ainslee, and himself
with drench mixture. The reason he'd eased up on the pressure wasn't just
due to the mess, but because his arms and shoulders and back were tired.
And sore. And telling him about it with every continued move. Lower the
empty bag. Walk to the stall door. Swap the bag with a full one handed over
the rail. MacCreary was overseeing that portion. Most of the stable-hands
had gone for some rest. Neal would have envied them if he wasn't exactly
where he wanted to be.

Ainslee needed him. And that was a very good feeling. So. He'd take a
deep breath. Pull the bag close, uncaring if it leaked or not, he was already
sticky and damp. There was a clear trail in the straw from his trek back and
forth across the floor. He'd reach Ainslee. Hold the bag while she reat-
tached the hose. Shuffle it into his hands, and then lift it above his head
again.

Squeeze.

After hours of it, Neal's arms visibly trembled. Ainslee didn't look
affected at all. She wasn't paying the least attention to her husband, or
much else. As if in a trance, she crooned, clicked her tongue, and whispered exclusively to the horse, communicating all kinds of messages Neal
couldn't understand.

But the horse sure did.

Neal still didn't believe in magic, but he could see why everyone else did. It was just as Mason had tried to explain what felt like a month ago. Ainslee possessed a fantastic gift. The horse was clearly enthralled. Neal considered it. The Clydesdale might as well be. Everyone else had that issue with her.

The stall was getting all kind of unsavory smells and muck as Nightfall's condition finally improved. Neal ignored it and took an empty bag from her. Ainslee blinked several times, in rapid progression. And then she smiled.

At him.

Neal's heart jumped into his throat and nearly choked him.

"It worked. Oh, sweet heaven, Niall! It's worked."

Her whisper was heard outside the stall, as well. MacCreary broke into a loud whoop. Several men applauded. Nightfall gave a noxious-smelling ovation. Ainslee wavered as she tried to take a step toward him. Neal had her in his arms before she even remotely looked like she'd fall.

And then he cradled her close. Against his chest. Any bit of tiredness evaporated. Along with any sore muscles. Nightfall nuzzled Ainslee's head and then nodded, as if giving his approval. That was fanciful. Neal shook himself mentally and started for the stall door. Somebody opened it for him. Neal smiled. The lad grinned back and doffed his hat.

"Her grace is dead on her feet. I need a plaid," he requested.

"And we've got one ready."

MacCreary fluffed a length of material out while Neal set Ainslee down. He had her bundled in it and back in his arms before she had a chance to gainsay anything.

The grounds about the stables and out into the yard were churned up and muck-filled. Neal skirted them, holding Ainslee as tightly as he dared without hurting her. Dawn glow touched the area he walked, lighting it. The area around his heart warmed markedly. That might be so there was space for the sensation of his heart enlarging. Neal had never felt anything so wondrous. Never had a day been filled with so much promise.

No wonder everyone spoke of love in such awe-stricken tones.

He probably smelled like a sewer and looked twice as grim. Neal didn't consider it. He didn't care. He might just as well have been floating. Ainslee's breathing grew heavier, and more constant. She was asleep before he'd climbed the steps to the front door. And that felt even more phenomenal. He walked into the great hall, nodding to anyone he passed. Crossed the huge span of floor without awareness of one step. Took the right side of the staircase leading to the chieftain's rooms. And hers.

A trio of servant woman started trailing him. Neal ignored them, bypassed his chamber door and approached the one to the duchess's suite. He lifted Ainslee slightly so she wouldn't feel him kicking at her door. It didn't budge.

"Here, your grace."

One of the maids hustled to his side, fussed with a large set of keys. Unlocked the door. Neal didn't wait for her to push it open. He shouldered it easily.

"Will her grace...be all right?"

Neal turned about. Faced the trio of maids, all exhibiting the same expression of concern on their faces, although only one was rubbing her hands together.

"She's exhausted. She needs a warm bath. Real warm. And food. Followed by a lot of sleep."

"Aye, your grace. 'Twill be seen to."

"Immediate-like. And make certain the water's extra warm!"

Two of them answered, bobbed him a curtsey, and rushed out the door. The other maid hastened past where he stood to the chaise lounge. Neal would have followed her except Ainslee spoke.

"Niall?"

Breath from her whisper touched his neck. Neal's heart stuttered again. It was such a remarkable sensation. It happened often, and only with her. He was already fond of it. He cleared his throat, but the answer seemed to have the same stutter.

"Y-Y-Yeah?"

"What...about our...talk?"

"Oh. We have time for that, sweetheart. Later. Right now, we could both use the rest, and I. Really need. To find my way into some soap and water."

She smiled slightly. Yawned. And Neal found out what people used to be talking about when they said a heart could be filled to bursting. It wasn't physically possible, but it sure felt it.

Exactly.

They reached the chaise, and he set her down gently. Reverently. Reluctantly released his arms from about her. Stood. And then Mason grabbed everyone's attention from the doorway to the connecting room.

"There you are, oh thank God! You are well! And the duchess—!"

"Mason?"

"I thought all manner of ills might have befallen you. I was about to ring for your Honor Guard!"

"Really? What on earth for? I could have been in my wife's chamber."

"I'm na' prone to hysterics, Neal, but the tracks from your balcony—"

"Whoa."

Neal interrupted him with the word and a hand up in his direction. Mason instantly stopped speaking.

"Niall?"

Neal bent back to his wife. Tried to project a reassurance he was far from experiencing.

"What, sweetheart?"

"You...fell from the balcony?"

"Ainslee. It's nothing. I'm certain my valet's mistaken. But I'll go and see what all this fuss is about. Okay? Ah, look. Just in time."

Her chamber door opened. It was one of her maids returning, bearing a breakfast platter. The aroma of bacon, fried meats, and toasted scones followed her as she bore the tray to a table. Behind her came two men lugging a large barrel tub. And on their heels was a manservant with a pail of water.

"I'll leave you now, love. Eat. Rest."

"You need to eat, too."

"Oh. Don't worry. I'll get Mason right on it. Until this eve, my love."

Neal lifted her hand to his lips, but thought better of kissing her fingers. He slid his thumb along her knuckles instead. Ainslee trembled. One of the maids sighed behind him. And then he was moving away. He reached the door. Hustled Mason through the salon and back into the Chieftain bedchamber. He waited until both doors were shut before speaking.

"All right. What's this about tracks?"

"Well. Look. I thought sure you'd taken a tumble or something equally drastic."

Mason pointed to what looked like a scuff mark on the floor. Neal squatted and looked it over. Mason wasn't mistaken. It did look like a partial boot print. There were more. He scanned the floor and saw another one, and another one beyond it. A fourth was just inside the door to his balcony. Neal stood and followed them all the way to the edge of his balustrade and then he looked over it.

He'd underestimated his foe, again. This balcony wasn't just a method for possible escape. Looked like somebody knew it was point of entrance, as well. Neal turned around, folded his arms, and leaned nonchalantly back until his butt hit the stone. There was a really good print right beside his boot. And it was the same size.

"Looks like a size twelve," he commented.

"Your grace?"

Oh. That's right. They didn't have shoe sizes yet. Neal looked up as Mason approached.

"I was in the stable all night, Mason. Assisting her grace with a horse. A big Clydesdale. These are not my prints."

The man straightened. His eyes might have gone wider, but they immediately narrowed as he looked down at Neal's boot beside the drying mud of an imprint. And if the rain hadn't let up, there wouldn't have been anything to see.

"I thought it was you, Neal."

"Nope. You know what that means?"

"I'm a-feared to put it into words."

"It means if we hadn't been at the stable last night, I might not be here talking to you right now."

The man gasped. "And Ainslee?"

Emotion hit Neal like a brick wall. And then it turned to fire. Red. Hot. Enraged. Neal sucked in a breath and held it. Listened as his heart pounded furiously. Exhaled. He'd never felt murderous hatred until that moment. It took several moments to speak. Even then, his voice was harsh. Guttural.

"Do we know where that path leads?"

"Aye."

"I will need Honor Guardsman posted there. It needs to be done quietly. No need to alert anyone."

"Your grace?"

"Oh. I meant...there's no need to alert anyone...*yet.*"

"I'll see to it myself, Neal."

"And see to finding me something to shoot with."

"A pistol?"

"No. I was thinking more along the line of something you use to go grouse hunting."

"Grouse hunting?"

"I have an invitation to do so. With my cousin. I'll need to do some target practice first. Figure out fire power. Range. Accuracy. Artillery. Things like that. You see. I may have been a dismal shot before my accident, but trust me. I'm an ace now."

Neal was already fond of Mason. Trusted him implicitly. The man was worth double whatever salary they paid him. The look they exchanged only sealed the deal.

"So. How about you go in and order me up a breakfast while I make use of the rain barrel. I think I've sullied the house enough with stable muck."

"I'll fetch a towel."

"You need a raise, Mason.'

"I am already compensated."

"We're gonna have to talk, buddy. When you get a raise offer, always take it. It's like a breath mint."

"Breath mint?"

"We don't have those either?"

"I can order them."

Neal hid the smile. It wasn't easy. And then he lifted a foot and yanked off a boot.

CHAPTER TWENTY-FIVE

NEAL HAD NEVER SLEPT BETTER. Nor with as much abandon. He woke at almost three in the afternoon, on his back, without a stitch on, and with a magnificent hard-on.

Wow.

This was rare. And he wasn't thinking about the erection. The twenty-first-century Neal Straithmore was a poor sleeper. Rarely had two hours of restful sleep. He'd thought it came with the territory. If you attempt global domination of new energy markets and have a finger in world financial markets, you can expect some side effects. V.I.P. treatment at hotels and airports. Sporting events. Banks. Suspicion at stock holder meetings of companies he had his eye on. Instant adherence to his orders. Immediate gratification of just about every whim.

But dreamless, restful sleep was one thing you learned to go without.

Hmm.

Neal stretched, sat up, and looked around. He wondered if Ainslee had slept as well. Or if she was still resting. Neal's entire body relaxed slightly and then warmed. He already knew he loved her. This was just another sign. He had to have the most beautiful wife in existence. One with a soul that matched. She was the epitome of womanhood...

Oh.

That was stupid.

Neal looked down in defeat as his dick got the message, as well. This couldn't continue. And it wasn't going to. The duke and duchess needed to talk. He needed to tell her who she was really wed to. But...not yet. Tonight, they were going to alter this marriage. His groin throbbed as if in agreement. Neal snickered, scooted to the side of his jumbo-king mattress, supported his erection with a hand, and slid off the bed.

Hmm. That was another thing the world needed. Athletic cups. Maybe he'd see to their invention. But first, he'd need to figure out elastic. But, that was going onto another back burner in importance. As far as he knew, they didn't even have zippers yet. If memory served him right, the inventor was a Japanese chap. He'd specialized in zippers and nothing else. Made a fortune in the billions. Over a little clothing device.

Neal proceeded to do stretches, not only to limber up, but make sure parts of his anatomy weren't going to be an issue. He moved from the stretches into push-ups, stopping at a hundred, went right into accomplishing an equal amount of sit-ups, finished up with over two hundred jumping-jacks. Following that, he jogged onto the balcony so he could dump a bucket of water from the rain barrel over his head.

He almost broke into song.

Neal stood there, dripping, listening to his pulse sing. His heart beat. His lungs expand and contract. He'd spent hours at gyms throughout the world. Paid premier prices for the best personal trainers. Ate all kinds of healthy foods.

He'd never felt this good.

Then again, he was away from Electro-Magnetic waves. No invisible electrons shot through his body as millions of people used their wireless communication technology and he happened to be in the way. That could be it.

All of which meant he really needed to get back to his goal. He needed to do something about the world pollution, global carbon emissions, polluted water, and renewable energy situation two hundred plus years from now. He was here for a reason. He had to get to New York. Put his destiny into play. It was in his hands.

And—

Wait a minute.

He could always travel as the duke. Take Ainslee with him. Along with however many other people would need to accompany them. They'd probably go by ship – and while he'd been willing to go as a crewman in the bowels of a cargo vessel – if he had Ainslee with him, they'd travel in style. Ainslee could get her new wardrobe. But she wasn't wearing the gossamer fashions Lady Blair said were in fashion. Perish the thought. Ainslee could set her own fashion. Set the world on its ear.

And he'd be at her side.

Shivers accompanied the mental image.

What the hell?

Neal blinked the ocean view back into focus. Scattered clouds were on the horizon. Nothing hinted at the amount of rain they'd experienced. And he'd air-dried while he stood here, oblivious to the surroundings. That was so unlike him. Neal Straithmore was never lost in thought. He utilized every available second of every day. Time was his enemy. And it was always ticking by. Just as it was now. He needed to get this new plan underway.

Neal hurried back into his chamber, slipped into a robe that Mason had left lying across the foot of his bed, crossed to the servant bell, and pulled on it. Mason may have been hovering just outside. The guy arrived in moments.

"Good afternoon, your grace." The man greeted him with the title. It was probably due to the fact that Barnes was behind him. The door shut behind them.

"Hi, guys. And it's better than good. I have to tell you, it's great."

Barnes approached the bed and started pulling covers back into place. Smoothed out any creases. Mason was the one who replied.

"Ah. I see you have recuperated from your veterinary foray into the stables."

"Yeah. You could call it that. And I'm starving. Order up a really nice-sized luncheon. Unless her grace is having another tea or something."

"I believe she is still resting."

"Good. Well. Have the kitchen send up everything they can spare. I could eat a horse."

Mason's brows shot up. Neal didn't know what expression Barnes might have on his face.

"I'm joking, guys. It's an expression. For being famished."

"Oh. Verra good. Barnes? Why do na' you go to the kitchens and see to a meal for his grace?"

They waited until the under-valet left. Nobody said anything until the door shut.

"I really have to learn to watch my tongue," Neal commented.

"You have certainly changed in the twelve years since you left."

"Twelve years? I was a kid."

"Nigh on fifteen."

Neal sent a glance the valet's way. Looked away before Mason noticed. Tried not to sound sarcastic. "That old, huh?"

"You were angry. You late uncle was the same. It was for the best."

"Ah. I see. I ran away. Well. That's makes it really odd that he'd leave the dukedom to me."

"I believe he had his reasons."

"Yeah. Two clowns and their ringleader. Garrick. Lachlan. Aunt Margaret."

Mason grinned. "I do enjoy your quips, Neal. They are—"

Someone knocked loudly on his chamber door. "I shall be right back."

Neal waved him off and tried not to bounce with suppressed energy. This was really weird. Even if he was excited and energized, the old Neal would have hidden it. A half hour felt like is passed while Mason discussed something in quiet tones at the door. And finally he shut it.

"I have news, your grace."

"My meal is on its way?"

"Oh, no. Na' that. I have news of your paper order."

"Paper? Oh, yeah. The roll. You found some?"

"Indeed. It will be here within the month."

Neal caught the laugh. It wasn't easy. Mason approached a wardrobe and started eyeing the shirts hanging there. As if Neal would need them.

"That quickly, eh?" Neal finally replied.

"Transportation has improved so, it near takes the breath. I was unable to find anyone who knew of markers however."

"Oh. That. Well. It's a writing implement for writing big things on large paper."

"I see. And you have seen these markers?"

"Well. Yeah. In...uh, the Far East. But, it's no big problem. I can always start playing around with used candle wax and soot."

"Candle wax and soot?"

"I might be able to fashion large crayons. They'll work."

"Crayons?"

Neal tightened his lips before he swore. Mason had one of Neal's linen shirts hanging over his bent arm and was regarding Neal without expression. This could get sticky real quick. He needed to get his brain into gear.

"See? This one of the changes I refer to. You are truly different, Neal. I am na' the lone one to note it."

"Well. I did suffer a head injury."

"I do na' mean that. It's more – pardon the impudence – as if you'd had a life-changing event."

Neal stared at his valet. He *had* experienced a life-changing event. It wasn't the Bermuda Triangle time travel, either. It was—

"I've fallen in love with my wife," he said aloud.

The valet beamed. "Exactly."

Neal cleared his throat. "Why are you gathering my clothing, then? I plan on attending her grace in her chamber this eve. The most I'll need is a robe."

"That may na' be a good idea, Neal."

The valet placed the shirt atop Neal's bed and started looking through drawers until he found a length of plaid he liked. He placed it on the bed, too. Then he opened the top drawer and fished out cuffs.

"Why not?"

"Apparently, Lady Blair invited several guests for the evening. They've been arriving as you slept."

"So? Let them party. I'll be in my wife's room."

"You may na' wish to do that."

"You're joking, right? That is exactly what I wish."

"The guest list could be problematic."

"Oh. I'm sure Lady Blair can handle it. Isn't that what she did all these years? Play hostess?"

"The guest list includes the solicitor fellow who drew up the late duke's will, as well as two of his colleagues. I saw them arrive. They have been in Lady Blair's wing ever since. I need to alert you. They do na' inspire my confidence."

Neal hissed through clenched teeth. "Damn it! That manipulative bi—!"

He bit the rest off. Mason nodded as if he'd finished it, and at this point in time it meant something other than a female dog.

"'Twill na' be that difficult. You and the duchess need only make an appearance. Mill about. You may na' need to stay."

"Really? And why is that?"

"'Tis perfectly obvious your marriage is a love match, Neal. Anyone seeing you two would know that. You have a glow about you. Both of you have it."

Neal's heart gave a powerful thump. He looked down at the valet. Ainslee had a glow about her, too? He wondered if it was possible. Hoped like hell it was.

"So. Would you like to wear the otter pelt sporran? Or the silver-embossed leather one tonight?"

"Which one is hardest?" Neal asked.

Mason's brows lifted, but he didn't say anything. He squeezed the sporrans one-at-a-time. Held out the leather one. Neal regarded him for a long moment. Made a decision.

"You know...I was planning on taking the duchess on a trip to New York. A honeymoon, as it were."

"Now?"

"Ainslee will be safe with me."

"There are a lot of others...about the estate...that may na' be."

Neal looked over his valet. Soundlessly read the concern being demonstrated by the man's stiff stance. Neal realized he actually cared about what might happen if he left his aunt and her offspring unsupervised. How much harm it could cause to other people. And then he dealt with the shock and surprise without showing any of it.

"Mason. I must be getting good at reading your line of thinking. You're right. Now is not the proper time. I can see it will be trouble. But...let me see here. I don't really have to go. I can send an emissary."

"You would send an emissary on your honeymoon?"

Neal burst out laughing. "Sorry. I'm working this out. I actually need to purchase stock over there. They'll need funding. Say...a hundred pounds for the stock purchase. Oh. He'll also need travel expenses."

The valet gasped. That gave Neal the clue he needed.

"I know. It's a lot. But can we raise that?"

"You will need to speak with the comptroller, but...it may be possible."

"I need it like...today."

"I'll have him report to you."

"Good. And I know just the man to choose for this assignment. Have him report to me, too."

"If you do na' mind me asking...?"

"Iain Straithmore. My Honor Guardsman."

"Ah. Good choice. If you'll allow me, I'll just go and see that these gentlemen report to you."

"One more thing. You did say you had a copy of the will?"

"Oh. Aye."

"I'm going to need it. Oh! While you're at it, send for the housekeeper. Tell her to start preparations on the Dower House."

Mason went completely out of character and grinned widely. Realized what he'd done. And then tried to act like it was nothing. Neal tried not to smile as the valet cleared his throat.

"Would...you wish it also kept quiet?"

"Oh, hell no. Make a huge production out of it. Shout it from the rooftops if you wish. Make sure everyone knows."

Mason had a jaunty step. Neal hadn't noticed it until now. Mason opened the chamber door, and then stood aside as two menservants entered with platters, bearing all sorts of savory items. Neal's belly growled in appreciation. The rest of him was too annoyed and on edge to do anything other than scowl.

CHAPTER TWENTY-SIX

THE SEAMSTRESS, MISTRESS AGGIE, CONTINUED to work miracles with Lady Iliff's old wardrobe. Even if she said she had help, the woman was a magician with her needle. Thank goodness! Ainslee hadn't known the workings of a large estate, nor that she'd be required to dress and attend every sup in gowns fit for a princess. She touched the gold netting that floated atop her scarlet satin skirt with nervous fingers. The scarlet material came out of hiding to form her tightly-fitted square-necked bodice, while the gold became the piping along her neckline and sleeves.

She'd call her mirror a liar, if this was any other time. And place. Had she really been the girl who chased after horses, wishing to be male?

It didn't seem possible.

Being a woman was wondrous, despite feeling like a stranger in her own skin. It was fanciful, but she wouldn't be surprised if the wizard who had done this miracle would appear, wave his magic wand...and she'd be back to that moment when she'd hidden behind a standing stone awaiting the new duke's morning ride. Hair tied back in a long braid, skirts hiked up so she could run.

Her maids, Beth and Doreen, continued to work wonders with her hair, when all it used to be was a braided mass tucked out of the way beneath a collar. Tonight, they'd pulled the hair at her temples back and braided it, entwining gold ribbons throughout. The rest of her hair was free. She looked so different. And entirely ladylike.

She sincerely hoped Niall thought so. He'd sent a message to meet up with him on the landing of the chieftain steps. He'd made it sound as if he'd be there momentarily. Ainslee pushed a lock of hair back over her shoulder and sighed resignedly.

Lady Iliff had possessed slightly smaller feet, however. Or the fashion had been for a tight fit. Ainslee's toes were pinched in these particular slippers. That was the lone reason she wasn't pacing back and forth, too nervous to stand still. Too excited to keep a train of thought. She moved to the stair rail and looked out at the great hall before her. They'd lit all the torches in the brackets along the walls. The room was alive with light and shadow. Flames reflected the weapons displayed on both walls, as well as the array of shields at the far one. It was a magnificent room. Worthy of a strong, powerful clan.

Completely worthy of her husband.

The thought brought a pleasant tingle. A feathery sensation to her belly. A weak feeling to the backs of her legs. All mysterious. All exciting. A cadence of steps resounded from beneath her vantage point. Ainslee bent her neck to watch two Honor Guardsmen emerge from the shadowed area beneath the staircase and walk into the great hall. They looked massive. Impressive. And intent.

The duke had guards patrolling the great hall? She wondered if that was a normal event, or one just put in place. And that thought sent a tremor of unease through what had been all kinds of building excitement.

"I see punctuality is another of your virtues, wife."

Ainslee spun at the duke's greeting. He was walking toward her, looming from the dark maw of hall. She raised her glance. Caught a gasp at his magnificence. Quickly looked back down as heat flooded her cheeks. No matter how many times she saw him, especially wearing the Straithcairn chieftain regalia, this happened.

It was disconcerting. Exhilarating. And exciting.

"Your grace."

Ainslee dipped into a curtsey. He was before her within moments. She watched as the tassels of his socks settled. He held out his hand for hers. Ainslee glanced at it. Up to the approximate area of his chin. Back at his hand.

"You have no idea how difficult this eve is for me."

Was that due to her?

Ainslee swallowed. Stammered two words that hurt her throat. "It...is?"

He gazed into her eyes, sending a look that pierced her heart and soul. Ainslee was enraptured. Completely still.

"Oh, yes. Because all I really wish. Is to be in our chambers. With you."

Oh, my. Oh, my. Oh, my!

It was a hesitant gesture, but she placed her hand within his. And lightning struck the great hall behind her. It sent every piece of artillery to firing and bounced off the wall of shields before returning with a whoosh that took her breath. Lit her soul. Snatched her heart. And sent it winging.

He bent forward and lifted her hand to his lips. Kissed the tops of her knuckles. The slight scruff of whiskers on his chin brushed against her skin. He hadn't shaved. Her eyes widened as she realized it, and then he looked toward her. Small lines spliced his forehead as he looked at her. His eyes resembled candle-lit silver. He turned her hand over, and placed his lips against her inner wrist.

Ainslee's knees almost dropped her. She stumbled. He stood and pulled her toward him, making a bulwark of strength. Power. Vitality. And something she didn't know enough about to name. All she knew was her belly had daggers of thrills shooting through it, and her thighs felt the consistency of black pudding. She clung to his arm as he started down the steps. Thrilled to every moment of contact. Worried about what he must think. She knew he'd been in London with all kinds of ladies. The gossips spoke of their beauty. Availability. Rumor had it he'd been extremely well-liked. He'd enjoyed a lot of feminine company. They were probably witty companions, their conversation filled with double entendres.

In comparison, she felt awkward. Almost childish. She wished she could think of something clever to say.

"Evening, your graces."

They reached the bottom of the steps. The two Honor Guardsmen were at the base of the steps, one on either side. The nearest one greeted them. The other one nodded.

"Gentlemen. Thirty paces."

Niall didn't act surprised at their presence. And he gave them instructions. It must be a normal event. He and Ainslee waited while one of them opened the door to the foyer for them. They proceeded through.

"I assume you'll help me find the dining room again?" he asked.

Ainslee nodded. Sent a glance upward toward him. Quickly looked back down before he completely tied her tongue.

"I...understand you are opening the Dower House."

"You heard that, did you?"

"Um. Aye. The servants spoke of it. Oh. I suppose I should na' say that. You mustn't think I gossip with servants."

"Ainslee. You are perfection itself. You can speak with whomever you like. I spoke as I did because I'm gratified to hear word of the Dower House is getting out. I wonder if it's gotten far enough yet."

"Far enough?"

"Lady Blair's wing is a fair distance off."

"Has she...upset you?"

"And then some. But, that's all right. I'm not allowing her to do it again. Trust me."

"She will be livid."

"Really?"

"She has been...in control of the estate for many years."

"No wonder I left."

"She may...retaliate."

"Well. I can but hope."

Ainslee's footsteps faltered as she realized he was serious. "Are you certain-sure you wish that?"

"By the way, darling. In case I haven't mentioned it. You look gorgeous. And in the event that word isn't around, let me just explain it. It means beautiful. Fabulous. Stunning. Superb. I don't know who is behind your wardrobe, but I have to say. They're good. They have my utmost appreciation and approval."

Ainslee's smile nearly split the side of her mouth. She beamed. He leaned closer to her.

"Ah. We're almost there, love. Whatever happens...stay at my side."

Love.

At the endearment, she almost looked down to check that her slippers were still on the floor. She felt she might be floating. And he was being silly. He wanted her to stay close? He asked it as if it might be a hardship. Ainslee squeezed his arm. He tipped his head toward her and smiled.

"May I infer that you're all right with that?" he asked.

"Oh. Aye! Perfectly."

He winked. Her knees quivered. He pulled her even closer as if he knew it. And then he looked up and nodded to Rory, who stood at the portal to the salon and announced them.

CHAPTER TWENTY-SEVEN

NEAL SENT A QUICK GLANCE about the room. Did his best to relegate Ainslee to the back of his mind. Garrick was on his left. The man looked like he hadn't slept in days. He stood in the shadows, nursing a snifter half-full of brandy. Wore full weaponry. His mother, Lady Blair, appeared to be holding court at the back of the room. She wore another disastrously diaphanous gown. Neal moved his glance before he had an unfortunate physical reaction. At her elbow stood a portly gentleman in English attire. Long trousers. Jacket. A large cloth was folded about his throat, forcing his head up. The white cravat didn't hide the man's multiple chins. And it contrasted sharply with his ruddy skin tone. Beside him was a fit, mature gent in Scot attire. Neal assumed that was the Scot solicitor who had drafted and overseen the will. He had Mason to thank for that information. Another English fellow was on Neal's right. He was talking with the vicar.

Well. Neal hadn't expected the vicar to miss a meal.

Lachlan was on the right, beside the comptroller. Neal gave his cousin a half-hearted smile. Lachlan lifted his almost-empty brandy snifter in salute.

Behind him, he heard his Honor Guardsman enter the room and assume a post, one on either side of the door. Exactly as he'd instructed. He didn't check. He didn't need to. He watched his aunt's expression as she saw them. That was extremely pleasant.

"Ah. Niall. There you are. And looking so..."

Lady Blair dragged the English gent and the Scot fellow with her as she approached. Neal waited for their arrival. He averted his eye as Lady Blair curtseyed, sending her bosom to the edge of disaster as she did so. Caught a movement as Garrick put his drink goblet on a side table. Placed his right hand on the hilt of his sword.

That was interesting...

"Good evening, Lady Blair."

"Oh, Niall! You wretched lad. You can call me Aunt Margaret. Always did afore."

"Things change. I didn't know we had guests. Would you...handle the introductions?"

"You ken the clan solicitor, Reagan Fells, of course?"

"Reagan."

Niall nodded to the Scot gentleman. Received a bow in response.

"And this is Barrister Kingston. From the firm of Kingston and Bon. In London."

"Barrister Kingston."

"No need to stand on such ceremony lad! We've met."

That was a surprise. "Have we now?" Niall answered.

"Oh, come now, lad." The man leaned forward and jostled Neal's right arm. "We're tipped a few pints and had some laughs. Celebrated the armistice more than once. Why...there was one particular fest—"

"Which shall remain nameless. And unmentioned. Due to the presence of ladies," Neal interrupted him.

The man immediately sobered. He tilted his head back even farther so he could look a lot closer at Neal. "Oh. Yes. Of course. Begging pardon."

Lady Blair started walking away. "Follow me. Along here is Barrister Bon."

"Aren't you forgetting something?" Neal interrupted her.

"What?"

"Reagan Fells? Barrister Kingston. May I have the pleasure of introducing my wife, the Duchess of Straithcairn. Ainslee Straith? Reagan Fells and Barrister Kingston."

"The pleasure is mine," the Scotsman replied.

"Charmed," Barrister Kingston chimed in.

The men bowed. Ainslee sketched a curtsey at Neal's side. She was trembling. Her fingers gripped him like talons, but she didn't exhibit anything noticeable. Pride swelled throughout his chest. It was like a warm thick electric blanket. It enveloped him with security and comfort. And a buzzing sensation that tingled and then evaporated.

"Oh. Yes. Of course. How...impolite of me," Lady Blair spoke. "And I'm so gratified you two could make it out of your chamber long enough to join us."

Ainslee's gasp was nearly inaudible. Neal tipped his head to one side and considered his aunt for a bit. She was trying to be offensive. But she had the wrong target, and poor ammunition. Neal couldn't see a damn thing wrong with admitting he'd been in seclusion with the beauty at his side.

"I certainly hope you won't mind when we return there, then," he finally replied.

Neal struggled against snickering at the look on his aunt's face as he moved toward where the vicar was wiping his hands on a napkin. The other barrister was beside the vicar. He wasn't as rotund as his partner, but looked a lot more cagey.

Mason had been accurate. The men didn't inspire Neal's confidence, either. They finished the introductions. Moved on to greet Lachlan and the comptroller, and then Neal steered his aunt toward the door. And the two Honor Guardsmen standing there.

"Oh. While we are handling introductions, allow me to present two members of my guard."

"This show of force is ridiculous, Niall," Aunt Margaret hissed at his elbow.

"I would say that depends on who and what I'm dealing with."

Garrick moved out of his shadow. The guardsman on that side matched the move, stepping forward to stand beside Ainslee. On the left. Neal almost puffed out his chest. He'd heard and read about that happening. He'd never believed a man would want to do it until now.

"You sent orders to prepare the Dower House," Aunt Margaret informed him.

"You are correct. I did."

"Well. I am na' going to the Dower House."

"Really? What makes you so certain?"

"Because these gentlemen are here to contest the will."

"Oh. That's...entertaining."

Ainslee was reacting. Neal's arm sagged slightly as her weight pulled on it. He immediately moved his left arm from her grasp and around to her back. Did his best to bring her close and hold her against him with a nonchalant air. And then he held her there.

"You will na' be the one entertained, Niall Straith. I assure you."

"Truly? And what makes you say that?"

"You are na' the duke."

Neal chuckled. He couldn't help it.

"Laugh all you like. But you failed to fulfill the requirements. I have in my possession the will. It's a bit smudged, but it does state that the new Duke of Straithcairn will only keep the title if he weds an 'L' MacAffrey. You failed to do so. Garrick will na' make that error. All he has to do is wed the right woman. He will succeed to the title. Not you."

"How...distressing," Neal replied.

Ainslee went stiff. Neal tightened his hold on her. "How is the salmon, Vicar?" Neal asked it over Lady Blair's shoulder. The man nodded, lifted a cracker in his direction, and then shoved it into his mouth. Neal turned his attention to the Scotsman.

"Correct me if I'm wrong, Reagan Fells...but didn't you draw up this will?"

The man nodded.

"And you are willing to verify my aunt's contention?"

"Well. Lad. I—"

"Before you do so, I would like to ask some questions. Were there any copies made at the time? And were they perchance...also signed? And perhaps they were...verified by another party?"

"Well. I—"

"And was one of these copies handed to a witness for protection? In the event of a fiasco. Such as this?"

Reagan Fells started turning red. Neal didn't move his gaze.

"Now. Could it be that one of the witnesses at the signing was a man named Mason Millbourne?"

"That...was the name of the late duke's valet."

"And he was there. Am I right?"

"Aye."

"Well. By some strange coincidence, Mason Millbourne just happens to be *my* valet, too. Strange how that works, isn't it?"

The solicitor lost the extra color. The Honor Guardsman on Neal's right stepped forward to flank him on that side. This had to be one of the most gratifying experiences of Neal's life. Easily outstripping a forced company takeover. Neal was having a hard time keeping his voice from reflecting it.

He waited. Reagan Fells wouldn't meet his eye. The man finally mumbled the answer.

"Aye. I believe he was given a copy."

"Oh. I know he was. I've seen the copy he had. He doesn't have it anymore. Everyone want to know why? Because I sent it to Edinburgh. So it can be legally filed. And away from any...tampering that might occur. Or, didn't anyone notice that I sent Iain Straithmore on a mission this afternoon?" Iain had been headed to New York. It was a bluff, but they wouldn't know that.

Aunt Margaret looked like she might explode. She was turning a purplish hue that spread beneath her clothing darkening the fabric's hue. Neal had never seen skin that color. And he really did try not to look.

"Everyone. Please. Enjoy your meal. The duchess and I will be leaving you now. We won't be available until sometime tomorrow. Maybe the next day. Oh. And Lady Blair?"

She opened her mouth and shut it. It was a continual motion. She looked like a fish out of water. Dressed in shimmery scales. Ready for a butcher's blow on the chipping block. Neal regarded her for a long moment before he finished.

"Start packing."

Neal scooped Ainslee into his arms and brought her close. He felt her every breath. Warming. Bracing. Electrifying. He turned about and walked out the door. As if he'd ordered it, his two guardsmen immediately filled the portal behind him, creating a barrier. Rory was standing outside with his mouth open and his eyes bulging.

That was another bit of luck. News of this should be about the castle before Neal and Ainslee reached their chambers. Neal nodded to Rory. Pulled Ainslee even closer. And then he started jogging.

CHAPTER TWENTY-EIGHT

AINSLEE HAD NEVER BEEN INSIDE the chieftain's chamber. She'd peeked once, and then never again. It was sacrosanct space. She knew the room was very large, with high ceilings, even higher than the duchess's suite. The furnishings were constructed of heavy wood. It was very dark. Solemn. The chamber exuded power. Might. Majesty.

She wouldn't have entered it even though no one would have ever known.

Niall's steps had slowed as he'd reached the great hall, and then climbed one side of the staircase. He was breathing heavily, each breath lifted strands of hair at her forehead. His heart was pounding with mighty thumps, too. She felt every beat right against the side of her breast where it was smashed against him. They reached his chamber door. He moved her slightly to access the handle, and then shouldered the door open. The door sucked shut behind them. Niall set her on her feet.

"You're...not going to faint, are you?" He peered down at her to ask it.

"Um. N-no." She stammered the answer.

"Want me to order up a repast?"

"Sup...per?"

"I did just haul you away from one, Ainslee. Are you hungry?"

"Are you?"

Niall looked away for a moment. When he looked back, his gaze bore into her. She almost backed a step.

"Oh, yes. Very. But. Not. For. Food," he replied, breaking the words up as was his wont.

Ainslee gasped.

"So? Back to my original question. I'm going to leave you for a bit. Set a few things up. Are you going to be all right?"

"I *am* a Highlander," she replied with the slightest trace of indignity.

"Hold that thought."

He winked and spun before she could react. His kilt swayed with the quickness of his motions as he slammed the bolt down on the chamber door. The sound reverberated through the room, as if in accompaniment to Niall's steps. He reached the door that connected their rooms, pulled the bolt down to bar it. He did the same to a large wooden door that must lead outside. Then he moved along that same wall, raised an arm, and pulled drapes aside, revealing a vista of sea and sky lit with sunset hues of orange and red.

Ainslee slapped her hands to her breast and watched awestruck, as he opened the other side of the drape. His action put a warm hue of light on the entire room, lighting up all kinds of items. She glanced about with a slight niggling of nervousness.

Where the duchess's chamber had been altered over the centuries with wainscoting and fabric and all manner of elegant refinement, the chieftain chamber retained the original dark gray stone walls. The stone might have been smoothed, but it still looked rough-cut. Impenetrable. There was an immense fireplace opposite the window, the black pit looking massive and regal from behind a screen of Straith plaid with a stitched rendition of a roaring flame on it.

Long, narrow tapestries hung from close to the ceiling. Despite craning her neck Ainslee couldn't spot where they began. They covered a good amount of the stone walls. Not enough to mute the chill. Just enough to add a regal presence to an already majestic chamber. They were mostly worked in dark threads. Blood-colored reds. Dark gold. Deep blues. Teals. Grays and blacks. Here and there were touches of metallic threads that sparkled. The tapestries depicted scenes of battle, green, fertile dales, mature stags at hunting season, storm-whipped seas. They were all bordered with Straith plaid. Shields covered some of the space between tapestries. They were works of beauty and grandeur, especially visual when highlighted and caressed by the flame-colored radiance coming from beyond the span of glass Niall had revealed.

The sunset also touched on furniture. Armoires. Bureaus. A couch. A large round table with high-backed chairs. Here and there the light hit brass knobs, lamps and torch brackets, gilt edges. When that happened, the surface glinted. But the main piece of furniture was an enormous bed set atop a large platform. Ainslee's heart took a sudden dive. It felt extremely real. Her belly started pounding in rhythm with her heartbeat. The sensation wasn't remotely painful. It carried a lot of thrill. Excitement. Anticipation.

Niall's bed was immense, made more so by its position atop a foot-high dais. Ainslee swallowed nervously as she scanned upward. The footboard was a masterwork of wood, carved with thistles and Celtic knots and other images she couldn't quite make out. It probably stood above her head. The headboard was fashioned of the same wood, carved throughout to match. It was so high the top disappeared into the ceiling's shadow. Despite craning her neck, she couldn't see it.

And then Niall cleared his throat.

Ainslee dropped her gaze. He'd moved from the wall of window, but stopped in front of his footboard. She'd been off a bit. The footboard was way above her head even if she stood on the platform. It was twice Niall's height. But she should factor in that the pedestal started somewhere in the range of Niall's calf. Ainslee gasped and quickly looked back up to his face. Niall was just standing there, his arms folded, his chin lowered. He regarded her without expression. But she sensed something. A tenseness. Near anger. Something that was almost auditory. It raised the temperature. And her heart-rate.

"Have you ever been so close to losing control, that you had...but one choice?"

She blinked at the surprise. "What?"

He started undressing. Her eyes widened as he unfastened his scabbard and set the sword on the platform beside him. His next move was to pull daggers from beneath his belt. He placed them beside the sword. He did it without looking. He didn't take his gaze from her.

"It's akin to lock-down."

"A...what?"

"Lock-down. Of emotion. And motion. Because anything else...might prove disastrous."

"Disastrous?"

"If I scare you, you'll let me know?"

"You do na' scare me."

"Thus far."

He lifted a leg. Pulled off his boot. Slid a *skean dhu* from his sock. Tossed it atop the other daggers. Did the same with his other leg.

"I am going to make love to you, Ainslee. I will be gentle – to the best of my ability. But it is not. Going to be easy."

A loud gasp escaped in one breath. He regarded her for several moments, when all she could hear was her continued quick breaths and her rapidly increasing pulse.

"You make me afraid, my love."

My love.

Her heart stuttered. Her voice matched. "Y-you? Afraid?"

"Oh, babe. You have no idea. So. Let's just skirt that little issue for the moment. You ready to finish your thought?"

"What...thought?" she asked.

"The Highlander remark. Explain it."

Ainslee lifted her chin and stared at him. "How?"

"It means you're fearless. Strong. Brave. No matter what the odds. Am I close?"

"You are a Highlander too, Niall."

"You're mispronouncing it. The name is Neal. Rhymes with meal. And tonight. When you cry my name out. I want to hear Neal. Okay?"

Something shot through her. It electrified. Blazed. Instantly dissipated. Leaving her shocked and stunned. Ainslee trembled for a moment and then stilled.

"I...do na' understand," she relied.

"Oh. You will. All of which is a waste of time. You ready to answer? Or are you frightened?"

"Nae."

"Good. Because I think you're going to have to come here, babe. To me. Now."

"What?" Ainslee didn't have to feign surprise.

"I need you to come over to me. Trust me. It's not a good idea if I fetch you."

Ainslee's head went back slightly at his tone. Deep. Full of something close to menace.

"You want me to say it nicer?" he asked.

"Uh..."

"Forget I offered. I'm not certain I can. Come here, Ainslee."

"Niall."

"Close, babe. But it's Neal."

"Neal," she parroted.

"Exactly. Now. Are you going to come over here? Or am I going to have to come. Fetch you?"

"You are...scaring me."

"Well. Great. That is exactly what I'm trying *not* to do. It's bad enough one of us is already terrified."

"You?" Her feet started moving toward him. She hadn't even sent the order to do so.

"Oh. Yeah. Me. Terror has been my constant companion since meeting you, I think."

"It has?"

Ainslee stopped an arms-length from him. Looked up. He nodded.

"Yep. It's real. And it is always there. Abject. Complete. Are you wearing a sexy little corset tonight?"

Her eyes went wide. He groaned. Answered it himself.

"Of course you are. Turn about." He put a finger out and spun it.

"Why should I?"

"Because I asked you to."

"You are acting..."

"Yes?"

"Verra different."

"Oh, darling. If I acted the way I want to, things would get real ugly. Real fast."

She gasped. "They would?"

"You're...untouched. Yes?"

She nodded.

He licked his lips. Shuddered. "Translation of that – totally ugly. Now, turn around. Please."

She did. Every hair on her body whispered to attention as shivers flowed all over her skin. They raised goosebumps. Launched her heart into palpitations. Sent all kinds of sparks throughout her belly. And then the sensation went lower. Her private-most area experienced a series of quivers that shocked. Stimulated. And rapidly excited. Her nipples even hardened.

She felt his fingers along her spine.

"I had you turn around so I can slide every one of these little buttons out of their little buttonholes. It's the best I can manage. The alternative is to rip them off. Oh, God."

His voice got lower. More intense. Her thighs started quivering.

"You're wearing a red one."

The back of her dress ripped as he tugged at it. Little buttons bounced on the wood at their feet.

"Give my apologies to your seamstress. I didn't...uh. Mean to do that."

And then what had to be his lips touched the juncture between her throat and shoulders!

Ainslee jerked at the contact, gasped, and then felt something completely different. And truly unbelievable. A melting sensation went through her entire body as he kissed her skin. It thrilled. Enticed. And scared. Somewhere in the juncture of her thighs things sizzled and swelled. Her legs wavered. His arms snaked about her, his hands cupping her breasts as he yanked her back against him. She might have fallen if he hadn't.

But he wasn't using the hold to support her. His fingers massaged and toyed, each move sending thrills she'd never felt before. Her breasts grew wickedly heavy. Deliciously alert. Somehow enlarged within his hands.

Oh, my!

Ainslee caught breath after breath as her nipples turned into darts of sensitivity. Sparks shot from where they were jammed against the restriction of satin and ribbon to join the myriad of sensations pooling in her belly and nether area. And it just kept getting stronger. Hotter. And larger.

Ainslee tilted her head, making access easier for him. Niall pushed the bodice of her gown down, slid his hands beneath the boning of her corset, and touched flesh. And Ainslee's knees gave out. She sagged minutely before he lifted her, bending his knees to support her, all the while his fingers continued questing, reaching, and then toying with the crests of each breast. Ainslee grabbed a huge breath, slammed her eyes shut, and watched a spear of lightning flash through her vision. She arched back. Sent moans winging outward. Niall continued his circular motion. Sending sensation. Fire. And intensity. Ainslee arched backward.

"Oh, my. Oh, Niall. Niall. I did na'—"

"It's *Neal*, babe."

His voice was deeper than she'd ever heard it. With a sobbed sound at the end. Tormented-sounding, yet still commanding. It rumbled through her back where she pressed to him. Punctured through the bubble of bliss that gathered about her. His fingers continually played with her nubs, pulling. Massaging. Moving quicker and quicker. A riot of sensation built within her. Enlarged. And then it erupted.

"Neal!"

The name was a cry. It hovered in the room about them, blending with his groan. The suction of his lips grew harder. More fierce. He moved his caress up her throat, reached an ear, and sent a blizzard of shivers with every motion of his tongue and lips on the spot. Each of Ainslee's panted breaths ended in a moan.

"Ah!"

He yanked his head back, and gave a tormented-sounding cry.

"This is not working! I have to be gentle! Slow. Measured!"

He spun her around, and set her atop the platform, placing her above him and then stepped back. One step. Two. He was breathing harshly. His nostrils flared. He began shuddering.

"Oh, Ainslee. You are beautiful beyond belief. Beloved beyond measure.

And I am scaring the crap out of myself with just how much I want you and how difficult it is to keep it contained. Ah!"

This time the cry was long. Loud. And extremely deep. He'd pulled his arms close to his sides, and made such tight fists of his hands that the knuckles whitened. His head was flung back. Cords lifted out of the skin of his neck. Ainslee was transfixed. Enraptured.

Awestruck.

And then he lowered his head and caught her gaze.

CHAPTER TWENTY-NINE

THE LEATHER SPORRAN WASN'T HARD enough. Even filled with sundry items to create a weighted barrier atop his groin, it didn't help. All the sporran did was bob up and down with every twinge of his erection. This was beyond painful. Neal had never been this near to losing it. The combination of want, need, desire, and lust was at a combustible level. He hadn't exaggerated earlier, but terrified might not be a big enough word to convey this. He wasn't just dealing with testosterone. He was struggling with something volcanic. The driving force hammered at his restraint efforts with the same painful hits it was giving his groin.

His entire vision got colored with a red wash. It increased in hue with each throbbing beat of his heart. Dark red. Light red wash. Dark red. Light red wash. Dark red. That color coordinated with the bodice of her dress, gapped open now and hanging off her upper arms. It exactly matched the little red corset she wore, too. Neal struggled not to look. Nothing obeyed. This was insane. Her corset wasn't just sexily revealing. It shoved her breasts to the top of the lace, and he'd pushed it down enough that little dark nipples peeked above there.

Oh, shit.

Oh, shit.

Oh, shit.

He forced his gaze upward. Nothing on his body obeyed. Because of her. And...*crap*. Looked like he'd marked her neck. She had such delicate-looking skin. That was going to bruise.

"Neal?"

Pleasure rippled through him at hearing his name from her lips. Pronounced correctly. It sent a whiff of cool air atop a bonfire of emotion. It wasn't much, but enough that he managed to answer.

"Yeah?"

"I'm na'...afraid."

She sure sounded it. Neal snarled. That was an excruciatingly bad sign. He'd been attempting a smile.

"You should be," he finally answered.

"But I ken...what happens a-tween a man and woman."

Oh, shit.

Double shit.

She blushed.

All kinds of heat started accompanying the red hue before his eyes. As if fire licked at his ass. The backs of his thighs. His spine. Shoulders. Neal wrenched every muscle in his body into submission to keep from lunging for her. Grabbing her to him...

...and mauling.

"I mean...I am na' a bairn. I've seen horses. 'Tis na' that scary."

"I don't think we're dealing with the norm here, Ainslee."

The words were croaked. Guttural. Sounded like a man in torture. Something in his attire ripped. None of his shirts had much give to them. Neal had figured they'd taken his measurements when he'd first arrived and been sewing everything to his exact frame. One thing was obvious. He hadn't been flexing when they'd done their measuring. And linen didn't stretch. There wasn't room for the pressure he was putting on the garment right now. From the feel of it, a shoulder seam had given up the fight.

"But...I love you," she whispered.

A wall of elation hit him, bowing his legs. Sending him a step backward. It was accompanied by a shaft of light that arced across his vision and stabbed right into his heart. It penetrated, going deep. Neal's throat closed up. His eyes watered. His breath stopped. His heart went into hammer-mode.

She grabbed her skirts and jumped down. Her breasts bounced. Little nipples darted out before going back into hiding.

Neal was rooted in place as she approached. He needed to move. Step back. Do anything other than watch as she came closer. Watch. And feel. She pulled one of her arms from a sleeve as she approached, then the other. Her bodice dropped forward onto her skirt. Leaving his nemesis: the little corset. It wasn't exactly red. It had barely-there black stripes running vertically through it, crafted from some shiny material. She came closer. Reached arms-length. And then she ran a finger along the tops of her breasts!

Neal arched back to howl. The sound of fabric ripping accompanied his move. That felt like the shirt's other shoulder seam. She was right in front of him when he looked back down. Neal was shuddering. His heart was its own entity, thudding against his chest wall with forceful beats. And his breathing returned with a force that ruffled stray hairs at her forehead.

"Did you hear me?" she asked.

He snatched her to him, smashing her perfect breasts against his chest, and slammed his lips to hers. A high-pitched operatic note filled his ears. The crashing sound of tsunami-level waves joined in. And at the periphery of it was a long keening moan. From her.

Neal had never felt anything like this. The kiss turned into a riotous blend of furor. Passion. Unbelievable fervor. He moved his mouth atop hers, marauding at will. Conquering.

Taking.

Neal toyed with her lips. Split them apart. Delved into her depths with his tongue, and somehow kept from falling. She must be telling the truth because she didn't act remotely frightened. She'd flung her arms about his neck, and writhed against him as the kiss deepened. Her tongue touched his with a hesitant gesture. Neal went completely still at the first touch. But she explored farther. Moaned deeply. And Neal's chest felt like it might explode.

With a groan, he pulled back the kiss, grabbed her tightly in one arm, raced around the bed, leapt to the platform and then atop the mattress. It bounced twice at their landing. He didn't know how he managed it. The move had been pure instinct, and reaction. And they continued to be in command of his body. Ainslee's hands moved to his pecs, as if to support him. There wasn't much need for that. Neal was in a haze of perpetual motion. Intent. And focused. He held himself up with one arm, while the other grabbed bunches of her skirt and shoved it up. He touched skin. Ainslee reacted with a gasp and a jerk. His fingers found the top of her thigh-high stocking. He trailed down it. Reached a slipper. Slid it from her foot. Tossed it over his shoulder. It landed somewhere with a whisper of sound. He shifted higher, sitting in order to follow the same path down her other leg. With the same result.

His shirt was beyond tight. Ainslee's fingers alternately kneaded his pecs and pulled at the ruffled material down his front. Her lips parted. She panted. Each bit of air added to the fervor building within him. Her eyes were half-slit, sending dark blue sparks at him. He heard more fabric tearing. That was definitely the seam up his back. His chest felt the release.

"Oh, Ainslee. Oh, baby. Oh, love. Oh, shit."

He couldn't wait. His hand discovered what he'd yet to visually reveal. And she was perfection. Sleek calves led to supple thighs. The muscles trembled beneath his questing fingers. Each of her panting breaths now carried the slightest feminine sound. Adding encouragement. Neal's hand skimmed the lace top of her stocking, reached bare skin. Her legs tensed. Her trembling increased. Her cries grew more distinct. And a moment later, his thumb found her nub. Two fingers, her center.

So moist. So warm. So tight.

So...gloriously alive.

Neal's fingers began moving. Stimulating. Enervating. Ainslee lurched right up from the bed. Her eyes flew wide with surprise, while her hands yanked on the ruffled jabot, twisting and pulling. Her hold yanked buttons from their holes, so that when she dropped back to the mattress, his jabot came free. Her garbled cry probably carried shock, but it immediately changed to mews of delight as he continued vibrating. And that was followed by all kinds of screams.

"Oh, baby. I can't wait. I'll try. And be gentle..."

Kilts were really good for this.

Neal thrust his sporran around to his back, shoved his plaid up and out of his way and pivoted, neatly settling between her thighs. And then he just hovered there. Tensed. Poised. Waiting. Watching. She was trembling. Gazing at him with wide, luminous eyes. He couldn't tell her eye color from the light sent from the setting sun, but his mind colored them sapphire blue anyway.

"Neal?"

His name was whispered. Tremulous.

"I love you, Ainslee," he replied.

Her eyes opened wide. Her mouth matched the stunned expression. And then the most amazing look of joy transfused her features. The same feeling of joy shot right through him. Grabbed his heart. Squeezed. Neal maneuvered into position, using one hand for guidance. He reached her core. Pressed at her opening. And then he shoved.

Oh. God.

She was hot. Wet. Incredibly tight. He slid in a fraction. Her body went rigid. Neal eased back out. Did the same slow motion back in. Got a little farther. Did it again. Her every breath was gasped. Labored-sounding. He continued stroking. Barely entering her cavern. Sliding slowly back out. Each time he pushed, she went rigid. She relaxed as he moved out, only to go rigid again. Vise-like coils enlarged just enough for him to gain the slightest room. They tightened again when he moved away, only to grab at him the next time. Neal forced himself to go slowly. Fighting an insurmountable need. Unbelievable desire. Everything on his body hammered with need. The urge to shove was bad. Seemingly impossible to fight. It ordered. Commanded. He'd never struggled so valiantly against achieving something.

Nor had he wanted it so badly.

"Oh, baby. Oh, Ainslee. I love you. I do. But I—! Forgive me, darling."

He dropped his head and snagged her lips with his. Mingling their breaths. Entwining their tongues. Sending passion-tipped messages with each caress. Hoped she wouldn't notice how he grabbed her hips and held her. And then thrust. He broke through. Gained depth. And a vise-like hold. He caught her cry with the kiss. She helped.

And then he stopped.

Neal scrunched his eyes shut and focused all his energy on one thing; staying still while she absorbed him. He yanked every muscle to tautness. It barely worked. His entire body fought his attempt at restraint. His gut was a morass of fire. His loins burned. His lower back whorled with scorching agony. His thighs and legs muscles kept pulsing. Neal had to lift from the kiss to pant each breath. And still he started pulling out from her enclosure.

Damn it, Neal. Harder.

Everything fought him. Extremely enraged. And more than a little tormented. He shook. The mattress swayed with him.

"Neal?"

Her whisper dented his consciousness.

"Yeah." The answer came through gritted teeth.

"Is it...wrong?"

"No." The answer came with a groan that iced his teeth.

"What...should I do?"

"I'm trying not. To hurt you, love. I mean...any further."

The words were garbled. Nearly intelligible. Something within her moved. Slid along his length. Neal groaned and his shaking intensified.

"Neal?"

A hand touched his forehead, brushing a stray lock of hair back. Neal cracked an eye open. She was waiting for it. She licked her lips. He pulsed in place. Her eyes widened in something that didn't look like pain.

"It's na'...that bad."

And then she lifted her legs, hooked them about him, and started the movements herself. Neal went wild. As if an archer had just released an arrow, Neal churned. In. Out. Harder. Pulling out only to shove back in.

Again. And again. He pushed up to gain position. Making each thrust harder. Stronger. Deeper. Gaining the slightest cry from her each time.

The mattress began bucking in rhythm. Thumping along with each shove. Adding more dimension to an already unreal experience. The pleasure built. Went from a sliver of sensation along his spine to a solid knot of pressure at the base of his back. Just above his buttocks. Ready. Enlarging. Getting fiery hot with the delay. Neal yanked it into submission. It gave his muscles definition she seemed to enjoy. Her hands roved all over him. His belly. His chest. His back. Up his arms.

His movements became more strident. Deeper. Harder. Her cries longer in duration. Higher-pitched. Synchronized with their movements. And they started carrying his name.

"Neal! Neal! Neal! Oh! My—!"

She arched her neck, and screamed. And Neal exploded. Pleasure erupted absolutely everywhere. It was tinged with all kinds of hues. Infused with scent. Compounded with perfectly pitched notes of incredible beauty. Neal reeled with absolute joy. His mouth opened, sending a groan of uncontainable bliss outward. It surrounded them, giving sound to how his spirit soared upward, gaining the heavens. Everything was infused with light. Power. Wonder. And for an infinitesimal moment, Neal could swear he touched heaven.

The moment ended. Intensity started waning. His body continued throbbing in slower and slower pulses. He was very close to sobbing. He lowered his head. Opened his eyes. And locked gazes with his beloved. She gave him the most beatific smile. He couldn't return it for several moments. The lurch his heart gave him was too powerful.

Neal thought he had experience. He'd had sex countless times with numerous women, in nearly every conceivable position. And all of that had been obliterated and then over-written by this experience with Ainslee. He'd never felt this level of contentment. Perfection. And peace. It was almost magical.

He collapsed beside her. Pulled her into his arms. Held her close, stroking the waterfall of hair along her back.

He hadn't known love made all the difference.

He knew it now.

CHAPTER THIRTY

ERIC'S DOPPELGANGER, RORY, HAD AN older brother. His name was Cedric. He was one of the estate gamekeepers accompanying Neal this morning. There were three of them. All in their mid-thirties. Cedric probably looked exactly like Eric/Rory would once they reached that age. The man had shoulder-length sandy-colored hair. Neal couldn't tell if he was balding or not. Cedric wore a large tam on his head. It didn't really matter, but as a motorcycle enthusiast, Neal had seen thousands of men who looked like they had a full head of hair until they took their caps off. Regardless, Cedric was a nice-looking fellow. A few inches shorter than Neal, but large, well-muscled. Self-confident.

Despite the antagonism radiating off the fellow, Neal liked him on sight.

They'd met this morning, over a breakfast befitting a day of shooting on the moors. Coffee. Porridge. Fried eggs. Back bacon. Baked beans. Blood pudding. Fried tomatoes and mushrooms. Oatcakes. And fantastic-tasting scones dripping with butter and honey. Neal hadn't been this full in years. Couldn't remember a meal he'd enjoyed more.

Then again...he'd been famished by the time he'd arrived, dressed in another kilt, worn this time with a plain linen shirt above it. He sported a brown leather vest with myriad pockets, knee-high boots, and thick woolen socks that scratched. This outfit seemed to also require the normal amount of daggers about his waist, while *skean dhu* were tucked into either sock.

It was an incredibly perfect morning. A bit breezy, although sunlight banished most of the chill. But that wasn't what made it so perfect. He'd opened his eyes to the sight and feel of Ainslee snuggled against his side, a soft smile on her face. He hadn't drawn the drapes and dawn light had streamed into the chamber, bringing even more beauty to her features. If Neal hadn't been smitten already, he damn well would have been at that awakening.

He wasn't sure if he should leave her in his mussed bed. He didn't think Mason would say anything, but he didn't know her maids. And Neal didn't want a whisper of anything to reach Ainslee's ear. She'd already shown her shyness last night, after he'd fetched a pail of rain water for them to wash with. Neal slept in the nude. Always had. Always would. Ainslee was the opposite. She'd even asked him not to look, while a deep blush suffused her cheeks.

That had endeared her to him even more.

So, Neal had turned around, listened to her splashing, and when she said so, he swiveled to see her engulfed in one of his robes. He'd even managed not to snicker. She'd still worn it when he'd carried her through the connecting door to her room. It wasn't a hardship. His heart had been full to bursting with each step, and felt even more so by the way she'd nuzzled her nose against his throat. She hadn't awakened, even as he settled her into the center of her bed and tucked her in. He couldn't resist placing a kiss on her forehead.

And then he'd sprinted for his room, retrieved her clothing so it could be in her chamber. Piled it atop the chaise. Returned to his room. Rung for Mason. Neal didn't really need the valet to assist. But he realized he liked seeing him. And things he used to consider a time waste had changed. He hadn't looked at why too closely. He could guess. Being in love with Ainslee altered all kinds of things. But by the time Neal had reached the small dining room and the array of breakfast items, he was thoroughly ready to put a dent in the amount of food on display.

"This here is a blunderbuss, yer grace. Yer familiar with it. Or, so ye said."

Cedric brought Neal's attention back to the present with a jolt. The man had a slightly caustic edge to every comment. Neal looked across to Cedric and the thirty-inch long gun he held. The man had another gun slung over his shoulder. The gamekeeper standing behind Cedric carried another one. The blunderbuss resembled a sawed-off shotgun. The end of the barrel had been flared like a trumpet. Supposedly this was to scatter shot in a wider area to make a better kill ratio. But that hadn't been proven. There were blunderbusses in the Straithmore Collection, but Neal had rarely handled one, and never fired it. He probably could have, but he wasn't that interested.

What interested him was nailing a target with a thirty-thirty at a hundred yards without a scope. That gave him great satisfaction. Almost as much as hitting a bulls-eye with a *Lapua* 338 sniper rifle from a distance of one mile.

And these gamekeepers had set out ten bird decoys at about twenty feet away.

Twenty feet.

Neal had to turn aside before they caught his expression. Hell, if he missed at this distance, he could always throw the blunderbuss and hit something.

"Ye payin' attention this time?"

"Uh. Yeah." Neal nodded.

"Good. This here is a paper patch bullet."

Holy shit.

"Let me see that."

Cedric handed it over. Neal tested it for weight. Looked it over. It had a waxy feel. There had been replicas in the Straithmore Collection, but despite researching antiquities markets, he'd never found an actual paper bullet from pre-Civil War era.

"What's it loaded with?"

"A measure o' gunpowder. Some small shot."

"And the seal?"

"These here are lard. We like them more than the beeswax ones."

"Pork?"

"Aye. Makes it a bit more pleasant when you bite it open."

Neal nodded. Handed the bullet back. Cedric looked him over without expression.

"What is it?" Neal asked.

"Yer a bit different today."

"Than...I was...before?" Neal asked it as a leading question.

"Aye."

"You were there?"

"You do na' even remember?"

"I suffered a fall the other day. Hurt my head. Lost a bit of. Memory."

Neal lifted the hair at his temple. By now, it should be a nice purplish and green hue. And he hadn't even thought of it for days now. *Odd.*

"Well. At least this morn, yer sober."

Neal nodded. No wonder his gamekeeper was annoyed. Firearms and alcohol were a poor mix.

"Man. Was I a twit," he muttered.

Cedric gave him another long, measured look. Neal held the gaze. Cedric finally nodded and returned to his lecture.

"This is a hammer. It has two cocking mechanisms. Half-way is to lock it for loading. Fully back to fire. We're taking this to half-cocked."

...*half-cocked.*

Neal fought a grin as the explanation for that expression was demonstrated for him. He didn't dare show amusement. Not to the man who thought he handled guns while drunk.

"Got it," he finally answered.

"Now. This here's the firing pan."

Neal stepped closer. The man lifted a little lid beneath the trigger.

"You bite the end of yer paper bullet open and pour a bit in the firing pan. Like so."

Cedric bit the end of the bullet open and tapped about a half teaspoon into the pan. Neal nodded.

"Set the lid down gentle-like. Then, ye tip the gun barrel up and empty the rest of yer paper patch into it."

"Containing the gunpowder and lead shot pellets."

"Aye. Drop the paper down next. Then you take up the rod....like this. And ram the load into a nice solid mass."

Cedric pulled out a metal rod that had been in brackets along the bottom of the barrel. He shoved it down the gun and started tamping the mix. He then removed the rod and slid it back into its holder. He'd glanced occasionally at what he was doing, but for the most part, kept his attention on Neal. Neal returned the favor.

"Now you are ready to shoot. You need me to demonstrate, yer grace?"

"Nah. I think I'll just have a go at it."

Cedric held out the gun, keeping the barrel pointing up. Neal took it, pressed it to his shoulder. Brought it to bear as he turned a half-turn to the left, and fired. It wasn't as loud as he'd expected. Nor was there a lot of recoil. There was a bit of white smoke. But before it had dissipated, his success was clear by the others' reaction. All ten of the decoys had fallen.

"Good shot!" One of the other men exclaimed.

Neal looked over at Cedric. The man was giving him another level look. Pretty expressionless.

"Word is ye've changed."

"God, I hope so," Neal replied.

A ghost of a smile lifted the man's lips. It disappeared almost instantly. The man slid the spare blunderbuss off his shoulder. "Let me ready another round fer ye."

Neal held out the used gun. "Let me do it this time."

"Ye certain-sure ye ken what to do?"

"Why don't you watch? And...I think we could move my targets out a bit farther."

"Lads? Take them another ten feet!"

"Oh. Come on, Cedric. Give me something difficult. Let's try twenty more."

"Twenty feet?"

"What's the range of these guns?"

"With accuracy?"

"I don't shoot if I'm not going to hit a target," Neal replied.

"Forty. Forty-two feet."

"All right. Let's do forty."

"Take the decoys out another twenty feet, lads!"

Neal exchanged guns with Cedric. Waited for the man to hand him a paper patch bullet from his bag. Neal put it between his teeth and tore. Wasn't bad tasting. Had a bit of bacon flavor to it. He pulled the trigger to half-cocked until it locked. Lifted the lid of the firing pan. Tapped out a bit of gunpowder. Lowered the lid. Turned the gun, stock down, and finished loading. He pulled the rod out and tamped his load. Replaced the rod. Other than a couple of glances he didn't look at what he was doing. He kept his gaze on Cedric. The man raised his eyebrows, but didn't comment.

"We ready?" Neal asked.

"Aye!"

One of the other men answered. Neal put the gun to his shoulder, turned, and immediately lifted the barrel back up as a stag shot through the high grass just beyond the decoys. Beside him he heard Cedric's whistle. And that was a very satisfying feeling. He waited for the deer to disappear. Lowered the barrel and fired.

All ten decoys fell over.

The other two men cheered. Cedric nodded.

"Yer aim...has definitely improved, yer grace."

"Yeah. I know. Came along with that change everyone is talking about. Take them out to forty-five feet."

"Forty-five?"

"You heard me."

"Lads! Another five feet."

The other two men ran for the duck decoys. Neal waited while Cedric reloaded the first gun he'd used. Neither of them spoke. He had a slight breeze coming from his right. There wouldn't be a lot of momentum behind the shots, if he could even get them out that far. He'd have to angle the gun to the right and up about ten degrees.

"We ready?" he asked.

"Lads?"

"Ready!"

Neal turned and fired. He didn't have to wait for the cloud to clear to know the results. The whoops from the other two gave him the answer. He lowered the gun, and looked over at Cedric.

"Too bad my cousin Garrick isn't here again," Neal remarked.

"Again?"

"You mean, he wasn't here when we went shooting...before?"

"Nae."

"Where was he?"

"I do na' ken. It was na' my turn to watch him."

Whoa.

Neal sent a sharp glance toward the man. One thing was instantly apparent. He didn't radiate disgust anymore. Neal's brain clicked with thought processes. He could almost feel it. Cedric's reply meant one of two things. Either he wasn't the type to speak of others and he was giving Neal notice of that, or some of them did watch for Garrick and it truly hadn't been his turn.

"Were you three accompanying me?"

"Aye."

"Then which one of you has the big mouth?"

Neal narrowed his eyes, looked down at the man, and waited. It was his turn to be antagonistic. Height was a definite advantage in situations like this. He'd used it more than once. Cedric didn't shift his gaze, however.

"I do na' catch yer meaning."

"Well. Garrick has the same opinion of my shooting as you had. He thinks I'm a piss-poor shot. He got that from somewhere."

"Probably his brother."

"Who?"

"Lachlan."

"Lachlan?"

"That's who was out here with you last time, yer grace."

"Oh. Hell. I forgot about him."

"Ye forgot yer own cousin?"

"It's not hard. I mean...you've met my aunt, Lady Blair, haven't you?"

"Aye."

"Well. It's bad enough knowing her husband had sex with her once. That would be Garrick. But. Damn. Lord Blair must have been blind. Deaf. And mute."

"Yer grace?"

"Think about it, Cedric. The man had sex with my aunt more than once. That thought alone is enough to ruin sup."

Cedric regarded him for an instant, and then the man put his head back, and roared with laughter. That's when Neal decided it wasn't just a good morning. It was one of the best one he could ever remember.

CHAPTER THIRTY-ONE

RORY MET HIM AT THE front door. The fellow was agitated. He'd been pacing, and it wasn't a sedate pace. He saw Neal, spun quickly enough to swirl his kilt and raced toward him.

"Thank the saints! Yer back!"

"Did you desert your post, young man?"

"'Course na', yer grace. My under-footman is handling 'doo'-ties."

"You have an under-footman? Already?"

"The steward thinks I do a fine job. He promoted me."

"I see. So. What's the problem?"

"It's her grace, and—"

"Why the hell didn't you say so? Where is she?"

"Blue salon."

"It's too early for tea. And I'm not exactly dressed for it."

And I can't believe those words just came out of my mouth.

"It's na' tea. Laird MacAffrey has arrived. He brought clan."

Oh, shit.

Neal started jogging, Rory at his side. They reached the staircase. Neal stopped. Rory was a step behind. Two of his Honor Guard stood at attention in the shadow cast by the stair's landing above.

"Gentlemen?" Neal greeted them.

"Your grace."

Both men said it in tandem. Their head nod was in sync, as well.

"Do I have a constable?"

"Aye."

"Rory? Do you know who he is and where to find him?"

"I soon will."

"Good man. Fetch him for me. You two. On my six."

Rory sprinted for the front door. Neal headed for the double door, his mind racing. He basically needed to go right a lot. The blue salon was on the other side of one of the four fireplaces along the wall of the great hall behind him. It shouldn't be that hard to find again. And he could always ask one of the guardsmen behind him. Blame his injury.

But, what the hell could Ainslee's father want?

He'd been thinking of a nice leisurely lunch...followed by the same kind of lovemaking session. He hoped Ainslee wasn't feeling too sore or tender. Because he really looked forward to this. Maybe, they'd spend some time in the dark alcove of his balcony, sponging each other off with the water from his rain barrel.

Followed by a long, leisurely sup.

Another round of loving...

Damn MacAffrey. No matter what the fellow wanted, his timing was atrocious.

"Your grace?" one of the guardsmen enquired behind him.

Neal turned about. Both guardsmen had identical looks on their faces. Quizzical.

"What does 'on your six' mean?" the man continued.

"Oh. Sorry. It's a modern term for...never mind. Follow me. Closely. About three paces back."

Neal jogged the entire way, his heart keeping rhythm with his steps. The sound was echoed by the guardsmen's steps behind him. The blue salon wasn't difficult to find. He could hear MacAffrey's raised voice from down the hall. Neal jumped down the last set of steps and didn't remember how he reached the door.

There was a kid standing beside it. Looked to be in his late teens. Lean. No hint of beard growth. Resembled Rory, and the gamekeeper, Cedric. The thought that Neal might employ the entire family flashed through his head and then he discarded it. The kid caught sight of Neal before he reached the door. The under-footman gathered a quick breath and opened his mouth as if to announce the duke's arrival. Neal motioned for silence.

"You'll tell me where she's gone or—!"

"Laird MacAffrey!"

Neal entered the room with a boom, first by smacking at the door to send it crashing against the wall, secondly by using his orator tone. In this small room, it was probably enough to rattle bric-a-brac. Everyone jumped. The Laird of MacAffrey was standing before Ainslee, and the man had an arm raised. He lowered it and spun at Neal's entrance. Neal walked past him, ignoring him completely, and took a knee before his wife.

And then he held out his hand.

He'd seen Ainslee in all sorts of vivid colors. Knew she was the most beautiful creature he'd ever seen. Elegant. Graceful. But right now, dressed in a charcoal-shaded gown that matched the hair peeking from beneath a long veil of aged lace, she looked beyond beautiful. She looked positively ethereal. Like an unworldly creature had descended from the skies to bless mortals with her presence. But at any moment, if she wanted to, she'd disappear.

Neal's heart scudded when she placed her hand within his. So small. So delicate. He caught her glance and held it. She was pale and might be shaking, but the look in her eyes gave away that lie. Ainslee wasn't remotely frightened. Neal slid a thumb along her knuckles, lifted her hand to his mouth. Touched his lips to her skin. Rubbed slightly, enjoying the brush of whiskers from his growing beard. And then he lifted his head and addressed her in soft tones, as if they were the only ones in the room.

"Forgive my appearance, my love. I was out in the field with my game-keepers. I did not know. We were. Expecting company."

She smiled. And his eyes watered up. Neal blinked rapidly against that particular affectation. The last thing he needed was to be emotional. Not now.

Hell.

He'd thought her father had bad timing.

"My father arrived...unexpectedly," she answered.

Neal cleared his throat. "I see. Well. If you will allow it...may I address him?"

His query was clearly heard in the silence that had fallen throughout the room. She nodded. Neal released her hand and stood up. Took a deep breath. Straightened his back. And turned around to face her father.

Neal's two Honor Guardsmen were inside the room, on both sides of the door. Feet spread to shoulder-width. Lips lifted in matching sneers. Hands on sword hilts.

Damn. They were impressive.

Neal didn't puff up his chest to look bigger. It happened subconsciously with the dose of pride he experienced. A quick glance showed MacAffrey had brought eight men with him. Nine, if Neal counted the heir who was probably still in the throes of puberty. They were all smaller men. They didn't look like a band that wanted a fight. Even if they were about to get one. Neal looked down his nose at Ainslee's father. Spoke with his orator voice.

"Well. Laird MacAffrey. To what. Do I owe. The displeasure of your visit? Unannounced. And uninvited."

"Me daughter's run off."

"Lileth?"

"I only have but one more daughter."

"Hmm. I see. What I don't see is why this event in your household brings you into mine."

"I'll na' allow her to abort me authority."

The man's complexion darkened and he shoved a finger in Ainslee's direction. Neal regarded him for a long time, making the wait as uncomfortable as possible. He didn't reply until shuffling sounds could be heard coming from the men about MacAffrey.

"If you are referring to my wife, the reigning Duchess of Straithcairn. I suggest you use her title. Anything else, I will find offensive. Is that clear?"

"But, your grace—!"

"I asked if my instruction were clear. Or do I need to reiterate them for you?"

"Aye. It's clear 'nuff."

"Good."

"Just hand over my Lileth, and we'll be gone, your grace."

"What makes you think she's here?"

"She sent a note last eve to her!"

Dughall pointed at Ainslee again. Neal waited another long moment. "Are you referring to the Duchess of Straithcairn again? And failing to use her proper title?" he asked.

Dughall's skin went even darker red. His mouth worked behind clenched teeth. His eyes bulged out. Neal watched silently and decided this was highly enjoyable.

"Forgive me. Lileth sent a note to her grace, the Duchess of Straithcairn." The man finally replied.

"And you believe this means Lileth is here?"

"The wench will na' tell me wot was in the note!"

"Final warning, Dughall. You will address my wife with the proper respect or incur consequences. I don't know what they are, so I'll invent a proper penalty. And I need to warn you, Dughall. I intend to get very medieval with what I decide."

"Are you threatening me?"

"Gentlemen? Does the castle still have a working dungeon?"

Neal looked over the heads of the MacAffrey bunch and addressed his

Honor Guardsmen. Murmurs of reaction happened through the ranks of MacAffrey clansmen. Neal ignored them.

"Aye, your grace. More than one," one of the guardsmen answered.

Rory had arrived. He motioned from the door. Neal nodded. Rory had a gentleman with him. The man looked almost as wide as he was tall. And he was nearly as tall as the doorframe. Neal guessed him at mid-forties. He had silver-tipped hair at his temples, an air of authority, and looked like he could handle just about anyone. And anything.

"Ah. Dughall. It appears my constable has arrived."

More than one man jerked around. Dughall was the first to turn back to Neal. He'd lost quite a bit of color.

"Now wait. Just a moment, yer grace. All I wanted to ken was if my Lileth was safe. Things can happen to a young lass if she's away from the protection of her family."

"I see. Well. I shall ask. Are we harboring a fugitive?"

Neal addressed the guardsmen and Rory. Everyone shook their head. He turned back to Ainslee and went to one knee again. Softened his tone.

"Darling? Forgive the question. Has your sister...sought refuge with us?"

She shook her head as well. There was the cutest smile atop her lips, too. Neal's lips twitched in response. He settled with a wink. Stood back up. Turned back to Dughall.

"Well, Laird MacAffrey. There you have it. Your daughter is not here."

"That's it? Yer just gonna believe it? Have ye nae sense, lad? You have to beat the truth out of them!"

Neal's eyes narrowed. His jaw set. He hoped the anger was projected with his tone when he finally replied. "I sincerely hope you are not referring to my lady wife, the Duchess of Straithcairn again."

Dughall nearly swallowed his tongue. It was audible.

"Uh. O' course na'."

"Then. May I bid you a good day? And good riddance. You have sullied my wife's presence long enough."

There was an audible gasp from the assemblage. Neal ignored it. He was trying to be as offensive as possible. And enjoying the hell out of it.

"Ah. Look. Out in the hall. I see more of my Honor Guard has arrived. They will be escorting you gentlemen out. Oh! One more thing before you leave, Dughall."

The man didn't reply.

"I was told the will was written because you desired an end to an old grievance of some kind. Your clan and mine had been at war for decades. Did I hear this correctly?"

Dughall nodded.

"Well, then. If you ever arrive at the castle again. Unannounced. And uninvited. And accompanied by armed clansmen. And if you ever again threaten my wife, the Duchess of Straithcairn, I will consider it an act of war. And respond accordingly. Now. Is any of *that* unclear?"

A thumping sound started up out in the hall. Someone out there had a drum. The thump had a cadence to it. Like a battle march. That's when Neal decided there wasn't any need of reaching New York. Or a trading floor. Or building an empire. Gaining financial domination of world markets. He'd been driven to gain more and more his entire life. More money. More power. More influence.

Shock held him rooted to the spot as the Laird of MacAffrey and his troupe filed out of the blue salon and turned to their left. The MacAffreys were already smaller in stature. Once they got surrounded by Straith clan, they looked even more diminutive.

Neal had been so wrong. Money had no value when placed against the real power in the universe.

Love.

All these years. All the stupid striving for wealth. Avoiding love every time he chanced near it.

Well. He knew the truth now. And he had it. Right here. Right now.

He was exactly where he wanted to be.

CHAPTER THIRTY-TWO

"AH. THERE YOU ARE, YOUR grace."

Neal looked up from the journal he was reading as Mason entered his chamber, a white cloth draped across his arm as if in preparation for something.

"I have been on the hunt for your location for some time. I should have checked your chambers."

"On the hunt for my location?" Neal repeated.

"Exactly, and growing quite exasperated."

"You have such a droll way of speaking, Mason."

"Droll?"

"Yeah. Very. And never change. It's one of the things I like about you."

"And may I also repeat that request, Neal?"

The man lost all joviality as he placed the towel on the rack of Neal's shaving stand. He wouldn't need it. Neal had given off shaving. Unless Ainslee preferred him beardless. But she hadn't mentioned it, one way or the other.

"What request are we referring to?" Neal asked.

"That you never change. Again, I mean."

"Oh, I don't know. I thought the old me wasn't so bad."

"You were a moron, Neal. I realize it now. And I have to say this. I have served many members of the gentry before coming to work at Straith. I served the prior duke of Straithcairn. And I must say I have never been prouder to be in my position in my entire life."

"I did something...extraordinary?"

"But, of course! The castle is abuzz at the set-down you gave that MacAffrey! The nerve of the man! And the way you came, not only to your wife's aid, but demonstrated the level of respect she deserves! Oh. Neal. I only wish I'd been there to observe it."

"You liked that, huh?"

"And then some. To quote your grace."

Neal chuckled.

"But, I need to ask you, is it such a good idea to relocate Lady Blair?"

"Your thoughts?"

"I have always considered it much more beneficial to have an – and I sincerely hope you pardon my impertinence – enemy in one's sight. So as to ken what they are planning."

"True. But I'm actually checking the extent of Lady Blair's influence. See...when dealing with a spider, there are three options: Ignore it. Kill it. Or move it somewhere that it can't be an issue. I already know I'm not going to ignore her. Relocation is the next option on the list. And...spiders don't stop spinning their webs just because you move them. You just don't have to see them or care. Nor will anyone else. Which – in my aunt's case – sounds like a viable consequence to her meddling."

"A spider, Neal? How...apt."

"You didn't see it?"

"I do so like your manner of speaking. There's no beating about the bush."

"So. To the matter of my aunt? She is being relocated. I just don't know how far that might need to be. But I'm certain I will find out."

"The duchy does have a piece of nice property...inland a piece."

"Really? How far inland?"

"'Tis a huntsman's cottage. A good half-day ride at least."

"Excellent. I'm going to have to give you another raise. So. Hey." Neal lifted the leather-bound journal he'd been reading. "Did you know my father?"

"I did. The duke's younger brother was quite a fellow."

"Did he really meet my mother on a trek through...let's see. He lists Egypt? Sumer? A place I can't even pronounce."

"They were quite the explorers, your parents. 'Twas a sad day when a carriage accident took them from the world."

"Are there other journals like this one? Written by former...dukes?"

"Every duke has written a life history."

"What a spectacular idea!" Neal rose to his feet. Set the journal on a table. Almost clapped his hands.

"Neal?"

"Oh. I've been pondering something. I...have something I need to make certain future generations know."

Future generations?

Oh, my God.

What he'd just said hit him with the force of a blow. Neal reeled and almost fell back into the chair. A future generation meant he'd have at least one child. One, created with Ainslee. Held, and cradled, and nurtured to adulthood.

That realization changed everything.

Neal's entire body experienced a wash of something so amazing, it stole his breath. The sensation came in waves that crested and then subsided. They were combined with a light of such brilliance he had to narrow his eyes and blink rapidly against an instant film of tears. He didn't have any experience to draw from for how this felt. It went beyond any thrill the twenty-first century Neal had experienced when dealing with takeovers and monetary success and jet-powered flight. This feeling was indescribable. Beyond compare. It weakened his limbs, sent a tremor through his belly, and infused his chest with such warmth, he might be glowing.

He had to wait several heart-pounding moments, and then clear his throat in order to continue speaking. He was actually amazed he was still standing.

"I...uh...wasn't sure how to get the information to a future...Straith, although I told Iain exactly what was needed before he left. I see now that if I list the instructions in a missive, seal it with wax, and secure it in a journal for opening in say...1870? That might be exactly what I need."

"1870?"

"Oh. Um. I...have a hunch. I get them...occasionally. I usually go with them."

"I see. Well. I shall have the comptroller fetch you a journal so you can start. You have a fresh quill and ink at your writing desk. Or would you rather use the library desk?"

"Quill and ink pot? Truly? And fine grains of sand?"

"But, of course. Everything is strictly modern."

Mason walked to a tall armoire standing in the shadows against the wall that contained the door leading to Ainslee. His beloved. Taking a long bath. Preparing for him.

Neal banished the thought so he could pay complete attention to Mason. The man stood before a furniture piece that was a lot narrower at the top than the bottom. It had a slanted front. Mason unlatched two leather hoops, released the slanted portion, and brought it down to create a writing surface.

Wow.

That piece was worth a fortune on the antiquities market two hundred years from now. Then again, the same could be said for all of the furniture in Straith Castle. Even from here, Neal could see the writing surface had a leather top, affixed with brass studs. Cubbyholes containing little pots of ink. Feather-topped quills. All kinds of mysterious items. He'd never written with an ink and quill. Too time consuming. He might feel like he had to write in calligraphic script.

Hmm.

That challenge could prove highly entertaining.

"So."

Mason turned and walked over to one of Neal's wardrobes and opened it, revealing more shirts than had been there yesterday. The castle seamstresses were not only creating a spectacular wardrobe for Ainslee, but they seemed devoted to making certain Neal wouldn't shame anyone with his attire, either. He smiled at the instant thought. Mason's words cancelled the smile. Rapidly.

"What do you wish to wear this evening?"

"Oh, no. Uh-uh. I'm wearing a robe. And not a whole lot else. I'm spending this evening with my wife, Mason. In her chambers. Unless...and please don't say it. There can't possibly be a reason that is a bad idea."

"I think it a spectacular plan, Neal. But, might I suggest you wear the robe trimmed with ermine?"

I have an ermine-trimmed robe?

Mason went to another wardrobe and started shuffling, and then a knock on the chamber door stopped everything. Neal swore beneath his breath. Mason crossed to the door. Spoke for a bit. Shut it.

"It better not be a reason I have to get dressed," Neal told him.

"Well, I was under the assumption it would be the comptroller. With the selection of rings from the safe. If memory serves me right, I believe there is a sapphire setting that should fit her grace."

"Good man."

"You are too quick with your praise, Neal. I was mistaken. It is an invitation. To go grouse hunting on the morrow. Early. At Huntsman's Dale. With your cousin, Garrick. The man he sent has instructions to await your reply."

Neal whistled. "Hmm. My aunt certainly doesn't waste any time."

"Lady Blair?"

"Garrick doesn't have the smarts for this, but I'm not being generous.

Tell the man I gladly accept, but I think we need to make a party of it. Can you make certain the solicitor fellows are invited?"

"The gents from London?"

"They're still here, aren't they? Oh! And add in Reagan Fells. And the vicar. He might as well join us, too."

"That will be quite a party, Neal."

"Exactly. Write all that, will you? I'm going to quaff a really large dram of whisky, and then go dunk my head into the rain barrel."

Mason had just closed the door when Neal returned from the balcony. The man stood expectantly in the center of the room.

"Now. For the part they won't know about. You ready?"

Mason nodded.

"We need to get a message to the new captain of the guards, Iain Straithmore's replacement. On the sly. Extremely quiet. Nobody knows. Can you do this?"

"You're calling in the Honor Guard?"

"They're all good shots, aren't they?"

"The best the clan has to offer. 'Tis why we have games every year. To pick them out, make certain of their fitness for the position."

"Good. And here is what you need to tell him. I want every man dressed as a gamekeeper and on the field at Huntsman's Dale before sunrise. Armed. With a flintlock rifle. We have those, yes? If they like, they can also carry a blunderbuss. Or the small version, the dragon. Either way, I need them armed to the teeth and prepared for anything."

"The teeth?"

"It's an expression. I'll explain it one of these years. After we handle this new strand of the spider's web."

"The Lady Blair?"

"It's obvious my aunt heard of MacAffrey's visit."

"I assume so. Everyone did."

"So. She knows the heiress is missing. Now...I'm guessing the missing heiress eloped with her love, because she'd heard of her father's recent choice of bridegroom. My cousin, Garrick. But that's only a guess, so don't quote me. This moved my aunt's timeline up considerably. But then again. I am not surprised. I've been expecting this."

Mason was still regarding him with a blank expression, but he rarely gave much indication of what he was thinking. Neal continued.

"The MacAffrey heiress is missing, Mason. Nobody knows where. That means there are two ways left for Garrick to replace me and become the Duke of Straithcairn. Are you following my drift, yet?"

"Following your drift?"

"Do you see where this is heading?"

Mason frowned slightly and shook his head.

"Garrick will need to wed the widow to fulfill the requirement of the will. That is one way. The other one is obvious and connected to the first."

"What widow?"

"Ainslee."

Mason's eyes enlarged. His jaw dropped.

"I assume they expect me to have an unfortunate hunting accident, Mason."

"Garrick would na' commit murder. Not in broad daylight."

"Keeping an eye on Garrick will be Cedric's responsibility. But he may have compatriots. That is why I wish to know where the solicitor fellows, Kingston and Bon are. Not to worry. I'm a really good shot. I'm prepared. I'll have over a dozen men who are also good shots protecting my back. We'll need some sort of signal. Tell them to give a sharp whistle if they spot anything. And finally, my Aunt Margaret and her camp need to be completely unaware of everything."

"You can rely on me, Neal."

"I know. You need another raise. Remind me. But, before anything else happens, could you please find me that robe?"

Neal grinned, but the valet didn't return it.

CHAPTER THIRTY-THREE

HER ROOM WAS PROBABLY THE most elegant one in the castle.

Ainslee was reclining on her chaise lounge, looking about the chamber with a touch of awe. The maids had lit five sets of candelabra throughout the room. One had been situated on the headboard behind her. Candlelight flickered all about the chamber, highlighting the richness of the room. She was dressed in a gossamer pink nightgown made from a fabric so fragile it pulled slightly with the weight of the little white lace that had been affixed to it. That lace had been tatted by a master. It was interwoven with silvery strands that sparkled in multi-hued flashes when she moved. Ainslee had blushed, her skin reaching the same color of the gown as Mira and Beth had helped her into it. The accompanying robe was fashioned of finely woven wool and much more modest. Made of the same pink shade, it also had the same lace decorating it. Her maids had laced more silvery lace through little braids that pulled her hair back, but for the most part, it was left loose.

She was nervous. Expectant. Excited. The walls of her room seemed to breathe in accompaniment with her. And then something occurred to her.

She'd called the duchess's suite – *hers*.

And not just once, either!

Ainslee gasped as she realized it. And then the connecting door opened. Neal walked in. If she hadn't just inhaled a gasp, she'd have done so. The same thing happened every time she caught sight of him. Her heart ticked up. Her pulse raced. Her throat closed off. It wasn't just because he was so manly. Muscled and fit. Nor was it his handsomeness, although that was already eye-catching. The slight shadow of a beard on his jaw only heightened his appeal. He wore a long plaid robe with a white and black fur trim that did nothing to disguise how broad his shoulders were. Nor how narrow his waist and hips.

There was just something about him. Something that spoke just for her.

Ainslee's breath came out with a soft sigh. She couldn't tell his expression. He'd swiveled as soon as he entered and dropped the bolt down, barring the door. He walked past her without appearing to pay her much attention, reached the door leading to the hallway, and did the same thing to secure it. And then he turned. Lowered his chin. Regarded her for a long moment while her heart did antics within her chest.

"You hungry?" he asked.

Ainslee stood. Unfastened the front hoops holding her robe closed. Slowly slid the garment off her shoulders. And then she answered, using several pauses between her words, like he did.

"Oh, yes. But not. For. Food."

She didn't know who moved first. The robe dropped off, and the next second she was in his arms. Lifted above the floor. Her lips smashed to his. A groan erupted from his throat, but it was matched by her moans. She couldn't get enough!

Ainslee lapped at his lips. She was parched and he was liquid; cold while he was heat; famished, and he was sustenance. She darted her tongue through his lips in tandem with his motion. Her heart seized up as their tongues connected. Her belly sent all kinds of signals shooting through her and Neal's arms tightened about her. The combination of sound emanating from their throats swelled and grew. Enlarging. Encompassing.

He broke the kiss and moved. Ainslee clung. They reached the bed. The beautiful scarlet and gold coverlet was pushed aside by one of his arms. He set her atop the sheets with the other. And then he joined her with a lunge that sent more than one pillow flying. His side matched against hers, sending heat. Electrical stimuli. All kinds of tingling. And then he lowered his mouth to hers again. Their breaths entwined. Their tongues tangled. His hand slid up her side. Cupped a breast. His fingers flicked a nipple, sending absolute magic. Ainslee arched upward, subconsciously begging for more.

Without thinking, her hand grabbed for the ermine trim of his robe and pushed it from his shoulder. Down his arm. To his elbow. Moved her caress to his flesh. Neal released his hold on her breast in order to shrug out of the sleeve. She held to his arm as he moved, feeling his muscles ripple beneath her fingers.

Their kiss deepened.

Ainslee's moans intensified. She skimmed her touch to his shoulder. Moved from there to his chest, working her way across hardness that quivered and flexed beneath her fingers. Everything about Neal was hard. Masculine. There wasn't anything about Neal that wasn't taut. His belly was a collection of rope-like cords, bunching and moving as she quested across them.

"Oh, baby. Oh, love."

Neal rolled onto his back, taking her with him. And she immediately opened her legs to straddle his hips. Heavy inhalations for air filled the chamber. Exhalations matched, making a symphony of sound. She barely heard the sound of her nightgown as it ripped somewhere.

"I think...we are going to need. To remove this. So I won't need to apologize. To your seamstress. Yet again."

Ainslee gripped the neckline and pulled it open. The tissue-thin material gave easily as she separated it. She yanked her shoulders from it. Pushed it off her arms. Down to his belly.

"Or not."

Neal said it as he helped. The sensation of silk along her limbs was slick and cool. That impression was immediately followed by his hands. Heated and electrifying. It created all kinds of sensations. And then ignited them. The nightgown puddled into her lap, creating a mass of pink-toned mist, interspersed with the darker strands of her hair. It separated them. But it didn't obscure.

Neal was erect. Large. Shadowed. Pulsing. And making the fabric wave slightly as she watched!

Ainslee admired him through heavy lashes. She flashed her gaze back to his face. All kinds of muscles throughout his arms and chest flexed and moved as he pushed the mound of material out of the way. Ainslee dared a glance down. Back to his face. Looked again. The garment hadn't torn completely. There was a thin strip of lace across his waist. Glints from it speckled her vision. She'd seen stallions all her life...but never observed them mating. She'd never seen anything like Neal. Hard. Large. Dark-toned. Ainslee subconsciously tensed.

"It won't hurt, babe," Neal spoke. His voice was gruff. Whispered. "I promise."

"'Tis...na' that. I—"

Her words stopped. She didn't have an explanation for how awed she felt. How ready. How excited.

He reached for, and gripped her waist. Used it to lift her and bring her toward him, the move sliding her along his length. Ainslee's gasps were audible. They carried her surprise as sparks shot through her belly. Her back. Her thighs.

Her loins.

They sent stimulation. Restlessness. All kinds of incendiary reactions. He moved her back down. And then slid her up his length again. Over and over. Ainslee grew hot. Wet. Agitated. Her thighs shuddered in anticipation. His fingers tightened. His chest and belly grew even more defined as he continued.

"Neal. I—"

The words were moaned. Neal glanced from his ministrations to her face and back to what he was doing. Yet, still he moved, glossing his shaft with her moisture. Teasing.

Toying.

"I think it's time you learned how to ride, baby."

He stopped. Held her in position for a scant moment. His tip barely sheathed. Her entire being quivered. Silently pleaded. And then he slammed her down onto him. Ainslee screamed as a bubble of absolute pleasure ruptured, showering everything with ecstasy. She didn't need any instruction. She grabbed his shoulders in her hands, her lower legs latched onto his hips, and she rode him. Up. Back down. Using strong, massive lunges forward before slamming back down. His hands assisted, and every movement sent more and more pleasure. The wave of sensation grew. Then it overwhelmed. Lifting her to heaven and allowing her to stay there for the briefest time. It crested and was waning as another one began. And then built. Her breathing grew labored. Her pulse erratic. Everything went taut as she strove toward pleasure.

And this one carried her screams.

Throes of bliss pulsed through her again. She was still experiencing waves of wonder as Neal grabbed her to him, rolled, pushed up, and started pumping. His lips caught hers. His kiss adding immeasurably to the experience. Hot. Heavy. Thrilling. The mattress jumped along with his thrusts, sending thumping sounds into the room. They got faster. Harder. He lifted his head.

"Oh, baby. Oh, Ainslee. Oh, love. Oh, baby."

He gave her the same snarl she'd seen from their wedding night when he'd jumped on this bed. His movements got wilder. More intense.

"Oh, baby! Oh...Ain...*slee!*"

The last part of her name was a deep-toned yell, accompanied by a solid shove into her. Ainslee wrapped her arms about him, holding tightly as he shuddered in place. He'd ceased thrusting, but his loins pulsed with erratic movements within her legs. Everything else about him was immobile. Hard. For the longest time. And still he yelled. He sounded enraged. His eyes were crunched shut. He was turning red. Thick cords stuck out in his neck. Everything about him looked taut. Angered.

Completely dominant.

Ainslee stared, enthralled. Her skin rippled over and over with something that had her completely spellbound. Mesmerized. Almost shocked. She was still watching as his cry ended on a sobbed note. He sucked in another breath. Lowered his head. Caught her gaze.

"I love you," she told him.

He blinked rapidly. A sheen of moisture filmed his eyes. She'd thought they resembled molten silver. Right now they were glossy. Illuminated from within. He smiled and then chuckled, sending a puff of breath onto her skin. And then he whispered something she had a hard time catching.

"Oh, darling. I love you, too. You have no idea. I penetrated the portals of time to find you."

"The portals...of time?"

"Oh. Crap. Don't worry, love. I'll explain everything. But we have time. We have all the time in the world. Well...after tomorrow, we will anyway."

"After...tomorrow?"

He didn't answer. He simply dropped a kiss to the tip of her nose, and collapsed onto the bed beside her. The mattress gave a final lurch before it settled. He shuffled about on the far side of her for a bit, bumping his chest into her shoulder. She didn't realize he was gathering the bed covers until he settled the ivory shaded sheet atop them. He gathered her against him with one arm. Rolled onto his back. And then, he started breathing heavily. As if he slept.

"Neal?"

"Hmm?"

"What happens tomorrow?"

"I love you, Ainslee. And I might be young again, but I still need to recuperate a little. Okay?"

His words were mystifying. And something else. They sent a shiver of something like fear through her belly. It sounded in her voice despite how she tried to sound nonchalant. "What do you mean...young again?"

"Wow. Making love to you is an amazing experience. One, I can't even fathom. It even loosens my tongue. So now...I really have to beg for mercy, darling."

"Mercy?"

"From your questions."

"But—?"

"Do you love me?" He turned his head and tipped an eye open to watch her answer.

"Aye."

"Trust me?"

"Aye."

"Then trust me to explain everything. You may not believe me, but I will still tell you. But not...until tomorrow night. You have my word. Tonight I need to hold you. Make love to you again. Hold you some more. Revel in the sheer good fortune that I have found you. The world can intrude tomorrow. Please?"

Ainslee didn't answer for a long moment. He grew tense beside her while he waited although his expression didn't change. He'd given her everything she asked. Fulfilled her every dream. She loved him with every fiber of her being. Even if he told her he'd committed murder or some other heinous act, it wouldn't change her feelings. Love was too strong. Too vital. Too all-powerful. The breadth of it stunned. The scope amazed.

Ainslee smiled tremulously. Then, nodded. Snuggled against his warmth, wrapped within his arms.

And slept.

CHAPTER THIRTY-FOUR

EVEN BEFORE DAYBREAK, THE DAY was problematic. The sky was heavy with cloud cover, although it wasn't raining yet. Wind gusts ruffled the air. The temperature was brisk. Mist hovered near the ground, obscuring details. Each breath contained a hint of moisture. It wasn't an auspicious day for a grouse hunt.

But it looked perfect for murder.

Neal had watched his visage in the mirror with interest. He'd seen paintings in museums of sporting gentlemen from past eras. A few had even been depictions of Scottish gentry. All Neal needed was a couple of dogs at his feet and a blunderbuss cradled in his arm. He'd look perfect.

Mason had been anxious as he assisted Neal into a cuff-less, off-white linen shirt, beneath a brown leather vest with lots of pockets, followed by a thickly woven plaid that wrapped about his hips before Mason stepped up onto a stool in order to drape a length of it over one of Neal's shoulders. The end was tucked under his belt at the back. Fringe from the plaid skimmed the backs of his knees. His sporran was plain brown leather, the match to his vest. A handkerchief was folded and pocketed in the sporran, beside a flask that contained a dram of whiskey. A tam of brown tweed covered his head. He carried the usual assortment of weaponry. Multiple daggers lined his belt in the front, while two *skean dhu* were stuffed into his tasseled, woolen socks. Brown leather boots completed his attire.

The valet had wanted to cancel. Neal disagreed. The timing was too good. For once, time was on his side. He reassured the man while dressing. They had a good idea of the plot. Players were assembling. They had the best type of witnesses, in the form of the British solicitors.

All Neal had to do was avoid getting shot.

The plan was to stay within two feet of Garrick. The man couldn't shoot him from that distance without backing away, perhaps portraying a stumble. Neal would just have to move faster and trust in Cedric. The gamekeeper would be at Neal's other side, watching Garrick for any sudden move. But, Neal felt using Garrick was too chancy. Too many variables were involved. Aunt Margaret would want a surer thing.

That meant there would be an accomplice. Maybe more than one. The Honor Guard would be responsible. That's why they all carried rifles. Besides, as he told Mason, delay wouldn't end the threat. It would simply change the game plan. Diminish the timeline. And desperate foes usually did desperate things.

He didn't need Mason to tell him what the optimum time for a hunting accident would be. It was obvious. Early morning. With mist filling the meadow. Horses getting hobbled. Dogs running about. Men checking firearms. That's when Neal would need to be the most diligent. And Mason begged him to do so as he stepped back and pronounced Neal ready.

Two Honor Guardsmen in Straithcairn regalia met Neal at the base of the chieftain steps and accompanied him to the stables. They watched in silence as his cousin joined him. Men and horses milled about the stable yard, lit with torches. The air was fraught with storm-filled intensity. Shivers rippled along Neal's arm as he requested Dragonbreath. Garrick was waiting. He wore a light gray leather vest atop his kilt and a matching tam. The combination made him easy to spot in the dimness. Neal guessed the reason. He and his cousin were like in stature. His accomplice might need a way of making certain he hit the right man.

Garrick was amused by Neal's choice of mount, smiling widely as the huge stallion was saddled and prepared. Neal had a moment of worry that he'd make an easy target before they even arrived. Dragonbreath was the largest horse in the entourage.

But Garrick wouldn't have known which mount Neal would select. The odds of his cousin placing an accomplice anywhere before their arrival at Huntsman's Dale was remote. These rifles weren't that accurate. Even in the hands of a marksman. It was too chancy.

Besides, Dragonbreath had proven his docility. And that's what mattered to Neal.

The field of play looked just as bad as Mason had anticipated. Daylight wasn't putting much of a dent in the elements. A light, misty kind of rain was falling. Waist-high meadow grass was wafting with wind gusts. Neal dismounted, with the usual amount of thigh and ass showing, although nobody seemed to notice. The two barristers were standing off to one side, stomping their feet and grumbling – probably about the weather – although they shouldn't complain. They were both attired in long trousers beneath coats. The old Neal would have envied them.

Garrick appeared to be frowning as he looked over the assemblage of gamekeepers. Some held to dogs leashes, some cradled blunderbusses in their arms, some had the smaller version of a blunderbuss called *dragon* carried beneath their belts. And all of them had a flintlock rifle strapped to the back of one shoulder.

"Ready to flush some grouse, men?"

One of the men called out. There was a chorus of 'ayes'.

"I say...Niall?"

Garrick turned toward Neal. His gun negligibly swung with him. Cedric caught the barrel and lifted before it reached Neal.

"Careful, lad," the man cautioned, as if it was incidental.

"Yes?"

Neal replied in an off-hand fashion as if absorbed with his own gun. He shuffled it, and tried to act uncomfortable with the piece. Clicked his tongue and sighed as if dispirited and looked toward his cousin. Garrick had a gamekeeper behind him. The man wasn't familiar and his cap was too low on his forehead to make out his expression. Neal hadn't counted on him. He watched as one of his Honor Guard dressed in nondescript leather and kilt stepped toward the man, obviously intent on shadowing him.

Knowing he was protected with such vigilance gave Neal such a warm sensation, he looked quickly back to his gun before it showed somewhere. It was too dim to make out expressions this morning. Body language was going to tell the story. Garrick's was saying all kinds of things. The man was really pleased about something.

But what?

"The gamekeepers all...carry flintlocks this morn."

"Oh. Yeah. I heard we have a herd of red deer in the area."

"Red deer, you say?"

"I'm not amiss to fresh venison on the table. Do the rifles...bother you?"

"Oh, no. No. 'Tis nothing like that."

And the man snickered.

That was his clue. Garrick no longer had to worry over what might be said should a lead slug hit Neal rather than a load of pellets.

...because his accomplice had a rifle.

Damn it.

That extended the potential murder field from a maximum range of for-ty-two feet, to about fifty yards. Neal did a summary glance about the area. A strand of trees was situated within range. There was an arrangement of standing stones a bit to the right – sticking above the grass haphazardly, looking like a rough-hewn, miniature Stonehenge. A hill on either side delineated the valley. Both were too far for sniper distance. Not with a flintlock rifle. But every other inch of the area seemed to be covered in meadow grass. Thistle-strewn. Waving in the wind. Thigh-high on Neal, it provided a perfect camouflage. Everywhere he looked was a potential sniper spot.

But, wait.

A sense of déjà vu smacked into Neal. It took a moment to realize why.

This was where he'd had his 'accident'! Been spit out of a time portal. Jettisoned into a new life. And met the love of his. He probably glowed at the recollection. He kept his gaze on the ground while he tempered his heartbeats back to normal.

"We ready?" Garrick asked at his side.

"Oh. Sure. Why not?" Neal cleared his throat to speak loudly. "Gentle-men?"

"I say, Barristers Kingston? Bon? We ready?"

Garrick called out to the Englishmen. Dogs were set loose, baying almost the instant they started running through the grass, leaving a myriad of trails. Dark spots flew up from the grass before them. Perhaps twenty feet in distance. They rose ten feet. Fifteen. Twenty feet. Neal swung his blunderbuss upward. Fired. Beside him Garrick did the same. Several birds dropped.

Neal held out the spent rifle without looking. Cedric took it and handed him a loaded weapon. On his left side, Neal felt Garrick and his man doing the same.

"You aim appears to be much improved, cousin," Garrick remarked.

"Yeah. Go figure," Neal relied.

"Go...figure?"

"It's an expression. It means—"

Something glinted on the flattened trail of grass before him. Neal's glance dropped. He focused. It looked like...gold. He knelt to check it out, heard the sound of a rifle blast, followed instantly by a close thud. Then Garrick cried out, but his voice was lost amidst the noise of every gun in the area responding. There was a series of loud bursts that sounded like a Revolutionary War battlefield reenactment. Neal spun and brought his blunderbuss to bear on Garrick. It wouldn't have mattered. The man was reeling backward, his mouth wide while his hands clasped to his chest, attempting to stop a dark spot that just kept growing in the center of his vest. It was akin to watching a movie in slow motion. Garrick staggered another step. Fell. First to his knees. And then onto his face.

Cedric was on his knees beside Garrick, rolling him over. Neal could hear each gurgled breath the man took. He moved to crawl toward him, but the bit of gold he'd glimpsed bit into his knee. Neal lifted his leg, scraped mud and grass off the spot, and pulled his signet ring from the mess.

His spiral signet ring. The one he'd been wearing in the Cessna Citation X when this had all started. He stared at it uncomprehendingly. The ring shouldn't even exist in this dimension. But it did. And that bit of gold had just saved his life. He tucked it into a vest pocket and lunged toward Garrick.

"Chest shot," Cedric said.

"Yeah. Sounds like lung." Neal replied.

"Do na' so much as twitch."

The man sounded deadly serious. Neal stood. Looked about. A haze of smoke now added to the general melee. It was difficult to see anything with clarity. Men loomed out of the dimness as they approached. The Honor Guardsman who'd been watching Garrick's gamekeeper was the speaker. He had his dragon out and held within an inch or two of Garrick's man. The fellow dropped the pistol he'd been holding. Neal didn't need to ask where it had aimed. He could guess. A man reached them. Another. Dogs were still baying in the distance. The sound of flapping feathers as grouse took wing could be heard if he chose to listen for them.

He didn't.

Neal turned his attention to Garrick, and the man's fight for air. More men arrived. Cedric stood and started shouting orders that Neal probably should have given. He didn't know what was wrong with him. Everything felt surreal, as if someone else was standing here. Neal was just observing. His every breath was loud in his ears. He had the same issue with each heartbeat. It was difficult to hear over them.

"Somebody send to the castle for a litter! You, there! Take a horse and ride! And you! Go get the dogs!"

"What the devil just happened?"

The barristers arrived. One went to a knee beside Garrick. The other one looked from Neal to his cousin and back. Neal didn't know which one had spoken or who to address. Cedric answered.

"'Tis clear. We have a hunting accident on our hands."

"A hunting accident?"

"Aye. Garrick Straith's been shot."

"By who? You?"

One of the barristers pointed at Neal. Cedric answered again.

"Na' him. His weapon has na' been fired. Here. Check it yourself."

Neal probably should be embarrassed. With the exception of the barristers, his was probably the only weapon that hadn't been fired. Cedric gestured for the blunderbuss. Neal gave it to him. Cedric handed it to Barrister Kingston. The man sniffed the barrel. Handed it back to Cedric.

"Then who is the shooter?"

More men arrived, adding hulking masses to the scene. All kinds of shuffling noises. Low-toned words. Garrick was struggling for each breath now. His body arched upward with each effort.

"He's suffering shock. We need a blanket."

Neal's voice worked although it sounded like he was chewing gravel. Someone handed him a plaid. Neal bent to place it carefully about Garrick. The fellow looked almost as ashen as his vest. There wasn't anything anyone could do. Even if this was the twenty-first century, and Garrick had access to the most advanced trauma care, his injury would have been fatal. Neal stood back up.

"'Tis Lachlan!"

Someone shouted it from the tree stand, across the field.

"Lachlan!" Someone else reiterated it.

"What?"

A chorus of deep voices asked it. Neal's head felt pressurized. His ears filled with his own respiration. Heartbeat. And his voice as he added it to the mix.

"The bastard shot his own brother?"

"What?" The blend of voices asked again.

"'Tis a foul morn!"

"Nae! 'Tis murder! Of the most wicked! Brother against brother!"

"Murder!"

"No!"

Neal yelled it, using his largest voice. Everyone quieted almost instantly. He didn't have to raise his voice to be heard. He raised it anyway.

"Listen to me! Everyone. This is not murder. This is a hunting accident."

"A hunting accident? Are you daft?" Barrister Kingston asked.

"Think, men! Who among us wishes to walk into my aunt's rooms with the news that her eldest son was just murdered by her youngest? Well? Who?"

Grumbling could be heard from the crowd. A lot of whispers. A cough.

Neal went down on a knee beside Garrick. Gestured for Kingston to join him, so both barristers could hear. He bent close to Garrick's ear.

"Garrick! Garrick!"

The man shuddered and then spoke. "Aye?"

A froth of bloody foam accompanied the word. Neal pulled the handkerchief from his sporran and wiped at Garrick's lips.

"Was this murder?"

"I—"

More bloody foam spewed from the man's mouth. Neal sopped at it, too.

"Do we tell your mother it was murder?" he asked in a loud voice.

The man jerked. Did it again. And finally answered.

"No."

"Well. There you have it. Barristers Kingston and Bon. What say you? Was this a hunting accident or not?"

"Where is Lachlan?" someone asked.

"Uh. We will need a bag or two to fetch him."

"What? Why?" Neal asked.

"He was in the trees, yer grace. The men are verra good shots. The smoke gave away his position...and that means there is na' much left o' him."

"Oh."

Neal didn't know what else to say. He placed his handkerchief beneath Garrick's chin and rose to his feet again. Barrister Kingston followed him. Barrister Bon stayed beside Garrick. And then, they all heard the sound of Ainslee, calling his name.

CHAPTER THIRTY-FIVE

LADY ILIFF'S WARDROBE HAD INCLUDED more than one riding habit. Ainslee had fallen for this one the moment she'd spied it. Crafted of a sapphire blue satin with black velvet piping, it was extraordinarily luxurious for the Highlands. The satin exactly matched her eyes, according to her maids. Beth, Mira, and even Doreen had voiced the same opinion. The seamstress, Mistress Aggie had let out seams in the back and sides to give Ainslee breathing room, but the jacket was still a tight fit. The skirt had the opposite issue. Beyond voluminous, it was meant to worn with no fewer than eight petticoats and a set of ruffled drawers. Ainslee had opted out of most of that. It was a good choice. The excess width gave her the ability to ride astride without violating too much decorum.

She hadn't slept in. She hadn't known why. Something had awakened her earlier than usual. She'd rung the servant bell. She had a day planned of touring the first floor, checking stores and whatever else was down in the windowless bowels of the original tower. She was the chatelaine of Castle Straith now. She wasn't looking to Lady Blair for help, nor would she accept any. Ainslee had been debating between a light-blue day-gown and the tan one, neither of which should show much dust, when Beth and Mira had arrived, alert as if it was broad daylight and not pre-dawn.

That's when Ainslee learned of the grouse hunt. It was all her maids could speak of. The castle was abuzz with it. The duke could be in danger. Storms filled the sky – an ill omen to be sure. The weather was dire. Danger imminent. The duke didn't realize the extent of his aunt's hatred. Or his cousin's jealousy. Someone needed to do something.

If the duke perished...?

Beth hadn't finished the words. She didn't need to. But nothing they thought came close to Ainslee's reaction. Her maids might think they knew what would ensue, but no one could guess the pain that had stabbed nearly through Ainslee at the thought of losing Neal. Her eyes blurred with tears she rapidly blinked from existence. That's when she'd directed Mira to this riding habit. But everything took too long!

She was the Duchess of Straithcairn. She stood at the head of a proud, Highland clan. She could no longer ride about the countryside willy-nilly. She had responsibilities. Duties. A position to uphold.

Ainslee stood in shock as she realized it.

How had she changed this much?

In two days?

She knew what had happened. She'd fallen in love. Completely. Totally. And she wanted him to be proud of her. So, she'd stood and worried, caught up in a personal purgatory of possibilities as her maids helped her don long stockings with bows at the thighs to hold them up. A set of bloomers. Two petticoats. She'd trembled while all the buttons were fastened up her back, but hadn't betrayed her impatience or anxiety.

Exactly as a duchess should.

Ainslee had walked at a sedate pace down the chieftain's stairs, carrying a cloak over one arm. She crossed the great hall, holding her skirts aloft. Listened to the heels of her riding boots as they clacked on the wooden floor. That seemed to take forever, too.

As did the walk to the stables.

One of Neal's Honor Guardsmen met her at the front stoop. He nodded in greeting as she covered up with her cloak. The guardsman shadowed her all the way to the stables. His presence warmed Ainslee considerably. He stayed five paces behind her as she walked from stall to stall, greeting horses. MacCreary joined her at the second stall. They discussed a potential mount for a morning ride. A groom. The best place for a run. As if she had nothing better to do this morning.

They'd reached Nightfall's stall. He'd been brushed and groomed, and accepted her presence with a head toss in her direction. He ignored MacCreary and the guardsman. Just as he ignored the stable hands milling about. She talked over Nightfall's recovery and how well he looked. Opened the stall to what sounded like a combined inhaled breath from those watching. Greeted the stallion with a rub along his blaze. He whickered in response.

And then, her façade fell apart.

Shouts sounded at the stable opening. The sound of thudding hooves came next as a rider arrived. Ainslee stood, listening intently, and that's when she heard the words that sent her heart to the pit of her belly. The messenger had ridden hard. He spoke through gasps for breath.

"There's been...a hunting accident! Send...a litter! Huntsman's Dale!"

"A hunting accident?"

"Hunting accident?"

Hunting accident. The words kept repeating, accompanying each heartbeat. Ainslee didn't think. She acted. She grabbed a handful of Nightfall's mane, pulled him around, and launched off his water trough, straddling the stallion. He was wider than she'd expected. The skirts rode up her ankles with her move. He shook his head, loosening her grip, so she grabbed higher up his head with both hands. Scooted up to whisper toward his ear. He trembled but didn't otherwise react. It's all she had to go by.

"It's the duke! You must get me to him, my big handsome *gaol*. You must!"

Nightfall started moving. Muscles rippled everywhere she touched as he trotted through the stables. Groomsmen jumped out of her way. Ainslee ducked to clear a beam. Another one. She heard MacCreary shouting orders behind her. Assumed he'd get someone up on horseback to accompany her. But Ainslee didn't care a fig about a groom, or decorum at the moment. All she cared about was reaching Neal.

The stallion broke into a canter when they cleared the portcullis. Ainslee lost the cloak as a spike grabbed her hood, yanking the cloak from her, as well as loosening some of her braids. She bent closer to Nightfall's neck, matching to him, so that when the walls opened up she was securely attached. Even as he bucked twice before breaking into a ground-eating gallop.

Nightfall was amazing. Ainslee had never been so high. Nor moved so swiftly. He also seemed to know where she needed to go. He turned, leapt a section of the wall, and went through high meadow grass as if it were nothing.

Wind lifted her hair into a veil. Ruffled her skirts along Nightfall's sides. Lightning crashed in the distance. The rolling boom of thunder accompanied it. The horse surged forward with each one, but didn't falter otherwise. They leapt a burn, running high with water. Started up a hill, covered in shale. Ainslee clung in place, tightening her thighs as he crested the hill and started sliding the other side, slipping occasionally on loose rock. Raindrops splashed her face, wetting her dress. They cooled. Raised goose bumps. But hampered her vision even more.

Ainslee narrowed her eyes.

The standing stones came into view.

Moments later, Nightfall reached the arrangements of monolithic stones. Passed between them. Crested the next hill. Groups of men were standing in the bottom of the valley. Several more were near the trees. Some were walking between them. And she couldn't see Neal.

"Dear God! Not Neal. Please, God. Not Neal. Please? Please?"

The litany didn't stop. She kept repeating the prayer in time with Nightfall's strides.

"Please, God? Not Neal! Please?"

Someone saw her. Shouted. Pointed. Nightfall bore down on them at full speed. Hooves thudding. Chunks of turf flying. She clung to him. Her hair was a loose mass that streamed behind her. It blended with Nightfall, and gave the horse the appearance of wings. The skirts of her dark habit rippled in waves along the stallion's sides. She looked like a banshee.

And none of that mattered.

She started calling for him.

"Neal! Neal!"

One of the men waved. Another. Nightfall sped past anyone walking, bore down on the group. The stallion stopped just shy of blasting through the gathering. Without one hint of instruction from her. He stood there, sides heaving, breath fogging the air before his nose. Ainslee slid from his side. Stumbled.

But she couldn't see him!

Ainslee scanned faces with rising anxiety. Most of the men were wide-eyed and slack-jawed with astonishment at her arrival. She didn't care. She couldn't spot Neal.

"Ne-al!"

She tried to shout it, but the name came out sobbed. Broken with fear. The gathering started moving back, parting for her. And in the midst of them she saw him.

Alive.

"Neal!"

Her cry carried relief. Absolute joy. He stood with his mouth also open at her appearance. Nothing had ever looked so wondrous. Ainslee didn't know how she got there, but a moment later she was in his arms. Wrapped within them, and then lifted off the ground.

And that's when she burst into tears.

CHAPTER THIRTY-SIX

THE DAY FULFILLED ITS PROMISE. The storm broke as the cart arrived. Everyone carried extra plaids in their packs. Ainslee sat atop Dragonbreath wrapped in one. She was completely covered. Impossible to verify identity.

Her presence still affected him.

Neal caught himself glancing more than once up to the lone figure sitting atop the large stallion. Dragonbreath was an impressive horse. He was eclipsed by the dark stallion that stood beside him. It was unbelievable that she'd ridden Nightfall. Even more so, since she'd done it without a saddle, reins, or even the bit thing in its mouth. Nightfall still hovered next to Ainslee as if she held an invisible rope connecting them. Neal hadn't been the only one stunned as the big horse had borne down on them, and stopped dead. He'd been so amazed his voice hadn't worked to answer her.

He shook his head, spraying droplets. Swiped at his brow. There was no longer any rush to their movements, although they'd all be glad to reach shelter. There was nothing anyone could do. Garrick had breathed his last. The men were all solemn as Garrick's body was draped across his saddle. The gamekeeper he'd had with him was trussed up and draped across another horse. He'd probably still be proclaiming innocence except for the gag Cedric had used on him. What remained of Lachlan rested in the cart, covered with at least two plaids.

Neal approached Dragonbreath and eyed him for a moment. Ainslee caught his glance before shifting closer to the horse's neck, giving Neal room. Nobody appeared to be looking. He'd just have to mount by himself. Neal gathered the reins in his left hand before holding to the pommel, stuck his left foot in the stirrup, and heaved up and into the saddle. He was fairly pleased with himself, too, except for the puddle of plaid material between his legs. That took a moment or two to adjust before he was situated.

He blinked more rain from his eyes, and then swiped his hand across his hair, plastering it to his skull, sticking the ends onto his shoulders. He probably should have pulled the kilt band from his back and covered his head with it. It made a rain shelter. He'd seen others doing that. It made sense.

And then Ainslee leaned into him and made everything on his body vibrate to an entirely different frequency. Warmth radiated from where she touched. Contact with the elements no longer mattered. She looked up at him, and smiled tremulously. It didn't match her eyes. Even in a rain-soaked mid-morn, he could see her worry.

"What is it?"

She shook her head and turned forward again. The top of her plaid was just beneath his chin. Neal wrapped his right arm about her and pulled her up and over the pommel and onto his lap. And then held her there. Someone gave the signal to proceed. It wasn't him. Neal settled into line behind Cedric. The big black stallion Ainslee had brought started walking alongside Dragonbreath. Nightfall's head was down. Rain dripped off his mane, tail, and fetlocks. Defining musculature. That horse was like a big black shadow. Devilishly dark. With a temperament that matched. And she'd ridden it? Bareback?

He still found it difficult to believe.

"Ainslee?" he prompted.

"Forgive me."

Her whisper was slight.

Neal stiffened with surprise. "For what?"

"I was...indecorous."

"In-what?"

"Decorous."

"Please say you're joking."

"I am...the Duchess of Straithcairn. Duchesses do na' ride about the countryside at a gallop. And they never ride unaccompanied."

"Oh. Honey. If that's indecorous, please? Don't let me stop you. Or anyone else."

"My behavior...shocked everyone. I know. I saw their faces."

"Oh. Babe." He chuckled. It lifted her. "What you saw was pure amazement. There isn't a man here who wasn't stunned at your arrival on Blackie there. Bareback? At that pace? I thought you were going to run us over before you stopped him."

"I did na' stop Nightfall."

"Right. Look. I was told you were fey. I didn't believe it. But your ability with horses? I got to tell you. That's pure magic, babe. Pure."

She giggled. His heart lightened.

"I mean, come on. They call Nightfall a devil horse. And, if you'd looked around, you'd have noticed that nobody went near him. Know why? They're afraid of him. I know the feeling. I'm afraid of him."

"There's naught to fear."

"For you. And look. He's following you like a puppy. It's pretty unbelievable. *That* is what the men were stunned over. Oh. Crap."

"What is it?"

"We're running."

The horse started moving at an odd pace. Neal jerked his thigh muscles tight in response. It was a subconscious move. It lifted both of them from the horse's back. Ainslee chuckled. It wasn't remotely funny.

"This is a trot."

"It's a death-defying run."

She snorted back what was probably laughter. "You act as though you've never ridden afore."

"You don't say."

"Aye. I do."

Neal smiled to himself. It was déjà vu again. Back to when he'd first arrived and Rory repeated what he'd said. "Well. That's just one of the things we will be discussing, darling. Later. After I meet with my aunt. And take a shower."

"A...shower?"

"Rainfall means I get a shower. I'll show you that, too. You'll like it. I think. We should invent one...except we need to figure out how to warm the water first. I know. You haven't got the foggiest idea what I'm talking about. I have a lot to explain. After I speak with Lady Blair. I'm not looking forward to that particular interview, in case you wondered."

"You do na' have to be the one to tell her."

"I'm the laird, darling. It's my duty. But I'm taking her solicitors with me. And Cedric."

Dragonbreath's motion wasn't too difficult to follow, after all. It was like a steady jog with a hitch to it. Neal eased back down into the saddle and rolled forward and backward with the horse's motion. He was rather pleased with himself. Ainslee gave a low whistle. Beside them, Nightfall whickered in response. Neal swiped at his forehead again and looked over at the big stallion. Dragonbreath had been the largest horse they'd taken out for the hunt. Nightfall was a good six inches or so taller. He was rain-soaked. Black as pitch. Silently trotting alongside them in perfect sync with Dragonbreath.

And she wondered why the men had been open-mouth and stunned at her arrival?

"What will you tell her?"

Ainslee brought his attention back to her with the question.

"Who?"

"Lady Blair."

"Oh. Her."

"You can na' tell her the truth."

"Why not?"

"Oh, Neal. She'll be devastated."

"So? It's her fault. She meddled with destiny. If I hadn't bent down at that exact moment, it would be me draped over a horse back there. Not Garrick. And my aunt would be celebrating. Forgive me if I do not feel empathy. She tried to orchestrate events. Now she gets to reap the consequences. You can't manipulate the future, darling. There are too many variables. Human nature is just one of them. Unseen events another. That's why—"

Neal's voice stopped. His heart felt like it did the same thing. His ability to breathe got affected next. His brain wasn't frozen. It raced ahead. What in the hell had he just said? Verbally figured out? *Done?*

Oh, shit.

Oh, shit.

Oh, shit.

"Fu—!" Neal caught the expletive. But not the growl that emanated from deep in his chest somewhere.

"Neal?"

"I could really use cell technology about now!" He muttered it from between clenched teeth.

"Cell tech...nology?"

"A way to get a message out. And received. Instantaneously. I need to recall a messenger. Ah!"

Neal lifted his chin and sent the cry into the air. Murmurs sounded from about him as the men heard and assigned a supposed reason. He didn't notice much, and cared less. Rain splashed his face. It chilled. Carried dread. The afternoon wasn't just filled with gloom anymore. It carried a large helping of foreboding as well.

"Neal?"

Ainslee was shaking. Her voice reflected it. Neal pulled her closer to him as if to provide shelter. He bent his head toward her.

"Forgive me, darling. I...have to work things out. And—crap. I wish I had that paper roll. And stinkin' markers!"

"Markers?"

"I need to get this down. I work better if I can draw visuals. Large ones. Interconnected. Random and continuous. So I can step back and look at it. Ponder. Evaluate. You know. Brainstorm."

"Brainstorm?"

"Oh, Ainslee. We have a lot to discuss. Trust me. An awful lot. We may have to pull an all-nighter. We'll need tea. Pots and pots of it."

She tipped her head to give him a puzzled look.

"I'm not fond of the coffee around here. It's barely drinkable. That's one thing I might be able to solve. Without incurring future world consequences, that is."

The black rock wall of the castle entrance came into sight as a dark smudge against a lighter sky. It loomed closer. The horses slowed. The entrance to the corridor swallowed them. There were puddles about the ground. Neal could hear the splashing of hooves. Heavy breathing of their mounts. But not much else.

He was using the time to prepare mentally. Steel himself for the upcoming meeting.

Lady Blair's screams followed Neal down the hall. Through the arched entrance to the east wing where she still resided. And farther. They even seemed to leach through solid wooden doors that shut behind him.

Her expression had changed the moment she'd caught sight of Neal amidst his Honor Guard. That was unfortunate. He'd hoped she'd been given a recounting of the hunting accident already, and wouldn't be expecting her sons. Her lack of the correct information was instantly apparent. Lady Blair had gone from an expectant and pleased countenance to one that was tight-lipped and ashen-colored. And that was just from hearing of Garrick's demise.

She'd crumpled when told of Lachlan's death.

Neal hadn't stayed. To commiserate or observe. Despite how his heart had twinged with her soul-wracking sobs. He didn't know what to say. Or do. So, he'd turned about and walked away, leaving her in the company of Barristers Kingston and Bon. He had no affinity toward them. They'd come to discredit him. At Lady Blair's invitation. They could earn their stay.

Neal hadn't just been accompanied by Cedric, either. Eight members of his Honor Guard had been at his back. Neal had ordered the physician sent for. Given instructions. He didn't couch it in what would be futuristic terms, but Lady Blair was on suicide watch.

He fully expected her to do so.

Neal told himself Lady Blair had earned everything she now suffered. Her grief didn't bother him. He knew it for a lie the moment the thought occurred. Her agonized cries raised goose bumps all along his skin as he walked. Up sets of stairs. Back down others. Beneath arched entries. Down tapestry-lined halls. His Honor Guard accompanied him, one man leading. Neal hadn't been in the chapel before, nor seen the vicar in muted attire. The place exuded an aura of sanctity. Reverence. Things he'd never suspected existed before. They discussed interment. The castle had a crypt beneath the chapel, but it hadn't been used in decades. There was the cemetery outside. On land sheltered by castle walls. That would do.

For both men.

The entire time, Neal swore he could hear Lady Blair's agony. It was like a shroud he couldn't shed. It added to unease that had started up when he realized he'd done basically the same thing. He'd tampered with fate. Tried to align destiny. Put things in motion toward a certain outcome. But he shouldn't reap a like penalty. He hadn't done it for personal gain.

Well...not wholly.

Oh, man.

The vicar was a long-winded speaker. Neal's mind wasn't paying much attention. He had a lot to mull. He reassured himself that he wasn't splitting hairs here. He hadn't done what Lady Blair had. She, and her cohorts, had planned murder. Neal was different. He was planning on saving humanity.

That was altruistic.

Not selfish.

He hadn't looked at all the pitfalls, because he hadn't taken the time nor drawn it up, but his plan couldn't go far wrong. And if he could solve the global warming issues due to carbon footprint problems before they even started, shouldn't he?

If everything went according to plan...

And nothing untoward happened...

Ah!

There were so many unpredictable events! So many years to account for!

He'd sent Iain with clear instructions, but those could be misinterpreted. He hadn't written them down. They were to be given to a broker, but what if the man wasn't trustworthy? What if Iain Straithmore misinterpreted them? Neal wanted stock in iron first. As steel became available on the market, sell iron and buy steel. By the late nineteenth century, that stock needed to be sold so they could buy into electricity...and back pretty much anything Nikolai Tesla was working on. Make certain to buy a major share of Ford Motor Company stock. Enough to assure the design engineers put electrical engines in the Model T and not gasoline combustion ones. But whatever happens, do not buy petroleum stock.

Ever.

Even with variables, none of that sounded disastrous.

The vicar apparently finished his recitation of the memorial service he'd provide on the Sabbath. A long span of silence was Neal's only clue. He thanked the vicar and left. Honor Guardsmen accompanied his every step. Along the same, or similar halls. Up and down short flights of steps. They finally reached the oldest section of the castle, the one containing the dungeons. There was a plain wooden door in the main foyer. It opened to a set of narrow spiral stone steps. Walking down them felt like entering something akin to purgatory. The stone down here was rough-cut. Never smoothed. It looked more than secure. This place was impenetrable. The constable met him at the bottom of the steps. Gave him the news. They had a confession. It was exactly as they'd thought.

That should have broken through the strange aura that surrounded Neal, the one resounding with the sound of Lady Blair's anguish.

It didn't.

Neal didn't linger in the dungeons. Torches may have lit the interior but it was still dark. Dank. Cold. Hopeless-feeling. There was nothing more to do. The fellow was secured. Fed. Given water. A blanket. A bucket. He could be dealt with later. After the funerals. Neal and his escort walked back up the spiral stone steps. A sense of light permeated each step upward. They reached the second floor. The door to the dungeon was shut behind them. Neal took a large breath. It tasted of freedom and life. The Honor Guardsmen accompanying him all matched with their own deep inhalations. They might have felt the same. Neal didn't ask. They didn't offer.

Neal and his retinue entered the double doors beneath the chieftain stairs. The guardsmen removed their tams. Held them over their hearts. Bowed their heads toward Neal. Still in complete silence.

Neal's heart swelled. His chest warmed markedly. A knot closed off his throat. He cleared his throat and nodded in response. Six guardsmen turned about and left. Marching down the hall in cadence. Shoulder-to-shoulder. Two abreast. Their kilts swayed. Weapons jangled. It was extremely impressive.

The remaining two took up a post, one at either side of the chieftain steps. Neal climbed the right side, absorbing a silence that had a presence. Like a withheld breath.

Just waiting to exhale.

CHAPTER THIRTY-SEVEN

AINSLEE HAD BEEN PACING HER room when he knocked. He knew because her face lit up at the sight of him, she made as if to rush to him, but then she checked it, and a moment later resumed her steps. All highly interesting. Neal pondered her for a bit. She reached one wall of her room. Spun around. Started back. He didn't think he'd taken that long, but he must have. Her maids had attended her. She'd probably bathed in her chamber. Had her hair re-braided into a barely contained waterfall of tresses down her back. She was definitely re-dressed.

Well.

It was all probably for the best.

A joint shower on his balcony was bound to be cold, and she'd been covered in a soaked plaid when he'd last seen her. At the front steps. He'd lowered her to the ground, watched, as did everyone else, while she said something to the big black stallion that kept him meekly following Drag-onbreath, and then she'd mounted the steps into the castle.

Now, she wore a dark rose colored gown that made her skin pristine clear, her eyes strikingly noticeable, and her waist even tinier. The gown hadn't been altered yet. The amount of material used for her skirt was an entertaining feature, since she wasn't wearing pontoon things beneath it. With her movements, she snagged more than one scatter rug. She also appeared to be sweeping the floor at the same time.

Neal tried not to smile at the thought. She turned and caught him at it. Her chin lowered and she gave him a remonstrating look that should work wonders on their children. Neal immediately sobered and attempted to look contrite. And he couldn't imagine why.

"Did...you meet with Lady Blair?" she finally spoke.

"Yes."

"How did she take it?"

"Poorly."

"Should I...offer to assist?"

"I don't believe either of us would be welcomed, love. We might even be in the way. She's under the care of a fellow who calls himself a physician. He's using leeches. Uh." Neal couldn't prevent the grimace before he continued, "he's also concocting some sort of preparation for her to take. Remind me to never get ill around here."

"'Twill be laudanum. She takes it for head pain."

"She gets headaches? Really? I thought she only gave them."

She straightened, lifted her chin to regard him from across the room. That remonstrating look of hers apparently held full censure. Her disciplinary tactics appeared to already be in place and functioning well. She wouldn't have to use much more than an expression to berate a future Straith. He almost pitied them.

"Have I...done something wrong?" Neal asked.

"Of course na'."

"Oh. I get it. You are attempting the decorous thing again, aren't you?"

She blushed and dropped her gaze. Her voice was difficult to hear. "I am the Duchess of Straithcairn. I need to start acting like it."

"Not around me, babe. I love you just as you are. Spontaneous. Loving. Young."

"I...shamed the position."

"Says who? I'll sack them immediately."

"No! Please. No one said anything. I have been thinking." She looked back up at him. "I should be a bit less...um. Spontaneous. A bit more... regal. So you will be proud of me." The last was whispered.

"Oh. Babe. I *am* very proud of you. Immensely. Completely. Crap. The last thing we need is protocol. Especially not when we're alone. Everybody needs a place where they can let their hair down."

She frowned. "My hair is usually down. I do na' think I can get it all up unless I cut it."

"I didn't mean that. See? There's an example. I continually say things you don't understand. I need to explain why."

"You were in the navy. You have seen a lot of the world. I have only read about it. Seen pictures in books."

"Right. Well. I have to admit. That is a really good cover story. You have no idea. But...getting back to topic: the phrase 'letting your hair down' means...um. Let's see. Relax. Yeah. That's it. It means to be yourself. Not worry over projecting an image. Not have to guard your tongue or thoughts every second. Everybody needs a place where they can do that. I love you, Ainslee. I wouldn't change a damn thing about you. We have a lot to go over, darling. A lot. You may think I've gone mad before I finish. Um. May I suggest...a change of venue?"

"To where?"

"Let's use my room. It's larger. And the floor could use a good dusting."

Her eyebrows met in another frown. Neal had a hard time stifling the grin. She was just so cute!

"I do na' understand."

"Your skirts are doing an excellent job on the floor. I can tell where you've walked by the shine."

She glanced down. Lifted her skirts to reveal a wadded rug before a slipper. Looked back over at him.

"Are you...poking fun at my attire?"

Neal chuckled. He couldn't help it. "Oh. Honey. Never. Not in a million years. And that is a fairly decent segue to what I have to say. Only it's not a million. More like two hundred. And then some."

"The woman must be suffering horribly."

Neal regarded Ainslee for several moments. Sighed heavily. Assumed a somber expression again. "Well. I can see that our early-dinner conversation is going to be a bit stilted."

"Early...dinner?"

"The kitchen sent up stew. Scones. All sorts of meats and cheeses. Some fresh peaches from a hothouse I didn't even know we had. The horrible stuff they call coffee. I sent them back for a pot for tea."

"You thought...of food?"

"I didn't order it, if that's what you're referring to. But it smells delicious. We should eat."

"I do na' feel hungry."

"Me, either. But I could use a change. Come along. I'll shower. Then, we can eat. Drink some tea. And I can get on to the business of explaining... uh. Lots of things."

"My heart hurts."

She walked slowly toward him. Her eyes were filmed with sudden tears. Neal had never seen anything so heart-rending. It affected his voice. The words came out in a deep soft grumble.

"I know, darling. Want to know something truly odd? My heart hurts, too. The old Neal would have taken a flight to some far-off place. Perhaps...Budapest. Stayed at an exclusive hotel. Turned off all internet and cell communication. Ordered the most expensive item on the menu. And then gone to bed with a clear conscience that things were right and just in the world. Which is all part and parcel of what I need to explain. You ready for your sup, yet?"

She gave him an unreadable expression. Neal took a mental stab at why.

The flight?

Budapest?

Internet and cell communication?

Hotel menu?

He was wrong on every guess.

"That is na' odd, Neal. Your aunt lost both her sons today. Regardless of why and how, I canna' imagine how devastating that must be."

"I know, babe. And...like I said, the new me is quite a bit different than the old one. That guy wouldn't have lost a moment of sleep. I was called a heartless cold bastard. It was true. But I've changed. I have learned how to feel. Because of you. I love you. Eternally. Whole-heartedly. It's the most amazing feeling in the universe. Well beyond anything I thought was pleasure. Love has opened my eyes to so much!" He cast a glance at the floor, then raised his head to continue his heartfelt confession. "Including heartache. I've discovered...it's not always fun and games. I heard Lady Blair's screams. I can still hear them. But I have to temper it with the knowledge that today could have gone so much differently. That could be my body lying on cold stone."

"Oh, Neal! I would have wanted to die, too!"

Tears spilled from her eyes, making her even lovelier. Neal sniffed against an answering emotion. It made his voice sound more gravelly.

"That...is probably how my aunt feels right now. But I have to remind myself of the facts here. That woman is guilty of attempted murder, sweetheart."

"You have...proof?"

"You mean beyond how her face fell when she caught sight of me walking into her apartments? Alive. Well. And talking?"

"Oh. I can na' imagine!"

"Lachlan's bullet was meant for me, Ainslee. He wasn't the lone shooter, either. We've got a confession. They had another accomplice, the fellow posing as Garrick's gamekeeper. His job was to make certain of my death, should Lachlan's bullet. Fail."

He separated the last word. She gasped. Neal continued his narrative.

"Not to worry. He's having a nice stay in the castle dungeons. It's not too onerous. He got a warm sup. Pallet. Blanket. I suppose I should draft up charges and hand him over to whatever legal system is in place...except I'm trying to keep this quiet. I suppose that is my contribution toward the decorous stuff."

"This is all so...unreal. I feel strange. Expectant. Anxious. As if something else needs to happen, but I do na' ken what."

"Ah. Good description, babe. Entirely apt. Come with me. You need some sustenance, and I could use a double shot of whiskey. For courage."

He held out his hand. She placed hers in it. Neal regarded her ring-less left hand for a moment.

"I just remembered something...and it might actually fit."

"What?"

"The reason I am standing here. Right now. Is because I bent down to retrieve something. It was in the ground. It's a ring." Neal fished about in his vest pocket. "Now, that I think of it, this little ring is another good way to start the conversation we need to have. There. See? It's my family ring. In the shape of a spiral. It's the logo for all my companies - Straithmore Enterprises."

She glanced at it. Back to his face. And she didn't even ask the obvious question about his companies.

"'Tis verra pretty."

"Might be small enough. Here. Try it on." Neal lifted her left hand. Slid it onto her ring finger. The spiral ring dangled. He tried it on her middle finger. It was still too large. He palmed it with a sense of defeat and stuck it back in his pocket. "I'm not giving up. You need a wedding ring. Mason tells me we have tiny rings in the Straithcairn collection. One is a sapphire that might match to your eyes. Or so, I'm told."

"I have...the Straith emerald ring already."

"Yeah. I know. But you need a wedding ring that fits. One you wear all the time. So the entire world knows you are taken. By me."

She smiled. Her eyes had a patina of moisture atop them again. Neal was hooked. Rapt. His shoulder struck the doorjamb, knocking them back a half step, and breaking the spell. Ainslee giggled.

Neal shook his head, and tried not to flush. It was useless. He could feel the heat.

"Well. Glad to see that still works," he remarked, and swept her up into his arms.

CHAPTER THIRTY-EIGHT

THE STEW WAS DELICIOUS. AS were the scones, the oatcakes, the meats and cheese. Ainslee hadn't realized how hungry she'd been until she finished her second bowl of stew and sat back. Replete. Warmed. And entirely relaxed in the big, upholstered chair Neal had set her in. She stifled a yawn. Looked across the table at her husband. Felt a thrill from it.

He was just so impressive. So manly.

And he was all hers.

Neal had matched her appetite, bite-for-bite. He'd finished right behind her. His bowl fell with a clatter, as if it slipped. He was acting strange... almost nervous. Edgy. And he wouldn't meet her gaze. But, she hadn't known him that long, and it had been a trying day.

She waited.

Ainslee didn't know what to say. The silence after his bowl settled was strange. It wasn't an uncomfortable quiet, though. Rather, the opposite. He'd had a fire lit in the fireplace. Flames occasionally sent popping and hissing sounds into the chamber from behind her. The wall of windows was to the left of him. They hadn't completely covered the glass panes. The day's rainfall had turned into a raging storm. Lightning occasionally lit the space, sending strips of light into the room that matched the drapery openings.

Neal slid his chair out. It made a screeching sound against the floor. If she'd been any less comfortable, she'd have probably jumped. Ainslee craned her neck up to look up at him.

"I think...I should go get a shower. About now."

"Shower?"

"Yeah. The rain sluicing off the roof makes a great shower. It'll be a bit brisk, but I like showers better than baths."

"Like...a waterfall?"

"Yeah. Exactly like that."

"Oh. We have lots of showers. There are waterfalls all over Straith land. Gruder Loch has one. Ram Point another. Huntsman's Wood also has a small one above the burn."

"Have you...bathed in them?'

"Aye."

"I hope they're secluded."

"I believe so. 'Twas never an issue, though."

"You bathing naked is not an issue? You're joking, right? I'm surprised we weren't at war over that."

Ainslee glanced down, toward her lap. She couldn't help the blush. "No man ever...looked at me afore you wed with me. I was na'...the bonny MacAffrey."

"Well. Lucky for me, everybody was blind. I think you are the loveliest thing ever born. I'm pretty sure most of the countryside agrees. If not, they haven't met you yet."

Ainslee's eyes widened. Her blush deepened.

"All of which is not helping me one iota at the moment."

"What?"

She lifted her head. He was regarding her with a slight smile and an expression she couldn't describe. It sent an immediate swell of heat through her. Everywhere.

"I have...things I need to tell you. I'm actually wondering what I should say. And how much. So. I'm thinking I might go stick my head under some cold water first. I'll just take a chunk of this lye stuff with me."

He picked up a bar of soap. Sniffed it. Ainslee smiled.

"That is na' lye. 'Tis made with olive oil and wood ash. A bit of herbs for fragrance. Lye soaps are used for house cleaning. And laundry."

"Right. Well. I'm not a history buff. I haven't the vaguest idea what was used in soap right now. Which...is a good place to start, I suppose."

"What is?"

"I don't know what ingredients are in soap in 1803."

"Why would you ken what soap is made of?"

"Well, you do."

"'Tis a housekeeping function. I should ken it."

Neal turned and started pacing. Ainslee smiled and pulled her feet up beneath her. Arranged her skirts over her legs. Leaned back into the plush embrace of the chair. Rolled her head to watch his progress to the dais his bed stood upon. Didn't quite stifle the yawn as he swiveled and began to walk back toward her. He started speaking as he went.

"Ainslee. Sweetheart. I'm trying to find a lead-in here, and this is...truly difficult. H. G. Wells hasn't even written his classic novel, Time Machine, yet. Crap. And then some. How about we talk about...Napoleon Bonaparte? We'll try him. He's around. I know a little about him. The man just got back from Egypt. He'll publish a set of really large, incredibly beautiful volumes about Egypt. It starts the field of study called Egyptology. A complete set is worth a fortune. I know. I purchased one at auction."

Ainslee perked up. "Oh! Is it here?"

He chuckled. "No. Sorry, love. It's not."

"Can you...get it?"

"Sure. We'll put it on our wish list for when it's published. Scratch the Napoleon idea, okay? It's not working. And I can't prove anything for years yet. Napoleon doesn't mount his disastrous campaign into Russia for what? Ten years or so? He'll eventually be defeated at a place called Waterloo and exiled to someplace called Elba. He'll try and re-start his campaign, but... that fails, too. Then he'll die. As do we all."

Ainslee's mouth dropped open. "Are you a seer?"

"Um. No. It's actually...a bit more, uh. Mind-boggling. Far-fetched. Completely implausible. But...you do believe in paranormal stuff. Right?"

"Para...normal?"

"The world is full of weird things. Things that defy explanation. Like... your gift with horses. I was told you were fey. Do you believe that?"

"Fey?"

"Yeah. It's akin to witchcraft."

"Are you accusing me...of being a witch?" Her voice dropped on the last word. A log fell as it in concert.

"Oh. No. No. No. No. No, honey. Darn it! I'm already treading water and I barely got started swimming. I forgot that witchcraft is a bad thing in this day and age."

"It has ever been a bad thing...according to the church."

"Well. That may be, but society will change. Nobody burns witches at the stake in the future."

She gasped audibly. "You *are* a seer."

"Not really. It's more—uh. Wow. I'm trying to explain how I know what I know. This is a lot tougher than I realized."

"But you have seen so much! Things I have only read about."

"Good one. Let's try that. What did you read? Exactly."

"Lot of things! I found the best source, too! The Encyclopedia Britannica. The MacAffrey library had the third edition!"

"You read the encyclopedia? Cover-to-cover?"

"Aye."

"I'll bet that was fun."

"It was! There is so much to learn! And 'twas printed by Scotsmen, you ken! In Edinburgh!"

"Oh. Right. I forgot that part. Scotland is actually a goldmine of inventors, love. But...that's another thing I know that I can't prove I know. Nor, can I prove *how* I know it. So. Let's go with what we have. Was there anything in encyclopedia about...oh. I don't know. I'll just throw out a term. Watch your reaction. Was anything written about...time travel?"

The last two words were rushed.

Time travel?

Ainslee regarded him for long moments while the lightning flashed, the fireplace crackled and popped, the candle flames flickered. He'd stopped his pacing and stood on the other side of the table watching her.

"Well? Was time travel covered in the encyclopedia? Have you ever even heard that term? Ever?"

Ainslee didn't know how to answer. Something was familiar about the phrase, but she couldn't quite place it. She had to think...

"I'm blowing it, aren't I?"

"Blowing it?"

"You are giving me *the look* again."

Ainslee tried to blank her expression. "What look?"

"Whenever I say something that sounds – uh. Well. Let's go with 'not entirely sane', shall we? Whenever I say something that sounds not entirely sane, you give me a quizzical look. It's really quite cute."

"Oh."

"And I'm trying to explain here without getting more looks because I sound like a complete knot-head. That's probably another new term. Means...idiot."

She remembered! She'd discovered a book in the library back home. She'd found it last season, dusted it off, and tried to read it, but grown bored. She clapped her hands. "Oh! I ken what you speak of! You are referring to the 'Memoirs of the Twentieth Century', are na' you?"

"The memoirs of what?"

"There is a book in the library. 'Twas written by an Irishman, a Samuel Madden, I think. 'Tis a verra rare book. Verra old."

"There is a book about time travel in the library? Here? Right now?"

"I am na' certain of the ducal library. It may have it. The one I speak of 'twas at my father's house. Printed in seventeen-thirty-three, I think."

"Somebody wrote about time travel in the eighteenth century? Seriously? That's wild. So, tell me. What did it have to say?"

"But you had to have read it. Why else would you ask?"

"Uh..."

"I'm afraid I did na' finish it. I am na' fond of epistolary novels."

"Epistolary?"

"'Twas written in correspondence form. I find that style of writing... boring."

"You're an amazing woman, Ainslee. I really hope you know that. If not, I'll just continually tell you. Beautiful. Intelligent. Self-educated. Extremely loving." He cleared his throat. "So. Where were we? Oh yeah. The book about time travel. How far did you get with it?"

"The letters are from a man who had been to the year nineteen-ninety-six. Or perhaps it was nineteen-ninety seven."

"Nice. What did he have to say?"

"The Jesuits are in control."

"Religion? That's what the book features?"

"Aye."

"That figures. Some things never seem to change. Sounds like we are back to square one, sweetheart." Neal took a deep breath. "I'm going to try something different. Let's go back to the beginning of all this."

"The beginning?"

"My...accident. Do you remember that?"

"Your accident?" Ainslee didn't feign the confusion.

"The one where my horse bucked me off and I hit my head. That accident."

He lifted the hair from his forehead. There was a purplish-hued bruise at his temple. It was faded about the edges but still looked nasty. She'd forgotten all about it.

"Oh. That accident."

"You were there just before it happened? Right? You said something about Thundercloud. I remember that."

Ainslee gulped. Looked away for a moment before looking back at him. Now, she'd have to confess. Her voice wavered. "'Twas actually...my fault," she whispered.

"How do you figure?"

"How...do I figure?" she asked.

He sighed heavily. The sound was accentuated by a log falling in the fireplace behind her. Ainslee's pulse leapt. Nothing on her body betrayed it. She was proud of that.

"That means I'm waiting for an explanation to something I find unbelievable. I'll rephrase it. What makes you say it's your fault?"

"I needed to speak with you so I hid behind a standing stone. My appearance is what startled Thundercloud into bolting. I...am so sorry."

"It wasn't your fault, babe. Truly. But...did you see me fall?"

She shook her head.

"Did you see anything that would make you suspect he – uh. I mean *I* – had perhaps...perished?

Ainslee frowned. Thought back. And then remembered. "Oh. Aye. I did see you just before the lightning struck. You were lying in a bad position. Your neck was...rather skewed. I thought for a moment, you'd broken it."

"Ah! Broken neck. Would have been instantaneous. Poor fellow. So...after you saw him, there was a lightning strike?"

"It hit the meadow. 'Twas so bright, it blinded me for a moment. And the thunder knocked me off my feet. And...then I heard you groan. I was so relieved."

"I see. That explains...quite a bit of this."

He blew another sigh. There was a knock at the chamber door, the one leading to the hall. Ainslee craned her neck to watch as Neal passed her. She would have leaned over the chair's arm to observe, but that might seem too unmannerly. So she waited. Listened as he exchanged words with another male. A lot of words. Something was said about Lady Blair. The poor woman. Ainslee should ask.

And she would...if she wasn't so tired.

"They've come for the supper dishes, love. And look. They brought us a pot of tea. And more buttered scones. With honey. Hmm. Good thinking."

Ainslee shook herself aware and watched the servants clear off the table. A silver tea service was placed in the center of it. An oil lamp was set beside it. She watched the flames glance off the silvered surface of the tea set. That was interesting. Mesmeric. The door shut. She barely heard it. Neal caught her yawning this time.

"It's been a really long day. Full of all kinds of...stuff."

He poured a cup of tea. Looked at it for a moment, and then moved his gaze to hers. Ainslee had a hard time focusing. Her eyelids felt leaden. She didn't know what was the matter with her. He was so thrilling to be with, and yet...

"Ah. Darling. You're exhausted. Come. I'll undo some of the hooks up your back so you can breathe. Put you atop that great big bed of mine. Go grab my shower. We can talk tomorrow. The next day. Next month. We have time. We've got an entire lifetime of it."

The mattress felt like a large hug wrapped about her. Something tapped against her throat. Neal glanced there, before picking something up. She was listening to the sound of his voice more than his words. She heard snippets. Everything felt too wondrously secure. Protected.

Warm.

"Oh. Look...out of my pocket. My spiral ring. This is...truly far-fetched... love. How did...bit of gold...time warp? And...the one spot...save me from a bullet?"

Ainslee murmured an answer.

"I love you. I'll just...shower...back."

I love you, too.

Her heart whispered it as she snuggled into pillows, inhaling the aroma of clean linen. Fresh herbs.

She slumbered.

She didn't see a blaze of multi-hued light that sent slices of brilliance through the chamber, lighting it to a blinding level. She failed to hear or feel the crash of thunder that followed. And she completely missed Neal's agonized cry.

CHAPTER THIRTY-NINE

THE MOMENT NEAL PUT HIS signet ring on, he knew.
He *knew*!

It was the ring.

The same thing that had saved his life today was now taking it away.

Every hair on his body lifted, as if preparing for an immediate and close electrical surge. Clouds that had been dark came close, whirling, spiraling to pitch black. Tornado-force winds slammed him back into the rock wall next. The sluice of rainwater that had been a shower now pelted him with a blast of droplets that stung. A hole formed in the mass before him. Lighting continually flashed across the blackest area…right in the center. It grew closer. And then it started swirling.

It was just like the Bermuda Triangle incident. Only so much worse. This time, he knew exactly what he was losing!

Everything that mattered.

"Ainslee!"

Wind stole his cry. Neal couldn't get the ring back off. Panic made him clumsy. Inept. He twisted and turned the piece of gold. Yanked on it. Lifted his foot to snag a *skean dhu* so he could cut it off. He'd father lose a finger than Ainslee. His whole hand. He'd cut off his arm if need be!

"No!"

This time Neal was vividly conscious as a vortex sucked him into it; conscious, and alert, and completely distraught. His cry echoed with anguish. The sound followed him. His body slipped and rotated along a frightening tunnel of lightning bolts that kept flashing. Blindingly bright. Leaving incredible color in their wake. The space spun faster. More rapidly. Moving sickeningly quickly.

And then the steering column of a Cessna Citation X materialized out of nowhere right before him. Neal grabbed for it, the move instinctual. That one act may have saved him. He didn't know. But the moment he had the wheel, the vortex about him gave an immense groaning sound as if metal was bending and rending. Then it started slowing. The electrical lightshow turned into a series of random sparks that emitted a cloud-like vapor that fogged the view. Coated his face with moisture. Neal lifted a hand to swipe a palm across his eyes, and push back long hair that no longer existed. He replaced his hand on the wheel, then watched the fog become a reddish glow.

And then it dissipated.

Before his eyes, the view morphed from a steering column into a wide span of monitors, all blinking or fuzzy with skewed images. Switches. Gauges. Controls. Levers.

Oh. No.

It couldn't be.

No.

No.

No!

Neal's heart sent pain with each denial. It didn't change anything. He gripped the steering wheel and fought a wave of grief so vivid, it nauseated. He'd received more than the pot of tea. Mere minutes ago. In his chamber. At Straith Castle. Neal had received the news that Lady Blair had taken an overdose of laudanum. The woman had ended her life. She had too much loss to deal with. She couldn't handle the agony.

And right now, Neal knew exactly what that felt like.

No!

His chest was a mass of pain. Each heartbeat sent more of it, while every breath fanned the flame to a more torturous level. This wasn't probable. Or possible. Or credible. But nothing changed the facts facing him right now. He was back in the Cessna Citation X. The cockpit was swinging wildly side-to-side, but didn't overturn like it had been. Outside the glass, however, the world was a different story. The dark mass that surrounded them was still spinning. Emitting bolts of lightning. Flashes of brilliantly hued light.

But, wait.

A pin-dot of something appeared in front of them, in the very midst of all the dark. A tiny bit of light. Barely discernible. It grew. Became a glimpse of daylight. Ocean waves. Blue sky. The spot enlarged as they raced for it. Inside, the cockpit was awash with flashing red emergency lights. Alive with continual pings and buzzes. And Eric's cursing.

"Damn it! Hold, you bitch! Hold!"

Eric?

Neal jerked his head to look at the co-pilot seat. Eric's forearms were bulging with muscle as he fought to keep the plane on an even keel. The rotation of the cloud mass outside the plane began to slow. There were pauses between the lightning flashes. Now and again the darkness still surrounding them lit up, but it wasn't close anymore. The view of sea and sky and sun looked to be several yards in circumference. And growing.

And pain seized his chest like he hit a wall. Neal had rarely prayed in his lifetime. He didn't believe in an almighty deity covering the entire planet's woes. He started praying now.

Please, God. I'm begging you. Please...? Please, put me back. Show me the way back. Please, God...

The view blurred. Went awash with moisture. Neal blinked tears back and tightened his jaw, and tried to absorb a hellish pain he hadn't known existed. His heart was a solid ball of anguish. Fiery-hot. Acid-filled. It leached the mixture into his throat. Down his arms. Through his belly. His legs. Neal had never experienced such a combination. Nor anything at this level.

Please God. I'll do anything. Make any sacrifice. Please...?

"Holy shit! We're gonna make it!"

Eric's triumphal words interrupted Neal's concentration. "No!" He snarled it this time. The word came out loud. Angered. It resounded through the fuselage with a boom.

"Hey, boss! You're back? Oh. Wow! I was so worried!"

"No," Neal said again.

"Fifteen minutes ago, I thought you were a goner."

Fifteen minutes?

"No," Neal repeated.

"Not that I had time to check, but I was really afraid you'd bought it, man."

"Fifteen minutes?"

It wasn't conceivable. Neal's voice reflected it. He'd been gone more than four days. *Was it four days?*

Could have been five.

He hadn't been counting. He'd been living life. Truly living it. For the first time that he could remember. And...now?

He'd lost everything.

"Yeah. It was about that. You gave a strange cry, and then nothing. You didn't answer me. You didn't make any sound. Nothing. I really thought— well. It was about fifteen minutes ago – give or take. I don't know for sure, because...well. I was fighting the Bermuda Triangle. Holy shit! Times two! We just went through a vortex in the middle of the Bermuda Triangle! And survived! Can you believe it?"

"No," Neal replied.

His voice sounded lifeless. He only wished he could deaden the continual spurts of pain his heart kept sending through him.

"And look! Blue sky and sunlight! Dead ahead!"

A sizzling slithered through the row of monitors facing them. It was followed by colorful images as one-by-one everything came back on-line. The plane shot out of darkness and into what would have been blindingly bright light except they both still wore sunglasses.

How is that even possible?

Eric fished his communicator off the floor with his left hand without looking. He must have tossed it off at some point. Neal didn't know. And he didn't care. He was still trying to absorb hellish pain. It had reached his fingertips where he had them clenched about the wheel, his toes inside his leather shoes. And his heart just kept sending more. Because he'd found there was only one thing that mattered in the universe.

Love.

And he'd lost it.

Neal listened as the kid began speaking into his microphone.

"This is NC4082. NC4082. Enroute to Miami! Any traffic controllers out there?"

"This is Fort Lauderdale-Hollywood."

The controller's response came with a lot of static. Which was weird, but not as much as the fact that Neal was still wearing his headset along with the sunglasses.

"I can barely hear you, Fort Lauderdale. Come again?" Eric replied.

"This is Fort Lauderdale-Hollywood. State your call numbers please."

"NC4082. Enroute. Aruba to Miami."

"Miami? You're a mite off course, bud. Did you say...NC4082?"

"That's an affirmative," Eric replied.

"We don't even have you on radar. Wait a moment. You just showed up. You're currently flying...east over the Atlantic. New flight plan?"

"What the—? Um. Yeah. New flight plan. And we'll be landing at Fort Lauderdale-Hollywood rather than Miami-Dade. Turning west now."

"Cancelling mayday."

"You guys got our mayday?"

"Puerto Rico reported you missing over an hour ago."

An hour ago?

"An hour ago?" Eric echoed Neal's unspoken thought, his voice sputtering. "No way! This is too much. My watch says it's nine thirty-five. On the dot."

"Time check. Eastern zone. Ten forty-six, man."

"What? Oh. This is too much. No way. We encountered something weird out here, guys."

"Come again, NC4082?"

"We're just flew through...something...uh. Not normal. We...experienced a really weird cloud. A lot of turbulence! We got sucked in! We barely made it out alive!"

"Come again?"

"We just flew through something in the Bermuda Triangle! Aren't you listening? We just escaped a UFO! Or something weirder. I don't know! We can't have lost an hour. And you can quit laughing. It's true!"

Neal clicked off Eric's headset and spoke into his. "Fort Lauderdale-Hollywood? This is Neal Straithmore. NC4082."

His voice was deep. Authoritative. Calm-sounding. Relaxed. None of his inner anguish came through. The change in the controller's voice was instantaneous.

"Sir!"

"We will be requesting permission to land shortly. We will keep you apprised of our approach. Out."

Neal clicked off the headset. Turned his head toward at Eric. The kid had a militant look to him. Neal didn't blame him, but now wasn't the time to divulge what had happened. Neal might never speak of it. A glance about showed absolutely nothing in the sky about them. They had clear visibility for miles. He banked the plane to the left, turning it around, watching the sun move from their front to behind them. The monitors all showed his action.

"Boss. You *know* what just happened."

"Do I?"

"Well. Yeah. You were here. You saw it."

"I don't know what I saw."

"We went through a time portal or something!"

"I don't know that."

"What would you call it, then?"

"Severe unexplained weather phenomena."

"Oh. Come on, boss-man. That was real. We were caught up in some-thing major! It was really dangerous. Touch-and-go. Pretty frickin' scary. And they're saying we were caught up in it for an hour? Holy shit! No wonder my arms ache. And you're really gonna sit there and say *nothing* happened?"

"No. I'm saying I don't know what happened. And until I know. I'm not discussing it."

"Are you saying that to be politically correct? Because I'm not buying it."

"I was blacked-out, Eric. I don't know what happened." *And, just like that, I automatically have another good cover story?*

"Sir. We almost died. In fact, I thought you had."

The coast of Florida came into view. Not because of land mass, but because there was a distinct haze of smog visible in the sunlight. Neal's shoulders sagged slightly. Looked like carbon footprint was still a problem. How was that possible...unless?

He'd dreamt it.

"What happened was real, man," Eric said beside him.

Neal clicked on his headset again. Spoke into the microphone. "Fort Lauderdale-Hollywood? This is Neal Straithmore. NC4082."

"Fort Lauderdale-Hollywood. We have you on approach."

"Excellent. Permission to land?"

"You are cleared for your usual runway, sir. Over and out."

There was a runway he usually used? At an airport he rarely visited?

Neal pondered that for a moment. Dismissed it. Someone could have set something up without his knowledge. He should have known about it, though. Sounded like he needed to check the chain-of-command at the board meeting.

Oh.

Wait.

They'd apparently lost an hour. The meeting he'd ordered had probably been cancelled. That was all right with Neal. He didn't want to handle pub-lic speaking at the moment. And then he realized he faced a conundrum. He didn't know which runway was the usual one. Neal considered that for a moment. Turned to Eric.

"Why don't you take it in, kid?"

"You're letting me land this baby? Really? Oh...sweet!"

"I think you earned it. Don't you?"

Eric acted like a kid in a candy store, his face alight with dignity and excitement, anticipation...a real treat. He could handle it. Neal settled back into his leather seat. Lifted his hands. Yep. He was looking at forty-nine-year-old hands. And there was his spiral signet ring. He moved it about on his little finger. He decided to test things. The ring wasn't remotely tight. Came off easily. He had a definite tan line. Neal put the ring back on. Flexed his hand.

Eric coasted them to an almost perfect landing. They taxied up to an enormous hangar. It had the Straithmore spiral logo on every side of the building. Including the front doors. It was painted in black. That was incorrect. His logo design was trade-marked. They'd used all kinds of colors. Red. Green. Blue. Yellow. Rainbow.

Never black.

Black was a reminder of the issues facing the planet – and the culprit behind it: petroleum. Neal's companies dealt in renewable energy resources. He sponsored technology to lessen, or even mitigate, carbon footprint problems. That was his trademark. Corporate mission. Political forum. He would never have a logo painted in black. Ever.

CHAPTER FORTY

THE IMAGE ACROSS THE HANGAR front separated as the doors opened. Eric taxied the plane inside. Parked it between a gargantuan 747, and a large-belly cargo plane. Both planes were fuel hogs and emblazoned across the sides with black Straithmore logos. Now that Neal looked at it closely, the end loop appeared to have a suspicious droplet hanging off one end.

It resembled a drop of crude oil.

Neal narrowed his eyes. Focused.

What the hell was going on?

He'd wanted financial dominance in the world, yes – but not at the expense of the planet. That had never been his agenda. Straithmore Enterprises was known as a sponsor of green incentives. Apparently, he'd been lax with his leadership. Somebody in his organization was sabotaging his efforts.

Neal wondered how far it went. How many members of his staff he'd have to fire. And then he wondered if he really cared enough to handle it.

Wait.

What?

Had he really just thought that?

Neal stared at the cockpit but wasn't seeing anything before him. He was stunned into immobility. Making money was *the* driving force in his life. It always had been. Saving the planet was part of that, but secondary. Nothing else had been of any consequence.

And – right now – none of that even mattered. Because, even if he'd dreamt it, loving Ainslee had been too real an emotion. Too all-encompassing. Too wondrous. There was no descriptor vast enough for what she meant to him. Neal had been wrong all these years. He'd been blinded by the materialistic. He hadn't known.

Love was the real force in the world.

It always had been.

Neal sucked in a breath as his heart pulsed painfully. As if he needed a reminder.

"We made it here on fumes, boss. Which is more weirdness. We had a full tank when we left Aruba."

Neal grunted.

"I'll go order a refill truck."

The kid spoke from the cabin door. Neal waved a hand toward him, then he peeled off his headset. Held it for a moment while he took another pain-filled breath. He hadn't unfastened his belts yet. He was moving on auto-pilot.

How could this emotion be linked to a fantasy? Had he really imagined being in the past?

Everything?

Because – if so – why did it feel like he had a ton of weight pressing down on his shoulders, while something resembling a hatchet had slammed into his chest, deep enough it could continually press against his heart.

From nowhere, he recalled a writer saying it is better to have loved and lost than never to have loved at all.

That was complete horseshit.

Neal had never dealt with this level of anguish. This amount of pain. This depth of emotion. He'd much rather be innocent of love and every-thing that went with it.

Then again...

Neal's mind drifted back to his wife. As he'd last seen her. Her dark lashes against her cheeks as she slept. Safely snuggled atop his bed. The dark pink of her gown contrasting with the off-white linen of his bedding...

Neal's eyes grew moist. His breath caught. The hatchet in his chest twinged tortuously. He needed to cease reliving this. Especially if it had been a hallucination.

Or. Maybe. Just maybe. He was losing his sanity here. That was a distinct possibility.

Neal sighed heavily. Pulled off his sunglasses with one hand, wiped at his eyes with the other, and then unfastened his belts. He eased out of the seat next. The cockpit wasn't tall enough to stand. He felt like he'd been on a three-day drunk. He was stiff. Sore. Every muscle was in on the act. He even had a cramp in the arch of one foot.

But above all that was pain that his heart just wouldn't cease pumping out. His situation didn't improve once he reached the door, either. Neal held to the doorframe of the Cessna and took a step down. Another. He felt frail. Drained. Oh. *Hell.* This was ridiculous. There were only four steps. He could do it. The sound of a truck engine caught his attention. Neal looked up, and watched a fuel truck enter the hangar. It parked next to the Cessna. A driver hopped out. He wore a red shirt bearing the Straithmore spiral logo. In black. The truck had the same emblem on the door, as did the tank in back.

There was a definite drip of oil hanging off the right end loop.

"Eric."

Neal's voice was weak. He cleared his throat and tried again. "Eric." This time it was heard. His assistant turned from greeting the driver and jogged over.

"Yeah, boss?"

"Why is a Straithmore logo on that truck?"

The kid looked over his shoulder as if to verify things and then turned back. "Because it's one of ours."

"One of our...what?"

"Trucks."

"We don't have fuel trucks."

"Yeah we do. You've got an entire fleet of them. And semi-trucks. And oil tankers. How else would we get Straithmore Petroleum delivered?"

"Straithmore *what?*"

Shock was a debilitating event. Neal's knees buckled. He sagged onto his butt on the top step of the ladder. That hurt. The linen pants didn't have enough padding in them. He stared at Eric. The kid looked unsure. Confused. But entirely honest.

And exactly like Rory.

"Straithmore Petroleum," Eric repeated.

"I don't own petroleum."

"What? Uh. Did something happen out there that you're not telling me? Because this is coming from way out of left field, boss. Petroleum is your family business. You're like, the definition of an oil magnate. Fifth richest man in the world, but that's about to change."

"*Fifth* richest? *Fifth?*"

Neal was reeling. He was amazed Eric didn't notice. But maybe nothing showed physically.

"Heck, you might get to number three when the congressional vote goes through. Straithmore stock is going to go through the roof."

"What...congressional vote?"

It felt like darkness was closing in. On all sides of him. And the kid didn't even seem to notice.

"You've been lobbying for years to get the arctic opened up for drilling. It's about to pay off. Looks like the vote will finally go our way this session."

"No."

"Well. Yeah. And it was a long, hard fight."

"This can't be happening. It can't."

Because that meant it had really happened.

Neal didn't dare consider it. Not even momentarily. He could barely handle the agony of every heartbeat now. He was actually afraid.

"What can't be happening?"

Go with what you know, Neal. "What about global warming? Climate control? Carbon footprint?"

"Whoa. Boss. I can't believe I'm hearing those words coming from you. You know global warming is something that happens all the time. It's cyclical. Part of earth's evolution. Climate control is just a couple of words used for political hype. And, as you continually point out, the idea of carbon footprint is not based on solid scientific data. We've had studies done to back our side."

"*Our* side?" Neal shook his head.

"You know the business inside and out. Your family has been in oil since...I don't know. The very beginning. You helped design the current ads. 'Oil is what made the country great. And Straithmore Petroleum *is* oil'."

"Oh, my God." Neal felt faint. He lowered his head to his bent knees and started hyperventilating. This couldn't be happening.

It just couldn't.

For this scenario to be true...

It meant Neal had really been back in 1803! He'd traveled through time. Messed with fate, just like Lady Blair had done. This was the result.

This was also proof he'd met Ainslee! Fallen in love. Wed her by proclamation. She'd existed! Everything had really happened. At the thought, the hatchet in his chest turned into a live thing that started eating away at his heart, elevating everything to an agonizing level. Neal fought sobs. The ladder shook, rattling along the concrete floor.

"Are you...all right, boss?"

Neal shook his head. He was devastated. Ill. Making words was beyond him at the moment. Taking each breath was about the most he could handle.

"Is there anything...I can do?"

Eric was so young. So capable. He didn't know he was the sole benefactor of Neal's estate. It was time the kid found out.

The darkness surrounding him began to subside.

Neal felt a vestige of hope.

The weight he'd felt on his shoulders eased. But the feeling of a blade within his chest cavity didn't budge. He wondered how long a human could live with such a sensation before they couldn't take it anymore. And ended it. Like Lady Blair had done.

Wow.

The future looked pretty damned bleak.

"Boss?"

Eric's voice grated. The shouting he started up was worse. Neal hunched his shoulders.

"Somebody get me some water! Cold! Of course, bottled! He doesn't drink anything else."

No. Not bottled. Damn it.

Neal took a deep breath. Tensed the muscles in his gut. Stood up. He'd never been the type to wait for destiny. He made his own. Always had. And, while he couldn't do a darn thing about his future, he could definitely work on the global issue.

"Eric?"

"Yeah, boss?"

"Go run me a glass of tap water. Not bottled. Plastic is one of the world's pollution problems."

"All right. Who are you? And what have you done with the real Neal Straithmore?"

Eric didn't sound serious. A glance showed his wide grin. Neal almost smiled in response. And then the irony hit him. Here he was – the real Neal in the correct body – and somebody actually asked for identification?

"I'm definitely Neal Straithmore, kid. And, before you question it, I'm in full control of my faculties. I'm about to change a lot of things. I've just had...why don't we call it an epiphany? That's a good word. Which isn't that unbelievable, given the circumstances."

"What circumstances?"

"We just cheated death. Remember?"

"And it was really cool! We should tell someone. Everyone. The media! You want to give a press conference?"

"Eric—"

Eric's face fell at Neal's tone. "Can we at least discuss it?"

"Maybe. Do I still have a...place in Miami?"

"You don't remember?"

"Eric. I didn't tell you before, but I've been experiencing TIA episodes. They're called mini-strokes. They can leave one...disoriented. A little forgetful."

"Holy hell! Are you all right?"

"For the moment. Yes. Thanks. But we have bigger problems. Do we have a way to get to Miami?"

"On it."

Eric snagged a cell phone from his back pocket. Neal watched him scroll a finger across the screen. Good. Technology hadn't altered much, if any. That was one plus to his return.

"The Hummer will be here in five."

"The Hummer?" Neal was actually surprised that the words came out without one hint of inflection.

"Yeah."

"I have a Hummer, too?"

"Everyone in the company drives them. They have the highest safety rating. They're roomy. And they look really cool."

"I suppose I have a fleet of helicopters at my disposal, too? Big, fuel-guzzling ones?"

"Well...yeah. Would you rather take a flight?"

Eric pulled out his cell phone again. Neal stuck his hand up.

"No. No. A drive is fine. And I have some...research to do. I don't think I can do that in a chopper."

"Good thing we equipped the executive Hummers with command centers. You'll have everything you need."

He had a command center. In a Hummer. The fuel rating had to be worse than dismal.

Well.

Neal knew where to start with the changes.

CHAPTER FORTY-ONE

A VEHICLE ENTERED THE HANGAR. IT wasn't just a Hummer. It was a stretch Hummer limo. Charcoal-toned with a black chromed Straithmore spiral logo. The unit came complete with black windows, too. Neal had to admit, as it pulled to a stop and a driver stepped out, the vehicle was really cool. And that was before he saw the command center.

The entire back section was a mobile office. It came complete with swivel chairs, small desks, computers, monitors. Compact. Masculine. Black leather swivel seats surrounded and massaged. Neal slid into one, and turned on his monitor.

Ah. Excellent.

His passwords were still the same. He barely heard Eric join him. The door shut. The driver got back in the front. They began moving. The motion was a barely noticeable waver of his body in the seat. Neal didn't even notice it. But he was busy typing letters into the search engine.

'Iain Straithmore.'

The search took micro-seconds. And he had a lot of entries for Iain Straithmore to look over. Neal added clarification to his search bar.

'Iain Straithmore. 1804.'

A couple of links showed up. Neal clicked on one. It was a listing in an ancestry site. A marriage had taken place in the state of New York between an Iain Straithmore from Scotland, and a New York woman, Rebecca Township.

Well. Well. Well.

His progenitor had also found love, and not long after he'd arrived in

New York, either. That explained why Neal had an American passport and not one from the UK. It didn't explain the oil mess. Neal went back to the opening search screen.

'*Straithmore Petroleum.*'

The screen loaded with thousands of sites to look through. Neal went back to the search bar. Added a codicil.

'*Straithmore Petroleum, first stock purchase.*'

The fourth site down was an article from a business magazine. Neal scanned it rapidly. And...finally!

His great-grandfather had been interviewed in nineteen twenty-one. The reporter had asked about the Straithmore family's uncanny luck in the stock market. Great-grand-dad was quoted as saying every Straithmore received one word when they inherited. It had been passed down from Iain Straithmore. On his death-bed he'd said some cryptic words. Neal enlarged the letters on the screen. Apparently he needed reading glasses all-of-a-sudden.

Damn aging issues.

'Iain Straithmore said he'd been told to buy iron and then steel from a very wise man. He knew to buy them even before they were available. And...while Iain couldn't remember the exact instructions, one word stuck with him. Petroleum. He didn't know what it was, but when it was available, they needed to do something with it.'

"Damn it!" Neal swore aloud.

"Boss?"

He should have written the instructions down! Then again, he shouldn't have even sent Iain to New York in the first place. And if Neal ever made it back to Ainslee, he was never messing with the future again.

Ever.

His heart pinged painfully at the thought of her. He started another search before pain overtook his mental exercise. He typed in 'Straith Petroleum'. No hits came up for that combination. Neal tried again with 'Straith stock'. Then 'Straith fortune'.

Nothing came up that mattered.

This was really strange. Neal had sent Iain to New York with a hundred pounds. He was supposed to buy stock in the Straith name. Iain had enough for the journey, and Neal had added ten more pounds for Iain to buy stock if he so wanted. If Iain's purchase made his heirs so rich, what had happened to the Straith family fortune that should have ensued? Could Iain have stolen the hundred pounds?

Had Neal misread the man's character that badly?

No.

It had to be something else.

Neal typed in 'Duke of Straithcairn.' Scanned for the most recent one. And..

There!

The current Duke of Straithcairn was forty-five. He was the eleventh in an unbroken line stretching back to the seventeenth century. His name was Reagan. He was married. Had two children, a son and a daughter. His son's name was Alexander. His daughter Annabelle. His wife...?

Neal's heart stopped. His entire chest hurt. He'd rather take a blow.

The current duchess was named Ainslee.

Neal swiped a hand across his eyes to clear his vision. He'd been avoiding it long enough. He typed in her name and the year.

'Ainslee Straith. 1803.'

There was a record of a marriage between Niall Straith and a Miss Ainslee MacAffrey. Nothing more. Neal broadened the search.

'Ainslee Straith – nineteenth century.'

There were a lot of Ainslee Straith's. Apparently, it was a family name. Neal went through site after site after site. Read nothing about his Ainslee. If she'd had a child, Neal couldn't find a birth record. He couldn't even find a death certificate for her. He couldn't find anything. He smacked the keyboard in disgust.

And then he knew his next move.

He needed to get back there. To Castle Straith. The current duke would know what had happened. Everything was entered in the family bible. There would be a record of his Ainslee.

And he really needed to reach Huntsman's Dale. Get to the exact spot it had happened. Wearing the ring. And hope like hell a storm showed up. It was a long shot. Chances were slender, at best. But, if he was going to perish of a broken heart, he'd rather have it happen on Scot soil. So he could, at least, feel close to her again.

"Hey. Eric?"

"Yeah?"

The kid had been doing social networking on his monitor. His interest in his boss hadn't changed. He obviously still had little of it. He cocked his head to listen.

"What are your feelings about oil?"

Eric swiveled in his chair and looked at Neal for a long time. Then he replied with something very interesting.

"We've had this conversation before."

"Really?"

The kid nodded.

"And. To refresh my memory. Your thoughts are...?"

"I think we should diversify. Get into some of the energy renewal initiatives. Work toward saving the planet, not just using its resources."

"With an opinion like that, I'm surprised you work for me," Neal commented.

"Well. I did graduate at the top of my class. Made it through an applicant process that eliminated more than a few. But I had an edge. We're related."

Neal stilled. "How closely?" he asked.

"We're from the same area of Scotland. Same clan. My grandma was a Straith. She married an Irishman, hence my last name."

And just like that, Neal got the explanation of why Eric was Rory's doppelganger. "Ah. We're cousins," Neal said. "That's...interesting. Thanks."

"That's all you wanted?"

"For now."

The kid went back to his multi-screen conversations. Neal turned back to his monitor.

Wait.

He'd inadvertently clicked something that brought up images. His photo appeared in multiple shots all across the monitor. Apparently, he went to a lot of events that required a tuxedo. He looked bored in most of them. The recent ones had a gorgeous blond on his arm.

Oh. Shit.

Lindsey.

Neal had completely forgotten her. He swiveled his chair to face Eric again.

"Hey. Eric."

"Yeah, boss?" Eric asked from over his shoulder.

"Did we leave a woman in Aruba?"

The kid chuckled. "Well. Yeah. We did. Lindsey. I don't know what happened. You didn't say. I didn't ask."

"I see. Send her a huge bouquet of flowers. An apology. A plane ticket back. Tell her I'll explain everything after I return from a sabbatical."

The kid turned back to face Neal. "You're taking a sabbatical?"

"The moment I get packed. And a flight booked."

"Why don't you just take a corporate jet?"

"Because I'm going on a sabbatical. I will not be available. I may not even take my phone."

"You're going off-grid?"

"And then some." Neal smiled as he recited the words.

"Um. Who is gonna run the company while you're...not available?"

"Good point. Have the driver stop by my attorney's office."

"Your attorney's office?"

"They still have an office in Miami, don't they?"

"They're located in one of the buildings you own."

"Well. Of course they are. With my interest in blocking anything that might save the planet, I probably need lawyers under my feet. I hope they're not getting a bargain on the rent."

Eric snickered.

"You told me I'm the fifth richest man in the world, right?"

"Yeah. You are."

"Well, I'm going to transfer that problem, Eric."

"It's not a problem that I can see."

"You are about to find out, young man. But. Before I give you. Power of Attorney. Will you promise me something?"

Eric's jaw dropped. His mouth kept opening and shutting, but nothing came out. That was almost entertaining enough to break through the ache Neal was living with.

"Buy yourself the new Tesla. Take it out on a race track. I think you'll love it."

CHAPTER FORTY-TWO

IT TOOK THREE DAYS TO get to Scotland.
Seventy-two hours.

Neal would have been counting every minute if they hadn't been so crammed with things he had to handle. Do. Take care of. The Power of Attorney was just the start. Unless he wanted long legal entanglements, he had to transfer all kinds of properties and titles. Being fifth richest man came with a lot of baggage. Eric already looked older. His grin flashed a little less often. Neal hoped the responsibility wouldn't wear him down too quickly.

Neal finally gave the kid his personal cell phone – complete with private numbers for some of the most influential people on the planet. Neal bought a disposable one, with just enough technology he could get flights and rentals taken care of. Make sure of directions. And then he was finished with it.

Not that he questioned his self-control – but Neal had forgotten the power cord. Wouldn't matter, actually. He hadn't brought any credit or debit cards with him, but he was still Neal Straithmore. He had offices all over the world, one as close as Inverness. Another in Edinburgh. He was well-known. If he wanted cell technology, all he had to do was walk into one of his offices.

He'd also used the three days to acquire a good used backpack. Hiking wear. Long sleeves shirts. Jackets. Wool socks. Trekking shoes. A fedora. And then he had to figure out how to get all of that into the backpack. He'd stopped shaving. His whiskers grew in fairly quickly, leaving him with a grizzled look. It was a familiar brownish-red, but there was a lot of gray in there, as well. He looked light-years different than the tuxedo-clad CEO of Straithmore Enterprises, which was exactly what he wanted. Eric commented on it the last time he saw him. Said Neal was looking pretty 'Old Country'.

Good description.

The asphalt he'd been driving only went so far. Neal wondered absently if they called it tarmac out here. If not, they should. Neal smiled slightly. He hadn't been exaggerating to Ainslee when he'd told her Scotland was a mother lode of inventors and inventions. Tarmac was just one of them. A John McAdam had come up with a way to bind the surface stones together with coal tar. They'd called it 'Tar McAdam' – hence the name.

It was desolate out here. Nothing in sight except a few sheep and a lot of yellow meadow grass. There had been a dogleg to the left, a mile or so before the road ended. Neal had ignored it, although the pavement down that particular deviation had been in great shape. That was probably where any traffic exited on this road. Neal didn't notice and he didn't care. His objective was Straith Castle.

Neal maneuvered his four-door sedan onto the non-maintained gravel trail and managed to get another half mile before the ruts and overgrowth got too difficult for the car. He parked the vehicle where it was. Left the key in the ignition. Fished his cardigan out of the back seat. Buttoned it. Pulled the fedora onto his head. Hefted his backpack. And started walking.

It was a nice day. Especially for a morning in October. A chilly breeze teased him as he started to walk. It carried a possibility of rain, as did the cloud cover. Neal inhaled the scent of moisture. Heather. Thistle. Fresh air. This corner of Scotland was like an oasis of nature. Pure. Untouched. Clean. He stopped at a stream.

Wait.

It's called a burn, Neal.

He lowered the backpack, went to his knees, cupped his hand, and quenched his thirst. The water was icy cold. Refreshing. Clear. Tasted perfectly clean. Neal stood, re-shouldered the backpack, and continued on. He already felt healthier. More alive. His heart was beating in tandem with his steps. He could hear each breath as he filled his lungs and then expelled the air. The tip of a standing stone came into view. Neal's heart ticked up a notch. He jogged to the crest of a hill, and stopped to look over the area known as Huntsman's Dale.

It hadn't changed much.

Grass still covered the area. It waved and bowed with the wind. A strand of trees stood on the opposite side of the bowl-shaped valley. Neal looked over at it. The trees looked different without their foliage. A little taller. A lot less sinister. They couldn't hide a sniper such as Lachlan today.

Neal was a bit winded from his jog, so he walked down toward the spot where it had all started. The place where he'd usurped Niall Straith's barely deceased body. First met Ainslee. And where Garrick had met his end.

Neal narrowed his eyes against the wind. Looked about. There wasn't any sign of a trail through the area. A boulder stuck out of the sod off to one side. He'd never noticed it before. Then again, he hadn't had a reason to observe things this closely. Neal set his backpack down beside the boulder. Settled onto his butt on the rock. Extended his legs. Used his backpack as a back rest. Lowered his hat to shield his eyes.

And waited.

He may have dozed off. He wasn't sure. The sun had moved. Clouds had gotten darker. Nothing else had changed.

But he hadn't really expected it to.

Well.

Time was passing. Still. Always.

Neal stood. Brushed off his khakis. Re-shouldered the backpack, and started walking again. He wasn't on horseback. It took a lot longer to reach the start of Castle Straith's outer wall on foot. Eventually it came into sight. Neal walked until the castle wall was waist high, so he could lean against it and prop his backpack at the same time. Catch his breath. And look over the bay toward the cliffs on the opposite side. It was exactly as he remembered. Easily as regal. Majestic. His heart was still sending ache with every beat, but for some reason, it was muting slightly. He felt reenergized.

Almost hopeful.

Neal's steps grew quicker as the walls narrowed to make the entrance path. Each stride lengthened. Shivers lifted along his skin. The arrow slits were the same. The arch the same. Everything the same.

Wait.

The portcullis was missing. There was a ridge in the rock where it had been. And nobody called out as he approached. Neal's heart started hammering for a different reason. He hadn't noticed it before, but the entire place reeked of dereliction. Desolation.

Almost like...

He was loping as he turned the corner. And then he stopped dead. The backpack rocked atop his shoulders. The tower that had stood so proud and tall was a good story shorter than before. There were gaping holes where windows used to be. And even a casual observer could see the interior was gone. Open sky was in every aperture. No matter how high he looked.

"No!"

Neal's cry was lengthy. It carried the shock. Dismay. And defeat.

He lowered his backpack. He didn't care where it landed. His boots crunched with every step as he approached and climbed the flight of stone steps that had once led to such grandeur. The front stoop stone was still there. Neal stood on it and gaped. The entire great hall was missing. Only stone remained. Walls with large fireplace openings lined the sides, while the chieftain stair was basically intact, but impossible to reach. The bottom steps were already separating, leaning precariously in midair. Because there wasn't any roof. And there wasn't any floor. Above the landing of the chieftain steps was a view of sky. His chamber was gone. The duchess's chamber. The rooms where he'd found such bliss but four days ago...

All gone.

His life with Ainslee had never felt farther away. Neal shook with emotions he'd never experienced before. Worse than even heartache. Sometimes he'd rather be a cold, heartless bastard. Because now, he knew how what dying hope felt like.

Neal covered his face with his hands. Sagged onto his knees. And wept.

CHAPTER FORTY-THREE

"HELLO, THERE!"

Neal didn't know how long he stayed hunched over. Absorbed with grief. It had been a long enough span of time his sobs had ceased. Any tears dried. He lifted his head from his hands. The elements intruded. Wind ruffled his sweater. His hair. Raindrops dusted his face intermittently. He shivered with chill.

"Hello!"

The young female voice hailed someone again. Her words penetrated the elements. It took a few moments to realize the words were meant for him. Neal swiveled, and looked across the courtyard. A young woman was walking toward him, coming from the direction where the stables had been. She was leading a very large horse. It was a Clydesdale. The horse had a reddish toned coat. And a big white blaze on its nose.

The girl lifted her arm and waved at him.

"I said, hello!" she called out.

Oh, my God.

"Ainslee!"

Neal shouted the name. Joy filled him. It was a great motivator. Neal hadn't known that. He was on his feet and racing down the stone stairs, his legs pumping, his heart thumping, and his breath coming in great heaves for air. He leapt the final two steps and started across the overgrown courtyard at a dead run. His fedora flew off. He was halfway to her before he realized the obvious. She was hatless. Her charcoal-shaded hair was blowing freely. It didn't look much longer than shoulder-length. She wore a cranberry-colored cardigan. Tan slacks.

This wasn't Ainslee.

Neal's steps slowed. Then stopped. His heart didn't match. It was pounding away with powerful beats that hurt his chest. His legs were complaining. Muscle spasms spurted through his thighs and lower legs. He locked his knees so he wouldn't fall. And he was out of breath. Neal bent forward, supporting himself with hands on his thighs as he gasped for air. He'd forgotten he wasn't a young athletic twenty-six-year old anymore.

Now, he was paying.

He barely heard her approach. She stopped about six feet from him. The horse followed suit.

"I did na' ken we had a visitor scheduled."

"Uh—" Neal couldn't make words yet. He didn't have enough breath.

"I'd have met you. Given you a tour."

"Tour?"

He should have waited. The word was a huff of sound. He was surprised she understood it.

"'Tis na' tourist season, but we're grateful for anything we get."

"You...have a tour?"

"Oh, aye. We conduct full tours all year round. The old castle is verra special. Some say 'tis haunted. The span you were looking over? That was the great hall. 'Twas said to have been a magnificent room. Over ninety feet in length. Eight fireplaces. And the double-staircase at the end? That led to the chieftain rooms. There is a wall of windows up there that once looked out over the ocean. 'Tis a breathtaking sight...but um. You must na' tell anyone I said that."

"Why not?" Neal asked.

"I climbed up the back balcony to view it. There is a sheer drop to the ocean. 'Tis na' safe. You will na' tell on me, will you?"

"Of course not," Neal replied.

"Um. Sir?"

"Yes?"

"You called me...Ainslee. Do you perhaps...ken my mother?"

Neal shook his head. "You reminded me. Of someone."

"Ah. I'm told I take after one of my ancestors. A previous duchess. From a long time ago. She was half Irish."

Neal's heart twinged sharply, as if someone had just stabbed him with a hot blade. He barely kept the sound of agony from leaving his lips.

"They say she was verra beautiful. But I should na' say that."

"Why not?" Neal asked.

"My family would say I'm fishing for compliments."

Neal glanced up at her. She definitely bore a resemblance to Ainslee, especially since she was blushing. And then she tipped her eyes up to his and stunned Neal. She had silver-colored eyes! They were the exact match to the ones he'd viewed in the looking glass when he'd been in Niall's body.

Neal went to a knee before he fell. Bowed his head. Felt a smattering of raindrops against the back of his neck. He resembled the stable hands when they'd encountered Ainslee after he'd made her his duchess. A clansman swearing fealty. Neal didn't care. He wasn't shaking with cold, anymore. It was barely containable sensation, a rush of jubilation that damn near took his head off. He'd rarely encountered emotions before meeting Ainslee, and now he dealt with an emotional rollercoaster that sent him from euphoria to the depths of despair and then rocketed him back to the heights of elation and joy.

Ainslee had borne him a child!

This stunning young woman standing before him was proof.

"Are you all right?" she asked.

Neal nodded, although 'all' and 'right' were lames words for how he felt at the moment.

"Oh, dear. I did na' bring any water or snacks today. But, I was na' expecting tourists."

"It's...okay," Neal managed to reply.

"Perhaps you should come up to the manor."

"The manor?"

"That's what we call it. 'Tis a bit more. That's where the Straith family moved after the fire."

Neal gathered a breath. Stood back up. Turned to view the decrepit-looking tower. It looked pretty forlorn against a backdrop of dark gray clouds.

"There was a fire," he remarked. "That explains it."

"Aye. 'Twas a long time ago. 1860. They managed to save some things. Not a lot."

"The journals in the library?" Neal asked hopefully.

"Nothing so wondrous. I wish they had. The family lost every record. Almost everything. They only managed to save items on the main floor. But that included a weapons collection from the great hall. It's still extensive, although we've had to sell some it off."

Neal swallowed. Hard. "That's...a shame."

"Oh, well. Time's change. And life...is expensive. Would you like to see the collection? I can waive the entry fee, if you like."

Neal regarded her for a moment in surprise while raindrops started sprinkling his features in earnest. He hadn't realized he looked so destitute.

He didn't even have his backpack with him.

"I had heard somewhere...that the Duke of Straithcairn...owned a lot of stock in the New York Stock Exchange," he prodded.

"Oh. I heard that rumor, too. If so, 'twas sold off."

"Sold off?"

"The duke at the time sold every holding he had to build the manor house. 'Tis a fine house. Large. Well-built."

"The duke at the time sold – did you say – *every* holding?"

"Aye. The worst was the land over yonder."

"What land?" Neal asked.

"Did you note a bay as you approached? There is a spit of land on the other side. With a big cliff."

"I saw it. I was...awed by it." Just as he'd been that the first time he'd seen it over a week ago.

"We had to sell it, too."

"The Duke of Straithcairn doesn't own it?"

"We have na' owned it for over a century. We can buy it back. The papers give my father first refusal if the owner ever sells...but that is na' ever going to happen."

"He'll never sell?"

"Oh. Nae." She smiled, but it wasn't a happy expression. "My father received a letter just yesterday about intent to sale. 'Tis a pipedream. We could never raise the funds to purchase it."

Great job, Neal. Chalk up another variable to the mess he'd made by tampering with fate. Even if he'd written a letter and secreted it in a journal with instructions to be opened in 1870, it wouldn't have mattered. The journal had burnt to ashes by then. No wonder his plan for the future had gone completely bust.

"I'm sorry. I should na' have said that. I am ever saying things I should na'. My grandmother calls me indecorous, whatever that is."

She flashed Neal a smile. He returned it. She had no idea how closely she resembled Ainslee. Nor how beloved that made her.

"Would you like to see the weapons display?" she asked.

"I...think I'll come back for that another time, miss. Thank you for the mini-tour. And for all the information. Truly. Thank you."

"Oh. I didn't introduce myself. How rude of me. I'm Annabelle Straith."

"Pleasure to meet you, Miss Straith. My name is Neal. Neal Straithmore."

Her eyebrows rose. "From the 'States?"

Damn it, Neal. He'd been so caught up in her revelations, his mind racing on potential options, that he'd forgotten to use a pseudonym. "Um. Yes," he replied hesitantly.

She clapped her hands, the move lifting the horse's reins. The horse nodded his head, as if in agreement.

"Oh! You're one of the American Straithmores, aren't you? I thought you looked familiar. We're related, you know."

Neal smiled. "Really?"

"You certain you do na' wish to come for a visit? It's about to storm. And there aren't many places to shelter out here."

She was right. The wind had grown to gusts that whipped her hair, the horse's mane and tail. It also sliced right through his cardigan, sending bone-chilling cold. The raindrops had become a medley, hitting his nose. Cheeks. Hands.

"I have something I need to do first, Annabelle. Perhaps...later?"

"Would you like to come for supper?"

"Thank you. I would like that."

She flashed him a smile. Neal froze. She looked so much like Ainslee right then, he was afraid of what might happen. What he might inadvertently say.

"To find us, just take the first right when you go back down the road. You can na' miss it."

"Ah. Yes. I remember it. The well-maintained pavement."

She nodded. "Seven o'clock?"

"I'll...try."

"I'll tell my mother to expect you."

She held out her hand. Neal took it. Looked at her fingers momentarily, almost raising her hand to his lips before coming to his senses. He shook her hand. Released it. And then watched as she mounted her horse and waved. The rain was pelting him as he watched her ride away. He didn't move until she'd disappeared around a bend of black stone. That's when he snagged his hat and shoved it back on his head, then the backpack. He hefted it, and started jogging. He was wheezing before he reached the place where the portcullis used to be. His thighs were burning with effort. He didn't let it stop him, although he slowed.

He had a mission.

He only hoped he had enough power left on his phone to complete it.

CHAPTER FORTY-FOUR

THE RAIN HAD TURNED TO sleet. Day to near-night conditions. The road to muck. Neal's steps had slowed to a desultory jog. He was bare-headed. Wind had whipped the fedora off somewhere near the beginning of the wall. He hadn't wasted the effort or time to chase after it. He'd pulled the backpack off and cradled it in his arms to make the load feel lighter.

And...finally!

The rental car came into view.

Neal yanked the left side back door open, tossed his backpack in. Slammed the door. Pulled the driver's door open and dove into the space. The disposable phone was in a cubbyhole on the console. Neal powered it on.

He had two bars of communication available.

Ten percent power.

He punched in the numbers of his personal cell. It took forever to connect. All he heard was dead space, and then...thankfully! It rang. Eric answered on the third ring.

"Hello?"

"Eric!" Neal shouted.

"Boss man! Long...! You coming back? Because I...tell you, I'm already...! You didn't say...trade unions. And...worse...when they argue."

"Delegate. Call in one of the negotiating firms."

"You never did."

"It's my forte. Not yours. Delegate what you don't know. That's the number one rule. Now, listen! We don't have much time on this call!"

"You keep fading. Where...you? The Amazon?"

"You need to do something for me!"

"Sure. What do you need?"

Eric's words were interspersed with static. The signal sometimes strong. Sometimes so weak, Eric's words were barely discernible. Neal gripped the phone harder.

"Transfer half my holdings to the Reagan Straith family. In Scotland!"

"Half...to Reagan who? Where?"

"The Duke of Straithcairn! Make it an anonymous donation."

"To Duke of what? Where?"

"Reagan Straith! And, forget being anonymous. Deliver the news personally!"

"Reagan...? Straith. Where again?"

"Straith Castle! Northern Scotland."

"You want me...Scotland?"

"Yes! And, while you're there, make sure and meet Miss Annabelle Straith."

Neal chuckled. Shook his head. Eric would be perfect for Annabelle. And – *what the hell*. Since Neal was messing with fate again, he might as well add in matchmaking.

"You want me to transfer...the Duke...Straithcairn...Scotland. Half. You want...half? Of everything? That's...lot of zeroes! Billions!"

Eric's words were breaking up, but it sounded like he had the basics. Neal relaxed as he realized it. Muscles moved in spasms throughout his jaw. Neck. Shoulders. Lower back. He hadn't known he'd clenched them that tightly.

"Yes! That's exactly what I want!"

"Can I transfer companies...trade unions?"

"Good bye, Eric! And good luck. And, since I've never told you this – I love you. If I'd had a son, I would have wanted it to be you."

"What...that?"

"I love you!"

The phone connection went dead. Neal tossed the cell phone onto the floorboard. He didn't know if Eric had heard the last, but the kid would figure it out. Neal had wanted to adopt him. That part was in his will. If Eric didn't get the idea then, he wasn't the man Neal thought he was.

The storm had gotten worse. Neal's lower legs were hanging out the door, getting pelted with sleet. Already, he felt frozen. It took an act of will to get his legs in. He'd forgotten this was a right-hand drive car. He slid along the seat, and managed to get his legs into position so he could drive. He sat up. His left arm was acting up. Neal leaned over to pull the door shut with his right arm. Grabbed for the ignition key. Started the engine. His left side wasn't responding. He had to adjust the fan blower with his right hand. Neal set the heat blower to high. Then sat, looking at the frosted windshield, while he absorbed the chill from an instant dose of cold air.

He hadn't noticed it before because he'd been so intent on reaching the car and his phone, but he had a myriad of dots blocking his view. Neal flexed his right hand. Then the left one. The left responded visually, but he couldn't feel it happen.

Great.

He was experiencing another transient ischemic attack. He hadn't brought a clot-blocker pill with him on this trip. He hadn't brought any pharmaceuticals. He must have been too used to being in a young, physically fit, young man's body.

Or he'd made another subconscious move, setting himself up for disaster.

The engine gradually warmed. The air coming through the vents was a blessed relief. Neal moved his hands to the defroster to dangle his fingers in the blast of warmed air. Get them flexible enough so he could steer. Only his right arm moved. Neal had to physically lift his left arm with the right one and manipulate it to the top of the dashboard. He couldn't even feel the heated air. His forearm rested on the steering wheel. His fingers dangled above the defrost vents. Neal couldn't feel any of it.

He needed to get indoors. Settled in a quiet, dark room. He wondered if the Straith family would assist, and automatically knew they would. Goodness radiated from Annabelle just as it had from his Ainslee. The Straith family would help him. At the very least, they would have an aspirin tablet he could take.

But to get there, he needed to rely on his right side. Good thing this was a right-hand drive car. Automatic transmission. His left arm was useless.

He leaned across to program the wipers with his right hand. Move some of the heat to the floorboard as well as the window. Turned it down a notch. Switched on the headlamps. The sleet had turned to snow. It filled the bottom of the windshield when he was back in position to drive. Neal reached across his body to change the wipers to full power. He put the gear selector into drive next. The car lurched forward before he was ready. He braked with a jerk.

That was stupid, Neal.

But he'd moved. Neal changed the gear selector to reverse. Angled the tires. Lifted his foot off the brake, and the car immediately lurched backward. He braked again. The car slid quite a bit before it stopped. He repeated the process a half dozen times, with resultant jerking motions and sliding, until he was fairly certain he faced the correct way. It was nearly impossible to tell. What had been a track before was barely discernible in the headlamps.

This was bad.

He was suffering a T.I.A. Left-side movement was impossible. He had a half mile to go before he'd reach asphalt. The ground was slick. His tires had dug all kinds of ruts into it, making traction difficult. The weather was near blizzard-conditions. Night had fallen rapidly. He didn't have any power left on his cell phone. He hadn't packed for winter conditions. And, there was more.

Neal glanced at the fuel indicator.

Damn it.

He hadn't refilled the gas tank before driving the final leg. The fuel gauge was showing just above empty. Things couldn't get much worse. But the instant he thought that, they did.

The car acted like it had a mind of its own. The engine whined. Neal didn't have to step on the gas pedal. Every time he let off the brake, the car lurched forward uncontrollably. Neal fought the steering wheel for control with his right hand as much as he directed anything with it. Snow began building up on the windshield. He needed to let go of the wheel and reach across in order to move the heat from the floor to the defrost mode again. That sounded tricky.

He was leery of putting the vehicle in park. The car was stuck in drive. But he needed to do something about the window situation. The wipers were thumping in concert with his heart as they smacked into the obstruction of packed snow.

Neal leaned heavily on the brake. The car continued sliding forward. He reached for the wiper control knob, and the moment he looked up, the ghostly white visage of a standing stone blocked his path. It was right in front of him.

What the hell?

Neal yanked the steering wheel to the right. The car shuddered, responded, and then began sliding. It jammed into something next. Rolled. Neal smacked a hand to the ceiling to keep in place. He wasn't wearing the safety belt? Had he really been this stupid?

His right arm responded. His left was still paralyzed. The car rolled again. Neal moved to the door handle. He'd rather be out in the elements than inside this death trap. He shoved the handle down. Pushed with everything he had against the door. Nothing budged.

The car rolled again. He crashed against the inside of the left door, smacking his head on the lever. The door popped open. Neal shot out. Slammed into the ground with a shoulder-crunching force. He gave a pain-filled grunt. Caught a glimpse of snow-covered rock. Sheets of blinding snow. And the edge of the ground. Neal curled into a fetal position. He'd broken his shoulder. Probably had internal injuries. The car was still stuck in gear. Neal watched open-mouthed as his rental disappeared over the edge of a cliff.

He gasped for each breath. Waited to hear the sound of the car smashing against the rocks at the base of the cliff. Or maybe it would reach ocean. Sink out of sight. Nobody would ever know what had happened.

Unless he survived.

And then it hit him. Why hadn't he just gone down with the car? Ended this existence? He had a better chance of finding Ainslee in the next realm than this one. Would he really rather live with heartbreak for the rest of his life?

Neal put his head to the ground. Shook with the anguish that came from losing love. The one that dogged his every second anymore. Found that the agony of never being with Ainslee overrode even the pain of his injuries.

But, maybe.

If, he was lucky.

He wouldn't survive this.

It was possible. Nobody knew where he was. He had internal issues. It hurt to breathe. He might have fractured a rib or two. His shoulders were ablaze with fiery pain. He might expire of his injuries. Or exposure might get him.

He could hope.

Nobody would be looking for him. He hadn't even committed to attending supper with the Straith family. They probably wouldn't check up here for him. And by the time anybody realized he was missing, it might be too late. Who would suspect he'd escaped the car? Hadn't gone over the cliff in it? They'd find the car. His cell. Belongings. Passport.

God. This hurt.

Death couldn't be any more painful.

And that's when he started praying for it.

CHAPTER FORTY-FIVE

A LIGHT APPEARED ABOVE HIM. NEAL groaned. He was on his belly. Lying flat.

How had that happened?

He lifted his head. Caught sight of the glint of something. About two inches away from his nose. The light got brighter. A pin-dot of illumination in a world of dark. The thing that had caught his attention sparkled again. Neal pushed hair out of his eyes, sluicing off rain as he did so. Narrowed his eyes. Brought the item into focus.

It was his spiral signet ring.

Damn thing.

He reached over with his left hand and picked it up. Looked at it for a moment. This little piece of jewelry had such power. It was hard to fathom, actually. Too bad it didn't have the power to fix things.

Neal palmed the ring. Moved it to the little pocket of his vest. Lowered his cheek to the rock surface. He felt rough. Like he'd taken a spill. Nothing drastic. That was really odd. He should be in massive pain from his car wreck by now.

And he was getting drenched.

"Neal? Are you there? Neal!"

Neal's mouth gaped open. His eyes widened.

I'm back?

He pushed up with such a swift motion, his bottom half slid off the cliff face. And he was *not* willing to die now! He grabbed for rock. Clawed and scrambled his way back onto the ledge. The move scraped his palms. Elbows. Knees. Ripped fingernails. And it all felt miraculous. Beyond wonderful.

He was on his knees and looking up as Ainslee's face came over the balcony edge. Which was the perfect position for the prayer of thanks his heart automatically gave.

Oh, dearest God! Thank you!

It really was her – his Ainslee! She held a lantern aloft in one hand. The flame inside was secured behind glass panels. It fought for life against the maelstrom. Her other hand held her cloak hood above her head, making a shelter as she peered toward him. She was still wearing the dark rose colored gown. He caught a glimpse of the neckline through the cloak opening. She had an anxious look on her face.

But it was her face.

There was no mistaking it.

"Neal?"

"Right here, babe." Neal's voice was jubilant. Wildly excited. Loud. He was surprised he didn't burst into tears, or bust into song. He'd heard of that sort of emotional overload happening. Right now, he knew exactly what it felt like.

"Oh, no! What happened?"

"Um. I. Fell."

In love.

"Do you need help?"

"Shouldn't. I mean...if Garrick could climb this thing, I sure can."

"Garrick?"

"Oh. Uh—."

Crap.

He'd forgotten. Garrick and Lachlan and their mother had just passed away. It felt like he'd been gone a year. Aged ten of them. Neal stood shakily, pressed his back against the rock face. The wind-driven rain whipped his kilt about him. Nothing had ever felt as glorious.

"I'll be right back!"

"Wait!"

The light disappeared with Ainslee. That put everything before him into perspective. He faced a black void.

Unwritten history.

His to live.

At Ainslee's side.

Neal pressed his pocket. Felt the outline of the ring. He wasn't quite finished messing around with fate. He had to get this piece of jewelry to Iain Straithmore in New York. Somehow. It needed to be passed down from father to son, so that Neal could receive it two hundred years from now and use it to get back here.

Was time really that...set? Cyclical?

"Neal? You still there?"

The light came back. So did Ainslee. Her question was entertaining. And profound. Of course he was here. There wasn't anywhere else he'd rather be.

"Yeah!" he called back.

A rope dangled over the balcony ledge.

"You found a rope?"

"'Tis from the servant bell. We can always restring it."

"Oh. Good call. You secured it?" he asked.

"Aye!"

"Not to any of the furniture, I hope. Except...maybe the bed?"

"'Tis tied to the door handle."

"Oh. Smart. Very smart. Thanks, love. Be with you in a moment."

Being twenty-six and athletic were fantastic things to be. Neal climbed the rope without any trouble. Heaved a leg over the balcony. Raced to Ainslee. Snatched her up into a heart-filling hug. Followed by a soul-searing kiss. Any notice of wind or rainfall disappeared. Time stopped. The lantern fell. Glass shattered. The flame went out.

But none of that made the slightest dent in how bright his soul felt. Nor how high it soared.

ABOUT THE AUTHOR

Jackie Ivie lives in the enormous state of Alaska with her husband and three very spoiled pets. She started her writing career writing hot highland historical romances for Kensington Publishing. There are now ten "Clans series" books, available in seven languages. Keeping her head in the clouds most of the time, Jackie now spends her time researching, developing, and writing her three paranormal series – the Vampire Assassin League, the dark angel series Chronicles of the Hunter, and time traveling with the Portals of Time – and her other historical line, the Brocade Collection.

Jackie loves hearing from fans, who can contact her at www.jackieivie.com or www.VampireAssassinLeague.com

Want to keep up with the assassins of the Vampire Assassin League and each new release? Sign up for Jackie's newsletter at http://jackieivie.com/para/news.htm.

Or for insider news, consider joining the Assassin Street Team at http://www.facebook.com/groups/379151425455048/

www.ingramcontent.com/pod-product-compliance
Lightning Source LLC
Chambersburg PA
CBHW071120170626
46809CB00002B/433